Praise for Debbie Macomber's
Bestselling Novels from Ballantine Books

Rose Harbor

"A heartwarming, feel-good story from beginning to end . . . No one writes stories of love and forgiveness like Macomber." —*RT Book Reviews*

Silver Linings

"Macomber's homespun storytelling style makes reading an easy venture. . . . She also tosses in some hidden twists and turns that will delight her many longtime fans." —*Bookreporter*

"Reading Macomber's novels is like being with good friends, talking and sharing joys and sorrows."
—*New York Journal of Books*

Love Letters

"[Debbie] Macomber's mastery of women's fiction is evident in her latest. . . . [She] breathes life into each plotline, carefully intertwining her characters' stories to ensure that none of them overshadow the others. Yet it is her ability to capture different facets of emotion which will entrance fans and newcomers alike."
—*Publishers Weekly*

"Romance and a little mystery abound in this third installment of Macomber's series set at Cedar Cove's Rose Harbor Inn. . . . Readers of Robyn Carr and Sheryl Woods will enjoy Macomber's latest, which will have them flipping pages until the end and eagerly anticipating the next installment."
—*Library Journal* (starred review)

"Uplifting . . . a cliffhanger ending for Jo Marie begs for a swift resolution in the next book."
—*Kirkus Reviews*

"Mending a broken heart is not always easy to do, but Macomber succeeds at this beautifully in *Love Letters*. . . . Quite simply, this is a refreshing take on most love stories—there are twists and turns in the plot that keep readers on their toes—and the author shares up slices of realism, allowing her audience to feel right at home as they follow a cast of familiar characters living in the small coastal town of Cedar Cove, where life is interesting, to say the least." —*Bookreporter*

"*Love Letters* is another wonderful story in the Rose Harbor series. Genuine life struggles with heartwarming endings for the three couples in this book make it special. Readers won't be able to get enough of Macomber's gentle storytelling. Fans already know what a charming place Rose Harbor is and new readers will love discovering it as well."
—*RT Book Reviews* (4½ stars)

Rose Harbor in Bloom

"[Debbie] Macomber uses warmth, humor and superb storytelling skills to deliver a tale that charms and entertains." —*BookPage*

"A wonderful reading experience . . . as [the characters'] stories unfold, you almost feel they have become friends." —*Wichita Falls Times Record News*

"[Debbie Macomber] draws in threads of her earlier book in this series, *The Inn at Rose Harbor*, in what is likely to be just as comfortable a place for Macomber fans as for Jo Marie's guests at the inn."
—*The Seattle Times*

"Macomber's legions of fans will embrace this cozy, heartwarming read." —*Booklist*

"Readers will find the emotionally impactful storylines and sweet, redemptive character arcs for which the author is famous. Classic Macomber, which will please fans and keep them coming back for more."
—*Kirkus Reviews*

"Macomber is an institution in women's fiction. Her principal talent lies in creating characters with a humble, familiar charm. They possess complex personalities, but it is their kinder qualities that are emphasized in the warm world of her novels—a world much like Rose Harbor Inn, in which one wants to curl up and stay." —*Shelf Awareness*

"The storybook scenery of lighthouses, cozy bed and breakfast inns dotting the coastline, and seagulls flying above takes readers on personal journeys of first love, lost love and recaptured love [presenting] love in its purest and most personal forms."
—*Bookreporter*

"Just the right blend of emotional turmoil and satisfying resolutions . . . For a feel-good indulgence, this book delivers." —*RT Book Reviews* (4 stars)

The Inn at Rose Harbor

"Debbie Macomber's Cedar Cove romance novels have a warm, comfy feel to them. Perhaps that's why they've sold millions." —*USA Today*

"No one tugs at readers' heartstrings quite as effectively as Macomber." —*Chicago Tribune*

"The characters and their various entanglements are sure to resonate with Macomber fans. . . . The book sets up an appealing milieu of townspeople and visitors that sets the stage for what will doubtless be many further adventures at the Inn at Rose Harbor."
—*The Seattle Times*

"Debbie Macomber is the reigning queen of women's fiction." —*The Sacramento Bee*

Blossom Street

Blossom Street Brides

"[An] enjoyable read that pulls you right in from page one." —*Fresh Fiction*

"A master at writing stories that embrace both romance and friendship, [Debbie] Macomber can always be counted on for an enjoyable page-turner, and this Blossom Street installment is no exception."
—*RT Book Reviews*

"A wonderful, love-affirming novel . . . an engaging, emotionally fulfilling story that clearly shows why [Macomber] is a peerless storyteller."
—*Examiner.com*

"Rewarding . . . Macomber amply delivers her signature engrossing relationship tales, wrapping her readers in warmth as fuzzy and soft as a hand-knitted creation from everyone's favorite yarn shop."
—*Bookreporter*

"Fans will happily return to the warm, welcoming sanctuary of Macomber's Blossom Street, catching up with old friends from past Blossom Street books and meeting new ones being welcomed into the fold."
—*Kirkus Reviews*

"Macomber's nondenominational-inspirational women's novel, with its large cast of characters will resonate with fans of the popular series." —*Booklist*

"*Blossom Street Brides* gives Macomber fans sympathetic characters who strive to make the right choices as they cope with issues that face many of today's women. Readers will thoroughly enjoy spending time on Blossom Street once again and watching as Lydia, Bethanne and Lauren struggle to solve their problems, deal with family crises, fall in love and reach their own happy endings." —*BookPage*

Starting Now

"Macomber has a masterful gift of creating tales that are both mesmerizing and inspiring, and her talent is at its peak with *Starting Now*. Her Blossom Street characters seem as warm and caring as beloved friends, and the new characters ease into the series smoothly. The storyline moves along at a lovely pace, and it is a joy to sit down and savor the world of Blossom Street once again." —Wichita Falls *Times Record News*

"Macomber understands the often complex nature of a woman's friendships, as well as the emotional language women use with their friends." —*NY Journal of Books*

"There is a reason that legions of Macomber fans ask for more Blossom Street books. They fully engage her readers as her characters discover happiness, purpose, and meaning in life. . . . Macomber's feel-good novel, emphasizing interpersonal relationships and putting people above status and objects, is truly satisfying."
—*Booklist* (starred review)

"Macomber's writing and storytelling deliver what she's famous for—a smooth, satisfying tale with characters her fans will cheer for and an arc that is cozy, heartwarming and ends with the expected happily-ever-after." —*Kirkus Reviews*

"Macomber's many fans are going to be over the moon with her latest Blossom Street novel. *Starting Now* combines Macomber's winning elements of romance and friendship, along with a search for one woman's life's meaning—all cozily bundled into a warmly satisfying story that is the very definition of 'comfort reading.'" —*Bookreporter*

"Macomber's latest Blossom Street novel is a sweet story that tugs on the heartstrings and hits on the joy of family, friends and knitting, as readers have come to expect." —*RT Book Reviews* (4½ stars)

"The return to Blossom Street is an engaging visit for longtime readers as old friends play secondary roles while newcomers take the lead. . . . Fans will enjoy the mixing of friends and knitting with many kinds of loving relationships." —*Genre Go Round Reviews*

Christmas Novels

Dashing Through the Snow

"Wonderful and heartwarming . . . full of fun, laughter, and love." —*Romance Reviews Today*

"This Christmas romance from [Debbie] Macomber is both sweet and sincere." —*Library Journal*

"There's just the right amount of holiday cheer.... This road-trip romance is full of high jinks and the kooky characters Macomber does so well."

—*RT Book Reviews*

Mr. Miracle

"Macomber's Christmas novels are always something to cherish. *Mr. Miracle* is a sweet and innocent story that will lift your spirits during the holidays and throughout the year. Celebrating the comforts of home; family traditions, forgiveness and love, this is the perfect, quick Christmas read."

—*RT Book Reviews*

"[Macomber] writes about romance, family and friendship with a gentle, humorous touch."

—*Tampa Bay Times*

"Macomber spins another sweet, warmhearted holiday tale that will be as comforting to her fans as hot chocolate on Christmas morning." —*Kirkus Reviews*

"This gentle, inspiring romance will be a sought-after read." —*Library Journal*

"Macomber cheerfully presents a holiday story that combines the winsomeness of a visiting angel (similar to Clarence from *It's a Wonderful Life*) with the more poignant soulfulness of *A Christmas Carol* to bring to life a memorable reading experience."

—*Bookreporter*

"Macomber's name is almost as closely linked to Christmas reading as that of Charles Dickens.... [*Mr. Miracle*] has enough sweetness, charm, and seasonal sentiment to make Macomber fans happy."

—*The Romance Dish*

Starry Night

"Contemporary romance queen Macomber (*Rose Harbor in Bloom*) hits the sweet spot with this tender tale of impractical love.... A delicious Christmas miracle well worth waiting for."

—*Publishers Weekly* (starred review)

"[A] holiday confection . . . as much a part of the season for some readers as cookies and candy canes."

—*Kirkus Reviews*

"A sweet contemporary Christmas romance . . . [that] the best-selling author's many fans will enjoy."

—*Library Journal*

"Macomber can be depended on for an excellent story.... Readers will remain firmly planted in the beginnings of a beautiful love story between two of the most unlikely characters."

—*RT Book Reviews* (Top Pick, 4½ stars)

"Macomber, the prolific and beloved author of countless bestsellers, has penned a romantic story that will pull at your heartstrings with its holiday theme and emphasis on love and finding that special someone."

—*Bookreporter*

"Magical . . . Macomber has given us another delightful romantic story to cherish. This one will touch your heart just as much as her other Christmas stories. Don't miss it!" —*Fresh Fiction*

Angels at the Table

"This delightful mix of romance, humor, hope and happenstance is the perfect recipe for holiday cheer."
—*Examiner.com*

"Rings in Christmas in tried-and-true Macomber style, with romance and a touch of heavenly magic."
—*Kirkus Reviews*

"The angels' antics are a hugely hilarious and entertaining bonus to a warm love story." —*Bookreporter*

"[A] sweetly charming holiday romance."
—*Library Journal*

New Beginnings

A Girl's Guide to Moving On

"Debbie Macomber's finest novel. Betrayal and sorrow can happen in any stage of life, and, in this wonderful story, her very nimble hands weave a spectacular kaleidoscope of courage, struggles, and finally joyous redemption and reinvention. Macomber totally understands the human heart. I absolutely loved it!"
—DOROTHEA BENTON FRANK, *New York Times* bestselling author of *All the Single Ladies*

"Whispers a message of love, hope, and, yes, reinvention to every woman who has ever wondered 'Is that all there is?' I predict every diehard Macomber fan—as well as legions of readers new to the Macomber magic—will be cheering for Leanne and Nichole, and clamoring for more, more, more."

—MARY KAY ANDREWS, *New York Times*
bestselling author of *Beach Town*, *Ladies' Night*,
and *Summer Rental*

"Macomber is a master at pulling heartstrings, and readers will delight in this heartwarming story of friendship, love, and second chances. Leanne, Nichole, Rocco, and Nikolai will renew your faith in love and hope. The perfect read curled up in front of the fire or on a beach, it's as satisfying as a slice of freshly baked bread—wholesome, pleasantly filling, and delicious."

—KAREN WHITE, *New York Times*
bestselling author of *Flight Patterns*

"Beloved author Debbie Macomber reaches new heights in this wise and beautiful novel. It's the kind of reading experience that comes along only rarely, bearing the hallmarks of a classic. The timeless wisdom in these pages will stay with you long after the book is closed."

—SUSAN WIGGS, #1 *New York Times*
bestselling author of *Starlight on Willow Lake*

"Debbie dazzles! A wonderful story of friendship, forgiveness, and the power of love. I devoured every page!"

—SUSAN MALLERY, #1 *New York Times*
bestselling author of *The Friends We Keep*

Last One Home

"Fans of bestselling author Macomber will not be disappointed by this compelling stand-alone novel."
—*Library Journal*

"Family, forgiveness and second chances are the themes in Macomber's latest stand-alone novel. No one writes better women's contemporary fiction, and *Last One Home* is another wonderful example. Always inspiring and heartwarming, this is a read you will cherish."
—*RT Book Reviews*

"Tender, real, and full of hope."
—*Heroes and Heartbreakers*

"Once again, Ms. Macomber has woven a charming tale dealing with facing life's hard knocks, begging forgiveness, and gaining self-confidence."
—*Reader to Reader*

"Macomber never disappoints me.... She always manages to leave me with a warming of the soul and fuzzy feelings that stay for days." —*Fresh Fiction*

"A very heartwarming novel of healing and reconciliation . . . that touches on life's more serious moments and [will leave readers] hoping to revisit these flawed but lovable characters in the future."
—*Book Reviews & More by Kathy*

Dear Friends,

Welcome back to Rose Harbor! Jo Marie, the owner of the Inn at Rose Harbor, is eager to greet her newest guests, and she's badly in need of a distraction. Nothing is working out the way she wants, though isn't that life? We seldom get what we want, but we almost always get what we need. And at this juncture in hers, Jo Marie has plenty of needs and wants . . . most of which involve Mark Taylor, her handyman.

As for those guests: The teenage years have always intrigued me, especially the angst and torment of falling in love for the first time. After reading several wonderful young adult novels recently, I found my mind conjuring up a story of young love.

You're about to meet Coco and Katie, who are returning to Cedar Cove for their ten-year high school reunion. They each have a specific reason for attending: an agenda to right wrongs and mend the wounds incurred by their first high school loves. And naturally they plan to stay at the Inn at Rose Harbor.

My hope is that you enjoy this next installment in the Rose Harbor Inn series and that your own mind will wander back to those high school days, when every emotion was so new and intense.

Hearing from my readers brings me great joy. I personally read every letter and post and thank you for your comments. What you've shared over the years has had a serious impact on my career. You can reach me at my website, debbiemacomber.com, or on Facebook. Letters are welcome as well, mailed to P.O. Box 1458, Port Orchard, WA 98366.

Thank you for your ongoing support and encouragement.

Warmest regards,

Debbie Macomber

Silver Linings

For a complete list of books by Debbie Macomber, visit her website at debbiemacomber.com.

DEBBIE MACOMBER

Silver Linings

A Rose Harbor Novel

BALLANTINE BOOKS • NEW YORK

2016 Ballantine Books Mass Market Edition

Copyright © 2015 by Debbie Macomber
Excerpt from *Sweet Tomorrows* by Debbie Macomber copyright © 2016 by Debbie Macomber

Published in the United States by Ballantine Books, an imprint of Random House, a division of Penguin Random House LLC, New York.

BALLANTINE and the HOUSE colophon are registered trademarks of Penguin Random House LLC.

Originally published in hardcover in the United States by Ballantine Books, an imprint of Random House, a division of Penguin Random House LLC, in 2015.

ISBN 978-0-553-39182-4
ebook ISBN 978-0-553-39180-0

Cover design: Belina Huey
Cover illustration: Tom Hallman, based on a photograph © Emanuele Capoferri/age fotostock

Printed in the United States of America

randomhousebooks.com

9 8 7 6 5 4 3 2

Ballantine Books mass market edition: July 2016

To Rick Hamlin

Trusted Friend

Talented Writer and Singer

All-Around Good Guy with a Big Heart

Happy 60th Birthday

The first year of being a widow was by far the most difficult. When I got the news that my husband had been killed in a helicopter crash in Afghanistan, it felt like an atomic bomb had gone off inside my head. My entire life, my body, my heart felt as if I'd gone into a free fall. For weeks I was reeling with pain and loss, stumbling from one day to the next. It felt wrong that the world would continue when it had come to a complete halt for me.

With no other choice, I struggled to make sense of this new reality that was mine. Only a few months after I received word of Paul's death, against everyone's advice, I left the corporate world and purchased a bed-and-breakfast. I moved from Seattle to a quaint community called Cedar Cove on the Kitsap Peninsula.

The first night I spent as the inn's new proprietor I felt Paul's presence as keenly and profoundly as if he were sitting by my side and speaking to me. He told me I would heal at this inn and all who came to stay would find a harbor of healing as well. It was for that reason that I named my bed-and-breakfast the Inn at Rose Harbor. *Rose* for my husband, Paul Rose, and *Harbor* for the promise he had given me.

Over the last eighteen months, I have seen that promise come to fruition and witnessed it with many of my guests as well. Slowly, one day at a time, I forged a new life for myself, a life without Paul. Recently I read the last letter my husband had written to me—a love letter he'd penned in case he didn't return. It took a long time to find the courage to absorb what he had to say, mainly because I didn't want to accept the fact he was really gone. As I knew he would, Paul wrote that he loved me and that he would always be with me. He asked that I live a good life for the both of us.

I'd taken Paul's words to heart and built a new life without him as best I could. As he'd foretold, the inn became the focus of the new me. Every day was a learning opportunity, a season of personal and professional growth. For one, I became far more proficient in the kitchen, creating tasty breakfasts for my guests. I also made friends in the community—good friends. I adopted a dog from the local animal shelter, Rover, who'd been named that because when he was found, it looked as if he'd been roaming on his own for quite some time. Rover had become my constant companion, my comforter, and my guard. I found it uncanny how well he sensed and reacted to my moods. It was almost as if Paul had directed Rover into my life.

One of the strongest friendships I forged was with my handyman, Mark Taylor. Mark can be prickly and mysterious, and while I considered him a friend, he could irritate me faster than anyone I'd ever known. I like to think of myself as even-tempered and not easily riled. Not so with Mark. Only a few words from him could drive me up the wall. At times he can be so unreasonable and demanding.

A good example of that happened last spring. I was washing the outside windows, balancing on a ladder. Out of the blue Mark insisted in the most unpleasant way that I climb off the ladder. I refused and he became so infuriated that he'd walked off the job. Really, he had no right to dictate what I do or don't do. It took a while for us both to cool down and be reasonable.

Ever since I read Paul's last letter my emotions have been on a roller coaster. I felt as if I was losing Paul. I'd stopped dreaming about him, and when I held his favorite sweatshirt, I could no longer smell the essence, the aroma, that had been my husband's.

As I slowly let go of Paul, I distracted myself by trying to crack the mystery that was Mark. He'd always been secretive, and never talked about his past. He was hiding something and I knew it. I plied him with questions, which he either refused to answer or completely ignored. I quizzed people who knew him before I moved to Cedar Cove, all to no avail. I went so far as to invite him to join my parents and me for dinner one night about three weeks ago. My mother has a gift for getting people to talk about themselves, and if anyone could weasel information from Mark it would be my mother. He thwarted me once again by refusing the invitation.

When I realized I'd used my curiosity about him as a diversion from my fear that Paul was slipping away from me, I apologized to Mark. It was then that Mark had shocked me with a confession. He claimed he'd fallen in love with me.

Mark loved me? I still had trouble wrapping my mind around that fact. If that wasn't shocking enough, what followed was even more eye-opening. Mark mentioned that he'd used every excuse imaginable in order to spend time with me. Until that very minute I'd been completely oblivious, but then everything came together like one giant thunderclap in my head. Although he declared his heartfelt feelings, he added that he couldn't, he wouldn't, allow the way he felt to develop into a long-lasting relationship. He intended to nip it in the bud.

As you can imagine, my thoughts started spinning like a windmill in a storm. It was then that Mark announced he was leaving Cedar Cove. Of course I objected; he was being ridiculous. I'll never forget what he said—it's burned into my memory.

A faraway look came over him and he refused to meet my eyes as he told me, "You were married to Paul Rose, and he was a hero. He gave his life in defense of our country. He's everything I'm not. I'm the antithesis of a hero, make no mistake in that." He went on to say that he was digging himself out of a black hole and that he should have been the one who died, not Paul.

Mark made it seem as if he felt guilty that he was alive and Paul was dead. I couldn't believe he was serious about moving away from Cedar Cove. It was such a rash and unreasonable decision I could only assume he wasn't serious, but I was wrong.

I suspected he would have packed up his bags that

very night if I hadn't convinced him to stay long enough to finish the gazebo I'd hired him to build. I was forced into reminding him that we had a contract, not one written in ink and legally binding, but a verbal one. If I knew anything about Mark—and really, when it came right down to it, I knew more than I realized—he was a man of his word. He'd already started the construction. I could tell he wasn't happy to remain in town any longer than necessary, but he reluctantly agreed.

I'd hoped that given time I'd be able to convince him to stay. After his declaration of love, I needed to delve into my own feelings, and I couldn't do that if he pulled a disappearing act.

The three weeks that followed proved to me exactly how serious Mark was about leaving Cedar Cove. About leaving *me*. Whereas before, any job I hired him to do took weeks—often months—he couldn't seem to finish this latest project fast enough. He started work in the early mornings and then he worked well past dusk, pushing himself to the point of exhaustion, until it became impossible to see in the dark any longer.

When I'd originally hired Mark to build the gazebo, I guesstimated that it would take him three to four months to finish the project, thinking I'd be lucky if he finished before Christmas. Yet in just a matter of weeks he had it nearly completed. For Mark to finish anything in three weeks was unheard of.

In fact, I could hear him outside this morning. It was barely light and he was already at work. I'd been up for about a half hour and had breakfast in the oven for my guests. It was one of my favorite recipes, stuffed French toast, which I'd assembled the night before and placed in the refrigerator. The coffee was brewed and the table set.

Rover wanted out and so I carried my coffee outside and stood on the porch watching Mark work away. He knew I was there but didn't acknowledge me. I wasn't surprised. Ever since our talk he'd basically ignored me as much as possible. I grappled with him, unable to understand how it was that he could claim to love me in one breath and then pretend as if I were invisible. I'd always found Mark difficult, but this was crazy.

"Morning," I called out cheerfully.

He nodded, without looking in my direction.

"Good morning," I repeated, louder this time.

"Morning." The greeting came grudgingly.

"You're in a grand mood this fine day. What's your problem?" He was often like this, taciturn and grumpy, but I was determined not to let it bother me.

As I knew he would, Mark ignored the question. I tried a different tactic. "Would you like a cup of coffee?"

"No thanks."

"Can I get you anything? Cookies?" I swear the man was addicted to my baking, especially my cookies.

"Nothing."

The *thanks* was missing this time. He had a five-gallon container of white paint sitting on the lawn, which meant that he was about to start the last stages of the project. My stomach tightened.

"It's going to be a busy weekend," I said, sitting down on the top step and cupping my mug between my hands. The morning had a chill to it and the warmth from the coffee inched its way up my arm. Autumn was approaching and I could feel it in the air, with a light scent of pine and sunshine on the turning leaves. Rover sat down at my side, nestling close to me, almost as if he felt my anxiety.

Mark didn't comment.

"Two women are due to arrive later this afternoon. They both live in Seattle, but it's their ten-year class reunion. They said they didn't want to worry about getting back to the city in case the parties went late and so they booked for both Friday and Saturday night."

He answered with a halfhearted shrug.

The silence between us felt oppressive. I found it difficult to carry on a one-sided conversation. The air seemed to throb with tension. It went without saying that Mark didn't want me anywhere close to him. He'd made it plain that he'd prefer to be just about anyplace I wasn't. If he truly did have feelings for me, then why the avoidance? Questions filled my head until I thought it would explode, but it did no good to ask. I'd tried that countless times and it was like butting my head against a brick wall.

When I heard the buzzer go off in the kitchen, indicating the French toast was ready to come out of the oven, I was almost grateful for the excuse to break away. Just before I entered the house, I looked back and saw his shoulders relax as if he was relieved to see me go. It was almost as if being close to me made him uncomfortable, and that was so unlike what it had once been. I missed the man who was a friend, who used to sit with me in the late afternoons. The one who listened as I talked about my day. Yes, he challenged and irritated me at times, but for the most part he made me think. He made me feel again when my heart had gone numb. I could laugh with Mark.

My guests, a couple in town for their only granddaughter's birthday celebration, lingered over breakfast and then checked out of the inn. They were headed to the airport. I went outside, stood on the porch, and waved them off, but I was more interested in Mark than I was in my departing guests. I looked for a way to break through that concrete wall he'd erected. At first I assumed he was embarrassed for confessing his feelings for me, but that didn't appear to be the case. I'd tried several times to get him to talk about it, but time and again he'd rebuffed my efforts. He was having none of it.

"The gazebo is looking great," I commented, trying yet again. I folded my arms around my middle.

"You'll be finished soon." He'd done an amazing job with this latest project. The gazebo was exactly as I'd pictured it and big enough to use for weddings and small gatherings, just the way I'd hoped. I could easily picture couples standing in the very structure as they pledged their love and their lives to each other.

Up to this point the bed-and-breakfast was barely breaking even financially. I needed a way to generate additional income, and offering the facility as a wedding venue seemed like a good idea.

"I see you've got the paint."

No comment.

His lack of response irritated me, so I returned to the house and grabbed a light sweater and Rover's leash. Walking my dog would help burn off the frustration. If Mark wanted to ignore me, then fine. I could give him all the breathing room he wanted and more.

When I returned with the leash, I found Rover lying on the grass close to where Mark worked. He rested his chin on his paws and kept close tabs on my handyman.

"You ready for a walk, Rover?" I asked. Generally, the instant he saw the leash Rover was on his feet, tail wagging energetically, eager to get going. Not this morning. Rover looked at me with dark brown eyes and then at Mark and then back again.

"Rover," I said again, with a bit more emphasis. "Let's take a walk."

"Go on," Mark said gruffly, nodding toward my dog.

"You talking to me or Rover?" I asked.

"Both of you."

"Fine." I walked over to Rover and attached his leash. He didn't seem all that interested until I tugged a little. He stood and we headed out of the yard. Rover paused and looked back at Mark much the same way I had earlier.

As soon as we left the driveway, I walked at a clipped pace to work off my irritation. The way I was feeling now, I considered myself well rid of Mark Taylor. If he wanted to move away from Cedar Cove, then it was fine by me. Good riddance! He was moody, cantankerous, and a pain in the butt.

By the time I'd walked two or three blocks, all uphill, I was winded. I'd walked so fast that I'd probably set a personal best, time-wise. The one positive was that the irritation I felt when I left the house had lessened. I took in several deep breaths and slowed my pace. Rover seemed grateful.

For reasons I didn't want to think about, I decided to walk past Mark's house. I remembered the time I'd found him in his workshop. A table had collapsed and pinned him down. He'd broken his leg and must have been in horrific pain.

Although he'd strongly objected, I called for help and followed the Aid Car to the hospital. After he was X-rayed and had a cast put on, I'd driven him home. One thing I could say about Mark was that he made a terrible patient. He'd snapped at me, complained, and issued orders as if I was personally responsible for his injury. He made it sound as if I was the very bane of his existence. Heaven only knew how long it would have taken for someone else to have found him—one would think he'd be grateful, but oh no, not Mark.

To be fair, he did thank me later. Weeks later, and even then the appreciation had come grudgingly.

Although Mark claimed to be in love with me, the thing was, I didn't know how I felt about him. I'd hardly been given the chance to absorb his declaration, let alone react to it. I wanted to talk about it, but he was having none of that.

The thing with Mark was that we disagreed on almost every subject. It took me a while to catch on that he purposely egged me on. At first he infuriated me. Not until later did I realize that arguing with him stirred my senses. I'd wallowed in my grief for months. Arguing with Mark lit a fire under me and proved my emotions hadn't stagnated. I still had the ability to feel.

I'd gotten used to spending time with Mark. We played Scrabble and would sometimes sit out on the porch at the inn and watch the sun set. He'd helped me plant a garden and I shared the produce with him. I'd enjoyed being with Mark and missed the times we shared. I missed him. And this was only a foretaste of what was to follow if I believed that he was indeed moving away.

The question was whether I cared for him the same way he said he cared for me. The truth was I didn't know if I was capable of loving another man after Paul. Perhaps Mark sensed that, read my doubts, and felt he couldn't compete with a dead man. I shook my head, certain now that I was grasping at the thin strands of a spiderweb.

I turned the corner to the street where Mark lived. As if he knew exactly where we were headed, Rover strained against the leash.

"Mark isn't at his house," I reminded my dog.

"There's no need to rush; he isn't home." Rover barked as if discounting my words and pulled ever harder on the leash.

"Rover, Mark's at the inn."

I had to half run in order to keep up with my dog. It was as if Rover had something to show me, something he felt was important for me to see. I didn't understand what was happening until I came closer, and when I saw Mark's house, I came to a dead stop.

The sign was prominently posted in front of the house, square on the edge of the grass, for anyone and everyone who drove by to see.

It was a local Realtor's sign that read in large red letters: FOR SALE.

This was no ruse, no trick. Mark was serious. He was leaving Cedar Cove, and more important, he was leaving me.

Chapter 2

Kellie "Coco" Crenshaw found it difficult to believe ten years had passed since she was in high school. Her overnight bag was laid open on top of her bed as she tried to pack for the reunion weekend. She had several outfits carelessly tossed across the bedspread as she sorted through her choices. She had to look great.

The window was open and the scent of Puget Sound and late summer filled the apartment. Coco lived close to the University district in Seattle, in a quaint brick building that had been constructed during World War II. It'd been updated a couple times over the years but had managed to maintain its distinctive charm. Coco loved her apartment, small as it was.

It'd been a major decision for her to remain in Washington State after her father had accepted a job transfer to the Chicago area. Within a matter of weeks, the family had moved, including her two younger sisters. That had happened six years ago, just about the time Coco graduated from college. She'd opted to stay in Seattle along with her older brother. For a long time afterward she feared she'd made the wrong decision, but she was happy to be in familiar territory. Aunts, uncles, and cousins were scattered all across western Washington, so she was never really alone.

Her phone buzzed and Coco quickly checked the text. It was from Katie Gilroy, a high school friend.

You home yet?
Yup. You?
Having second thoughts. Not sure I want to do this.

Coco typed furiously. She'd half expected this would happen.

Too late now. Be there soon.

No way was she letting Katie off the hook—they were attending this reunion, and she wasn't taking no for an answer. Coco had made the reservations at Rose Harbor Inn for two nights. She'd gone through all kinds of hassles to get this Friday afternoon off. She wasn't going to let Katie back down now.

It hadn't been easy to convince Katie to join her, but Coco had an answer for every excuse Katie tossed her way. They were doing this.

She was scheduled to pick up Katie at two that afternoon and then they'd take the ferry from Seattle to Bremerton and drive around the cove to the town they both knew so well—Cedar Cove.

Unlike Katie, Coco looked forward to attending this reunion. According to Lily Franklin, the reunion organizer, Coco had been the first person to mail in a check. But her eagerness to reunite with her high school class wasn't for the reasons some might assume.

Coco was going back to her hometown, to the school and classmates she'd known for the majority of her life, for one reason and one reason only.

Ryan Temple.

Just thinking about Ryan caused her blood pressure to spike. Nearly everyone in Cedar Cove viewed him as some kind of athletic Adonis who could do no wrong. He'd been the quarterback of the football team for all three years. He played baseball, too, and was good enough that after two years in college he'd been picked up by a professional team, and played in the minors for a couple years before heading to the majors.

She forgot which team he'd played for. Saint Louis? New York? Knowing what she did about him, she'd purposely not paid attention. Ryan Temple had become a hometown star, the All-American hero. It wouldn't surprise her if Cedar Cove threw him a parade. Legions of fans would line the streets, women would swoon; kids would chase after him and ask for his autograph.

Not Coco, though. No one knew Ryan the way she did.

Ryan had done her wrong, way wrong, and she was determined to finally tell him exactly what she thought of him. For ten years Coco had held on to her anger and pain. No longer, though. The time had come for Ryan Temple to own up to what he'd done.

Taking in a deep breath, Coco calmed her pounding heart. She had everything planned out in her mind and relished the thought of embarrassing him in front of their classmates the way he had her. It was what Ryan deserved.

Wanting to hit the road before Katie changed her mind, Coco finished the last of her packing, grabbed her overnight bag, purse, and car keys, and was out the door within ten minutes.

While on the drive to Katie's apartment, she heard her phone buzz, indicating another text. She ignored it, knowing it had to be from Katie.

Her friend's apartment was less than five miles from Coco's place, but with heavy traffic it took her nearly as long as if she'd jogged over. Just as she suspected, Katie wasn't out front waiting, as they'd discussed. That meant Coco had to find a parking spot, no easy task in the Denny Hill neighborhood. It seemed every street had some form of construction, which meant she had to drive around the block several times before she was lucky enough to secure a spot.

Grabbing her purse, she leaped out of the car and hurried down the sidewalk to Katie's building. She found her friend on the third floor, pacing the hallway.

"You're upset, aren't you?" Katie asked nervously.

"Of course not."

Katie's dark eyes rounded with surprise and gratitude. "I thought you'd be furious with me . . ."

"Why should I be? You're coming to the reunion just the way we planned."

Katie's shoulders slumped forward as though someone had forced her to lift a hundred-pound barbell.

When she managed to speak, her voice was a plaintive cry. "James doesn't want to see me."

"You don't know that," Coco insisted, although if everything Katie told her was true, then she might be right. Still, she knew her friend needed to do this, to get some closure. That was why she felt so strongly she must convince Katie to go.

"He's the only reason I even signed up," Katie said, and then added, "Well, other than you telling me I needed to do this. The thing is, I hardly know anyone and I doubt anyone will remember me."

"You know me."

"Well . . . okay, but only a few of the others. James made it clear he doesn't want anything more to do with me. I've accepted that."

Coco balanced her hand on her hip and snorted. "You have a say in this, too!"

Katie's eyes revealed her misery. "I have to accept it. James has rejected my friend request on Facebook. He's ignored my LinkedIn invite and blocked me from email. I got the message. What's done is done."

"He signed up for the reunion, didn't he? This could be your one and only chance to talk to him. Do you seriously want to let this opportunity slip by? If you do, you'll regret it for the rest of your life."

Katie briefly closed her eyes. "You're right."

"My guess is that he wants to see you, too, although he would never admit it."

Katie doubted that, and her look said as much.

Coco felt otherwise. "He had to know you were on the list."

"Not necessarily," her friend argued. "He made sure I know how he feels, and frankly it's just too painful to face yet another rejection. What happened between us was a long time ago. He's moved on with his life and so have I. Attending the reunion will only dredge up painful memories for us both."

"Do you want to set the record straight or not?" Coco asked, because she knew that was exactly what Katie wanted most.

"I do," she admitted reluctantly.

"Then get your bag and let's go."

What Coco wasn't telling her friend—or even admitting to herself—was that facing this reunion wasn't any easier for her. There was no need to burden Katie with her own emotional baggage when Katie had enough of her own to deal with.

Still, Katie hesitated.

"You may never have a chance like this again," Coco reminded her.

Whenever she was nervous or uncertain, Katie chewed the inside of her bottom lip, a habit she'd had from the time they were in high school. Coco noticed that she did so now.

"Okay, okay," Katie said. "I just hope I don't live to regret this."

"Trust me, you won't."

Katie made a scoffing sound as she opened the door to her apartment and hurried inside. Thankfully, her suitcase was already packed. Coco grabbed the handle away from her and raced down the hallway, dragging the carry-on behind her. She wasn't giving Katie a chance to change her mind . . . again.

Katie reluctantly followed Coco to the parked car. It went without saying this weekend would demand every ounce of courage her friend had.

Coco unlocked her vehicle and loaded the suitcase into the trunk next to her own while Katie slipped inside and latched the seat belt in place. Her shoulders were rigid, as if she were physically preparing herself for battle.

Coco placed her hands on the steering wheel and hesitated. She loved Katie and genuinely believed that going to the reunion would be the best thing for her. Her reasons for insisting Katie accompany her were partly selfish, too, though. She didn't have a significant other in her life and it would be hard to walk into the reunion alone. Katie was her security blanket, a friend she could hide behind when everything hit the fan with Ryan.

Feeling mildly guilty for forcing Katie to accompany her, Coco's hands tightened around the ignition key. "You still love him, don't you?"

Katie nodded. "Funny, isn't it? Does anyone ever really get over their first love?"

"It's going to work out, I know it is."

Katie didn't look as though she believed her, but she smiled, as if grabbing hold of that one small thread of hope and holding on to it with every ounce of strength she possessed.

Weaving their way through roadwork, detour signs, and traffic, Coco headed down to the waterfront. They paid their fare and queued up for the ferry that would take them back to Cedar Cove.

"It's going to be a good weekend," Coco insisted, more to bolster her own spirits than out of any real conviction. Every detail of what she wanted to say to Ryan had been reviewed countless times. Ryan Temple was finally going to be forced to face her and own up to the hell and humiliation he'd put her through. If everything went as she expected, Ryan wouldn't dare show his face in town again. His good-boy image would be forever tarnished.

Although it was only in the midsixties weather-wise, the car soon felt stuffy and overly warm. Katie scooted back her seat and leaned her head against the headrest.

"James has never forgiven me, you know," she whispered, without looking at Coco.

"Yeah." Forgiveness didn't come easily to her, either.

"You're going because of Ryan, aren't you?" Katie was a good enough friend to know Coco had her own motives for attending this reunion.

"I'd rather not talk about it, if you don't mind."

"I understand." Katie's cheeks reddened, but it might have been the heat inside the car.

"It's okay, no big deal." Looking for a distraction, Coco started the car's engine and rolled down the windows to let in the cooler air. The scent of the sound was more pungent this close to the water. Seagulls circled overhead, their cawing echoing over the parking lot as they waited for the ferry's arrival.

"Is Ryan married?"

Coco stared out the driver's-side window, avoiding eye contact. "I wouldn't know." Heaven help the poor woman who was foolish enough to get involved with the likes of Ryan Temple. Coco felt her friend's eyes boring into her.

"You have good reason to hate him."

"Why would I do that?" Coco downplayed her bitterness, not wanting Katie to guess how strongly she felt about the jerk. "It was ten years ago. I've put it behind me." That was only half true. With her busy work schedule, Coco didn't date often. No time, although if the right man came along she'd find the time.

A silly faraway look came over Katie. "You were the cutest couple. I remember watching you and Ryan walk down the hallway and thinking the two of you were perfect together. Who would have guessed what he was really like?"

Coco snorted with disbelief, searching for a way to turn the subject away from Ryan.

"You were," Katie insisted. "I thought you were, anyway."

"That was a long time ago."

"Ten years," Katie murmured. "Can you believe that it's been ten years since we were all together?" All at once she sat up straighter and her eyes went wide. "The time capsule. We buried one, remember? As part of the reunion we'll be digging it up, right?"

"Not until our twentieth class reunion."

"Oh right."

"If the next ten years pass as quickly as these ten, we'll be opening that capsule before we know it."

The ferry could be seen approaching in the distance. It wouldn't be long now before they boarded. Thankfully, the car had cooled off.

"Before we graduated, did you ever think about what our lives would be like in ten years?"

Coco mulled over the question. "Not really." By graduation day she'd been sick at heart, confused, and angry. The first two emotions had faded away over the years, but not the anger. Never the anger. It had become a part of her, an extra appendage like a third arm or leg.

The ferry docked and a long line of cars disembarked, rolling single file into the street with the waterfront traffic. Coco started the car and put it in gear, following the truck in front of her onto the ferry.

Katie didn't say anything for a long moment and then whispered, "I'm glad you made me come this weekend."

"I'm glad you came, too."

"It's going to be a great weekend for us both, meeting up with old friends and learning about one another's lives, although I doubt anyone will remember much about me."

"They'll remember," Coco promised.

"I doubt it," Katie countered, "but it doesn't matter. There's only one person I want to see."

There was only one person Coco wanted to see, too.

Chapter 3

As much as she was dreading this reunion, Katie had accepted the fact that Coco wasn't going to let her back out, especially at the last minute. After so many sleepless nights Katie would finally have the opportunity to explain to James what had happened. This reunion could very well be her one and only chance, and like Coco said, if she gave up now she would always regret that she'd let this opportunity pass her by.

Without a single word of communication, her high school sweetheart had let it be known that he wanted nothing more to do with her. She'd tried by all the normal routes to connect with him, but he'd ignored each one, shunning her efforts. Katie hated the thought of leaving matters between them as they were. She didn't expect anything to change, but she just had to have a chance to explain herself.

Coco drove onto the ferry and parked close to the vehicle in front of her. Cars lined up in designated rows, one after another, in the belly of the boat.

"Do you want to get a soda or something topside?" Coco asked.

Katie shook her head. "I don't think so."

"You sure?"

"Positive. You go ahead and I'll sit here for a few minutes and sort through my thoughts."

"Promise you won't even think of backing out."

"Promise."

Coco got out and headed upstairs. Katie stretched in her seat; the cool air was fresh and clean, and she breathed it in. It really was a lovely afternoon. The reunion committee couldn't have asked for better weather for this get-together. It was as if they knew exactly which dates to book.

This weekend had the potential to be life-changing, as uncomfortable and awkward as it was. She could hardly believe that the last time she'd seen James was the summer after their graduation.

In all her life no one had ever loved Katie as much as James Harper had. He'd been willing to sacrifice everything for her. As much as she had loved him in return, Katie couldn't allow that. If he'd given up college for her, it would have forever tainted their relationship. Closing her eyes, she leaned her head back and forced herself to think positive thoughts.

Because she wanted it so badly, she pictured seeing James at the reunion and his reaction once he saw her. She couldn't help wondering if he'd changed. She had. Not physically so much—the years had matured her, shaped her, and she assumed they had him as well. She wondered if he knew she'd gone into social work, helping young teens. He'd been the one to suggest she'd be good in that line of work. Was it possible that he remembered saying that to her all those years ago? She hoped he did.

The car door opened, momentarily startling Katie. Coco was back, holding two cans of soda. She handed one to Katie. "I brought you one anyway."

"Thanks." The can felt cool in her hand.

Her friend joined her and they both opened the soda cans. The cracking sound seemed to echo in the confines of the car.

"Worried about the reunion?" Coco said before she took the first swallow of her drink.

"A little." A lot, actually, but admitting that didn't come easily. "You?"

Coco shifted in her seat. "Not at all."

Katie snorted her drink. "You never could get away with a lie. Your body language gives you away, hon."

"Okay, I'm a little nervous, but no more than you or anyone else."

"Yeah, right."

Coco grinned. "I haven't kept in touch with a lot of people."

"Me neither." Between working two jobs, attending night classes, and finally obtaining her degree, there'd been little time for socializing. Other than Coco and one or two others, Katie hadn't made a lot of friends from their graduating class. She'd started Cedar Cove High School in October of her senior year. If it wasn't for swim team she probably wouldn't have connected with Coco, either. Their friendship had been key for her. If not for Coco, any connection Katie had with her classmates might have completely dissolved. Thankfully, almost from the first day Katie arrived at the school, shy, withdrawn, and feeling out of place, Coco had taken her under her wing.

They sat side by side for several moments without speaking, each caught up in her own thoughts.

"Can I ask you something?" Katie asked softly.

Coco shrugged. "Anything." Then she hesitated. "Let me revise that. Except if I don't know the answer, find it embarrassing, or just plain don't feel it's any of your business."

"Tell me how you really feel," Katie said, not bothering to disguise her amusement.

"Okay, fine, what's your question?"

Katie set the soda can aside. "Have you ever had a hard time forgiving someone?"

Right away Coco bristled, and Katie realized it was a loaded question and one she should never have asked her friend.

"What makes you ask?" Coco wanted to know.

Katie exhaled hard enough for her shoulders to lift as she expelled her breath. "I'm trying to look at this meeting with James the way a wronged party would."

"Have *you* ever had to forgive someone?" Coco demanded.

"Of course." She couldn't have made it this far in life without learning to let go of hurts from the past, especially the pain her parents had brought into her life. To the father who'd been a drunk and who'd abandoned her and her mother when Katie was a toddler. She'd had to move past the anger she carried about a mother who had then sought release from the pain of that rejection in drugs and alcohol as well.

"Was it easy?"

Katie wasn't sure how this all had gotten turned

around and she was the one answering the questions.

"No. It was hard, but I knew it was necessary."

"Why?"

"Why did I forgive or why was it necessary?" Her friend had grown quiet and intense. Coco's fingers clung to the soda can as if trying to strangle it.

"Both."

"I haven't seen or heard from my father in over twenty-five years. He didn't ask for forgiveness, nor did he seek me out. As a kid, especially when I got into my teens, I wanted to see him just so I could cuss him out. It never happened, though, and I suppose it was just as well."

"Did you hate him?"

Katie considered the question. "Hate him? No, not really. I figured in the end he probably got what he deserved. Life is like that, you know?"

"Like what?"

"It's the old 'what goes around comes around' philosophy. At least that's the way I like to think it works. My father treated people badly and he ended up alone."

"That gives me hope," Coco murmured.

Katie reacted quickly. "Hope?" she blurted out.

"I mean without hope. Those kinds of people usually end up without hope, right?"

"Right." Katie was fairly certain she hadn't misunderstood her friend. She studied Coco with fresh eyes. Although Coco never talked about what happened with Ryan, Katie was well aware her friend longed for some kind of payback. But then, how could she not? If the situation were reversed, Katie was fairly certain she'd feel the same way.

"You forgave your father, though," Coco asked.

Katie glanced down at her hands. She didn't want to mislead her friend, so she told the truth. "It took time. It didn't happen overnight."

"But how?"

Katie leaned her head back again. "It was around Christmas one year. At the time I must have been about twenty, maybe twenty-one. I was getting out of class. The night was cold and dark, and snow was threatening. As I walked to the bus stop I saw a man spread-eagle on the lawn, passed out with an empty liquor bottle at his side. Someone had called campus security and a couple of officers were trying to rouse him. My bus arrived and I wasn't able to follow what happened after I left. While I was on the bus I had the weirdest sensation that the drunk man could easily have been my father. I didn't see his face clearly or recognize anything about him that would remind me of my dad. Right away I felt sad and this overwhelming sense of pity came over me. I pitied him. His was a life wasted."

"So you went from hate to pity?" Coco took another long swallow of her soda.

"I don't think I ever truly hated him. I was angry and hurt and as little as I was when he left, I felt responsible somehow. That doesn't make sense, but in my line of work I see it all the time. Kids, no matter how young, blame themselves for what happens to their families. Even though this makes about as much sense as a kid thinking that not finishing his homework is the cause of global warming."

Coco's look grew intense and thoughtful. She went

quiet for several seconds. "Some things can't be forgiven though."

"Not easily, that's for sure. The thing I've learned—and trust me, I'm no expert—is that forgiveness isn't a gift we give the offender. It's something we do for ourselves."

"That's easy enough to say . . ."

"I know." In the distance the Bremerton ferry dock came into view. In order to distract herself from the inevitable, Katie looked away. All this talk about forgiveness had brought to the surface her hopes, and in equal measure her fears. Just because she'd learned how to forgive, that didn't mean that James had the will or the desire to lay the past to rest when it came to her.

"Do you feel it's in you to forgive?" she asked, hoping to turn the questions around on Coco.

"What makes you ask that?"

"You know why . . ."

"Well, I guess all of us have fallen short now and then . . ."

"Amen," Katie said with a halfhearted chuckle.

"And just as easily we might have inadvertently hurt someone without even knowing what we've done."

"That's not true," Coco darted back. "We know."

Although she disagreed, Katie wasn't going to argue.

This reunion would certainly prove to be interesting. Coco was outgoing and friendly, whereas Katie was much quieter, intense, and shy. Their differences were one reason why they were such good friends. They balanced each other.

Katie remembered the first day of school and how

dreadful it'd been to start yet another high school, especially in her senior year. She'd been moved to the third foster home in twelve months. It wasn't that she was a problem case or difficult to place—she'd never been in trouble in her other foster homes. Each move had been plain old bad luck. One set of foster parents had gotten a job transfer to another state. Then, with the second family, the wife had been diagnosed with cancer. Two major moves within a short amount of time. Her next family, the Flemmingses, were wonderful, as far as foster parents went.

"It looks like we're almost to Bremerton," Coco said, as if eager to change the subject.

The ferry docked near the Bremerton shipyard, which could be seen in the distance. Several mothballed battleships and carriers lined the waterfront, along with a number of nuclear-powered submarines. The shipyard and navy base were a large part of the local economy, both in Bremerton and Cedar Cove.

Ralph Flemmings, her foster father, had worked as a nuclear engineer at the shipyard until his recent retirement. Soon afterward the Flemmingses had sold their home in Cedar Cove, purchased a motor home, and traveled around the country. Every few weeks Katie got a postcard from a different part of the country. Ralph and Sue had taken to their new lives like a helium balloon to the sky, drifting in whatever direction the air took them. They were good people, and Katie would be forever grateful for their generosity toward her, especially that last year of high school.

Chapter 4

I stood for a long time staring at the Realtor's FOR SALE sign in front of Mark's house. It shouldn't have been this much of a surprise. Mark hadn't misled me. He was doing exactly what he'd said he intended to do. He was moving away. And yet I was shocked.

I don't know how long I stood in front of the house as a gnawing sensation attacked my gut. Like the liquid in a cauldron, it churned and brewed and swelled, and then all at once I was so angry I could barely contain myself. And at the same time I was unbearably sad. A profound sense of loss settled over me, that familiar pain I experienced in the first weeks after I'd gotten word that Paul was missing in action and presumed dead.

Rover sat on his haunches watching me as if he expected some sort of response on my end. I had none to give. The Realtor's sign blurred before my eyes.

It went without saying that any further attempt to talk Mark out of leaving would be pointless. I'd already tried that, but my words appeared to have no impact on him. It was as if he couldn't get away from me fast enough. Well, so be it.

The return trip to the inn was taken at a much slower pace than when I left, as my head and my heart assimilated what I'd found. As I drew closer to the inn, my thoughts whirled around inside my head. I was saddened and angry in equal measure.

When I walked up the driveway, Rover strained against the leash in his eagerness to get to Mark. I held on tightly, but Rover half dragged me forward even while I struggled to hold him back.

Mark glanced up, but when he saw it was me, he returned to his task at hand, indifferent to me. My intention had been to walk directly past him without a word and get inside the house without a display of emotion.

The silent treatment was what he deserved. If I could pretend I didn't care, maybe he'd feel the need to explain himself. Okay, admittedly, my thinking was probably skewed, but I was starting to feel desperate and lost. I had to believe there was some logical explanation for Mark's behavior, something he wasn't telling or couldn't tell me.

I wasn't halfway onto the property when, against all reason, my mouth took over. "You couldn't wait, could you?" I demanded, so angry that I barely sounded like myself.

Mark paused, turned around, and looked at me. He frowned as if he didn't have a clue what I was talking about. "Wait? For what?"

"To list your house." My anger was front and center and seemed to throb with every syllable.

"What's the big deal? I told you I was moving on."

"You had to rub it in . . . you couldn't put it off until you were sure this was what you wanted, could you?" My anger was to the point that I had trouble speaking coherently.

He set aside his paintbrush and turned to face me directly. "There was no reason to wait. The decision to leave has been made, so I listed the house."

"You didn't tell me."

"Why should I?" he snapped.

"You're right," I shot back, unbelievably hurt. "Why should you? Our . . . friendship, our relationship, means nothing to you. Why would you want to share anything with me?"

He appeared perplexed by my outburst, which said everything. He hadn't given my feelings the least bit of consideration. Any hope I'd clung to that he would change his mind dissolved like ice in boiling water.

He braced one hand against his hip. "I don't get why you're so angry."

I couldn't explain it myself. I felt the compelling urge to lash out and hurt him in the same way I was hurting. "I should have known I couldn't depend on you. You're doing what you've always done. You're running away. So run. Be a coward. If friends, if relationships, if love is more than you can deal with, then good riddance."

We squared off face-to-face. His face was red with anger and I felt the heat radiate off my own. My hands were bunched into tight fists at my sides, my nails digging hard enough into the skin of my palms to leave indentations.

His eyes narrowed and hardened. "I don't owe you any explanations. I'm my own person."

"Fine, be your own person. You don't need anyone; you're an island, an entity unto yourself. That's great. Perfect, in fact. Have a good life, because I don't need you, either."

Rover howled, but I ignored him and so did Mark.

"What I do or don't do is my own business," he reminded me. "If I choose to put my house on the market, then it's none of your concern, got it?"

Oh yes, I got it. "Loud and clear."

Neither one of us moved. The leash wrapped around my hand bit painfully into my flesh, cutting off the blood supply to my fingers. I ignored the discomfort.

"You're not my mother, or even my sister," he said between gritted teeth.

He'd never mentioned either his mother or a sister before, which served only to punctuate how little I knew about him. I'd wanted to introduce Mark to my family and he'd refused. It shouldn't have surprised me that he chose to ignore his own relatives, if indeed he had family. Nor should I be shocked that I meant little or nothing to him. People flowed through his life like creek water, never standing still for long.

"In other words, I'm nothing to you. Absolutely nothing."

He blinked, as if my accusation hit too close to the truth. "If that's the way you want to look at it, then go right ahead."

It irritated me that he had the ability to hurt me like this. I blinked furiously in an effort to hold back tears.

All at once without prior warning, all the anger drained out of me. I felt emotionally and physically exhausted. For a long moment all I could do was stare at him.

It took me a moment to find my voice. "Now you're purposely being cruel. I would have thought better of you," I whispered. In the months I'd known Mark, I'd never seen him like this.

Turning away, I returned to the house, softly closing the door behind me. Bending down, I released Rover from his leash and then, without meaning for it to happen, I crumbled to my knees and hugged my dog close. Adrenaline surged through my system. Such intense emotion needed a physical outlet, but still the shaking took me by surprise.

Rover licked my hand as though seeking to comfort me. When I could control the trembling, I stood on wobbly legs and walked aimlessly into the kitchen. Standing at the sink, I looked out the window and breathed in deep, even breaths in an effort to calm my racing heart.

Several minutes passed and I was just beginning to come to grips with my anger and frustration when I heard the front door open. I didn't immediately register that it was Mark until I heard his footsteps approach me. I had no desire to continue our argument.

"Jo Marie."

I ignored him.

He stood directly behind me. I could feel him as strongly as if he'd pressed his body flush against mine.

"Jo Marie," he tried again.

I refused to face him. "You can go, Mark . . . or Jeremy, or whatever name you prefer to be called these days. I won't hold you to the contract for the gazebo."

"I'll finish the job."

"No need. You're free to go."

"I said I'd finish the job."

I didn't think I could bear to see him again. "Frankly, I'd rather you didn't."

He paused and then reminded me, "I gave you my word. Don't worry. It won't be long; I should be done today, tomorrow at the latest."

"I'm absolving you from any further obligation." Despite my best effort to be cool and detached, my voice trembled.

Mark cupped my shoulders and I reacted by holding myself stiff. "You can mail me a bill for your services to this point."

He edged closer. "I'm sorry," he whispered, his breath warm against the back of my neck.

Shivers scooted down my spine. "Yeah, I'm sorry, too." I tried to sound flippant, but I wasn't sure I succeeded.

"The last thing in the world I'd ever want to do is hurt you."

If that was the case, he'd failed miserably. The hole in my stomach had doubled in size in the last thirty minutes. "I'd rather you left now."

"I can't."

"I'll find someone else to finish what you started," I said. "It shouldn't be difficult."

"I can't leave you like this," he said. His voice was so low it was nearly inaudible. "It's going to kill me to leave you, no matter when I go."

"Then why are you doing this?" I demanded.

As I expected, he didn't answer me.

"Is whatever it is that's driving you away so terrible you can't tell me?"

Again, he had no answer for me.

I bit into my lower lip, fearing I wasn't going to be able to hold back the tears for much longer. It infuriated me that Mark Taylor could reduce me to this emotional level.

Mark sighed and forced me to turn around and face him. The instant I did, he wrapped me in his arms and clung to me as if he was holding on to my very life.

My arms remained dangling at my sides. I refused to let my guard down, refused to give him the power to hurt me any more than he already had. But the longer he held me the more difficult it became not to put my arms around him.

"You have to know I love you," he said.

He released me and took one small step in retreat. I lowered my eyes, unable to look at him. Mark cupped my face, his callused hands rough against my soft skin.

"Jo Marie," he said, his voice strong and sure. "If you remember nothing else, remember this. I will always love you."

I tried to turn my head, discounting his words because his actions said otherwise. "If you love me so much you wouldn't do this."

He braced his forehead against mine.

"Go love some other woman," I urged. "Because, frankly, your love hurts too much."

"I can't."

I fully intended to break away, but he stopped me,

tilting my head up to receive his kiss. It'd been three weeks since Mark declared his feelings for me. Three weeks in which he'd jumped through hoops in order to ignore me. It was almost as if being in close proximity to me was unbearable for him. He went to great lengths to avoid any association with me. In that same time the most physical contact we'd had was a hug, and that had happened just before he announced he was moving away from Cedar Cove.

I stood perfectly still as his lips descended to mine. I hadn't been kissed or held since Paul left for a tour in Afghanistan. Even now I wasn't convinced I was capable of feeling any response from another man's touch.

It didn't take two seconds to discover I was wrong. Mark's kiss went through me like a laser. I didn't want to feel anything, but I couldn't help myself. I groaned, or maybe it was Mark who groaned. Perhaps we both did at the same time. My arms came around him and my fingers tangled in the small hairs at the base of his neck.

His kisses were urgent, fierce, as if he was desperate, as if he'd held himself in check for so long that when the dam broke, he was unable to control his pent-up longing and need another minute.

The intensity of his kisses nearly caused me to stumble backward. I might have, if not for the edge of the sink pressing against the small of my back.

"Jo Marie," he whispered, "Oh no . . . no . . . this shouldn't be happening." He interrupted himself by kissing me again with that same urgency. He held me so close and so tight I found it difficult to breathe.

I clung to him, too, hoping he'd have a change of

heart now that he'd held and kissed me with such abandon.

When he tore his lips from mine, his breathing was harsh and heavy. He hung his head, refusing to look at me, and then slowly, gently, he eased me away. He wanted to pull back more, but I wouldn't let him. My arms circled his waist and I hung on to him, afraid that once he let me go I would lose him forever.

For a long time we held on to each other.

Even then I knew.

Nothing had changed.

Mark had made up his mind, and kissing me, holding me, declaring his love, made no difference. The anger was gone now, replaced with a brooding sense of sadness. I dropped my arms and stepped back.

Mark maintained contact. "I'll finish the gazebo," he said.

I nodded.

"I finish what I start."

I wanted to challenge him and say he wasn't finishing what he'd started with me. Earlier, in anger, I'd accused him of being cruel. I hadn't meant it, and had spoken from my own pain. But now I realized how right I'd been. Mark Taylor was cruel in both word and deed.

"I'd give anything if things were different," he added.

I bit back a sarcastic reply. This was territory we'd already covered.

"How much longer will you be here?" I asked, without letting any emotion leak into my voice.

"I hope to finish today."

That wasn't what I was asking, but I didn't want to explain further.

"If the weather holds."

"And then?"

"And then I'm leaving."

"That soon?" I swallowed against the painful knot in my throat.

He nodded.

Chapter 5

As Coco and Katie exited the Bremerton ferry, Coco noticed how quiet her friend had gotten. It went without saying that Katie's head was full of James. All those uncomfortable questions about forgiveness were a dead giveaway. Her friend had never been able to forget James. He'd been her first love. Breaking it off with him had nearly destroyed her. Now here they were, both of them, ready to face the past, as painful as that was.

Coco was caught up in her thoughts as they rounded the curve that would take them past the lighthouse and into Cedar Cove. After her parents moved to Chicago, she'd avoided her hometown. It'd been four or five years now since she'd been back. Funny how everything seemed the same and yet it all felt so different. She looked up and down Harbor Street, and while several of the signs above the shops had changed, it remained basically the same. The hair salon was next to the flower shop and several restaurants. The library and totem pole could be seen in the distance.

"There's the marina," Coco squealed. "Do you re-member when Sally was messing around after gradu-ation and fell into the water?"

Katie smiled. "Sort of."

"Sort of? How could you forget? She completely lost it! Who knew the pastor's daughter had such a foul mouth?"

"Do you have the address for the inn?" Katie asked.

"Address?" Coco repeated. "I know where it is. It's the B-and-B the Frelingers once owned."

"Frelingers? Who are the Frelingers? I thought you said the inn was named after the owner?"

"New owner."

"Oh."

Coco made a right-hand turn and started up the steep hill, turning right again. A large sign hung out in front of the driveway announcing The Inn at Rose Harbor. Coco turned and drove down the long drive-way and an immediate sense of homecoming filled her.

"Wow," she said involuntarily. "I don't remember it looking quite like this." The three-story structure was breathtaking with its wraparound porch and large rose garden. A gazebo looked like a new addi-tion. A sign hung from a rope stretched across the gazebo's opening read WET PAINT. A profusion of roses bloomed in the attached garden, red and yel-low, white and pink.

"I don't know that I've been here," Katie said, but she, too, seemed to be in awe.

Coco parked in one of the allotted spaces. She climbed out of the car and stood, studying the B&B

with her hands braced against her hips. "The new owner has had a lot of work done. I don't remember this place being so beautiful or nearly this big."

Katie joined her and then walked around to the back of the car. Coco released the trunk latch and got out both their suitcases and set them down on the gravel.

The front door opened and a woman who didn't look much older than Coco stepped onto the wide porch. She was joined by a midsize dog, who wagged his tail in greeting.

"Welcome to Rose Harbor," she said, and while she smiled Coco noticed that the warmth she exuded didn't quite reach her eyes. "I'm Jo Marie Rose."

"Hi," Coco answered, hauling her suitcase toward the front porch.

"Come inside," Jo Marie invited. "We'll fill out the necessary paperwork and then I'll take you to your rooms."

"That would be great."

"You must be Kellie and Katie," Jo Marie said, as they made their way up the porch, lifting their suitcases.

"Kellie's my given name," Coco explained, "but most people call me Coco."

"You're both here for your class reunion?"

"That's us."

"Once we get settled, Katie and I are going to make a run over to the high school."

"We are?" Katie looked surprised.

"Sure, why not? I'd like to see if any of our old teachers are still around. It'll be fun."

"The only teacher I remember is Mr. Kloster."

And Coco knew why. The math teacher's aide had been James, and Mr. Kloster had been the one who asked James to tutor Katie. That had been the start of everything for her friend.

They finished the paperwork in short order and Jo Marie saw them to their rooms. Coco wasn't sure why she'd suggested they stop by the school. It'd been an impulsive idea, especially when she couldn't be at the high school and not remember how Ryan Temple had humiliated her.

It had all started in October of her senior year. Coco remembered that afternoon as clearly as if it had taken place just last week, instead of more than ten years ago.

She'd been practicing with the other members from the drill team. The wind whipped bronze and gold leaves across the carefully manicured grass. The football field had been especially prepared by the maintenance staff before Friday night's big game.

Even the small details remained vivid in her mind. She recalled the opposing team they were set to play. Tacoma. Funny how a small detail like that would linger in her mind. Tacoma High School had a much larger student population to draw players from, but Cedar Cove had a secret weapon.

Ryan Temple.

He was their ultratalented quarterback. A slight knee injury had kept him off the field for the first few weeks of the season, but now he was back, and according to rumors floating around the school, he was in excellent shape.

Coco was part of the drill team that was scheduled to perform at halftime during the game on Friday night. Living in a small town had several advantages. For one, the entire community supported high school sports. The stands at every home game were filled to bursting with students and faculty members along with family and friends and those looking for entertainment and a little excitement to add to their weekend.

The drill team's uniforms were standard fare, but Coco had come up with a design that changed boring into ingenious. By tucking up one edge of the pleated skirt and adding a huge madras flower, she changed the entire look. When she'd showed her fellow team members her idea, everyone had been enthusiastic.

Coco loved clothes. As a teenager she'd lived and breathed fashion and spent copious amounts of time poring over magazines and books, studying the different looks, gathering ideas she hoped to sew one day herself. She dreamed of the day her own line of clothing would be displayed on a New York runway.

She found it interesting and funny how dreams have a way of morphing in different directions. Life had taken her down a different path, but one that was equally challenging and exciting.

It was that Thursday afternoon before Friday's game when Ryan first sought her out after practice.

The football team had been on the field, and the drill team had gone over their routine in the gymnasium several times while waiting for the field to become available.

The boys had headed to the locker room to shower

when the drill team started toward the grassy field. At some point the two groups intersected.

Coco heard her name called and stopped to look around.

It was Ryan.

"Coco," he called again. "Hold up."

Her friends flew past her. Coco was struck dumb in front of Ryan, hardly knowing what to think. He held his football helmet under his arm and his maroon-and-gold uniform showed several grass stains.

"Hi," he said, looking a bit sheepish.

"Hi." His eyes were the most amazing color of emerald green. Coco wasn't sure she'd even noticed his eyes before. His hair was a deep, rich shade of auburn. He had a small scar just above his left eye, directly below his thick brow.

"I've been wanting to say hi."

This information completely tongue-tied her. This inability to speak wasn't normal for her. Coco had an outgoing personality and made friends easily. That said, it wasn't every day that the cutest and most popular boy in school sought her out. She managed to swallow without choking, which was something of a feat, considering how nervous she was. "Hi."

"Hi," he returned, and dazzled her with his smile. He kicked at the dirt with the toe of his shoe. "You going to the dance after the game?"

"Me?" She pressed her hand to her chest and felt her pounding heart.

He grinned, making his eyes sparkle all the brighter.

"Yeah, you."

"I guess." She'd been working hard on the drill

team's uniforms, and Coco hadn't given the dance much thought.

Ryan's smile widened. "Great, then I'll see you there."

"Sure." A one-word reply was all she could manage.

"See ya," Ryan said, and took off in a trot after his teammates.

"See ya," she called out after him.

It took Coco several minutes to realize that Ryan Temple had as good as asked her out on a date. As soon as Coco joined her friends on the field, they pelted her with questions.

"What did Ryan want?" Josie Sharp asked.

Coco wasn't sure what to say. "He said he'd wanted to say hi."

"Hi? That's it?"

Coco nodded.

The team members formed a circle around her.

"Wow."

"You were talking for longer than that," Laurie Burke insisted.

"He asked if I'll be at the dance after the game."

A shocked silence followed, one mingled with disbelief and awe. "He asked about the dance?" Josie whispered, as if Ryan had fallen to one knee and proposed marriage.

How dramatic they'd all been. It made Coco want to roll her eyes in retrospect.

"What did you tell him?"

"What do you think she told him?" Brittany Coolidge barked. "Of course Coco's going to the dance."

"I'm going, too," Ruthie said, and several others chimed in.

Friday night, the drill team's routine was flawless, but the talk was all about the updated uniforms. Coco received lots of compliments. The Cedar Cove Wolves pulled out a win, due to a last-minute touchdown pass by Ryan Temple.

The dance was in full swing by the time Ryan arrived with other members of the football team. As soon as he stepped into the gymnasium, he paused and searched the crowd.

Coco watched as his gaze fell upon her. It felt as if Coco's heart was going to break into song. It took restraint not to raise her hand to her heart as if that would hold back the excitement that bubbled up from the very tips of her toes.

Ryan started across the floor and was stopped several times along the way by friends and schoolmates wanting to congratulate him on the Hail Mary pass that saved the game. Coco remained frozen to the spot, afraid if she moved he would look elsewhere for a dance partner.

When he was able to break away, Ryan sauntered up to her. The music swirled around them. For a long moment all he did was look at her. And she at him. Coco was afraid to breathe, sure if she did the spell would be broken.

After a long moment, he smiled. "Hi." Just the way he said it made it sound as if he'd been waiting all day for just this moment. She knew she had.

"Great game." Her mouth felt dry, which made it difficult to speak.

"Thanks." He looked away briefly, as if uncomfortable with compliments. "Awesome routine."

"You saw it?" This surprised Coco.

"Only the last few minutes. Coach kept us in the locker room longer than I would have liked, so I was only able to see the end. You looked great."

Coco was sure she must have blushed.

"The new uniforms look hot. Someone said you thought up the flower."

She shrugged off his praise. "I enjoy doing stuff like that."

"So I heard."

The comment implied that he'd asked about her around school—otherwise how would he know? Okay, someone might have casually mentioned it.

"Would you like to dance?" he asked, glancing over his shoulder at the couples on the floor. They were playing one of Coco's favorite songs.

"Okay."

He reached for her hand and led her onto the dance floor. It might have been her imagination, but it felt like they were walking through the middle of the Red Sea. A pathway immediately opened up for them as couples scooted aside in order for Coco and Ryan to walk to the middle of the polished wooden floor.

Coco felt like every eye in the room was on the two of them. The fact that Ryan had sought her out in such a public way on the football field yesterday and again at the dance didn't go unnoticed.

They danced every dance for the rest of the evening, and when the dance ended Ryan offered to drive Coco home.

"Thanks, but I came with a few of my friends," she said regretfully.

Ryan looked disappointed. "You sure?"

She nodded. It didn't seem right to abandon Josie, Natalie, and Laurie just because she had what they might consider a better offer. Besides, everything was happening too fast. "I appreciate you asking."

"What are you up to tomorrow?" He didn't seem inclined to drop it there.

Coco's heart sank. "We're driving over to see my grandmother in Yakima. It's her seventieth birthday and the whole family is getting together to celebrate."

"You won't be back Saturday night?"

She shook her head. "No, we're staying over with my aunt and uncle." Coco wished with all her heart that her grandmother had been born a different time of the year.

"So your entire weekend is taken up." His face relayed his disappointment.

"Yes. Sorry."

"Can I call you?"

She brightened. "That'd be great." He pulled out his phone and she gave him her number.

"I'll be in touch."

"Okay." Out of the corner of her eye Coco could see her three friends impatiently waiting for her. They stood by the door, huddled together, whispering. She didn't need to speculate who they were discussing.

Coco was about two feet away when Laurie grabbed her by the arm and jerked her closer. "Oh my!"

"I can't believe it!" Natalie groaned.

"He danced with you the entire night!" Her friends gathered around her like a flock of geese, each one asking questions Coco didn't want to answer. She feared saying too much would jinx it.

"Ryan Temple likes you," Josie insisted with a dreamy look.

"What did you do to get his attention?" Laurie asked.

"I . . . don't know."

"Of course you know," Josie argued. "You have to know."

Coco wasn't sure she'd said or done anything worthy of Ryan, but she wasn't about to question it.

"He just broke up with Dakota Schmidt." Natalie was the one who kept track of such matters.

The only thing Coco knew about Dakota was that she was a class officer and was destined to be salutatorian for their graduating class.

"What happened with Dakota and Ryan?" Coco asked.

None of her friends knew, not even Natalie.

"Who broke it off?"

Again, silence.

"Who knows and who cares," Laurie insisted.

"Not when Ryan has his sights on our Coco."

"You know what this means?" Josie cried, as they headed out the school doors and into the parking lot.

"We can all hang out with the football team now."

"Hold on," Coco protested, and raised both hands.

"Ryan and I are not together."

"Not yet, but you will be soon enough."

"Right," Natalie agreed. "He wants you."

Coco remained unconvinced. "It seems to me you're taking a lot for granted."

"Did he ask you out?" Natalie pried, looping her arm around Coco's.

Coco wasn't sure she wanted to volunteer that information. "It wouldn't have done any good if he had. It's my grandmother's birthday weekend."

"He did ask, then," Josie squealed.

"You're all getting ahead of yourselves," Coco insisted, wishing now that she'd accepted Ryan's offer for a ride. If she'd gone with him she would have been able to avoid this inquisition from her friends.

They reached the car. Natalie unlocked it and Coco took the backseat the same way she had on the drive to the football game.

"Coco, get in the front."

"The front? Why?"

"You're dating Ryan Temple now and that grants you certain privileges!"

"Stop," Coco cried, embarrassed now. She would have said more, but her phone chirped with a text.

"It's Ryan," Laurie whispered.

The entire car went silent.

"You don't know that," Coco said.

"Aren't you going to check it?" Josie asked.

"I will later."

"Do it now," Natalie cried. "You can't keep us in suspense like this."

"All right, all right." Coco reached for her phone. Sure enough, the text was from Ryan.

"What did he say?" Natalie had all but climbed over the seat to get a look at Coco's phone.

"Nothing much. He said we'd talk."

Josie placed both hands over her heart. "Why oh why couldn't I be so lucky?"

Coco sighed. Little did she know then what she did now. If she had, she would have done everything possible to make sure Ryan Temple looked elsewhere for a new girlfriend.

Chapter 6

In her room, which was across the hall from Coco's, Katie unpacked her suitcase, hanging her clothes in the closet. Coco had mentioned stopping by the high school, but Katie wasn't sure she wanted to go with her. It was likely, however, that Coco would need her for moral support. The fact was Katie needed her friend for much the same.

It was hard to believe that in a matter of a few hours she'd see James. The worst-case scenario was that he'd continue to make it clear he wanted nothing more to do with her. That wasn't what she wanted, but there was every likelihood she would have to accept his decision. Perhaps there was a chance for them, but either way, she needed closure to this unsettled, unresolved issue.

They'd met when Katie transferred in October of her senior year. Changing schools had been the worst. Her social worker had tried hard to keep Katie in the same school district, but there were no spaces available for a girl who was nearly eighteen years old. Mrs. Gillian did the best she could for Katie, placing her with the Flemmingses, who were personal friends of hers. They had taken in foster kids in the past, but hadn't for several years. Mrs. Gillian assured them that Katie would be no trouble and that she'd be with them for only a few months. The Flemmingses agreed, and Katie had found a temporary home with a wonderful family. She made sure to always be polite and did what she could to be a help. She never asked for anything beyond what was absolutely necessary, wanting with all her heart to finish the school year in one place and graduate from high school.

In order to graduate with the class, she needed a math credit. Katie was placed in second-year algebra, but it didn't take her longer than one class period to realize where she'd been in her last school was way behind this class. She'd never get a passing grade without help. After class she'd timidly approached her teacher, Mr. Kloster, and explained her situation.

The teacher mentioned his TA and called to James just as he was about to leave the classroom.

"James," he said, stopping the tall, athletic-looking boy. "You met Katie earlier, right?"

James glanced at Katie and nodded. She knew what he must be thinking. Her hair was red and wild after hurrying from swim class, the shoulder-length curls flowing in every direction. She had freckles all across her cheeks and the bridge of her nose, and her clothes were secondhand. She wasn't exactly the coolest kid in class.

"Katie needs help catching up. Would you be willing to tutor her over the next few weeks?"

James looked as if he'd been asked to babysit a kindergartner. "I guess," he said, with a complete lack of enthusiasm.

"Fine. I'll leave it up to the two of you to work out a schedule." Mr. Kloster reached for his books and headed out the door. This was the last class of the day, so he must be eager to leave, and from the disgruntled look James tossed at her, he was just as eager to escape. Instead, he was stuck with her.

James walked out of the classroom with her. "Would twice a week work?" he asked.

She kept her head lowered and nodded.

"Can you meet before school?"

Katie shook her head. "Sorry, no, I ride the bus."

"When's your study period?"

She told him and he groaned. "I should have guessed. Mine is second period."

"What about after school?" she asked, willing to walk home instead of taking the bus.

He hesitated. "Is that the only time you can meet?"

He glanced toward the gym, which was off the cafeteria, and she realized that by tutoring her he would be missing out on time with his friends. She nodded. "Sorry."

"Great, just great," he muttered. They set a place to meet and then he asked, "How far behind are you?"

"I . . . I'm not sure." All Katie knew was that she was completely lost.

"Do you have time today?"

Clutching her books to her chest, she nodded.

"Perfect." He said it as if it was anything but.

And so they started meeting after class two times a week. In the beginning it was terribly awkward. They sat at a table in the corner of the cafeteria, across from each other. She rarely spoke unless prompted, and James didn't seem inclined to chat, either. This time together was strictly for solving for x and looking for y.

Katie lost count of how many times he said, gritting his teeth, "This isn't that hard."

Maybe not for him. "I'm not good with numbers."

Not long after they started meeting he grew impatient when she reached for a scratch pad. "There's a calculator on your phone," he muttered impatiently. Katie had trouble meeting his gaze. "I don't have a phone."

He looked stunned. "Who doesn't have a phone?"

"I don't," she whispered.

"Okay, whatever, use mine." He slid his cell across the table.

Those first two weeks were dreadful for Katie. Apparently, James had had to give up time playing basketball with his friends because of her and she guessed that was the reason he resented having to spend time with her. It didn't help when one of the guys taunted him, calling Katie his girlfriend.

Katie didn't dare look at James; it wasn't necessary, she could well guess his reaction. She tried, she honestly tried, but anything math-related was like learning a foreign language to her. By the time they started work on the quadratic formula her stomach was in knots and she felt hopelessly stupid.

"Just follow the steps," James said. "Come on, you're not stupid. You can do this."

"I can't if you're yelling at me."

"I'm not yelling," he said, lowering his voice as he glanced longingly toward the gym.

"You're upset because you'd rather be with your friends and you're stuck helping me."

"I'm upset because working with you is so frustrating."

"I'm upset, too," she cried, and shoved the book aside. "I can't understand any of this." She was close to tears and her voice wobbled. "I'll take whatever grade I get. You tried to help . . . and I appreciate that. Go play ball with your friends." Standing, she reached for the textbook and grabbed her sweater and started to walk away.

Almost immediately James caught up with her. "Okay, okay, I get it—math isn't your thing." He exhaled as if struggling to get a grip on his patience and keep his cool. He matched her step for step until they were in the hallway outside the cafeteria. When he spoke again it wasn't about algebra. "I heard you're on swim team now?"

She didn't look at him, fearing all she'd see was his annoyance.

"If you flunk the class, Coach will pull you from the team."

Katie swallowed hard. Swimming was the one area in which she excelled, the one thing in life that gave her pleasure. To have that taken away from her would be devastating.

She didn't say anything, but the lump in her throat thickened. This had been by far the worst year of her life. Yet another foster home. The social worker had told her that her mother had recently been sent to prison. She'd been arrested for stealing, most likely for money for drugs. Katie had no friends, and even James hated her.

His voice gentled. "The team needs you."

She needed the team, too, and swimming, although she wouldn't tell him that.

"I'll try to be more patient," he promised, exhaling. Katie slowed her pace and then stopped walking as she weighed her options. "Okay, I'll try, too."

With his hands in his pockets, James leaned against one of the lockers. "I'm sorry I yelled at you."

Katie looked up then, brushing the wild red hair away from her eyes. "I'm sorry, too."

"You aren't stupid," he said again, straightening and leading her back to the cafeteria.

"You could have fooled me."

"You've got to stop thinking like that," he chastised. "That's part of your problem. You keep telling yourself you don't get this math stuff. If you gave yourself half a chance you'd do a lot better. Try a positive attitude."

"You think that will actually help?" Katie couldn't help being skeptical, although she had to admit he was right. Her attitude was rotten, but then so was his.

"It can't hurt."

"Then I'll try if you do."

"Me?" he sounded surprised.

"Oh come on, James, admit it. You got trapped into being my tutor and you don't like it. Not that I blame you, but your attitude isn't exactly helping matters."

He arched his brows as if shocked she was capable of stringing more than two or three words together at a time.

It took a minute, but then he smiled. He actually smiled, and Katie smiled back.

"All right. Let's try this again with a fresh attitude from both of us."

"Okay," she agreed.

The tutoring sessions went better after that.

Making friends with Coco had been a big help, too. They were on the swim team together. The girl was open, friendly, and a little flamboyant, whereas Katie was withdrawn and shy. The one area where Katie excelled was in the water. Even now she remembered the first words Coco ever said to her.

"Wow, you're fast."

"Thanks."

"We're really glad you're on the team. A few of us are going out after the meet. Do you want to join us?"

More than anything Katie wanted to go, but she couldn't. Mrs. Flemmings needed her back at the house to help with dinner. It would have been fine if she'd made arrangements with her foster parents before the meet.

"I can't," she said, reluctance weighing down her words. "Sorry."

"Next time," Coco said, and then hesitated. "Do you mind me saying something about your clothes?"

Katie was sure her face must have turned a flaming shade of red. "I know they . . ."

Stretching out her arm, Coco wrapped her hand around Katie's forearm. "I want to go to fashion school, so I do this all the time. I hope you don't mind. I was thinking if you left that top untucked, your outfit would be really cool. That's the look they're showing in the magazines this fall." Katie hardly knew what to say. "That's so nice of you."

"I love this kind of stuff. My friends are used to me dressing them up. It's all about accessorizing. If you want, I can show you a few tricks."

"Okay." And that was the beginning of a friendship that had lasted from that day forward. Spending time with Coco was fun. Her newfound friend was full of ideas and energy and dreams for the future. Just being with Coco gave Katie hope that one day she'd fit in with everyone else at Cedar Cove High.

After swimming the next day, Coco swept Katie's untamed red curls back and tied them at the base of her neck. The day after that she loaned Katie a pair of dangly silver earrings with a matching necklace. She had a dozen thin bangles to go with it, but Katie found it too hard to wear them and write, so she returned the bracelets. But the earrings and necklace felt glamorous.

That afternoon was another tutoring session with James. With her heart pounding so loud she was sure he must hear it, she approached their table. She wondered if he'd notice the jewelry.

She sat down and dug her textbook out of her backpack.

James didn't say anything for a moment, and then said, "You look nice today."

Katie lowered her head in order to hide the pleasure his compliment gave her. "Thank you."

"Did you come with a positive attitude?" he asked.

"Did you?" she returned.

He laughed. "I did. Now let's get down to work."

To his credit, James didn't get annoyed with her once during that session. Katie continued to struggle, although she wasn't as willing to give up. Once she conquered the quadratic formula she'd be caught up with the class. As best she could figure, it would take another week, possibly two.

She wasn't sure what changed, but following their blowup, she found they were working together instead of against each other.

For the next session, Katie arrived at the cafeteria first. James was only a minute or two behind her, but instead of sitting in the chair across the table from her, he sat next to her.

Katie looked up in surprise, afraid to mention the change in position and even to guess what it might mean. Her heart started pounding like a runaway horse, and when she reached for her pencil her hand trembled.

James acted as if nothing was out of the ordinary, but it was, and Katie didn't know what it might mean.

He was reviewing her homework assignment that she'd started in class when one of the guys from his group of friends strolled past.

"James," he called out. "How long are you going to be? We're one man short."

"It'll be a while."

The other boy trained his look on Katie. She'd seen him around but didn't know his name. His scrutiny made her uncomfortable.

"How long is it going to take before you're back, man? The girl is taking all your playing time."

"The girl has a name: Katie Gilroy," he snapped.

In that instant it felt as if the entire world had stopped. Katie's heart shot into her throat. She hated that James had been put on the spot. He would never ask someone like her to Homecoming, and so she answered for him.

"No," she blurted out, feeling the telltale blush fill her cheeks with color. Her face burned with it and she lowered her head so low her forehead practically touched the textbook.

"I'll stop by the gym later, Brandon," said James.

"Sure."

Brandon left and Katie felt the tension ease from James and realized it had from her, too.

"Sorry about that," he said after a moment.

"That's okay, you don't need to apologize."

He rolled the pencil between his open palms. "Has anyone asked you to Homecoming?"

"No. It isn't for another couple of weeks, right?"

"Right."

She thought for a minute that he wanted to talk about the dance, but he dropped the subject and she was just as glad. Even if by some miracle a boy asked her, Katie wouldn't have been able to attend. She didn't have money for a dress or shoes or anything else and she wouldn't ask the Flemmingses.

When she'd finished the assignment, Katie closed her book and returned it to her backpack. She expected James would want to go and join his friends in the gym right away. Instead he lingered behind.

"I saw you walking home the other day."

Whenever she stayed after school, she missed the

"You taking her to Homecoming?"

bus. "The buses have all left by the time we're finished here. The house isn't that far." The Flemmingses' home was more than a mile from the school, but Katie didn't mind the exercise.

James glanced outside. "Would you like a ride?"

His invitation left her nearly speechless. "What about your friends? Aren't you going to go play basketball?"

"No."

She wasn't sure what to tell him. It felt like he was offering her a lot more than dropping her off on his way home.

"Do you want a ride or not?" he asked, smiling, when she didn't answer right away. He grabbed hold of his own backpack and swung it over his shoulder by one strap.

Katie smiled and nodded. "Thank you."

"No big deal," he said. "It's on my way."

When he smiled at her it felt as if the whole world was smiling on her.

Chapter 7

It wasn't until early afternoon that I looked outside and saw that Mark was busy painting the gazebo, clearly hoping to finish the job today.

As far as I could tell he hadn't even stopped to eat lunch, working straight through. I raised my fingers to my lips, which remained slightly swollen, even now, from his kisses earlier in the day.

Standing out of view of the gazebo, I watched the hurried pace he'd set for himself, my stomach in knots. For whatever reason a memory came to me of the day I'd gotten the news that Paul was missing in action and presumed dead. An army chaplain and officer had come to deliver the news. It had been early—just after six in the morning. I was up and had coffee brewing, getting ready for the office.

Little of our meeting, the actual words spoken, stayed with me. Everything stopped when I heard the words *missing in action—presumed dead*. The shock of it had knocked me so far off balance that I'd started orbiting another world.

What stuck in my mind from that terrible morning

was how desperately I needed my mother. I don't know how long it took me to reach for the phone. It could have been hours or minutes. I was completely numb. I don't think I said anything more than "Mom." Reeling, my head spinning at warp speed, I wasn't emotional or sobbing. Shock had a tight grip on me and yet just the desperate way I cried out her name, my mother knew.

The next thing I remembered was that she was there with me. I didn't cry until my mother had her arms around me. She held me close as I wailed. I rocked back and forth in a strange effort to absorb the wave upon wave of pain, this body blow of over-whelming grief.

As I stood watching Mark work, I had the strongest desire to reach out to my mother, needing her comfort once more and not knowing how to explain why. I resisted as long as I could before walking into my office and slumping down in the chair. For a full five minutes all I did was stare at my landline. When I found the courage to pick up the receiver I dialed my family home.

It took three rings for Mom to answer. "Jo Marie, what's up?"

"Hi, Mom. You busy?"

A short pause followed. "What's wrong?"

"What makes you think anything is wrong?" I asked, already regretting the urge to call her. I should have known my mother would see through my attempt to be casual. She knew me well enough to realize I was upset even before I could tell her.

"Something's up," Mom insisted, "so you'd best

tell me without pretending this is just a checking-in kind of call. I know otherwise, so cut to the chase."

Leaning forward, I braced my elbow on the desk and pressed my hand against my forehead. "Mark's leaving."

"Ah . . . so it's Mark," Mom said, as if that explained everything. And perhaps it did.

I pinched the bridge of my nose in a futile effort to hold back the tears. "He's just about finished with the gazebo and then he's heading out."

"Yes, you'd said he was moving on," my ever-practical mother said.

Apparently, she didn't fully understand the significance. "Yes . . . he told me that a few weeks ago."

"Didn't you believe him?"

"I did, but . . ."

"So what you're telling me is now that it's actually happening, you don't want him to go?"

That was it in a nutshell. "I don't," I admitted. "He's become important to me. He's my handyman and builder and my best friend, and now he's leaving. He hasn't even left yet and I'm feeling lost and alone."

"Oh, honey, I'm so sorry."

"I feel . . . I don't know." It was hard to explain when I hadn't been able to put it into words, even to myself.

"When Dad and I were at the inn for dinner, your father was convinced then you had a soft spot for Mark, remember?"

"I remember."

Mom wasn't one to hold back. "You do have feelings for him, don't you, sweetie?"

My fingers went back to my mouth and I closed my

eyes and remembered the anguished way in which Mark had held and kissed me.

"Jo Marie?"

"Yes," I admitted, "I guess I do." It was the first time I'd been willing to say the words aloud. Until he kissed me I'd denied any emotional attachment to Mark. Now I had to ask myself if I'd been falling in love with Mark, and I was afraid of the answer.

"Does he feel the same way about you?" Mom asked me, her voice gentle and careful, as if she was afraid the question would bring me pain.

"I believe he loves me." Mark had as good as said he was in love with me. "He won't tell me why he has to leave, but whatever it is has to be serious. He's done something he refuses to discuss with me or apparently anyone else." Our conversation from three weeks ago lingered in my mind.

"Do you think he's done something illegal?" Mom's voice dropped to a whisper as if the FBI had tapped my phone line and was listening in at this very moment.

"No, I don't think so," I said, though I couldn't be sure. Almost from the first time I'd met him, I'd suspected Mark Taylor was hiding some deep, dark secret. Everything about him was mysterious. I'd done copious amounts of research to dig into his past and had come away with no significant information. At one point I'd considered making an appointment to talk to Roy MacAfee, a retired Seattle police detective who did a bit of private investigation on the side. In the end I'd decided against it.

"Okay." Mom didn't sound convinced. "What could it be, then?"

I so badly wanted the answer. "I don't know; I just don't know." Whatever it was tormented Mark. From the way he held and kissed me I knew that he no more wanted to leave than I wanted him to go.

"Oh, sweetie. I am sorry, but in some ways I think his leaving might be for the best."

I couldn't believe what I was hearing. "What do you mean?"

My mother's hesitation told me this was a matter that had weighed heavily on her mind. "I've watched you over the last eighteen months, Jo Marie, and you've used Mark as a crutch."

"A what?" She wasn't making sense.

"A crutch. He's become your friend and your confidant, and that's all well and good, but it's time, Jo Marie. Time for you to break out of that protective wall you've built, insulating yourself from the world. You were crazy about Paul and he about you. He was lost, alone, drifting, and then there was Mark . . ."

"Mom—" I started to protest, but she cut me off.

"My goodness, Jo Marie, look at your life—Your best friend is a cranky handyman you've kept at arm's length. You no longer go out with friends. You behave like a grandmother, baking cookies, pruning roses."

"I'm an innkeeper. I don't have a lot of free time," I argued.

"Make time," Mom countered. "You're young and full of life—it's time you started acting like it. Yes, I know you're grieving, but really, is this what Paul would have wanted?"

I didn't want to argue with my mother. "Okay," I

whispered, "I'll give it some thought." What I'd wanted were some gentle words that would ease the ache in my heart. "I called to talk about Mark," I reminded her.

"I know. Perhaps I shouldn't have said anything, but I've been worried about you for quite a while now and hesitated to mention it. I know it's for the best."

"He put his house on the market."

"Let him go, Jo Marie, and use this time to reach out and make new friends."

My mother had certainly given me something to think about. I didn't necessarily agree with her, but what she said was worth considering.

"Would you like me to come over and spend a few days with you?" my mother offered.

I was tempted to accept, but then decided it would be a hardship for my dad to be without Mom. If I said the word, she'd be on the next ferry to Cedar Cove, but it would disrupt their lives for my own selfish reasons. I'd survived much worse and I would get through this, too.

"I appreciate that you would be willing, but no thanks, Mom."

"You're sure?"

"I'm sure."

"Call me if you change your mind."

"I will," I promised.

We spoke for a few more minutes, exchanging family news. I'll admit by the time we disconnected I did feel better. Just talking to my mother had helped ease the ache in my heart.

Rover was asleep at my feet, his chin resting on the

top of my foot. I reached down and scratched his ears. When I left the office I noticed the sun was shining and the afternoon had grown warm.

I glanced out the window and saw Mark wipe his forearm across his forehead. I'd made a pitcher of iced tea earlier in the day, so I poured him a large glass and added a slice of lemon. The oatmeal-raisin cookies I'd baked earlier in the week were tucked away in the freezer. I removed the plastic bag and took out four and set them on a plate and carried the tea and cookies out to Mark.

He looked over his shoulder when I came onto the porch, and a frown marred his brow when he saw me.

"I come in peace," I assured him. "You look like you could use a cool drink and a few cookies."

For a moment it seemed as if he was going to refuse me. "Thanks. Set them down on the porch and I'll have them later."

"Okay." I was disappointed but said nothing. Doing as he asked, I placed the glass and the plate of cookies on the top step. "This works out best, as the cookies are frozen."

He frowned. "You put cookies in the freezer?"

"I *hide* cookies in the freezer," I corrected.

"Because I tend to eat them as fast as you bake them," he said and smiled.

I smiled back. "No, because I'm afraid *I'll* eat them. You know what they say, don't you? Out of sight, out of mind."

Right away his smile faded and his look sobered. "Is that how it will work with me, Jo Marie?" he asked, his gaze holding mine in a tight grip.

He was so serious that for a moment I couldn't find my voice to answer. "No," I whispered, "I won't forget you, Mark. You'll always be right here." I pressed my palm over my heart.

He continued to hold my look for a long moment before he turned away and resumed painting. I watched him, unable to move. Despite his effort to hide it, I caught a glimpse of pain and regret in him. For just a millisecond I thought he was about to drop the paintbrush and take me in his arms again. The look passed so quickly I couldn't be sure. Perhaps it was my own heart speaking, calling out to him.

I returned to the kitchen, where I stood looking out the window above the sink. Once again I reviewed the conversation with Mark I'd had three weeks previously when he'd first mentioned he had feelings for me. Something Mark had said then kept bugging me. He'd talked about climbing out of a black hole, but I didn't know what he'd meant. I'd tried to ask him questions, but he wouldn't answer. He had reminded me that Paul was a hero and in the same sentence claimed he himself was flawed and broken.

Even now I remembered how intense he'd gotten, regret coating each word. Although Mark had never said it, I was convinced he'd been part of the military. In my talks with Peggy and Bob Beldon, they'd said they had the same impression. Someone, I didn't remember who, had said they were fairly certain Mark spoke fluent German.

Last year when he'd broken his leg and was dopey on pain meds he'd muttered something unintelligible at me. At the time I assumed he was incoherent with pain and just babbling. In retrospect it might have been another language, one unfamiliar to me. I wanted to ask him and immediately realized I couldn't. Anytime I questioned him he grew impatient and either ignored me or changed the subject. He'd become a master at evasion.

If I had only a day or two left with Mark I was determined not to waste them digging for information he was intent on hiding.

The doorbell chimed and I glanced at my watch. I wasn't sure who it might be. The two women I'd been expecting had arrived and had already registered. They'd let me know how much they liked their rooms. I'd left them fresh flowers from my garden, and the windows were open so a cool breeze came through. September really was a lovely time of the year in the Pacific Northwest. I rolled my shoulders, resolving to set aside my concerns and worries over Mark, planted a welcoming smile on my face, and headed to the front door.

Rover beat me there and sat on his haunches, ready to greet whoever had stopped by.

It was Mark.

He rarely bothered to ring the doorbell. He held the empty glass and the plate in his hands. "Thanks," he said.

I opened the door wider, took the glass and plate, and set them aside, waiting for him to come in. He remained standing on the other side of the threshold.

"I've about finished with the painting," he said, and reached inside his hip pocket and removed a folded slip of paper.

My gaze fell on it. The bill.

"But you aren't finished."

"Close enough, Jo Marie."

Reluctantly, I took the paper out of his hand and lowered my gaze. I didn't want him to know how difficult I found this moment to be.

Chapter 8

After Coco unpacked her suitcase she sat on the edge of the bed and looked out the window of her room onto the cove below. Sailboats bobbed on the waters of the marina and the Olympic mountains framed the background. Coco had forgotten how beautiful the view was from the cove. Next, her gaze drifted to the high school set on a hill in view of the inn. Almost against her will, her attention lingered there.

Now that she was back in Cedar Cove, she couldn't stop thinking of those first few weeks when Ryan paid her attention. After the school dance that Friday night in which Ryan had made it clear he was interested in her, Coco had been on an emotional high that lasted the entire weekend. Overnight she'd gone from a girl who others viewed as quirky and eccentric, to something of a sensation. Everyone, it seemed, wanted to talk to her about what was happening between her and Ryan. As if she knew. One day she was just another girl on the drill team and the next she was being sought after by the most popular boy in school.

Coco didn't know what to tell those who were curious. She couldn't explain why Ryan was pursuing her. As far as she knew, she hadn't even been on his radar. And yet it was the most exciting thing to happen to her in her four-year high school career. Perhaps she should have stopped then and reasoned it out. If she had, then the events that followed might have been avoided.

By Monday morning when Coco arrived at school, the subject of her and Ryan had spread like a California wildfire.

He fanned the flames by seeking her out in the cafeteria at lunchtime. Despite the fact that she was surrounded by friends, he made a point of asking her to join him outside. Coco numbly nodded and followed.

"You look great in that skirt," he said, admiration in his voice.

"This old *thing*?" she joked. It *was* old. She'd picked it up at a secondhand store and worked her magic. Taking something discarded and giving it new life was her gift.

He smiled and Coco swore the sun grew brighter. This guy was drop-dead gorgeous and he was paying attention to her. To her! As they sat eating their lunch together on the grass with no one else around, Ryan mentioned Homecoming. The school hallways were lined with posters about the dance.

"Are you going?" he asked.

Her heart started to pound with such an erratic beat for a moment she feared that she might actually faint. "I . . . I don't know yet."

"Has anyone asked you?"

"No," she whispered, afraid to meet his look for fear he would notice how shallow her breathing had become. It was a half-lie. Hudson Hamilton, one of the nerdiest guys in their class, had made a bumbling effort to ask her but hadn't been able to get the words out. Even before he finished she'd told him she wasn't interested. She hadn't meant to be rude, but in retrospect it had probably come out that way. The truth of it was she'd rather sit home and watch reruns of *Lizzy McGuire* than attend Homecoming with Hudson. She doubted he'd ever kissed a girl and she could only imagine what it would be like to dance with him. It didn't take much imagination to know Hudson on a dance floor was a disaster waiting to happen.

"Would you like to go with me?" Ryan asked.

Coco had been too stunned to respond. It didn't seem possible that Ryan Temple had just asked her to attend Homecoming with him. A date with Ryan, who was sure to be nominated for Homecoming king, was beyond the realm of possibility. For what seemed like an eternity, all she could manage was to stare openmouthed at him, hardly able to believe she'd heard him correctly.

"Coco?"

She pressed her hand over her chest. "Okay," she squeaked. The lone word robbed her of oxygen and she gasped for air. In an effort to appear as nonchalant as possible, she smiled and added, "That would be great."

His face broke into a huge smile. "Perfect. What color is your dress? I want to be sure the corsage will match."

Flowers? Dress? She hadn't given the matter of

the dance, let alone a dress, more than a wayward thought.

From that time forward, Coco's world had gone into a whirlwind of activity and excitement. Ryan Temple had asked her to Homecoming. She was going to be his date! The entire school knew Ryan had asked her. It was as if it'd been announced over the school intercom.

By the time Homecoming rolled around, Coco swore there was less fuss made over a royal wedding. The week preceding the dance had been crazy. Though she wanted to find something secondhand and fix it up, her mother insisted that Coco buy a new dress, and so they had begun a shopping expedition to find the perfect one, along with shoes and other accessories. She had her hair and nails styled at the priciest salon in Cedar Cove. Her mother said Coco looked positively stunning. Her father took pictures.

The night of the dance, when Ryan came to pick her up in his father's car, it felt like something out of a fairy tale. He'd talked to her parents for a few minutes until she appeared. When Coco stepped into the room, he slowly came to his feet as if she were an angel who'd made a visitation to earth. Her beauty left him speechless, or at least that was the impression he wanted to make, and naturally she fell for it.

On the ride to the dance Ryan repeatedly told her how beautiful she looked and how it was hard for him to take his eyes off her to drive. Oh, how foolish she'd been. Once they arrived they danced to every song. Just as she expected, Ryan was named Homecoming king, but he wouldn't hear of her dancing with anyone but him. She was the entire focus of his attention. He acted as if he'd fallen head over heels in love with her.

After the dance, Ryan suggested they drive around for a while and she'd agreed. Most every other couple she knew were going to one of the after-parties. For her part Coco was caught in this magical fantasy, and if Ryan wanted to spend time alone with her, then that was what she wanted, too. Her head swam with joy.

After a short while, Ryan parked the car in a dark area that overlooked the cove. Lights from the navy shipyard sparkled in the distance. It was romantic and perfect in every way. It grew even more wonderful when Ryan kissed her.

Eagerly, Coco came into his arms, loving the taste and the feel of him. She didn't know how long they kissed before he groped for the zipper at the back of her dress and lowered it enough to gain access to her breasts. Coco wasn't completely naive and she knew matters were advancing far too quickly. She broke off the kiss and drew in several breaths in the hope of clearing her head before things grew any more serious.

Ryan paused. But then he brought his mouth back to hers, seducing her with his tongue, whispering how much he loved and needed her, until her head was swimming. This was his night. He'd been crowned king and she was his queen. His beautiful queen. When he started fondling her breasts she let him. It felt so right and so good, and the endearments he whispered were as heady as any aphrodisiac. A little while later he slid his hand up her dress. Again, she stopped him, only it was far more difficult this time.

She liked what he did to her, enjoyed this sensation of feeling desirable. Oh, how he wanted her. He was desperate for her, he claimed, his need so great that he was in pain.

"Ryan," she whispered, having trouble speaking. She drew in deep breaths in a valiant effort to end the lovemaking while she could. She held on to his wrist. "This is our first date . . . I think we should stop."

"Okay," he whispered, kissing her again. "Anything you say."

His hands continued to work their magic, and as much as she wanted him to stop, she couldn't make herself say the words. It was all so new and wonderful. She had some experience, but nothing like this.

Coco had been a full participant of what happened next. He'd been gentle with her, and while they'd made love in the backseat of his father's Mercedes, it hadn't felt cheap or demeaning. He'd held and kissed her afterward and thanked her for giving herself to him, for letting him be the first.

Later, once she was home, Coco hadn't been able to sleep. She was blissfully in love, floating on a dream, rationalizing what had happened. Losing one's virginity was a rite of passage, and a lot of the girls in her class had already given up their V-card. Ryan had made it as perfect as possible, and she loved him with all her heart. He'd made her feel like a queen just the way he claimed she was.

Sunday in church she felt the first stirrings of regret, but she managed to convince herself that once she talked to Ryan any unease she felt would go away.

She waited all day for him to call. When she hadn't heard from him by late afternoon, she sent him a text, but he didn't reply. He was busy . . . she was sure she remembered him saying something about being with his grandparents or his aunt or something and that he would be out of touch. He had said that, hadn't he?

Coco was busy herself, chatting with friends, reliving every minute of the dance, explaining that it'd been the most romantic night of her life. The big question she got was where she and Ryan had disappeared to following the dance. They'd received any number of invitations to parties and hadn't made a showing at a single one. Coco was able to sidestep the questions, although she wished she had discussed with Ryan how best to answer. What happened with them was private and beautiful and something she didn't want spread around school.

Monday morning, she waited for him in the school parking lot. She felt a deep sense of relief when she saw him. He was with three of his friends. They laughed when they saw her.

Laughed.

Ryan gave a high five to each one as they strolled past her as if she were invisible.

"Ryan?" she called, and raced after him. He ignored her completely. It was as if he hadn't heard or seen her. And so she tried again. "Ryan." She stood directly in front of him so that the only way to get around was to sidestep her.

"What?" he demanded.

Coco swallowed hard and didn't know what to say.

"I waited for you."

"So?"

"I thought . . ."

"I've got class," he said, and left her standing on the steps leading up to the school, numb with shock and disbelief.

Only later did she learn the awful truth. Having sex with her had been a bet, a challenge. She'd been known as a "good girl," and when Ryan had boasted that he could have sex with any girl he wanted, his friends had dared him to try to get her in bed. All it took was a bit of attention and one date.

Ryan and his sick friends acted as if they'd conquered Rome. Within a matter of minutes, Coco was convinced the entire school had heard about Ryan's game. He'd claimed he could have any girl he wanted and he'd proved it with her. Any girl—and Coco had been an easy conquest. Next time, he bragged, he'd look for a real challenge.

As soon as she learned the truth, Coco went home and didn't return to school for nearly a week. It was easy enough to convince her mother she had the flu, seeing that it wasn't far from the truth. She was sick to her stomach and even sicker at heart, spending her time in bed, unable to face her friends.

In the ten years since, the humiliation of what Ryan had done had never completely left her.

While she was home she heard that someone had slashed Ryan's tires. Suspicion quickly fell on her, though, needless to say, such a thing would never have even occurred to her. Coco never learned who was responsible, though whoever did it was a hero in her eyes.

When word got out that Ryan had slept with Coco, her friends had been sympathetic, but none more than Katie. Although a new friend, Katie had stopped by the house every afternoon with a list of homework assignments from Coco's classes. Katie didn't mention Coco's humiliation. She'd been kind and thoughtful and gentle.

The girls in drill team were less so. They said Ryan was a pig, but Coco knew that if he were to ask any of them out, they'd leap at the chance the same way she had.

Returning to school took courage. But at some point, hiding away in her bedroom and licking her wounds was no longer an option. The only way she could think to deal with Ryan and his friends or anyone else who brought up the subject was to pretend what he'd done didn't matter. And so she showed complete indifference to him and shrugged it off as no big deal. Who was to say she wasn't a virgin, anyway? Ryan could claim what he wanted, but no one would ever know for sure.

Thankfully, her ruse seemed to work, and by the time another full week had passed, Ryan's little challenge was old news. The gossipmongers had found fresh fodder. The holidays were fast approaching and Coco kept herself busy with school and family. Then her parents, whom she'd never confided in, suggested she invite Ryan over for Thanksgiving dinner.

"No." She nearly screamed at the idea. Her parents were baffled. It was embarrassing enough that nearly the entire school was in on the joke. She couldn't bear it if her family found out.

"I thought you liked him?" Her mother appeared surprised.

"He was such a polite young man," her father insisted. "I'd like to see more of him. From what I understand, he's got a bright future as an athlete."

Coco wanted to scream that Ryan was nothing like they believed. Not only had he fooled her, but he'd managed to deceive her parents as well. "We've both moved on," she said, hoping it would satisfy her parents, and luckily it did.

As time progressed, Coco's friendship with Katie grew. For the rest of the school year Coco avoided her old friends, shunning their invitations. She dropped out of drill team and kept mostly to herself.

After graduation Coco got a summer job at the same fast-food restaurant where Katie worked. A couple times friends of Ryan's came in. Without Coco ever asking, Katie stepped in to take their orders so Coco didn't have to.

As difficult as it was, Coco put high school behind her. But not Ryan. Her humiliation had festered and grown into such an intense dislike that she now relished the thought of confronting him at their reunion.

"Coco?"

Katie's knock against the door of her room broke into her thoughts. She slid off the bed and pulled open the door.

"You okay? I knocked a few times. I thought you might have gone to the high school without me."

"Sorry . . . I was thinking . . . you know, about tonight." This evening's party would be her first opportunity to see Ryan again. This was the moment she'd been waiting for for the last ten years and she wasn't about to let it pass without telling him exactly what a scumbag she thought he was.

"Do you think Ryan will definitely show?" Katie asked.

Coco was sure of it. "Of course he will. His ego is much too big to miss the adoration."

But adoration was the last thing Coco intended to give Ryan Temple.

Chapter 9

Katie's attitude toward algebra and James did change, and his attitude toward her did as well. She applied herself, made an effort to understand what he told her, and followed his detailed instructions. Now that the resentment didn't shimmer off him like the summer sun on concrete, she felt less nervous. Katie remembered the first time she caught on to the concepts James was trying so hard to teach her. Once she had that breakthrough, everything else seemed to fall into place. For whatever reason, she'd convinced herself that she wasn't any good at math and would never learn. Thankfully, after a few rough spots, James's patience and encouragement had helped her see the light, and it was bright and beautiful.

"I get it, I get it." She beamed with pleasure and turned to smile at James, so excited that it was difficult to remain in her chair.

He gave her a high five and seemed as happy and excited as Katie was herself.

At their next session she proudly showed him her test paper. She'd aced it and she had James to thank.

She would never have gotten a passing grade if it hadn't been for him and the hours and hours of work he'd put into tutoring her.

James's smile said it all. "See, I knew you could do it."

"Thanks." She sat beside him at their table in the school cafeteria. The afternoon tutoring sessions with James had become her favorite part of the week and she missed him on the days they didn't meet. They passed in the halls a couple times each day, heading in opposite directions. They had different times for lunch. The only class she could be assured to see him in was Algebra 2.

"It doesn't look like you're going to need a tutor any longer."

Immediately her happiness sank straight through the floor. That meant she wouldn't be seeing James anymore. Unable to hide her disappointment, she lowered her head. His comment explained his good mood, too. After today he would no longer be saddled with her. The sense of loss was instantaneous. She considered him a friend and was starting to have a bit of a crush on him.

"I guess this is it, then? Our last meeting," she said, forcing a bit of enthusiasm in her voice. It was all she could do to pretend she couldn't care less if she saw him again or not.

"What do you mean?"

"We won't be seeing each other again."

"What makes you think that?" he asked, frowning.

"You said . . ."

He looked confused. "You don't need a tutor, but

that doesn't mean . . . well, unless you'd rather not spend time together."

Katie chanced a look at him. "You want to hang out with me?"

"Yeah, definitely." He didn't sound overly sure. "I enjoy being with you."

The bubble of joy that burst through her was enough to make her want to cry, which of course she didn't. That would have embarrassed them both. "You do?"

"You tried really hard with this stuff, Katie. I know it wasn't easy for you, but you didn't give up. The thing is, I would rather be with you than play basketball."

Unable to stop herself, she smiled at him. "I'd rather be with you than anyone."

James smiled back and then shifted his gaze away from her. "I was thinking," he said, and hesitated, looking nervous all of a sudden. "Would you like to go to the dance with me on Friday after the game?"

The numbness started right in the center of her chest at her very core, right at her heart. This feeling of loss and bitter disappointment was what happened every time she learned that she was being transferred to a different foster home. That tingling pain quickly spread out to her arms and legs. Before she could stop herself, she grabbed her books and raced out of the cafeteria so fast she nearly tripped on the steps in her eagerness to escape. When she looked back she saw him standing in the hallway watching her, his eyes wide and sad.

She didn't know why him asking her out was so terrifying, given that she liked him. It just triggered every feeling of fear of abandonment she'd ever had. The next time she saw James was at a swimming meet right before winter break. Katie had gotten so flustered she'd lost the race she should have easily won. Afterward she felt terrible about letting her team down and mortified that James had witnessed her defeat. James had waited for her outside the pool, and when she saw him she'd been embarrassed and found herself unable to look at him.

"Hi," he'd said, falling into step beside her.

She pretended not to hear.

He tried again, louder this time: "Katie, hi."

"Hi," she'd mumbled, still not looking his way. She clutched her gym bag and her books close to her chest and walked as fast as she could without breaking into a run. The cold air hit her face and made her eyes water. All she wanted was for him to leave her alone. She hadn't seen him since he'd asked her to the dance and she didn't dare look at him.

James walked silently by her side until they were halfway through the parking lot. When he did speak, he said, "You're a good swimmer."

She didn't know how he could say that when she'd performed so poorly. "I lost the race . . . I let the team down."

He matched his steps to her own, his long strides meeting her much shorter ones without a problem. "You'll do better next time."

She remembered thinking she'd do better if he promised not to attend the meet. Seeing him had unnerved her more than anything anyone could have said or done.

"Let me drive you home," he said.

"No."

"Katie . . ."

"Why'd you come?" she blurted out, wanting to blame him for her miserable performance.

"I wanted to see you swim."

"Why?" she demanded again.

"I already told you."

Her grip on her books was so hard the texts painfully bit into her chest. Her hair fell in wet tendrils over her cheeks as she stared down at the rain-soaked pavement.

"Come on, Katie, I'll drive you home."

She shook her head. "I'd rather walk."

"In the rain?"

She nodded rather than respond verbally.

"Katie . . ."

She swallowed hard, not wanting him to see how unnerved he made her. "Promise me you'll never come to one of my meets again."

"No way."

"James, please . . . just leave me alone."

He tucked his hand beneath her chin and lifted her head up so she had no choice but to look at him. A tear slid down her cheek. His gaze followed it and then he leaned down and ever so gently he kissed it away. His lips were warm against her cool skin. Warm and incredibly gentle. Just feeling his lips against her skin caused her to suck in a small wisp of breath.

Against every dictate of her will, Katie closed her eyes, savoring the feel of his mouth on her face. He kissed her again, only this time his mouth was lower on her cheek, closer to her mouth.

Unable to stop herself, Katie released a soft sigh of pleasure.

When his mouth slid from her cheek to her lips, she all but dropped her gym bag and her books to the ground. Her knees felt as if they were about to buckle. His kiss was soft and moist. He was so tender with her that it made her want to weep.

When he broke it off, Katie leaned her forehead against his chest and his arms came around her. The rain started in earnest then, pounding down on them in a torrent. Neither moved.

After what seemed like an eternity, James rubbed his cheek across the crown of her head. "Will you let me drive you home now?"

Katie nodded.

"Why'd you run away?" he asked, as his hands cupped her shoulders as though he feared she was about to bolt and run again. "If you don't want to go out with me, it's okay. All you had to do was say so."

She kept her gaze focused on the blacktop. "I've never wanted anything more, but James, I can't . . . I don't know how to dance and . . ."

"Shh." He gently tapped his finger against her lips. "The truth is I wasn't psyched to go, but if I did, the only person I wanted to go with was you." He brought his arms around her and tucked his chin on top of her head. "I'm not a good dancer, either."

"I'm sorry I ran."

"I wanted to come after you. I should have." He kissed her again, his mouth lingering over hers.

From that point forward they were nearly always together. James picked her up on his way to school so she wouldn't have to ride the bus. He left her notes in her locker when she had a break, and she did the same for him. Silly notes scribbled in class in which she poured out her heart. She saved every one of his.

After school she went to his house so the two of them could do homework together. He was at every swim meet, cheering her on. His friends became her friends, and for the first time in her high school career, Katie felt as if she belonged. Always shy and withdrawn in the past, with him at her side she could laugh and joke without the fear of anyone making fun of her.

She met his parents and James told her she was the first girl he'd ever brought home to meet his family. His mom and dad let her know they were proud of James, as they had reason to be. James was smart. Really smart. He'd applied to Harvey Mudd College in California with an eye toward computer science and had been accepted. It was huge that James would have this opportunity. His grandparents were funding his expenses.

As prom rolled around that spring, she confided that she couldn't afford an expensive prom dress. So he'd created a prom night for just the two of them. "It'll be just us," he said. "We'll have our own prom." And with his sister's help he'd made all the arrangements.

James and his sister had decorated the back patio with Chinese lanterns. The card table was set in the center of the space with a white linen tablecloth. His parents were out for the evening and didn't know that he'd brought out the fine china. He got roses as a centerpiece and placed them between two tall candles.

That evening was a romantic dream come true for Katie. James's sister served as their waiter and they had Chinese takeout. Afterward they cleared away the table and two chairs, and as dusk settled he put on a playlist he'd made especially for that night. James's mission was to make prom night memorable and enchanting.

As the music whirled around them, James held his arms open to Katie. It seemed as if he was opening up his heart to her, too.

She hesitated. "I've never danced much." Her bungling attempts had left her feeling inept and embarrassed.

"Me neither," he whispered. "We'll learn together."

While James held her, they did little more than shuffle their feet. Dancing was merely an excuse for him to hold her close. She pressed her head against his chest and thrilled to the sound of his heart beating. Katie closed her eyes, determined to keep the memory of this perfect night with her forever.

"This has been the most wonderful night of my life," she told the Flemmingses after James drove her home.

Mrs. Flemmings hugged Katie. "All it takes is one look to see how James feels about you."

"I feel the same way about him." She didn't say it outright, but Katie was in love. This feeling she had when she was with James wasn't easy to describe or explain. When they weren't together she felt as if she was only half alive. It was as if their souls had connected and were destined for each other.

Even now, ten years later, Katie felt her senior year with James had been the happiest time of her life.

Nothing could compare to the love she'd felt from him.

James truly loved her. No one had ever cared as much about her as he did. As the time for graduation drew closer, he worried about her future. It was heavy on Katie's mind as well. Washington State's responsibility for foster kids ended once they were eighteen and had graduated from high school. Her future looked scary and bleak. It frightened Katie to think of having to support herself on what she made working in a fast-food restaurant.

Graduation night, James asked her to marry him. At first she assumed he meant in the future. Then it became clear he meant before the end of the summer—before he left for college.

"Oh James, we can't. You're going to Harvey Mudd."

"We'll get off-campus housing. My grandmother is paying my tuition and you can get a job. It'll all work out, trust me."

Katie so badly wanted to believe they could make this arrangement work. "Have you talked this over with your parents?"

His gaze skirted past her. "I'm over eighteen, Katie, and I want to marry you."

The temptation was strong, like swimming along with a powerful riptide. "Let me think about it, but James, I want to be with you more than anything." They might have both felt a bit young for marriage, but she could see he was trying to help her.

He held and kissed her then, and she was happier than she could ever remember being.

It didn't take long for the bubble to burst. James's

mother sought her out shortly afterward to talk about their marriage plans.

"You're both too young," Mrs. Harper insisted. "We like you, Katie, and you've been wonderful for James, but we have serious doubts that marriage is a good idea for either of you." She hesitated and bit into her lower lip. "When James told his grandparents that he wanted to marry you, they were deeply upset. My mother feels this is a terrible idea. Seeing that they're willing to invest in James's future, they felt they should have a say in this and are convinced it would be a mistake. Frankly, Katie, I agree with them. The two of you are barely eighteen years old. You're the first girl James has ever dated. I'm afraid that in time he will regret this marriage and you will, too. Because of that, my parents have made a stand. If he goes ahead with this, they have decided to withdraw their offer to cover his expenses."

Katie gasped. Deep down she knew Mrs. Harper was right, that they were probably too young, but it made her sick at heart.

"We know James cares deeply for you and we appreciate that you seem to care for him, too. That's all well and good. Trust me, if the two of you are meant to be together then it'll happen, but the timing is all wrong for now."

Tears gathered in Katie's eyes. "What . . . what should I do?"

His mother reached for her hand and held it gently in her own. "If you mention our conversation to James it will infuriate him. The only thing I can suggest is a clean break. Say whatever you think is best, but end it, Katie, for your sake and for his. If you truly love James, then you need to think of his future and what he needs, and frankly, what he doesn't need is a wife."

There wasn't anything more to say.

His mother was right. Knowing how deeply James cared for her, Katie suspected he would do whatever was necessary to take care of her, even if it meant sacrificing his future. Katie loved him, too, loved him enough to do what she needed to do, what needed to be done.

They spent the summer together, and when it came time for him to head off to school she told him she'd met someone else. He didn't believe her and she was forced to admit it was a lie. Next she made a little speech about how "marriage is serious business and while I love you, it isn't a forever kind of love." She told him she wanted to spread her wings, live a little, and she didn't want to be tied down. She wanted her freedom. Still, James didn't believe her, and he refused to take no for an answer. In time she'd come around.

She couldn't afford a phone, and so after he left for California, James wrote her letters.

Every single day.

After the first few letters she found she couldn't read them any longer. It hurt too much. It killed her to pile his letters up in a neat stack and ignore them, but that didn't last long. She was desperate to know how he was doing, so she sat and read them all in one sitting, weeping through each one.

When she learned through the grapevine that he was headed home to talk to her, Katie went away and stayed with Coco until she knew he was back at school. If she saw him face-to-face it would have been impossible to pretend she didn't love him any longer.

At Christmas he mailed her a gift, a heart-shaped necklace. Katie never acknowledged the gift, but she wore that heart around her neck even now. She'd never taken it off.

Still the letters came. Week after week. Month after month. Finally she could bear it no longer and she wrote him back. The hardest and most difficult letter of her life. Five words. Only five simple words.

Please, don't write me again.

Then and only then did he stop. Katie moved into a state-sponsored group home, worked two jobs, and attended night classes. It took her nearly seven years to get her degree in social work, but she managed. Her only remaining connection with Cedar Cove was Coco.

Once Katie had graduated from college, she called Mrs. Flemmings and asked about James. Her foster mother learned that James had done well in school, graduated with honors, and had been hired by Microsoft. He wasn't married.

She was twenty-five years old. It took a week for her to gather up her courage and reach out to him, hoping against hope that the timing that had been "all wrong" according to his mother might now be right. Not that it'd done her any good. He didn't respond to her email, and when she tried again, she found that he'd blocked her emails.

She wrote him a letter, but it was returned with a note that said: *Please, don't write me again.*

And so she hadn't.

This reunion was her one last chance to connect with him. All she wanted was the opportunity to explain why she'd broken things off with him the way she had. She wasn't seeking a romantic reunion or absolution, just understanding. However, if James wouldn't listen three years ago, there was nothing to say he would now.

Chapter 10

I tucked the invoice Mark had given me into my pocket and headed toward my office to write him a check. I didn't bother to look at what he'd charged me; Mark had always been fair. As I walked through the kitchen the conversation with my mother played back in my mind. Now that I'd had time to absorb it, what she'd said rang true. It was going on two years since I'd lost Paul and I had yet to find my new normal.

Like Mom claimed, I'd been hiding behind the responsibilities of the inn. She was right about something else, too. I hadn't kept in touch with my Seattle friends. Gloria, Gina, and Melody had reached out to me on several occasions, looking to include me in their get-togethers. Each time I'd had a convenient excuse to decline, and after a while they'd stopped inviting me. I couldn't remember the last time I'd laughed with friends, taken girl time, enjoyed a Saturday movie, or gone out to dinner. I hadn't attended a Seahawks football game since Paul's death, either.

I'd sort of dropped out of Facebook as well, checking it only intermittently.

The most exciting thing I'd done in the last six months was attend a book club discussion. No, wait, I'd been more adventuresome than that. I'd actually tackled a complicated knitting pattern; that had to count for something.

It pained me to admit it, but my mother was spot-on. I'd turned into a stodgy widow whose life had become insular and dull. I was afraid to live life at full speed. When I'd first met Paul I'd seen myself as fearless, willing to take on difficult tasks, travel on a whim; my laugh was easy and full. I wasn't that person any longer. Grief had changed me and I wasn't sure I liked the woman I'd become.

The phone rang just as I entered my office. It was my business line, so when I answered I put on my most professional voice.

"Rose Harbor Inn, this is Jo Marie Rose."

"Lindsey Johnson here."

I recognized the name but couldn't place where I knew it from. "How can I help you, Lindsey?" I asked.

"You might not remember me. I called a few months back regarding SOS, Survivor Outreach Services. At the time you were busy and said there wasn't anything you needed."

I remembered the call and realized now why the name had sounded familiar. "I hadn't gotten defini-tive word that my husband was dead . . . his body hadn't been returned," I explained. "I didn't think I should join the group when there was a possibility Paul had survived the crash."

"I see that he has since been identified and laid to rest."

"Yes." I couldn't hold back the small catch in my voice. "He's buried at Arlington Cemetery."

"I'm sorry for your loss, Jo Marie."

"Thank you," I whispered in return.

"I'm calling to let you know our support group is meeting next week and I wanted to personally invite you to give us a try. We've all lost a spouse here. We know what you're going through. We're here to help in any way we can."

"Funny you should call. I was just thinking about how I still haven't found my new normal," I said.

"Well, that's something you're going to need to do on your own, but we can offer you some tools to ease you along the way."

My first instinct was to decline. I had a hard enough time dealing with my own grief without taking on the pain of others who'd buried a husband, or in some cases a wife. I wasn't ready for this. I yearned to escape the pain of the past instead of wading through it in waters so deep I'd need hip boots. But I had to do something to get myself out of the rut I was in.

"Okay," I said, shocking myself. "I'll come." I reached for a pen and made a note of the date, time, and location.

After I hung up, I stood for several seconds, staring sightlessly at the wall. My heart beat in double time, which was completely illogical. It didn't make sense that I should be afraid of a support-group meeting, and yet that was exactly what I felt. Scared. Instinctively, I realized joining the group would be my first baby step toward forging a path to a new life.

I'd been sidetracked by Lindsey's call. I needed to pay Mark what I owed him for his work on the gazebo. I pulled the bill from my pocket and, sitting down, I reached for my checkbook. He hadn't stuck around long enough to be paid, the way he normally did, but then I suspected he'd been eager to escape before another emotional scene might happen.

I opened the ledger and smoothed out the bill that had crumpled inside my pocket. As was our practice, I paid for all materials up front. In this case the lumber, nails, and paint. When he completed the project, I paid him for his labor costs. One thing about Mark I liked was that his work was excellent and his prices were fair.

I looked at the bill and my breath froze. He'd written PAID IN FULL across the top of the statement. But I hadn't paid him in full. I owed him for his labor. If this was a farewell gift, then I didn't want it. He'd earned his fee, and if I had anything to say about it, and I did, he was going to collect it. The man had tried my patience for the last time.

It was a bit of a challenge to calculate how much I owed him. I wrote out the check in a rush, so angry I could barely read my own handwriting. Tearing the check from the ledger, I stood and started for the door.

Sensing my mood, Rover followed me, his short legs marching with equal determination. I knew he'd be upset if I left him in the house, so I grabbed his leash.

Coco and Katie were coming down the stairs as I attached the leash to my faithful dog.

"We're heading over to the school," Coco said.

I'd given each of them a house key. "I'm going out for a bit myself. If I'm not here when you return, make yourself at home."

"Will do," Coco promised.

I followed them out and locked the door after them. Rover waited impatiently at the top step. He didn't often get a second walk in a day, and he was eager to show me how grateful he was to be out and about this afternoon.

It was almost as if Rover knew where I intended to go. He led the way straight to Mark's house, nearly pulling me up the street in his eagerness. Seeing that it was a steep climb, I didn't complain.

When I saw the real estate sign again on Mark's front lawn I tensed. I hadn't wanted to believe that I had used Mark as a crutch, as my mother suggested. Well, I was going to need to learn to do without him now. I didn't like it, didn't want this. However, my options were limited.

The door to Mark's workshop was open and I could see him working inside. He seemed to be packing. A wave of regret washed over me and it took a couple moments for me to find my voice.

He must have sensed my presence because he straightened and turned to look my way before I could announce my arrival. For a long moment all we did was stare at each other. For just a fleeting second I witnessed longing in his eyes, but it disappeared just as quickly and was replaced with irritation.

He spoke first. "What can I do for you?" He wanted me gone, though, and he couldn't have made it more plain.

"This won't take long," I said. Rover made himself

at home, lying down on a rope rug just inside the workshop door. "You realize that when we first discussed the gazebo I mentioned I wanted benches."

"Yes. Unfortunately, I'm not going to be able to do that."

"I thought not."

"You can buy however many benches you want at a far better price than what it would cost for me to build them. I told you that initially."

If he had, I didn't remember it.

He shook his head. "I know what you're doing and it isn't going to work."

I met his gaze head-on. I refused to back down or flinch.

"You're making up excuses to keep me here, Jo Marie. It's too late for that, so give it up."

"Whatever you say." I certainly wasn't going to argue with him. I stepped over Rover, who'd curled into a tight ball, and handed Mark the check.

"What's this?" he asked, reading it over. His face was marred with a deep frown.

I held my shoulders stiff. "It's what I owe you for the gazebo."

"You don't owe me a thing. The bill is already paid." He had a disgruntled look I found achingly familiar.

"Wrong. I didn't pay you for the labor."

He returned to cleaning out his workshop. "Consider it a gift."

"Thanks, but no thanks." My back was as straight as a telephone pole, letting him know I wasn't backing down.

"Okay, fine, if that's the way you want it." He

folded the check in half and stuffed it inside his pocket. Turning around, he continued his packing, his back to me.

"Let's go, Rover," I said, tugging on his leash.

He didn't budge.

"Rover," I tried again.

He remained resolutely exactly as he was.

I bent down to pick him up and for the first time since he'd come into my life he growled at me.

"Rover," I snapped in shock.

Mark whirled around and looked as stunned as I did.

"He's never done that before."

Mark remained on the other side of the room, his hands in his back pockets. "It's all right, boy," he whispered. "You should go."

Rover didn't look as if he intended to budge anytime soon. The only thing I could think to do was leave him. "I'll come back later and collect him or you can drop him off on your way out of town," I suggested.

Mark nodded. "Okay."

I backed up a couple steps, scanning the workshop. I hesitated, my heart in my throat, unable to casually walk away.

"Was there something else?"

I lifted one shoulder. I'd grown accustomed to sharing a great deal of my life with Mark. Hardly a day passed when we didn't talk. It had become habit to bounce ideas off him. "It's nothing," I said, accepting anew that I wouldn't have the opportunity to bend his ear in the future.

That satisfied him, or seemed to for a split second. "Something's on your mind, so just say it."

"Okay, I will. It isn't important and I don't know why I even wanted to tell you this . . . I've agreed to attend a survivors' support-group meeting next week. It's time I did . . . earlier today I had a long talk with my mother and she mentioned a few things that shook me up."

"Like what?"

Mark tried to show indifference, but his attempt didn't fool me. "She thinks it's for the best that you're moving away," I told him.

He arched his brows as though curious, so I continued. "She thinks I've used our friendship as insulation."

"As what?"

"I've come to depend on you too much." I felt my throat thickening. "She's right, you know. I consider you my dearest friend . . . I've felt safe when you were close . . . I knew I could depend on you to help me and I became far too comfortable in my protected little world."

"Your mother's right; it's time I left so you can figure out things on your own."

I could have lied, but he would have seen through it. "I don't see it that way. It hurts to let you go, Mark. I'm going to miss you so much." My voice trembled as I struggled to keep from showing how emotional I felt.

"It's necessary."

"So you keep reminding me, although you refuse to tell me why."

"You're not going to sit around and mope after I'm

gone, are you?" His words were more challenge than question.

"You'd like that, wouldn't you?"

The spark of humor that had leaked into his eyes disappeared. "No, Jo Marie, I wouldn't. Attend those meetings; you'll find them useful, and in helping others you might find some comfort yourself."

He was right and I knew it. "I'm going to do more than attend meetings," I said, determined to prove that I wasn't going to waste time longing for his return.

"Good."

"I'm going out."

He'd turned away but quickly reversed motion.

"Out? You mean you're going to date again?"

"Probably."

He let the possibility soak in. It seemed to take a long time for him to nod. "You should."

"That won't bother you?" It was a ridiculous question and one best left unasked, but I couldn't help myself.

He emitted a low growl. "It's going to bother the hell out of me."

I couldn't restrain a smile if I'd tried. "Thank you for that. It soothes my ego."

"You're beautiful, Jo Marie, and you have a lot to offer, so don't cut yourself short and don't take second best."

"What do you consider second best?"

He shook his head, letting me know he had no intention of answering. "I'll bring Rover by later this afternoon."

It came to me why then. "You consider yourself second best, don't you?"

Ignoring me, Mark continued about his business.

"Like I said, I'll bring Rover back later."

"In other words, it's time for me to go."

"Exactly."

I chuckled softly. "Tell me how you really feel."

He straightened and whirled around to confront me, his look as dark and intense as I've ever seen him.

"Just trust me on this."

He was wrong. I hungered to know what had driven him to this point, why he refused to let himself love me, but nothing I said or did made as much as a dent in his determination to go. I'd lost the will to fight him.

"Don't worry about Rover. I've got a couple of errands to run. I'll leave him with you and be back in an hour or so. Does that work for you?"

"Works fine. Are you ready to go yet?" he asked.

"Ready," I returned, and I was.

Chapter 11

❧

The moment Cedar Cove High School came into sight, Katie was filled with nostalgia; the memories were a mixture of challenges and joys. Although she'd attended the high school only during her senior year, this building, the teachers, and the students had helped shape her into the woman she was now.

Apparently, classes were about to be dismissed for the day, because a long line of yellow buses rolled into the parking lot. Coco was fortunate to find a parking spot in the visitors area. A bell rang in the distance and within seconds a flood of students surged out of the building in a tidal wave of youth.

Katie and Coco climbed out of the car as the teens rushed past, seemingly oblivious to the two of them. Wide-eyed, Coco watched the swarm of bodies and slowly shook her head. "Were we ever that young?" she asked.

Katie had been thinking the same thing. "We must have been," she murmured, and while it didn't seem like that long ago, it felt like it might have been a lifetime.

"And we thought we were so smart." Katie smiled. "Weren't we?"

"Not as smart as we are now," Coco answered, moving out of the way so as not to be run over. From the urgency with which the crowd moved, one would suspect the school was on fire. "Makes me wonder what we'll think at our twenty-year reunion. In another ten years some of our classmates will have kids attending here."

That seemed beyond the scope of possibility, and yet her friend was right. "I just hope that we'll each have found the one by then."

"Me, too, and maybe have a kid or two. Who knows, by then we might even turn into regular soccer moms."

"Us?" Katie wasn't catching the vision.

"It's a possibility."

Katie would like to be married one day, and she knew Coco felt the same way, too. Her longtime friend would be a loving mother. Coco dated quite a bit. She was fun and friendly, and people were naturally drawn to her, especially men. What Katie didn't understand was why Coco never seemed to stay in relationships for long. She suspected it had to do with what happened with Ryan Temple, but she'd never asked her directly. Coco bristled whenever the subject was mentioned.

"You'll be good with kids," Katie told her.

"Thanks." Coco's tone was flippant.

"I mean it, Coco."

"I know you do."

Focusing her attention on her friend, Katie wanted to remind Coco that her chances would greatly improve if she'd be more open to getting serious with a man. Over the years Katie had watched the other woman leap from one casual relationship to another.

It always started out promising. Coco would call her, rhapsodizing about the new man in her life and how perfect he was and how deeply in love she was. She'd be convinced he was the *one*, and that she was totally enraptured.

That would last a month, maybe a bit longer, and then the next thing Katie heard, the love affair was over and Coco was ready to move on. When asked what had gone wrong, Coco never had a good answer. He wasn't who she thought he was; it hadn't worked out. Her excuses were vague and matter-of-fact, as if she should have known earlier she was chasing the wind.

"You, too, right?" Coco asked, catching Katie's look.

"Sorry?"

"You want children, right?" Coco pressed.

"Oh yes." Katie didn't elaborate. Her own childhood had been dreadful. She wondered what would have become of her if not for her grandmother. Both her parents had been trapped in the web of alcohol and drugs that became stickier and messier with each passing year. Her father had disappeared before Katie had any memories of him, and her mother became involved in a series of dangerous relationships that invariably ended poorly. Katie's grandmother had been the one constant in her life. It was after her Grandma Brenda died when she was twelve that Katie had been placed in foster homes, one after another.

"You don't date much, though," Coco pointed out.

"I date," Katie insisted.

"Just not often."

Katie hated to admit it, but what Coco said was true. She worked long hours on her caseload, which seemed to grow every year. She did what she could to help children, so many of whom reminded her of herself. She had a soft spot for children torn from their families. Sure, she went out now and again, but mostly with friends from the office. Unlike Coco, she wasn't outgoing or as socially adept. For the most part she kept her own company.

"Come on," Coco said, starting to walk toward the school. "I want to check out my old locker."

"Do you think they still use the same lockers?"

"Of course they do. Nothing ever changes."

Katie had been afraid of that. "I want to stop by the pool."

"Me, too. I wonder if anyone has beaten your record for the four-hundred-meter freestyle."

"I'm sure they have." A part of her hoped her record held, however unlikely.

The hallways remained crowded as students flowed toward the exits. The mass of humanity didn't bother Coco, who wove her way through the throng with Katie following closely behind. She'd gone about twenty or thirty feet when she saw her old algebra teacher.

"Mr. Kloster." Katie said his name loud enough for him to hear.

His gaze caught hers, and he paused. From the look, Katie knew he recognized her but couldn't remember her name.

She made her way over to him. "Katie," she reminded him. "Katie Gilroy."

His eyes lit up with recognition. "Katie, my goodness, it's been what . . . five or six years."

"Ten. Coco and I are in town for our class reunion."

"Ah, yes, I heard this was a reunion weekend," he said. "It's good to see you."

"You, too."

He paused and turned back. "Now that I think about it, the reunion organizers sent me an invitation to attend. Unfortunately, the wife and I had already made plans for this weekend."

Katie didn't know what else to say.

He frowned, and his brow formed three lines. "You were in the same class as James Harper, weren't you?" he asked.

Hearing his name so unexpectedly jarred her. "I was." Apparently, Mr. Kloster had forgotten that he'd asked James to tutor her.

"He was one of my star pupils," he said and then added, "You remember the ones that show promise."

"Which means you wouldn't have a clue who I am," Coco teased.

Mr. Kloster grinned and looked sheepish. "I remember you both."

"Sure you do." Coco's laugh was filled with good-natured sarcasm.

"Maybe not your names," the math teacher admitted, "but certainly your faces." He checked his watch. "It was good seeing you. Enjoy your reunion."

They walked down the long hallway toward the commons, which was next to the cafeteria. As they came into the area Katie stopped, her gaze automatically drawn to the corner by the window where she'd once sat with James for her tutoring sessions.

Coco went on a few feet before she realized Katie wasn't with her. She turned back. "You okay?" she asked.

"Of course." It was a lie, and a big one. Her whole body had gone tense. "Do you remember the fight James got into over me?" she asked her friend. Most days he drove her, but certain mornings, he couldn't.

Coco looked unsure. "Sort of."

He'd been expelled from school for three days and his parents had been justifiably upset. Being James, he'd accepted responsibility and the ramifications without argument, but he hadn't told his family what had led to the altercation.

Brian O'Malley, one of the boys in their class, rode the same bus as Katie. A bully, he had relentlessly belittled Katie. He purposely bumped into her and made fun of her hair, her clothes, her grades, which admittedly weren't the best, but then neither were Brian's. She never seemed to be able to catch up with her classes.

Katie chose to ignore his bullying, keeping her head lowered and pretending not to hear the hurtful things Brian said. He viewed her as weak and vulnerable and an easy target. Katie never knew who told James about Brian harassing her, but she suspected it was one of his friends. Brian was a good forty pounds bigger, but that hadn't stopped James.

James had confronted Brian after school. "I hear you're on the same bus as Katie," he'd said, walking into Brian's personal space and glaring at him eye to eye.

"What's it to you?"

"Lay off her. Understand?"

Brian must have thought this challenge was some kind of joke. "If I have to." "You gonna make me?"

Within a matter of seconds the two boys went at it. Katie would never have known about the fight if she hadn't been walking by. When she saw what was happening she instinctively knew James was fighting Brian for tormenting her.

Horrified that James was about to be badly hurt, she'd cried out his name and raced down the grassy slope, slipping and sliding in an effort to intervene and break up the fight.

James must have heard her small cry because he momentarily averted his attention. That was when Brian hit him square in the jaw. James crumpled like an accordion. Then Katie really panicked and threw down her books and raced to his side just as the bus driver arrived.

Both boys were taken to the office for discipline by the dean of students. Katie followed and waited out in the hall, pacing back and forth, sick at the thought that James had been hurt defending her. James wasn't a fighter. Brian, on the other hand, routinely got into brawls and was big and mean-spirited. Katie had dealt with others like him and learned the best thing she could do was ignore the taunts.

By the time James stepped out of the office a large bruise had already formed on his jaw. Katie didn't know what to do first, weep or shout at him for doing something so crazy.

"Oh James," she'd whispered, tears filling her eyes. She tried to blink them away, but it was useless.

Wordlessly he stretched out his arm and she'd immediately gone to him and buried her face in his chest, hugging him. For a long moment he simply held her close, leaving one arm dangling at his side.

He must have felt her tears, because he kissed the top of her head and assured her he hadn't been hurt that badly.

"But you are," she protested, raising her head and softly examining with the tips of her fingers the darkening bruise on the hard line of his jaw. The corner of his mouth was cut and blood had dried and crusted there.

"I got in a few good slugs," he'd told her with a certain amount of pride. He flexed his hands and she saw that his scraped knuckles were bruised and bleeding.

"Why would you fight Brian?" she cried, caught in an emotional cocktail of anger and concern, fear and regret. Anger was winning out and she slapped his shoulder as hard as she could with her open palm, and then instantly felt guilty when he winced.

James pressed his hand to his shoulder. "I couldn't let anyone say those things to my girl, could I?"

It was the first time he'd called her "my girl," and that made her want to weep all the harder.

"Your parents are going to hate me."

"The school contacted my mom and she said if I got in a fight with Brian O'Malley then I must have been provoked. Mr. Singer didn't say it, but I know he agreed. Brian has a reputation."

"What's going to happen to you?"

"I'm suspended for three days."

Katie covered her mouth, dismayed on his behalf.

"Come on," James said, draping his arm around her shoulders. "I'll drive you home."

From that point forward, no matter what, he always took her to and from school so that she wouldn't have to ride the bus again.

Katie never knew what James told his parents. Whatever it was, he'd kept her name out of it.

"You ready?" Coco asked.

Katie stared at her blankly. "Sorry?"

"I thought you wanted to go down to the swimming pool."

Pulled back into the present and out of her recollections, Katie nodded. "Right . . . the pool."

Coco led the way out of the high school cafeteria and down the steps to the building that housed the Olympic-size swimming pool that was shared with the community. "Being here brings back a lot of memories, doesn't it?"

"It does." But none as strong or as meaningful as the first time James had kissed her.

"Do you remember my first day of classes?" Katie asked, wondering if Coco had any comprehension of what a difference their friendship had made in her life.

"Sure . . . I think."

"The counselor signed me up for swimming class. I

tried to tell her I could already swim, but she said it was a requirement for the school district."

Coco laughed. "That was a joke if ever there was one. You could swim circles around just about everyone in the entire school."

"Which is how I managed to get a spot on the swim team." It didn't take more than a couple class sessions for the coach to show up during class time. Within the first month of her coming to Cedar Cove High Katie had become a valued member of the team.

"And we were lucky to have you."

"I've always loved the water," Katie said. "Still do." Even now Katie swam laps three to five mornings a week. There was something therapeutic about getting into the pool and working out her frustrations. Not only was it good exercise, but it helped her sort through her thoughts as she faced the day.

Unfortunately, the building that housed the pool was locked and they were unable to check the latest stats for the swim team.

"We probably should get back to the inn," Coco said. "We're going to want to change clothes for tonight's function."

"Right."

Katie hadn't given a lot of thought to her wardrobe choices for the weekend. Coco was the one who obsessed, even now, over every outfit. When packing her bag, Katie chose a few outfits that were comfortable and had earned compliments from her coworkers. That was the extent of it. She wished now she'd taken more care with her choices, but at the time she had been half convinced she wouldn't attend anyway.

The drive back to the inn took only a few minutes.

"I need to shower and do my hair," Coco announced, sounding harried already, despite the fact they had two hours or longer before they were scheduled to meet for that evening's event.

"Would you mind if I borrowed your car?" Katie asked.

"Sure, no problem." Coco handed Katie the keys.

Her friend raced up the steps to the inn, eager to get going on her beautification process, while Katie climbed into the car and then backed out of the driveway and drove down Harbor Street.

Out of nostalgia she went past the Flemmingses' old house, where she'd lived until October of the year they'd graduated. They'd been good foster parents and Katie would always be grateful that they had opened their home and hearts to her. Without them she would never have met James.

She circled the block, and not knowing what she'd find, she drove past James's address. She wasn't sure if his family still lived in the area.

A romantic fantasy played in her mind—James would be standing out front and he'd see her drive by and signal for her to stop. Then he'd walk over to the car and look at her, and they'd talk and all would be forgiven.

Katie drove past the house and at first she thought she'd missed it. The lawn was brown, overgrown, and unkempt. The front windows were boarded up and there was a foreclosure sign posted on the front door.

The house had been abandoned.

Chapter 12

Once I'd returned to the house and got my car, it didn't take me more than a half-hour to run my errands. I'd told Mark I would return and collect Rover, so I reluctantly drove back to his place. I parked on the street and was about to get out when I noticed someone else was with Mark. Bob Beldon's pickup was parked in the driveway leading to Mark's workshop.

Bob had backed his truck as close to Mark's workshop as he could get. Both men were involved in dismantling Mark's shop, loading Mark's expensive tools into the truck bed.

They didn't see me, which was just as well—I was in no mood for conversation. I'd said everything that needed to be said. I'd come to collect my stubborn dog and intended to be gone in a matter of minutes.

"You sure you don't want me to save any of this for you?" I heard Bob ask Mark.

"No." His reply was gruff, distracted.

"I'm willing to pay you for it." Bob didn't sound pleased by Mark's answer.

"Not interested. Keep it and use it in good health."

"I can store it for you," Bob offered next.

They lifted what seemed to be an especially heavy saw into the back of the pickup. Once loaded, Bob bent forward and rested his hands on his knees while he took in a couple deep breaths.

"I'm not coming back, Bob." Mark sounded tired of having to repeat himself. "Take what you want, sell the rest, it makes no difference to me."

I must have made an involuntary sound because Mark looked up in that half-second, his eyes connecting with mine. The hurt I felt in that moment left me without a voice. I wanted to lash out at him, but all I seemed capable of doing was standing there like some idiot, my hand pressed over my heart to hold back the pain.

Whirling around, I returned to my car and drove off. Just before I rounded the corner, I glanced in my rearview mirror and saw Mark standing on the boulevard, watching me drive away.

When I returned to the house I found I was shaking. I needed something to calm my nerves, so I brewed a pot of tea. This latest bit of information shouldn't upset me. If Mark wanted to give away his tools and woodworking equipment, that was his prerogative. It shouldn't matter to me. All he'd done was repeat what he'd already made abundantly clear. And yet it reinforced what I seemed to be unable to accept. Not only was he leaving, he had no intention of returning.

Not for me.
Not for the friends he'd made.
Not for anything or anyone.

The front door opened and Coco came barreling into the house. She stopped at the foot of the stairway. "I'm heading up to get ready for tonight. Actually, I've never been *more* ready than I am now." That said, she bounded up the stairs like a woman on a mission.

I didn't know what she meant, but there appeared to be some underlying message in her words. Then and there I decided to be ready, too. Ready for this next phase of my life. Ready to break out of my shell and live again. Ready to adjust to life without Mark. I felt like I had made this resolution several times already today. I guess I'd just have to keep making it until it stuck.

Reaching for my cell, I scrolled through my contacts. It had been months since I'd called Gina's number, which was a sad, sad commentary. Once we had talked almost every day. Gina and I had worked together for a long time and she was someone I considered a close friend.

Following the news about Paul, Gina Forester had been the most persistent of my friends in reaching out to me. I'd lost track of the number of times she'd invited me out on a Friday night. My excuses were varied and creative. Eventually she'd stopped asking. But I was ready now. Just like Coco, apparently.

"Jo Marie?" Gina answered, as if she didn't believe I was the one calling.

"Hi there," I said, forcing enthusiasm into my voice. "What's going on?"

Gina hesitated. "You tell me."

"Not much on my end. I thought it was time we caught up. Are you doing anything tonight?"

My question was met with a short, uncomfortable silence. "Jo Marie, have you been . . . drinking?"

"Drinking?" I repeated, and laughed out loud. "What makes you even ask such a question?"

"You sound like yourself."

I wasn't sure how to take that. "What's so different?"

Again the strained silence, as if she wasn't sure she was willing to answer. "You sound . . . not exactly happy, but excited. Maybe a little manic? Not yourself, anyway."

So that was it. I wasn't myself and I hadn't been since I lost Paul, but I was ready to change that. The best way to answer her was to ignore what she said, so I did. "How would you feel about going out tonight?" I pressed.

"I have plans. Actually, Rhyder is taking me to meet his parents. We're going to announce our engagement to his family."

"Rhyder? Not Rhyder Marlow?" You're engaged to Rhyder Marlow?" This was a shocker. The two had dated off and on but bickered constantly. They were both department heads and constantly clashed. It seemed impossible that I was completely unaware that Gina had gotten so serious with Rhyder.

"Yes, Rhyder Marlow."

I felt like I'd been living in a cave. "When did the two of you get back together?"

"About six months ago." She continued to sound a bit tentative.

Six months? Could it really have been that long since Gina and I connected? "Gina, that's great. Congratulations. I didn't know."

"It's been a while," she said, sounding more like herself.

"Too long," I said, moving about the kitchen, running my hand along the counter. "I want to make up for lost time."

"Oh, I'm so glad. I've missed you."

"Missed you, too. I figured it was time I get back in the game, back into life."

"You sure you're ready?"

I didn't need to think about my answer. "I am. I had a wake-up call recently and realized I'd been burying my head in the sand . . . oh my goodness," I said, chagrined and a little embarrassed, "I'm talking in clichés."

"Listen, did you know Rhyder has an older brother? Rich is two years out of a divorce and he hasn't met the right woman. I know you two would hit it off. We could all get together?" This last part was a question more than a comment.

I'd blurted out that I was ready to get back in the game. But dating? "Sure," I said, surprising myself. "What do you have in mind? Just remember I haven't dated anyone since Paul. I'm a little rusty." Mark and I had never technically dated. Oh, he came over for dinner and we spent a lot of time together, but that wasn't dating. As it turned out, it wasn't much of anything.

"Let me connect with Rhyder and Rich, and I'll get back to you."

"Sure." I pressed my hand to my forehead, wondering what I was getting myself into with this. I should probably ease back into the dating game instead of full immersion. Wouldn't it be easier to meet for coffee first, see if we clicked, before going on a double date? I was about to suggest that when Gina spoke.

"I'll be in touch sometime this weekend. No pressure, Jo Marie. If you don't hit it off with Rich, it isn't a problem."

That was reassuring.

Rover barked and I glanced over my shoulder to find Mark standing just outside the kitchen with Rover at his side. I had no idea how long he'd been there or how much of my conversation he'd overheard.

"I'll talk to you later," I told Gina, eager to get off the phone now.

"Later," Gina echoed.

"Later," I echoed. I disconnected and stuffed my cell into my jeans pocket.

For the longest moment all Mark and I did was stare at each other.

"I brought Rover back," he said. "You were going to come get him, remember?"

I glared at him, unreasonably angry that he'd overheard my conversation with Gina. How much of it I didn't know, but enough. More than what I was comfortable telling him.

"I saw you earlier. At the house," he said.

This wasn't news.

"Why'd you leave?"

"No reason," I lied, stiffening my back.

"You were angry."

The man was a genius. "Thank you for bringing Rover back. It wasn't necessary; I would have collected him." I walked over to the front door and held it open for him, letting him know I was ready for him to move on. I remembered after Paul died reading an article about the different stages of grief. Anger was one of the defined stages. It came as a shock to realize I was grieving the loss of Mark's friendship. I'd started off in denial, refusing to believe he was serious about moving away. I'd bargained with him, done whatever I could to get him to change his mind, and now I was angry. Really, really angry. I didn't remember the remaining stages or even if I was experiencing them in the right order, but I did recall the last stage was acceptance.

Mark stood next to the open door, but he didn't take the hint. "I heard you just now . . . on the phone."

"So what?"

"You're going out on your first date. A blind one, if I overheard correctly."

"Not that it's any of your business," I said.

He didn't answer right away, as if he had to carefully consider his response. "You might find this hard to accept, but I want you to be happy, Jo Marie."

I snorted a laugh. "If you were the least bit concerned with my happiness, you'd—" I stopped abruptly, unwilling to churn up the same ground we'd plowed countless times. "Never mind. Go, wherever it is you plan to run, and live your life. I doubt you'll be happy."

"Why's that?" he challenged, his gaze narrowing.

"Because people who run rarely are. They are constantly looking over their shoulders. Constantly worried they're going to be caught. They're never at ease or free to be themselves . . free to love."

My words seemed to have a strange effect on him.

He clenched his fists and it seemed as if all the blood had drained out of his face. "You're right. More right than you could ever possibly guess. People on the run don't have the life they need or deserve."

Mark crouched down on one knee and stroked Rover. "Good-bye, my friend."

"So now Rover is your friend," I bit out. "As I recall, you called him worthless not too long ago."

"I never meant that."

"It's hard to know what you mean and what you don't mean. I thought I meant something to you, too, but apparently not." I shrugged as if I couldn't care less, when in fact I felt like I was dying inside.

He didn't bother to correct me. "Yes, I suppose it does look that way."

Rover stretched his neck toward the ceiling and emitted a mournful howl as if grieving a great loss.

I stood by the door, my arms crossed, staring straight ahead, refusing to look at Mark.

"I'm heading out now."

I clenched my teeth so hard my jaw ached.

He started past me and stopped. I flinched as he raised his hand to my face and cupped my chin. "Good-bye, Jo Marie."

For just an instant I thought he intended to kiss me. He didn't, and I couldn't decide if I was glad he hadn't or if I wished he had.

He descended the porch steps, got into his truck, and drove off.

"Good-bye, Mark," I whispered, and struggled with the urge to weep. In the end, I swallowed my tears.

Chapter 13

Oh yes, Coco was ready. She had everything she intended to say to Ryan mapped out in her mind. It'd taken her ten long years to reach the point where she could confront him. She would call him a lowlife to his face. Nearly their entire graduating class thought he was a god—after all, Ryan Temple was a star athlete who played ball for the majors. Coco intended to remind Ryan and his friends how unworthy he was of their adulation.

She had her outfit, a classy black dress, spread out across the bed and was out of the shower, dressed in her robe, when there was a knock against her door.

"Is that you, Katie?" she asked, getting out her silver jewelry to wear with her dress.

"It's me."

"Come on in." The long silver chain with the large links was her favorite. She'd add a silk scarf. Gone were her days of sorting through the bins at the Goodwill. She could well afford this dress.

Katie opened the door and walked into the room.

She had on the same clothes she'd worn when they'd visited the school.

Coco planted her hands against her hips. "Hey, you should be getting ready."

Completely ignoring Coco, Katie plunked herself down on the end of Coco's bed. "Thanks for letting me borrow your car."

"No problem. Where'd you go?"

Katie's hands were clenched in her lap. "I drove by James's house."

"Oh? Did you see his parents?"

"No. The house looks like it's been abandoned. The windows are boarded up and it's vacant." Katie seemed to be seeing some kind of symbolism in this.

"Did you ever hear anything about his family moving away?" Katie wanted to know.

"No, I didn't," Coco said, a little taken aback that Katie would even ask the question. If she had any information related to James, Coco would have mentioned it, no matter how minute.

Katie looked devastated, as if she were personally responsible for whatever had befallen James's family.

"I didn't think you had."

"Don't tell me you've decided not to attend the reunion now." This argument was getting old.

"I'll go," Katie murmured.

"Come on, Katie, lighten up. Just because the house James grew up in has been abandoned doesn't necessarily mean anything."

"It feels like it does," she argued. "I don't know how to explain it." She straightened and expelled her breath in a long, deep sigh. "It's as if my trying to connect with James is a waste of time . . . everything we once shared was lost when he left for college."

"You're reading far more into this than warranted," Coco insisted. "Now go get dressed."

"I wish I felt more optimistic."

"Me, too. Try to think positive thoughts about you and James; that's what I'm doing."

Katie nodded. "As usual, you're right."

"Good girl, and be sure and wear that hot little red dress. You look fabulous in it."

"Tonight? I was saving it for the dinner on Saturday."

"What did you bring to wear for tonight, then?" To Coco's way of thinking, Katie needed to make a splash this evening, and the red dress would do that and more. It was important for her friend to look her best, especially if James was scheduled to show.

"I was thinking I'd wear the dark-wash skinny jeans with the teal top, blue scarf, and boots," Katie said. "Isn't that what I showed you earlier?"

Clearly, her friend's mind was on something other than fashion, thought Coco. If Katie wanted to stand out in the crowd, she was going to need more help than Coco could give her, although that teal top would be a nice complement to her curly red hair.

"That outfit was for Sunday, and even then I had doubts. I'm afraid you might come off looking like you're ready to attend a Seahawks football game." Tightening the cinch around her waist, she said, "Let me look at what you brought again."

"Okay." Katie led the way to her room.

It took several minutes to sort through the items Katie had unpacked. By the time Coco finished, the entire contents of Katie's closet were scattered across the top of the bed. They finally decided on a yellow sleeveless dress with a white sweater in case the air-conditioning was on high.

"You're going to knock everyone's socks off," Coco promised, approving her final choice. It was perfect. It complemented Katie's coloring and gave her a look of understated sophistication.

Katie didn't look nearly as convinced. "I certainly hope James is impressed."

"You okay now?"

"Of course."

"Good." Coco was eager to return to her own preparations for the evening.

Just as she was leaving Katie's room, an unearthly howl could be heard from downstairs.

"What was that?" Coco asked, startled.

Katie glanced toward the door. "It must have been Jo Marie's dog. Do you think he's hurt?" Katie asked, and then quickly added, "I better go check to make sure he's all right."

Before Coco could remind her they had places to go and people to see, Katie dashed down the stairs. Her friend was a soft touch when it came to children and animals. Coco might have followed if she was more appropriately dressed.

Standing at the top of the stairs, she waited for Katie's return. It seemed to take an inordinate amount of time, but when Coco looked at her watch she found that it was less than five minutes.

"What was it?" she asked, as Katie bounded back up the stairs.

"Just as we thought . . . it was Rover. He wasn't hurt."

"What did Jo Marie say happened?"

"She said he's mourning the loss of a friend."

"A friend?" Coco liked animals, too, but she didn't get mushy over them the way Katie did. "You mean another dog?"

"No, she said it was a human friend who's decided to move away. Apparently, Rover thought the world of him."

"The dog knew this person was leaving . . . for good?" Coco couldn't quite wrap her mind around that, but it was of little consequence. She was well behind where she wanted to be when it came to getting dressed and ready.

"Give me forty minutes." She started back toward her room and then abruptly turned around. "Make that fifty."

"Or another hour," Katie teased.

"No way. I'm determined to be on schedule."

Katie simply smiled. "You know there was a very good reason we called you Lightning in high school, don't you?"

"Very funny. I've changed my ways." After nearly being fired from two jobs, Coco had learned to set her watch ahead fifteen minutes so if she was late then she would actually be on time. The trick had served her well.

"I'll be ready when you are," Katie promised.

An hour later Coco had finished. When Katie saw Coco, her eyes widened appreciatively. "Wow. You look fabulous."

"Thanks. You look really nice, too." And Katie

did. The yellow dress was perfect with her auburn hair and dark eyes. Katie had worn her curly hair short for several years now. Its maintenance was wash-and-go with a misting of spray conditioner. Her hair looked perfect every time. Coco envied her friend the natural look. For her part, Coco used every hair product available. She spent copious amounts of time taming her hair with a straightening iron and a dry shampoo for extra volume before it was wrangled into shape every morning. While it might look effortless, it was anything but.

They left the inn ten minutes before the mix and mingle was set to get started. They could have walked to the Captain's Galley but opted to drive because they were both wearing four-inch heels. At five-eight, Coco didn't need the height, but those extra inches boosted her confidence. She'd paid full price for these puppies and they were worth every cent. And surprise, surprise, they were actually comfortable.

Coco found a parking spot close to the restaurant. She did an admirable job of parallel parking, something she usually avoided like the plague.

Under normal circumstances Coco would have opted to be fashionably late. Not so this night. She wanted to be there first so she was in place when Ryan Temple arrived.

The scene was set in her mind. He'd arrive and of course all her classmates would treat him like he was visiting royalty. And naturally he would bask in the attention. To this point he was by far the most successful member of their graduating class. Athletic and talented, he'd played football and basketball, and pitched for their baseball team the year they won the state championship. Coco wasn't sure where his standing was currently. Not being a fan, she hadn't followed his career.

"You ready?" Katie asked, opening the passenger-side door.

"Ready." *So, so ready.*

They walked into the restaurant and were immediately assaulted by the scent of stale beer. A pool table was set up in the back of the room and the bar had two or three patrons who looked them over and smiled appreciatively. Dinner must be slow, because only two or three tables were occupied.

"We're here for the reunion party," Coco mentioned to the waitress.

"Upstairs," she told them, pointing to the back of the room.

The staircase was next to the pool table. Coco remembered reading that the Captain's Galley had closed down. That happened just after she'd graduated from high school. She'd heard it'd reopened under new ownership after she'd moved away. The new owners had chosen to keep the name, as it was a well-known watering hole. As she remembered, the food wasn't half bad, either, although she'd eaten there only a couple times.

It felt as if every man in the bar was giving them the once-over as Coco and Katie wove their way through the mostly empty tables toward the stairs.

"We're fresh meat," Coco muttered under her breath.

A table had been set up at the top of the staircase

and Angela Palmer sat there, looking official. She'd been one of the key organizers for the reunion and was a bit of a snob, as Coco remembered. Following graduation she'd attended cosmetology school and worked at a successful salon as a stylist. Coco disliked her because she'd always been keen on Ryan.

"Coco," Angela cried, as if they'd been the very dearest and closest of friends. She stood and hugged Coco, leaning over the table and squeezing her neck.

Angela released her and then stared blankly at Katie. Coco could almost see her mind working as she struggled to put a name with the face.

"You remember Katie, don't you?" Coco asked, coming to the other woman's rescue. "Katie Gilroy. Sorry, I had a brain fart there for a minute."

"Oh, of course. Katie Gilroy."

"No worries." Katie was generous in her willingness to look past the unintended slight. "I only attended Cedar Cove High our senior year. There isn't any particular reason you should remember me."

"Yes, there is," Coco insisted. "There're plenty of reasons. Katie helped the swim team win the regional championship."

"Oh my, how could I have forgotten," Angela said, and covered her mouth with the tips of her fingers.

Someone came up behind them, a couple Coco didn't recognize, and Angela was all business once again.

"You'll find your name tags here; they're listed in alphabetical order. I used maiden names."

Coco picked up her name tag and so did Katie. She peeled off the back and pressed it on the shoulder of her black dress. Coco and Katie started to wander away, but Angela stopped them.

"Before you go," Angela said, stretching out her arm to Coco.

Coco and Katie exchanged looks.

"Sorry to delay you, but I need a favor. A few of us are decorating the school gymnasium for the dinner and dance tomorrow night. We're meeting at about one and we could really use your help."

"My help?"

"You always had such a great eye for these things. Would you mind?" Angela asked, her eyes wide and pleading.

Coco supposed she should be flattered. "Sure."

Angela smiled at Katie. "You can come, too, if you like."

"I'd be happy to."

Coco rolled her eyes. Angela made it sound as if she was doing Katie a favor by including her, when she should simply be grateful.

As soon as they were out of earshot, Katie leaned close to Coco. "What was that business about the swim team winning the regional championship? You know that isn't true."

"You and I know it, but apparently Angela doesn't."

"Why would you say something like that?"

Coco didn't answer. Frankly, she didn't like the way Angela had dismissed Katie as if she was someone unworthy of her attention. It irked her, and she'd wanted to put Angela in her place.

As they came into the room, there were high-top tables decorated with cardboard numbers of the year they'd graduated along with a sprinkling of those annoying confetti cutouts that people sometimes added to cards and invitations. Each table had four chairs.

"Do you know how many signed up for tonight?" Katie asked Coco, staying close to her side.

"No." All Coco knew was that she'd caught sight of Ryan's name tag. Knowing him, he'd arrive late and make some kind of grand entrance. The mere thought of him playing the role of the hotshot was enough to make her want to puke.

"I saw James's name tag," Katie whispered.

Coco heard the dread in her friend's voice. "Everything is going to work out . . . for both of us."

"Yeah, right," Katie muttered.

"Let's find a table and then get something to drink." She was badly in need of liquid courage, and from the look of her, so was Katie.

They scouted out what looked to be the prime location, offering them a view of the staircase and those who arrived. "I'll get us each a glass of wine," Katie offered.

"Sounds good," Coco said, keeping an eye on the staircase.

"Honestly, I don't know if there's enough liquor in the world to see me through this night."

Coco smiled. Her friend was overreacting. She suspected James was as eager to see her as Katie was to talk to him.

Katie walked over to the no-host bar and Coco made herself comfortable. She pulled out the chair and sat down. When she happened to look up it was just in time to see Ryan Temple walk into the room. In ten years he'd hardly changed a bit—if anything, he was more handsome. His shoulders had filled out, and naturally he'd brought a woman with him. And just as naturally, she was absolutely stunning—a model, no doubt. When the moment was right, this date of Ryan's would get to hear just what kind of guy Ryan really was.

Chapter 14

Coco was a social butterfly and far more outgoing than Katie. While Coco fluttered about the room, visiting with friends, Katie sat quietly at the table sipping her drink.

She recognized several faces, mostly because they were the more outgoing and popular members of their graduating class. She wanted to keep an eye on the staircase when people were arriving, but Katie felt silly and a bit awkward sitting by herself.

A couple claimed the seats at a high-top close to Katie and looked as lost and uncomfortable as she did. Katie felt she should at least make an effort to look like she was enjoying herself.

"Hi," she said, joining the two. "I'm Katie Gilroy."

"Becca Cousins," the other woman said. "And this is my husband, Troy."

"Pleased to meet you both," Katie said, keeping an eye on new arrivals.

"I'm sorry, I can't place you," Becca said, as she rearranged an off-white shawl over her shoulders.

"No real reason you should," Katie said. "I only attended classes our senior year."

Becca studied her and bounced her finger against the tabletop. "Were you on the swim team?"

Katie smiled. "I was."

"You dated James Harper, too, didn't you?"

A tingling sensation went down Katie's arms. Now she remembered why Becca looked vaguely familiar. She had lived on the same block as James. They'd been childhood friends.

Katie didn't get a chance to answer.

"It was you, wasn't it?"

She nodded. "James tutored me after school in algebra."

Becca's husband looked bored and smiled apologetically as he interrupted their conversation. "Honey, would you like something to drink?" he asked, scooting back the chair as he stood.

"Please. A Diet Coke?"

"Got it." Troy left them, cutting around the tables and chairs and heading toward the bar.

After her husband left, Becca leaned close to Katie. "James got in a huge fight over you. I remember it because James was never a fighter. Everyone was shocked to hear he'd been suspended from school."

Katie could feel her face heating up, and while it might have been the wine, it was as much the memories. "The fight wasn't *over* me, really. James was defending me."

A dreamy look came over the other woman. "That's love, you know. Real love. I think James fighting Brian O'Malley was probably the most romantic thing I ever heard. Brian was a horrible human being.

He loved terrorizing anyone he thought might be weak. I think he must have gotten a sick sense of pleasure from picking on others. I can't think of a single person who liked Brian. No one ever stood up to him, because they were afraid."

"Except James."

"Right. He took a pounding, too, didn't he?"

He had and he'd done it for her. Every afternoon of his suspension Katie had made an excuse to stop by his house. His parents both worked outside the home, so it was only James and his sister at the house. Katie sat with him and his sister and they played computer games, and when his sister wasn't looking, James would kiss her. Because she suspected his mother might disapprove of her being at the house, Katie made sure she left before his parents were due home.

Caught up in the memories, Katie had to force her attention back to Becca. "What are you up to these days?" she asked, wanting to change the subject.

"I'm a mommy blogger. Troy and I have two children. I love that I'm able to be with Justin and Janese and writing about our life. I'm getting a following, too. What about you?"

"I work for the state as a social worker."

Becca looked impressed. "I hope you don't mind me asking, but whatever happened with you and James? He was pretty hung up on you. He wasn't like some guys. The only girlfriend he ever had was you."

Katie's stomach clenched, unsure how best to respond. "We went our separate ways shortly after graduation."

"Really?" Becca's face showed surprise. "You two were pretty thick back then. I grew up with James, we went through junior high and high school together. Lots of girls were interested in him and he dated a few times, but you were the only girl who lasted more than a week or two."

"Things happen."

"That they do," Becca agreed. "Breaking up must have been hard on you both."

Katie couldn't deny the truth. "It was." Harder than anyone realized. Becca wasn't telling her anything she didn't know about James. He wasn't like Ryan or any of the other boys she'd met. James was loyal and dedicated, serious and studious. And so incredibly smart. And yet out of all the girls in school, he'd chosen her. He'd loved her—deeply, profoundly loved her—more than anyone before, or since.

"I was in your old neighborhood this afternoon," Katie said, striving to sound natural. "I noticed James's house is abandoned. Do you know what happened to his family?"

"From what my mom said, the shipyard transferred his dad to San Diego a few years back. A young couple bought the house during the housing boom and then lost it. Seeing it empty like that really bugs my parents. The house is a neighborhood eyesore. I don't know why the bank doesn't just sell it."

Katie was glad to know that nothing bad had befallen James's parents.

Troy returned with their drinks and sat down next to his wife. Sipping a Shock Top, he glanced around the room and shifted uncomfortably. Katie understood. It must be difficult being with a group of people who all knew one another and feeling like an outsider. The only connection he had to these people was through his wife.

"I should probably say hello to a few of my friends," Katie said, looking for an excuse to leave.

"Sure. Good chatting with you, Katie."

"You, too, Becca."

Katie wandered across the room, keeping an eye on new arrivals. Up to this point she hadn't seen James, and she was beginning to wonder if he would show. Her fear was that he'd gotten word that she'd signed up for the reunion and decided to stay away. Obviously, James wasn't one to back down from a confrontation, but then she didn't know him any longer. And he didn't know her, not the woman she'd become.

Katie found Coco, who was chatting with a group of women, none of whom Katie remembered. She joined the circle and Coco was quick to remind her friends who Katie was.

"Katie was on swim team with me."

A chorus of "hi," "good to see you" followed.

After a few minutes Coco broke away. "James arrive yet?" she asked the minute they were out of earshot of the other women.

"No. I'm beginning to think he'll be a no-show."

"Have faith, my friend," Coco said, giving her arm a small squeeze. "He'll be here."

Katie admired Coco's confidence. With everything in her, she wanted to believe that, too.

"Ryan Temple's here," Coco whispered, focusing her gaze on the other side of the room. "And just look at all the attention he's getting."

Sure enough, when Katie glanced Ryan's way there

was a circle of admirers gathered around him. Mostly men, Katie noticed, which might be attributed to the beautiful woman at his side.

"Looks like he's holding court," Coco muttered.

Katie could understand their classmates' curiosity. Ryan played professional baseball and was something of a school legend.

Naturally, rumors abounded about what had happened with them the night of Homecoming, but Katie had never been one to listen to gossip and she'd never pressed Coco for details. All she knew for sure was that Coco had been the victim of a childish bet the boys on the football team had made. Coco had always been friendly to her, and when she didn't show up at school for a week following Homecoming, Katie had taken it upon herself to repay her friend in kind. They'd been good friends ever since.

"I saw you talking to Becca Holiday," Coco mentioned.

"It's Becca Cousins now. She's married with two kids and is a mommy blogger."

Coco shook her head. "That's great."

Katie noticed a look in her friend that she didn't recognize. Katie knew Coco loved her work creating apps and had been successful beyond anything she'd expected or anticipated. What she saw was a look of longing for something more.

That brought up the question of what Katie herself wanted. If she was ever going to find out, she needed to make peace with James so she could move on.

She'd dwelled on this relationship for too long. She'd been a teenager when she fell in love with James and he was, too. She'd changed, times changed, and love changed. She didn't want to admit it, but there was every likelihood that they no longer had anything in common. All she could hope for was the opportunity to find out.

About thirty minutes after Katie and Coco arrived, the waitstaff started serving appetizers. They were snatched up quickly. Katie couldn't have swallowed a single bite if she'd tried, and she refused all offers. The food and the drinks flowed. After finishing her glass of wine, she ordered a second. Liquid courage. She would need it if and when James arrived.

Halfway through the evening, Katie couldn't bear not knowing any longer. She approached Angie Palmer, who continued to man the sign-in desk.

"Is everything all right?" Angie asked.

"Oh yes, it's a great party," Katie assured her.

"The committee worked hard on getting the events organized. Of course, there were those who thought we could or should have chosen a different restaurant or a better menu. Several people complained about using the gym for Saturday night's function."

"I . . ."

"I noticed not one of those who complained volunteered to be on the reunion committee, though. Isn't that just like people?"

"It is," Katie agreed, figuring the less she said, the better.

"I want you to know a lot of effort went into this. I just hope my classmates appreciate everything Lily and I did."

"How many were on the committee?" Katie asked, remembering a long list of names on the flyer that had been mailed out.

"Ten. But Lily Franklin and I did the majority of the organizing. The other eight all live in Cedar Cove. They volunteered to help, but we got one excuse after another. It seemed easier to do the majority of the work ourselves; it was plain we weren't going to be able to rely on anyone else. We put their names on the program, in appreciation for their support.

"By the way, would you happen to have the contact information for Karen Castillo? She was one we weren't able to locate."

"No, sorry."

"What about Jeremy McPherson?"

"No idea." The only person Katie had kept in contact with was Coco.

Angie sighed with disappointment. "No one seems to know where they are or what they're doing. Lily and I put their names out hoping someone had kept in touch, but we never heard anything back."

"If I hear news about either one I'll let you know," Katie promised.

"It'd be appreciated."

Katie glanced down at the table and eyed James's name tag. "I wanted to ask you about—"

"Did you know two of our classmates have died?" Angie said, cutting her off. "Two. I found that shocking. Darin Joseph died in a car crash two summers ago. She took a corner too fast and slammed into a tree. And of course everyone knows about Andrew Webs, who died in Afghanistan. Just tragic, both cases."

"Tragic," Katie agreed.

"Sorry, you started to ask me about someone?" Angie said, focusing her attention back on Katie.

"Yes. James Harper."

"Oh yes, James. He was one of the first to sign up. His response card came in right away and then yours." Angie reached for her iPad and scrolled through two or three screens. "Ah, here it is. He signed up for all three events. Tonight's social, tomorrow's dinner, and the picnic on Sunday."

Katie had hoped that was the case.

"You wouldn't believe how many people were against holding the picnic at Manchester State Park on Sunday. In my mind, it's the perfect location, don't you agree?"

"I do." Manchester State Park had been one of her and James's favorite spots. They'd sat on the beach and talked for endless hours with the view of the Seattle skyline before them. The park was walking distance from the Flemmingses' house and Katie had often gone there to sit on the beach and think. Once James learned that was her favorite spot, he would join her.

Those times with James had been the most peaceful of her life: sitting on the sand, their backs braced against a large piece of driftwood. James would place his arm across her shoulders and she'd rest her head against his chest. Sometimes they would talk for hours and other times they didn't say a word.

"I see James hasn't arrived," Angie said, gazing down at the name tags.

Katie noticed there were considerably fewer tags than there were when she and Coco arrived. Only a scattering remained, like a jigsaw puzzle with several pieces missing.

"He's a pharmacist, you know."

"James?" As a matter of fact, she didn't know. At one time she'd heard he worked for Microsoft; perhaps she'd heard wrong.

"He said he worked for one of the hospitals in Seattle. Swedish or Virginia Mason, I don't remember which one."

"He'd be good at that," Katie whispered. James had enjoyed all the sciences, she recalled. The very classes she found the most difficult were the ones in which he excelled. Katie scored higher in the humanities, and though he hadn't really needed her help, she'd read through his class papers and made suggestions. Being generous with his praise, James insisted he would never have scored as high without her help. She didn't believe it for an instant.

"As I remember, James had a tendency to be late," Angie said, as though familiar with his habits.

Katie didn't remember him that way.

"He isn't married, you know. He sent in his bio. Everyone will receive copies of the bios at dinner tomorrow night. I'm surprised how many of our class remain decidedly single," Angie said, conversationally. "I'm thinking several of our classmates who used to be couples might reconnect. I've always loved a good romance, don't you?"

Katie smiled, encouraged by Angie's words. "I do," she agreed.

Chapter 15

Coco and Katie were away for the evening and the house was quiet, too quiet. Rover was asleep on the rug in front of the fireplace and I was at loose ends. I had a pair of guests due to arrive later this evening. Their reservation had come in weeks ago—a honeymooning couple, Finn and Carrie Dalton.

The phone rang, my personal one and not the business line. Caller ID told me it was Gina.

"Hello again," I said. I hadn't talked to her in months, and now twice in a single day.

"Hi," she said, and then without a pause, she added, "Listen, I talked to Rhyder and then to Rich and everything is arranged for tomorrow night."

Surprised, my jaw dropped. "Everything? What do you mean by *everything*?"

"Your date with Rich," she said, as if it should have been obvious.

"But I can't . . . tomorrow is too soon."

"No, it isn't," Gina argued. "Jo Marie, I went to a lot of trouble to make this happen. You're not going to back out on me now. I won't let you."

It seemed I had lit a bonfire under Gina. She'd acted before I had the opportunity to properly think through what I'd suggested and change my mind. And I would have changed my mind. I'd been upset and angry at the time. No way was I ready to leap back into the dating scene.

"I have guests this weekend," I explained. "Time away from the inn has to be planned well in advance. I can't just lock up and take the ferry to Seattle for the night," I argued. "I have responsibilities."

"O-k-a-y," Gina said, dragging out the word as if she was thinking through this problem. "Then we'll simply come to you. There's got to be at least one decent restaurant in town."

I bristled, taken aback by the slighting of Cedar Cove. "Actually, there are a few . . ."

"Then that settles it. Rhyder, Rich, and I will arrive around six tomorrow night."

"The ferry . . ."

"Don't worry, I'll check the ferry schedule and work out the details. I'm not letting you out of this, Jo Marie."

She wasn't kidding.

"It's time you got back in the game, friend."

"But, Gina," I fussed, my head spinning, seeking an excuse to put this off. "I don't know the rules any longer. The last date I went on was with Paul, and that was years ago now."

"Nothing ever changes," my friend insisted. "If it gives you comfort, Rich is as nervous as you are."

"You mean to say he hasn't dated since his divorce?" This wasn't boding well for either of us. I could see this was a nightmare in the making. Gina and Rhyder would be happy and in love, doing their best to prove to Rich and me how perfect we were together. Blind dates like this were the worst.

"Rich has started dating, but he hasn't met the right woman yet."

He'd probably gone from one dating disaster to another. He was likely traumatized by the whole thing. I know I'd been before I met Paul. "How do you know we're a good fit?" I asked.

"I don't, but you're a good person and nice; both of you have been through hell."

This sounded more and more like a terrible idea all around. "Gina, seriously, I wish you'd talked to me before you set this up."

"I did talk to you," she reminded me. "Tell you what. I'll give Rich your phone number and the two of you can connect, and afterward if you decide you'd rather not meet him then fine."

"He has the same option, right?"

"Of course. Can you agree to that?"

"I suppose," I said, with some reluctance.

"Good girl. Now, don't get cold feet on me. You're going to like Rich. He's a great guy."

I'd lost count of how many times I'd heard similar statements only to be sadly disappointed. Apparently, some people's definition of *great* didn't exactly line up with mine.

Not twenty minutes after I ended my call with Gina my cell rang again. I didn't recognize the number, which pretty much told me it was Rhyder Marlow's brother, Rich.

"This is Jo Marie," I said, keeping my tone as even as I could manage.

"Hi, Jo Marie. I'm Rich. Gina suggested I call you."

He, too, sounded deadpan, as if amused about being dragged into this by my cheerleading friend.

"Gina thought it might be a good idea if we talked before meeting tomorrow night."

"Yeah."

Silence.

I swallowed, unsure what to say next. "I understand you're divorced?"

"Two years now. You're a widow?"

"Going on two years."

"You date much since your husband . . . since you've been a widow?"

I thought about Mark and decided against mentioning him. "No. You?"

"Some, and to be frank, they haven't been great experiences. I recently met a woman with ten cats. Ten. I'm allergic to cats and I won't go into what her house smelled like. Then there was this woman who had this diet thing going. I swear it took her thirty minutes to order dinner. She insisted on talking to the chef personally and, well, let's just say the night didn't go so well."

He hesitated and then said, "My last date wasn't all that great, either. I need to ask you something. I don't mean to be offensive, but are you one of those women who is starved for sex?"

My eyes widened. This wasn't the kind of question I expected. "Excuse me?"

"Sorry, I have to ask. The last woman, after the cat lady and the diet freak, seemed like a decent sort. After our dinner date she wanted to know how soon it would be before we had sex because she said her body needed that release every day."

"Every day?"

"That's what she said."

For a moment I was speechless. "Where did you meet this woman? A strip joint?"

"No, church."

"You met her in church?"

"Yup."

I couldn't help it, I laughed out loud. And then Rich laughed, too.

"You can rest assured I'm not a sex fiend. It'd been so long that I felt like a virgin all over again."

Rich chuckled and I could tell that we were both more comfortable. "I find that infinitely reassuring. Gina mentioned you own a bed-and-breakfast and that if we're going to meet for dinner we'll need to come to your side of the water."

"I have guests this weekend. I *casually*, and I emphasize *casually*, mentioned to Gina that I *might* be ready to date again and the next thing I know she's got this blind date arranged."

"That sounds like Gina. She's a real firecracker. When she gets going on an idea there's no stopping her."

"I'm still reeling with the news she's marrying Rhyder. The two of them could barely tolerate each other, the last I heard."

"You're telling me. I can remember shortly after

Rhyder started working at the bank that he was considering quitting because of this woman who made his life miserable." He paused. "You should see the two of them now; they can't keep their hands off each other."

"Interesting." It boggled my mind to think of Gina and Rhyder in love.

"It's been sort of painful, you know," Rich said, growing serious. "Seeing the two of them together and so much in love. I didn't think my little brother would ever take the leap into marriage, especially after what happened between me and Melissa."

"He must really love Gina."

"He does. I said it was painful to see them together, but it gives me hope, too, you know?"

"I do know."

"So," he said, expelling his breath, "what do you think? Do you want to meet? It's up to you; I'm good either way."

My inclination was to decline. I wasn't ready, but then I realized I might never be ready. I'd had nearly two years of living like a nun, cloistered away in my bed-and-breakfast. If anyone were to study my lifestyle they would assume I was in my sixties instead of my thirties.

"Okay," I said. "Let's give this a try."

Rich didn't respond right away, and when he did his voice betrayed him. He sounded relieved. "I was hoping you'd say that. I would like to meet you, Jo Marie. Be warned. I'm just a regular guy, and not particularly handsome."

"Are you on Facebook?" I asked.

"Sure. Isn't everyone?"

"I suppose, though I haven't been on much since Paul died. But I'll friend you so you'll have a chance to see what I look like."

"I already know. Gina showed me a photo of you and her from a few years ago. You're . . . lovely."

"Well, thanks." His compliment flustered me. "I'll send you a friend request so you'll get a look at me, too."

"Okay." We ended the call a couple minutes later and as I turned off my cell, I realized I was smiling. As soon as I thought about Mark, though, the pleasure vanished.

Mark was the one who'd driven me to this point. I remained angry with him and at the same time grateful. He was gone now, if not yet from Cedar Cove then from my life. And with his departure I was about to enter into a new phase, opening myself up to fresh possibilities.

I heard the sound of a car and Rover was instantly on his feet. He headed for the front door, which told me the Daltons had arrived. I walked onto the porch.

Finn Dalton climbed out of the car. He was a tall and chiseled man, dressed in a flannel plaid shirt and jeans. An outdoorsman, from the look of him. He could have walked off the pages of an REI catalog. He went around to the passenger side and opened the door. Before his wife could climb out, he leaned forward and kissed her. It was a deep, lingering kiss. His wife, when I caught sight of her, was petite in comparison to her husband. The two wrapped their arms around each other and started toward the door.

"Welcome to Rose Harbor," I greeted.

"Thank you. I'm Finn Dalton and this is my wife,

Carrie." He smiled down on her and repeated, "My wife."

Carrie smiled up at her husband and then glanced toward me. "In case you haven't guessed, we're on our honeymoon. Finn and I have one last night before we fly back to Alaska," she said, as they walked up the steps.

"You get us registered and I'll get the suitcases," Finn said, before turning back to the car.

Carrie followed me into the house.

"How is it you happened to book this inn?" I asked, unable to hide my curiosity. If they were flying out of Sea-Tac the next day, there were far more convenient hotels than Rose Harbor.

"Finn hates being in the city. He'd rather drive miles out of the way than endure the traffic and noise. He's lived in Alaska nearly his entire life and it's where we've decided to settle ourselves and raise our family."

I wasn't sure I had as adventurous a spirit as Carrie. "You're willing to move to Alaska?"

"We're both writers. I love my husband and I'll go wherever he goes, live wherever he lives. We've given it nearly two years to be sure this relationship will work."

"Congratulations."

"Thank you," she said.

I gave her the registration sheet to fill out, which she did in quick order. I took her credit card and processed it and then handed her the room key. "I have two other guests on the second floor. There's a third floor with only two rooms. I'll give you the entire floor."

"Thank you. That would be perfect." Her gaze held mine. "Like I said, we're newlyweds."

She didn't need to elaborate—I got the picture.

While I gave Carrie the keys to the front door and explained where to find what she needed, Finn re-turned with the luggage. I told him where to go and he hauled it up the two flights of stairs, taking the steps two at a time. He returned in what seemed like seconds.

"You ready, Mrs. Dalton?" he asked Carrie.

"Ready? Finn, please, there's no need to carry me over every threshold we cross."

"On our honeymoon there is."

Before Carrie could protest, Finn lifted her and carried her up the stairs. Carrie looked over her shoulder at me and grinned from ear to ear before laying her head on her husband's shoulder.

I don't know what it was that in the space of a sin-gle day I had been confronted by two deliriously in-love couples. First it was Gina and Rhyder and now the honeymooning Daltons.

I was surrounded.

Against my will, my thoughts went back to Mark for the millionth time. But I pushed the thoughts aside and focused on the fact that I was going on a date.

It was my mother's heart-to-heart with me that had gotten the ball rolling. Soon I'd be meeting Rich.

Rover came to stand at my side, then went to the door, which let me know he needed to go outside. I opened the door and watched as he trotted down the stairs and then over to the gazebo.

He turned and looked over his shoulder at me with the most mournful, sad eyes I'd ever seen. And then he did what he'd already done twice this day; he raised his head and howled as if he'd lost his best friend.

Actually, we both had.

Chapter 16

All along Coco had felt she was ready to confront Ryan. When the time came, however, she was trembling in her four-inch heels to the point she found it difficult to keep her knees from knocking.

She'd had a glass of wine earlier but decided to order something stronger. As she approached the bar, she wondered if they made a straight shot strong enough to fortify her for this conversation. Lost in her thoughts, she stood in line for a few minutes and then abruptly broke away. She didn't need liquor to face Ryan. She'd been waiting ten years for this and she wasn't about to ruin it by having too much to drink.

She started across the room, focusing on Ryan. If anything, the admiring crowd that had gathered around him had grown larger. Just as she suspected, her classmates hung on his every word.

Ryan glanced up and happened to catch her eye. Coco didn't flinch. He turned to the runway model on his arm and whispered something and then spoke to his flock of admirers. He must have had a premonition of what was coming, because whatever he said dispersed the crowd.

Coco continued making a path straight toward him, ignoring a greeting from another classmate. Her hands were clenched in fists. She stopped directly in front of Ryan and the bimbo on his arm.

"Coco," Ryan greeted her, as if nothing unusual had ever transpired between them. "I'd like you to meet my wife, Jennifer."

Coco briefly turned her attention to the other woman. "I hope you know what kind of man you married." She didn't bother to keep the sneer out of her voice.

"I do." The other woman's voice was soft and cultured.

"I sincerely doubt it," Coco said. She might be trembling on the inside, but outwardly she presented herself as cool as an ocean breeze. She felt ready to give Ryan the tongue-lashing of his life.

"I was hoping you'd be at the reunion," Ryan said, squarely meeting her look.

Coco laughed wryly. "I can't imagine that's true."

"It is," he said, and then exhaled slowly. "I owe you an apology, Coco. When I think back on what I did to you, how I used you and embarrassed you, I get sick to my stomach."

Coco froze. Ryan was apologizing? She couldn't possibly be hearing him correctly. This was the last thing she expected. "What did you say?"

"I'm sorry, Coco. You have every right in the world to hate me and I wouldn't blame you if you did."

"I do hate you." She left no room for misunderstanding. "I have hated you for ten years. I have nothing but contempt for you." She spewed out each word. "As far as I'm concerned you're the scum of the earth. Worse. What you did . . ."

"What I did was unforgivable," he agreed, looking contrite and miserable.

Coco swiveled her attention to Ryan's wife. "You know about this? Did he tell you what he did?"

Jennifer placed her hand on her husband's shirtsleeve and nodded. "He told me about it before we were married."

"And you went ahead and married him?" Apparently, the woman was badly in need of therapy. Anyone who would willingly accept a husband who could use a woman the way Ryan had used her needed professional help.

"I did decide to marry him," Jennifer said.

Coco shook her head in shocked disbelief.

"I married him because when he told me about accepting that ridiculous bet he had tears in his eyes. He said he's regretted it every day since, and I believe him."

"Not every day," Coco challenged. If that was the case he would have apologized while they were still in school.

"I'm not the same ego-driven immature teenager I was ten years ago, Coco," Ryan said.

"Thank God," she whispered.

"I do thank Him," Ryan countered. "I tried to look you up with every intention of letting you know how sorry I was. I yearned to ask your forgiveness but decided to wait."

"For what? The reunion?" The Second Coming?"

"For the reunion," he said, ignoring her sarcasm.

"If I was going to ask for your forgiveness, I felt it was better to do it face-to-face. Can you forgive me? Is it possible to find it in your heart to accept my sincere regret that I took from you what I had no right to take?"

None of this was going the way she'd hoped, the way she'd counted on and planned. "I . . . I don't know," she told him honestly. He couldn't realistically expect her to brush off this pain she'd carried with her all these years as if it was nothing. This intense dislike that bordered on hatred had become a living, breathing appendage she carried with her constantly.

"Can you try?"

Without really thinking, Coco nodded. Her legs started to shake then and she felt the need to sit down. Stretching out her arm, she grabbed hold of the back of a chair.

Ryan immediately pulled it out and helped her sit. He claimed the chair on one side of her and his wife sat next to him. He turned sideways on the chair and leaned forward, bracing his elbows on the high top.

"Is there anything I can do to make this up to you?" he asked.

Coco didn't want to believe he was sincere, but from the anguished look in his eyes, she knew that he was. Did he actually believe he could give her back her virginity or wash away the humiliation she'd suffered with a few words? Nothing had ever been the same for her after that night.

"A thousand times over the last ten years I've regretted what I did, regretted my behavior, and was sick at the way I treated you afterward."

"You wouldn't even look at me," she whispered, choking down a sob.

"That's because I couldn't bear to look at myself. Every time I saw you I had to face up to what I'd done."

Coco bit into her bottom lip, but she wouldn't let herself cry.

"If you can't forgive me, I can accept that. If I were in your shoes I don't know if I'd have it within me to find forgiveness."

All Coco was capable of doing was staring at him, shocked and taken completely off guard.

"What Ryan is really saying," his wife inserted, "is that like you, he's carried this weight, this guilt with him for far too long. My prayer is that there will be healing on both sides, and I know that's what Ryan has prayed for, too."

Despite her best efforts, tears clouded Coco's eyes.

"I came to tell you how much I hated you."

"I know, and I deserve it."

Jennifer reached for her husband's hand and held it in a death grip.

"You're the reason Ryan signed up for the reunion," Jennifer continued. "He gave up playing in an important game tonight—"

"It doesn't matter what I gave up," he said, cutting off his wife. "What was important is what I owed Coco. I'm sorry, Coco."

Her throat tightened all the more until it became nearly impossible to swallow, let alone breathe. "I'm sorry, too," she whispered.

"You're sorry?"

"For hating you, for letting what happened between us nearly destroy me."

"If ever I can do anything for you . . ."

She gave a hiccupping sort of laugh. "Like what? What could you possibly do for me?"

"Tickets to a play-off game?" he suggested lamely.

"That is, if you're a baseball fan."

Coco wiped the tears from her cheeks. "I'm not, particularly," she said shakily.

"Well, if you are ever interested . . ."

Coco was afraid if she stayed much longer she would soon dissolve in tears, and Ryan looked close to breaking down himself. Scooting off the chair, she stood and squeezed his shoulder. "We all make mistakes, Ryan. It takes a big man to admit it when he has. This was the last thing I expected from you."

He reached up and gripped hold of her hand in what she translated as gratitude.

"It's time we let this go before we give it the power to destroy us," Coco whispered.

"Thank you," Ryan whispered back.

"I don't ever expect us to be best friends," Coco felt the need to tell him. "But if I ever need tickets to a Red Sox game I know where to look."

Ryan smiled. "Yes, you do."

Coco walked away, her eyes blinded by tears. She wasn't halfway across the room when she inadvertently bumped someone. He held a tumbler with an iced drink in his hand, which splashed over the edges, landing on both of them.

Coco gasped at the shock of the coldness against her skin. "Oh my goodness, I am so sorry."

He looked at her in mute surprise. All he seemed

capable of doing was staring at her. He cleared his throat and then shook his head. "No problem."

"Please, let me buy you another drink," Coco offered, as she brushed off the front of his polo shirt.

He continued to stare at her. "Coco?"

Coco narrowed her gaze and studied him. "We graduated together?"

His nod was barely perceptible.

"You're not wearing a name tag," she said, and waited for him to introduce himself.

He didn't.

"Aren't you going to tell me who you are?" she asked.

"You're even prettier now," he whispered, and then blushed as if he'd give anything to grab back those words.

Her curiosity was piqued even more now. "Tell me who you are," she demanded softly. Now that she had a good look at him she had to admit he did look vaguely familiar, but she couldn't place him. He seemed flustered by her attention and at the same time he couldn't stop looking at her as if she were a Greek goddess. She had to admit she found his attention flattering.

"I should go."

He started to turn away, but she stopped him with a question. "Did we have any classes together?"

Some emotion flashed in his eyes that she was unable to identify.

"We did."

This was really bugging her. It was clear that he'd once had a crush on her, and apparently still did, if she was reading the admiration in his eyes correctly.

It sort of made sense that she didn't remember him. Following the disastrous date with Ryan, Coco had done everything she could to make herself inconspicuous. She kept her gaze lowered and her head down. If anyone paid her attention she wouldn't have noticed. "Why don't I remember you?"

He shrugged and looked uncomfortable. "No reason you should. I wasn't exactly on your radar."

She thought she heard a twinge of regret in his voice, but before she could question the comment she heard her name called.

"Coco."

Coco looked over her shoulder to find Brittany from the drill team. "Hey," she said and smiled. "Give me a minute." She turned back to continue her conversation with her unnamed admirer.

But he was gone.

She looked to Brittany. "Did you see who I was talking to?"

Brittany gave her a blank stare. "No. I didn't notice anyone."

Coco had the impression that whoever he was, he'd often been overlooked, and that troubled her. Their brief conversation had intrigued her and she wanted to know more.

"What happened to your dress?" Brittany asked.

Coco looked down and the entire front of her dress was wet. She was a mess. "I bumped into someone. I better head to the ladies' room."

"Good idea."

Once inside, Coco grabbed a stack of paper towels and moistened them to dab at the wet spots.

The restroom door swung open and Jennifer Temple, Ryan's wife, came in. She paused and looked toward Coco.

"I just made an idiot of myself," Coco explained, feeling like she needed to explain what she was doing. "I bumped into someone and his drink spilled down my front."

"It's hardly noticeable," Jennifer assured her. "Coco, I just want to thank you. I can't tell you how much it meant to Ryan to talk to you and have you hear him out."

A light feeling came over Coco. "I was all prepared to give him the lecture of his life."

"He deserved it. I hope you could see that he's genuinely sorry."

As much as Coco would have liked to believe it'd all been an act on Ryan's part, deep down she knew that it wasn't. He couldn't have been more sincere or regretful.

As soon as she'd finished getting rid of the stain on her dress and drying it under the hand air blower, Coco returned to the party. The first thing she did was look for her mystery man, but when she didn't see him she sought out Katie.

Katie took one look at her. "You okay?" she asked.

"Better than okay. I feel great." It was in large part due to her short conversation with Ryan, but also because of the chat with her mystery man. A light feeling came over her, a sense of release and even joy. It nearly overwhelmed her.

"I saw you talking to Ryan and the model."

"They're married, and she seems really nice. I can tell she's someone I would feel good about calling a friend." Coco smiled at the stunned expression that came over Katie.

"And Ryan?"

"He shocked me. He said he specifically came to the reunion to apologize to me."

"No kidding? Wow, that's great."

"It certainly wasn't what I expected." As she spoke she scanned the room, looking for the guy she'd run into . . . literally. "I know it's all sort of crazy, but I've forgiven him. Ryan and I are fine. What's weird is I'm the one who feels set free. I've been carrying a load of hate all these years and I think that after tonight, I might actually be ready to let it go."

What shocked Coco was the fact that she'd assumed venting her hatred, retaliating, was the only way she would ever be free of Ryan. She understood now that spewing her anger would have only tightened the ropes tying her down. By attending this reunion she hoped she'd feel this sense of release through insulting and ridiculing Ryan in front of their peers. Perhaps she'd have been relieved for a time, but it wouldn't have dissolved the pain, wouldn't have purged it from her mind.

It didn't escape her notice that as soon as she agreed to make an effort to forgive him, she'd run into someone who had clearly adored her at one time. If the admiration in his eyes was any indication, he still did.

"How about you?" she asked Katie. "James show yet?"

Katie shook her head. "No . . . I've about given up hope. Angie assured me he paid for the event, but he isn't here."

"He'll come."

"I love your confidence, but the night's half over and there's no sign of him yet. I'm afraid . . . I think once he learned I planned to come he changed his mind."

"You'll get your chance, Katie. You have to believe and trust that the two of you will get all this settled once and for all."

"I'm trying."

Whatever this sense of lightness and tranquility was that surrounded her, Coco wished she could share it with Katie. If possible, she would have liked to bottle it.

"Hang in there, okay? I need to check out a guy," she told Katie.

"What guy?" Katie glanced in the same direction she was looking.

"Someone I talked to earlier." Coco scanned the room and was disappointed when she didn't see him. However, now that they'd spoken, she was on a mission to find out who he was.

Chapter 17

Katie didn't actually see James arrive, but she was aware of him the minute he entered the room. Her whole body felt it.

For probably the first time that evening her back had been to the door as she chatted with another girl, Jules Benedict, whom Katie knew through swim team. Then a tingling sensation came over her. Perhaps she'd heard his voice over the clatter in the room, although that was unlikely. In retrospect, it might have been the anticipation she'd felt all evening, waiting to see him, talk to him. Whatever the reason—she knew James had arrived at last.

"John and I have considered becoming foster parents," Jules was saying. "I think it's just great that you went into social work and find adoptive homes for children. A good home—"

A shiver went down Katie's spine and her heart started hammering like one of those giant Chinese gongs. Right away her throat went dry. "Will you excuse me?" Katie said, cutting off the other woman.

"Oh sure," Jules said, looking surprised.

Katie reached for her drink and took a deep swallow. She spotted him at the table collecting his name tag. Thankfully he'd come without a date. After signing in, he walked into the room.

It didn't take him long to zero in on Katie, she noticed. Their eyes locked for just an instant before he forcefully looked away. He peeled the back off his name tag and stuck it to his shirt. Then he veered deliberately in the opposite direction from where she was standing.

He'd changed from the teenage boy she remembered—he was slightly taller and his shoulders looked broader—and he'd filled out in other areas as well. His hair was shorter now, too. He was good-looking, but not strikingly so. No one was likely to ask him to pose for a calendar. In Katie's eyes, however, he was everything she remembered and more.

Ten years and she felt this pull toward him as strong as it had ever been. She'd never loved anyone more than she loved James.

It went without saying that he wasn't going to voluntarily seek her out. Any chance she had of talking to him would need to be initiated by her. Katie's nerves were already on edge when she approached him. James was chatting with Bill Watson, one of his friends, and when she came to stand beside him, James ignored her.

Bill glanced her way and smiled. "Katie, good to see you."

"You, too." She kept her focus on James, who continued to pretend she was invisible.

Thankfully, Bill was quick to pick up on the undercurrents flowing between her and James.

172   *Debbie Macomber*

"Good to chat with you, James," Bill said. "I'll catch up with you later." He briefly made eye contact with Katie. She read the silent message he sent her, which seemed to more or less wish her good luck.

Bill left, but it took James a couple uncomfortable seconds to acknowledge Katie.

"Hello, James," she said softly.

Then and only then did he turn his attention to her. "Katie." His greeting was as stiff as his spine. He stood straight as a two-by-four, holding on to a bottle of beer.

"I'm glad to see you."

He focused his attention on the other side of the room and didn't respond.

"You've changed," she said. She found it incredibly painful to see and feel his coldness. She wanted to believe it was an act.

"We've all changed, Katie. It's been ten years. That's the way of life."

He was right, of course.

"I wanted to talk to you, to explain things."

"Whatever you have to say isn't important."

"It is to me. I've tried to connect with you before and you've blocked all my attempts."

"I'd hoped you would have gotten the message, then. I'm not interested in reconnecting."

"Whether you want to hear it or not, I need to say it."

"Why?" he asked.

"Because I know I hurt you, and I'm so very sorry. I wanted to explain."

He arched his brows.

"It nearly killed me to leave you the way I did, but it was the only viable option at the time. I—"

James looked decidedly bored. "Listen, Katie, if you want my forgiveness, fine. It's yours. I got over you a long time ago, so there's no need to worry. What's done is done, so let's leave it at that, shall we?"

"I don't know that I can," Katie said, and resisted the urge to wrap her arms protectively around herself. "I need you to hear me out."

"I deserved an explanation ten years ago. Whatever you have to say to me now is pointless."

"You need to understand that I couldn't tell you then," she rushed to say.

"You're not hearing me, Katie. None of it matters any longer." He stared into the distance and seemed decidedly bored.

"Your mother—"

"Katie, stop," he said, turning to her, his eyes hostile. "I don't want to hear it. All I know is that you decided to dump me when I would have sacrificed my entire future for you."

"That's just the point. I couldn't let you."

"The decision was mine. Not yours. You took that away from me. But that said, it all happened a long time ago. Let's just leave it in the past where it belongs."

Not knowing what more to say, Katie hung her head and placed her hand over her chest. "Then tell me, why does my heart hurt like this? Why can't I let go and move on as easily as you?" she asked in a whisper.

He looked beyond her then, as if eager to leave, as

if all he wanted now was to escape. "I imagine it's guilty, but really, you have nothing to feel guilty about—like I said, I got over you a long time ago. I'm sincere when I say this, Katie. I wish you well."

"That's it?" Katie couldn't hide her dismay. This had been her greatest fear. She had accepted that James might never love her as much as he did ten years ago, but she'd expected him to at least let her tell him what had happened. "That's all you have to say to me?" she asked, struggling to hold on to him for a few minutes longer.

"Should there be more?"

"I'd hoped . . . I'd wanted . . ."

"This is it as far as I'm concerned." Then, for some reason, for just a moment, his look gentled. "You look good, Katie."

"Thank you . . . you do, too."

"All that's important is knowing that I got on with my life and you did the same. Like I said, if you're looking for absolution, you have it. Hashing everything out isn't going to change anything. Now, if you'll excuse me."

Seeing that nothing she said would make a difference, Katie stepped aside and James walked away.

She felt numb. For months she'd built up their meeting in her mind, hoping, dreaming, wishing to set matters straight with him. There remained so much more she wanted to tell him, so much more that was in her heart. But James had no desire to hear it. No desire to have anything more to do with her.

She remained frozen, unable to move. It was difficult to breathe as the regret and discouragement washed over her.

"Katie?" Coco was at her side and gently wrapped her hand around Katie's elbow. "Come on, let's find a quiet corner."

Katie managed to answer with a nod.

Coco led her away to an open table, pulled out a chair for Katie, and then scooted one out for herself.

"I saw you talking with James."

Again Katie nodded.

"I told you he'd show."

Katie forced a smile.

"Were you able to explain what happened?"

"A little. He wasn't interested in listening."

Coco patted Katie's hand. "What did you expect?"

"I . . . I don't know. Not a . . . such a cold shoulder . . . total indifference."

"Did he know you were signed up for the reunion? I mean, was seeing you a shock? Because that might explain his reaction."

"I . . . don't know if he did or not. He didn't say."

"Give him a chance," Coco urged. "Even if he knew you planned to attend, I'm sure it was pretty intense seeing you again."

"I couldn't reach him. I don't think he even listened. He said he got over me a long time ago."

"It's been ten years," Coco reminded her gently.

"I'm not over him."

"You will be, Katie."

"I can't believe how cold he was . . ." James was right, they'd both changed. He wasn't anything like what she remembered.

"Katie—"

"I want to go," she said, cutting off Coco.

"Go? Go where?"

"Out of here . . . back to the inn."

"Okay, but I want to say good-bye to a few people first."

Apparently, Coco didn't understand. "I don't want you to leave . . . you should stay. I'll walk back to the inn. It isn't far and I could use the fresh air. I need to think."

Coco frowned. "You're sure?"

Katie stood and gave her friend's hand a squeeze. "I'll be fine," she lied, and forced a smile. "I'll see you back at the inn."

Coco's frown deepened. "I don't know about this."

"Stop worrying. You're right. I'm being unfair to James. We both need time to absorb seeing each other again."

Without giving Coco a chance to argue, Katie left the room. Once downstairs, she saw that the restaurant and bar area were busy. Every table was taken now and the room was filled with the sound of chatter and music coming from the jukebox in the back by the pool table.

The evening was cool and Katie was grateful for her light sweater. Dusk was settling over the waterfront and drew her in that direction. She crossed Harbor Street and walked the short block to the marina, past the library to the totem pole.

Katie lost count of all the times she and James had walked along this very sidewalk, holding hands, lost in each other. The setting sun sent pink shadows shimmering over the water's smooth surface. Not a ripple in sight. It astonished her that the cove could remain calm while her heart was in turmoil.

Coco was right, of course. Her expectations had

been unrealistic. In her mind, Katie had envisioned James eagerly listening to her explanation or at least being open to hearing it. It was important that he understand that she'd broken off their relationship because she loved him and wanted the best for his future, at no small cost to her own.

Back then he hadn't believed her, hadn't taken her at her word when she said she didn't want to be tied down to one boy. That was why he'd written her those letters. What he didn't know was that it had nearly killed her to get those letters. There'd been emails, too, plenty of those, but the letters had been the one constant for months on end, until she'd finally asked him not to write her any longer.

In the face of so much evidence to the contrary, she couldn't let go of the belief that his feelings for her hadn't changed. What they shared was too deep, too real, too profound to fade no matter how many years had gone by.

But apparently she was wrong. Apparently it was too late.

Chapter 18

I walked into the living room to find Coco had returned from the mix and mingle and was pacing the area in front of the fireplace, her movements rapid and agitated.

"Oh hi," I said, surprised to see her. "I didn't realize you were back."

The instant she saw me she blurted out, "Have you seen Katie?"

"No. Is everything all right?" Coco looked more than a little concerned.

"I don't know." She rubbed her palms together as if she was seeking warmth. "She left before me. And then I thought she probably shouldn't be alone, so I decided to head back myself. But now she isn't here."

"Did she say she was coming back to the inn?"

"Yes." Coco continued to pace, with frequent stops to look out the window.

"Have you tried calling her?"

"I texted her twice and called, too, and she's not responding."

"I'm sure there's no need for worry," I said, and I

believed that. "It's such a lovely evening, my guess is that she decided to take a walk along the waterfront. I often do that myself."

Coco didn't look reassured.

"Why don't I brew a pot of tea, and if she hasn't shown up by the time we've had a cup the two of us can go look for her."

Coco hesitated and then nodded. "Okay, good idea. The tea might help calm me down."

I went into the kitchen and put the water on. I'd been in my office, checking online for spin classes. If I was going to broaden my horizons, make new friends, then there was no better place to start than by joining a class. For now it was easier to focus on the physical aspect of this new page in my life.

The water had just started to boil when I heard the front door open.

"Katie, where have you been?" I heard Coco ask, her relief obvious.

"Walking."

"You left forty minutes ago. I was worried. I tried to call you and was freaking out when you didn't respond."

"It's okay. I'm fine . . . really. I couldn't fit my phone in my clutch, so I left it in my room."

In my humble opinion, she didn't sound fine. I put the tea leaves into the pot, set it on the tray with two cups, and carried it into the living room area.

"How does hot tea sound?" I asked, as I set the tray down on the coffee table.

"Sounds great."

Katie sat on the sofa next to her friend. "Please, join us," she said to me.

I thought the two might prefer time alone and didn't want to intrude. I looked from one to the other to make sure the invite was sincere, and it seemed like it was. "I will, thank you." After the topsy-turvy emotional day I'd had, I would appreciate the company and the conversation. Mark hadn't been gone twenty-four hours and I already missed him, missed our times together.

Rover wandered in from where he'd been asleep in my office and curled up in front of the fireplace, resting his chin on his paws.

I brought out another cup from the kitchen and sat in the chair across from the sofa.

"So how's the reunion so far?" I asked. One look at Katie told me it hadn't gone so well.

Coco looked at Katie and then spoke first. "I got a real shock," she said. "I came intending to confront a boy who broke my heart and humiliated me. I was going to call him out as the scumbag he was, but before I could say a word, he apologized to me."

"Sounds like a guy who has done a bit of maturing," I said, as I leaned forward and reached for the teapot, filling each of our cups. Steam rose from the hot liquid.

"I've despised Ryan all these years and now I have to learn not to hate him." She appeared to find this amusing and laughed. "Actually, it was a bit of a letdown, you know? Everything I wanted to say was on the tip of my tongue. I was ready to beat him down to the ground and then he took the wind out of my sails."

"Is that a bad thing?" I asked.

"No, but I'll admit it takes some getting used to.

The truth is I'm happy. I know it sounds odd, but I actually feel like something heavy has lifted off my back. For years I had to keep feeding that hate for Ryan and now . . . now it's out of my hands." She laughed a little, as if at a loss to explain this transformation. "I wasn't ready to accept his apology, but I could see that he was sincere. I realized it couldn't have been easy for him to talk to me, but afterward we both felt better. I know *I* did. Does that make sense?"

"It does," Katie assured her.

"I agree," I chimed in.

I tasted the tea, which had steeped beautifully. It was one of my personal favorites, a blend sold in the Seattle area called Market Spice, named after the Pike Place Market.

"What about you, Katie?" I asked, raising the cup to my lips and blowing into the hot tea to cool it down before taking my first sip.

"The party didn't go as well for me as it did Coco," she said, holding her own tea with both hands and peering into its depths as if looking for some prediction from the leaves. "I saw an old boyfriend with the hopes that we might be able to reconnect. But that, unfortunately, isn't going to work."

"Give James time," Coco urged.

"It's useless," Katie whispered. She sat back on the sofa, cradling the cup. "He could barely stand to look at me."

"Don't be so sure," Coco said. "After you left, I watched James."

Katie's head came up. "And?"

"He looked for you."

"He did not," Katie insisted.

"Okay, fine, I don't know for sure, but a couple of times I saw him searching the room. I really think he was hoping to see you. Don't get me wrong, he wasn't blatant about it, but I got the feeling James isn't as immune to you as you think."

Katie's shoulders sank with defeat. "I doubt that's true."

"When did you become such a pessimist?" Coco asked.

Katie's smile lacked any real amusement. "To-night."

I leaned back in my chair, too. "I've had a pretty rotten day myself," I told them, knowing misery loves company.

Both Katie and Coco turned their attention to me.

"I lost a friend today," I elaborated.

"*Lost* as in died?" Katie asked, her voice gentle and full of compassion. Sensing her genuine concern made me realize what an excellent social worker she must be.

"No, he didn't die," I clarified. "Mark was my handyman and my friend. Over the last couple of years we've become close . . . but not in a romantic way," I explained, and then added, "Well, not until recently."

"Did you have a misunderstanding?" Coco asked.

"I don't mean to pry, if you'd rather not talk about it."

"Actually, I don't know why I'm telling you this, but it's nice to be able to unload a little."

"Please," Katie urged. "Hearing about your troubles will help take my mind off my own."

I clung to my teacup and looked into the amber liquid. "My husband died in Afghanistan almost two years ago, and Mark and I became friends, good friends. Then, out of the blue about a month ago, he announced that he'd fallen in love with me."

"Did you know how he felt about you?"

"No, although in retrospect there were signs. But I was caught up in my grief and oblivious to his feelings. What's so strange is that right after he told me how he felt about me he said he was leaving Cedar Cove."

"Leaving?" Katie echoed.

I nodded.

"Did he say why?"

"Not a word. It's all very odd."

"Today is the day he left?" Coco wanted to know. A deep sense of loss settled over me. "He headed out this afternoon. He's never given me any indication of where he's going or why."

"What did he say when he left?"

I hiccupped on a half-sob, half-laugh. "All he said was good-bye."

"He must be hiding something," Katie suggested, frowning.

"You think?" Coco muttered sarcastically. They ran through a couple scenarios, all ones I'd entertained myself. "As far as I can find out, he isn't in legal trouble or anything like that."

"Is he a spy?" Coco joked.

I laughed. "Not likely. Mark is unconventional, cranky most of the time, yet probably one of the most generous men I've ever known. He enjoys woodwork and would often build the most beautiful, intricate furniture. Not long ago he gave away a cradle he built to a couple he barely knew who are expecting their third child." It continued to boggle my mind when he could have set his own price for that cradle. He'd carved intricate forest scenes into the headboard. Without question, it was a piece of art.

"Do you know where he went?" Katie asked.

"I don't have a clue."

"He just up and left?" Coco repeated, as if she had as much trouble understanding Mark as I did.

I nodded helplessly.

Both women seemed to find this as baffling as I did.

"He would have left sooner if I hadn't convinced him to stay long enough to finish the gazebo."

"He built that?" Katie said, sounding awed.

I nodded.

"Wow, he is talented."

Saddened, I slowly exhaled. "I'm going to miss him so much."

"Do you . . . think you're in love with him, too?" This came from Katie.

It was the same question that had haunted me for the last three weeks. What I felt for Mark was completely different from what I'd experienced when I fell in love with Paul. With my husband the attraction had been immediate and explosive. We were crazy in love almost from first sight. We married in a fever, and within a matter of weeks Paul had shipped out to Afghanistan. Within the first year of our marriage he'd been killed.

Even now I was unsure about my feelings for Mark. Under any circumstances I would have been afraid to fall in love again, afraid to risk my heart. But considering that question in light of Mark's announcement that he was leaving anyway made it all the more confusing.

Until this afternoon when I'd overheard him speaking to Bob Beldon, I'd assumed Mark intended to return at some point. But he'd made it clear that wasn't in his plans.

Coco looked as puzzled as I felt. "But he told you he was in love with you and then he left town?"

I shrugged. Whatever demons were after him were apparently greater than any feelings he held for me. "Strange as it sounds, I think falling in love with me might be *why* he's leaving."

It seemed Katie was about to say something more when the front door burst open and Finn and Carrie Dalton returned from dinner. They were flushed with laughter and excitement. They paused in the foyer with their arms locked around each other when they noticed the three of us intently watching them.

"Oh hi," Carrie said, looking a bit embarrassed. "I didn't realize we had an audience."

"No problem," I assured her. "Did you have a good dinner?"

"It was wonderful." From the way she looked at her husband, I guessed she wasn't talking about the food.

"Where'd you go?" Coco asked, and then she added under her breath, "I want to order whatever it was they had."

Finn kept Carrie close to his side and answered, "A place just down the street. DD's on the Cove."

"Good choice," I said.

Finn glanced longingly up the staircase. "Now, if you'll excuse us."

"Oh sure."

"Finn," Carrie warned, as her husband started to lift her to carry her up. "Not again."

"It keeps me in shape."

"I know better ways for you to get a workout," Carrie whispered, and started racing up the stairs with Finn right behind her. Their laughter echoed up the stairwell, their joy contagious.

Silence filled the room after the two disappeared.

"Honeymooners," I explained, although it probably wasn't necessary. "They're only here for the one night and leave for Alaska in the morning."

Katie cocked her head to one side and frowned as if deep in thought. "I read a book about Alaska and the author's first name was Finn. It's not a common name . . . it wouldn't be possible—I mean, what are the odds? But do you think it might be him?"

I didn't have a clue, although Carrie had mentioned that she and her husband were both writers, but really what were the chances? "I have no idea if that's him or not."

"Really a great book; made me want to visit Alaska."

"Like you said, Finn isn't a common name."

"Probably not him," Katie said. "From what I remember he was something of a recluse, didn't give interviews and kept himself out of the public eye."

Coco looked at her watch. "You ready?" she asked Katie.

"Ready for what?"

"To go out. A couple of the girls from swim team want us to meet up with them at the Pancake Palace.

We have a bet on whether Goldie is still there. She must be close to eighty if she's a day."

Katie shook her head. "I don't really feel like going out."

"Oh no you don't," Coco said with conviction. "I am not going to let you go to your room and sulk and feel sorry for yourself. We are here to par-tay."

Katie looked as if she wanted to argue. "I'll be a drag. Besides, I barely know the other girls."

"Wrong," Coco insisted. "Steph specially asked me to make sure you joined us, and I told her you would."

"All right, all right," Katie agreed reluctantly.

"Being with friends is exactly what the doctor ordered," Coco said, and then laughed. "That was something my mother used to say."

Together my two reunion guests headed out the door. It was barely nine, but I was tired. It'd been an emotional day.

Rover stood when I did and followed me into the kitchen when I carried in the tray. I let him out the back door and then stood on the top step while he did his business.

The moon was full and cast golden beams over my garden, the very one Mark had created for me. I looked toward the gazebo, wondering where Mark was this night and if he was thinking of me. I hoped he was.

I closed my eyes and blew him a kiss.

Chapter 19

It was nearly one in the morning before Coco and Katie returned to the inn. Katie had at least made an effort to enjoy herself, Coco thought. It'd been great to reminisce with their friends, although her own mind continued to wander back to the man she'd bumped into earlier that evening. For no particular reason she could explain, he'd piqued her interest. He had looked vaguely familiar, but she'd been racking her brain, and if they'd ever shared a class she didn't remember him. Once or twice she'd noticed him glance her way, and when he did he held her gaze for several seconds before she grew flustered and her heart pounded. It'd been a long time since any man had interested her to this extent. What bothered her most was her inability to understand why. He was completely unlike the urbane, polished professionals she usually dated.

Men often told her they found her attractive, as he had. She was accustomed to flattery. What struck her was how sincere he had been. And the word he'd used: pretty. It wasn't one she'd heard in a long while.

He made her feel that way, as if she was the most beautiful girl in the world. Who didn't like *that* feeling?

Following their instructions from Jo Marie, Coco locked the front door behind them when they came in. The inn was still and quiet, and she had to assume Jo Marie and the other guests were asleep.

"That was fun," Katie admitted, as they walked toward the stairs. A night-light softly illuminated the staircase.

"Told you," Coco said, unable to resist. "Going out was far better than stewing away the rest of the evening in your room by yourself."

Katie muttered under her breath and then said, "I knew you couldn't let the 'I told you so' pass."

"I'm not right that often."

"Oh hardly," Katie muttered good-naturedly as they climbed up the steps, doing their best to make the least amount of noise.

Now was Coco's chance to ask Katie: "Did you happen to notice the guy I was talking to earlier at the social?"

Katie paused, her hand on the railing. "No. Should I have?"

Coco hesitated, uncertain how much to say. "I spilled his drink and tried to buy him another, but he wouldn't let me."

"What did his name tag say?"

"He wasn't wearing one."

"Figures," Katie murmured, and yawned. "A tall, dark, and mysterious man shows up at the reunion. Naturally, you're curious; who wouldn't be?"

"I won't sleep until I figure out who he is." While

packing, at the last minute Coco had thrown the yearbook from their senior class into her bag. Now she couldn't wait to look through it and find the guy's photo the minute she was in her room.

As they reached the top of the staircase, Katie muffled another yawn. "I'm headed straight to bed."

"I won't be far behind."

"'Night," Katie said. "It might not seem like it, but I'm glad I came. Thank you for making it impossible for me to refuse." Her smile was huge. "Guess that's another 'I told you so' moment."

Coco had the key in her lock. "'Night, Katie. See you in the morning, and I won't say 'I told you so.' One a day is my limit."

Once inside her room, Coco undressed, removed her makeup, and slipped on her jammies before she climbed into bed. Sitting with her legs folded beneath her, she flipped through the pages of her yearbook, studying each face, unwilling to give up until she discovered the identity of the mystery man.

She paused any number of times as she came upon several who'd come to the party that evening. It surprised her how much the boys had changed in ten years. Other than hairstyles, the girls seemed to have remained much the same.

She was all the way to the *H*'s before she found him. As soon as she came upon his photo and name, she gasped.

Hudson Hamilton.

The mystery man at the social was Hudson Hamilton?

Coco had trouble believing it. They'd had two classes together the last semester of their senior year.

He had rarely said a word in class, but aced every quiz and every test.

Hudson was an eccentric nerd. It wasn't unusual for him to wear a plaid shirt with suspenders, like an old man. Hudson was completely oblivious to fashion.

He wasn't weird or anything, just different. She remembered he was incredibly shy and every time he talked to her, he seemed incapable of getting the words out. It was almost painful to listen to him.

And he'd asked her to Homecoming. He'd hemmed and hawed and shuffled his feet and it'd taken forever for him to get to the point.

In retrospect, Coco would give just about anything to have gone with him. Imagine if she had and the whole sick thing with Ryan had never happened.

Just recently she'd told the teenage daughter of a coworker and friend, "Pay attention to the smart ones, not the good-looking ones. The smart ones make for better husbands."

This seemed prophetic now, although she didn't know where Hudson was in life or what he'd done following graduation.

His Homecoming invite came to mind as if it'd happened just recently. Hudson had approached her after English literature class. She'd been ready to head out the door when he stopped her.

"Coco."

"Yes," she returned impatiently. She'd been on her way to swim practice and couldn't be late.

"There's this dance." He studied the floor tile as if the design was a treasure map.

"Dance? Do you mean Homecoming?" she asked, wanting him to get to the point.

"Yes. That dance. I'd really like . . . it would be an honor . . . I mean, would you consider . . . I know it's—"

"Hudson," she'd blurted out impatiently. "If you're asking me to the dance, I—"

"I am," he interrupted, looking up, his eyes bright with hope.

Coco couldn't imagine attending any social function with Hudson. Anyone but Hudson. "I'm going with friends. Thanks anyway." She hadn't meant to be rude, but in retrospect she probably had been abrupt and dismissive. His timing couldn't have been worse. She was in danger of being late to practice. It pained her to admit that she had thought of him as far beneath her on the social scale.

Hudson nodded as if he'd expected a refusal. "Have a good time."

"I will," she'd told him, brightening in hopes of taking away the sting of her refusal. She added, "But thanks for thinking of me." And with that, she was off.

Coco leaned back against the headboard and closed her eyes. She'd kept the draperies over her windows open and bright moonlight skidded over the surface of the cove.

After the utter humiliation following Homecoming, it had taken raw courage to return to school. Most everyone avoided her, which is exactly how Coco wanted it. The one person she was most comfortable with was Katie.

Hudson apparently hadn't read the memo, though.

Once again he approached her after class one afternoon.

"Coco," he said, stopping her.

At first she pretended not to hear and she started out the door, weaving her way among classmates in an effort to escape. It did her no good. Hudson caught up with her in the hallway.

"Coco . . . wait," he said, rushing to catch up with her.

Heaving an exasperated sigh, she stopped but refused to look at him.

"I want you to know . . . Ryan is an idiot . . . I'm sorry."

All Coco hoped to do was get away. The last thing she wanted or needed was Hudson calling attention to her humiliation, especially in front of their classmates flowing through the busy hallway.

"Hudson," she said with exaggerated patience, "I appreciate what you're trying to say. But can't you talk in complete sentences like everyone else?" she demanded. Then she added, "And more important, why can't you just leave me alone?" With that, she rushed out of the building.

To the best of her memory, Hudson never spoke to her again.

Katie knocked softly against Coco's bedroom door. Shaken from her memories, Coco sat up straighter and called out, "It's open."

Dressed in her fleece robe and slippers, Katie let herself into Coco's room. "I saw that your light was on. You couldn't sleep, either?" she asked.

"I wanted to see if I could find the mystery man." She closed their yearbook and set it aside.

"Who is he?" Katie sat at the edge of the bed.

"Hudson Hamilton. Do you remember him?"

Katie shook her head.

"Until this weekend I don't think I've thought of him even once since we left high school. I didn't recognize him."

"Has he changed that much?"

"He's nothing like I remember, that's for sure, but then we've all changed, haven't we?" she said, rather than answer the question directly. Coco was disappointed that she hadn't had more of an opportunity to talk to him. Since their brief encounter he'd been on her mind, and she realized she wanted to know more about him.

He'd appeared to be at the event alone. Of course, he could be married with a wife who'd just opted to stay home. Even as the thought went through her mind, Coco discounted it. Hudson wasn't married and he wasn't involved with anyone. The vibes she got from him said as much.

"Why are you so curious about him?" Katie asked, and reached for the yearbook. She flipped the pages until she found Hudson's photo. She looked up when she did and frowned. "This is him? He was in our class? I don't remember him."

The fact was Hudson wasn't one of the guys a girl would remember. "He had a crush on me and I treated him badly," Coco said, shamed by her memories. Regret filled her. "I was rude and heartless." By all that was right, she should apologize. If nothing else, it would give her an excuse to talk to him again.

She needed to know what it was about him that attracted her so strongly now, when she hadn't had the time of day for him ten years earlier.

"Coco, you were never heartless," Katie insisted.

"I was a complete witch. I considered Hudson beneath me. I wouldn't consider going to Homecoming, or for that matter, even the movies, with Hudson. I'm mortified at the way I treated him."

Katie shook her head. "You just weren't mean like that."

It humbled her to admit the truth. "I was with Hudson."

"You were young; we all did stupid stuff like that," Katie told her.

"Don't try to minimize what I did, Katie." Coco leaned forward and took the yearbook out of her friend's hands. "Really, I'm no better than Ryan. I embarrassed Hudson in front of everyone when he tried to tell me that Ryan was a jerk. All he wanted to do was tell me how sorry he was for what had happened to me. I laid into him because I didn't want to be reminded of anything having to do with that night. I'm going to let him know how sorry I am." Actually, now that she'd said the words aloud, Coco realized how much she wanted to get to know him.

"You'll see him again," Katie assured her.

"I hope he's planning on going to the dinner and dance," she said.

"It will be easy enough to find out tomorrow afternoon," Katie reminded her. "Angie has all that information, and she'll be helping with the decorations for the gym."

"Right. So what's keeping you up, Katie? You still

thinking about James?" Coco asked, eager now to steer the subject away from herself.

"I can't stop thinking about him." She bit into her lower lip. "Do you honestly think he might have been looking for me after I left the party?"

Coco didn't want to mislead her friend or raise Katie's hopes when it wasn't warranted. "I can't really say for sure, but I did see him scanning the room. I'm sure seeing you again had an impact on him."

Her friend's eyes revealed such hopeful expectation. "It was so much harder than I ever thought it would be."

"Then it was probably the same for James, don't you think?"

Katie disagreed with a shake of her head. "I don't think so. From his body language—not to mention his actual words—he made it obvious all he wanted was to stay clear of me."

Hoping to steer Katie's thoughts away from James, Coco brought up an entirely different subject. "It was interesting what Jo Marie told us about her friend, wasn't it?"

"Weird that he'd pack up and leave." Katie, too, seemed relieved to talk about something else.

"Really weird," Coco agreed. "She's having a hard time of it, it's easy to see." Generally, Katie was more astute when it came to discerning others' behaviors, but Jo Marie's feelings for Mark were right there on the surface: visible. The innkeeper might not have admitted how she felt about the handyman, but it was apparent to Coco that the other woman had fallen in love with her friend. Coco hoped that whatever had driven him away would be quickly resolved.

Katie yawned and Coco realized she was tired, too. It felt as if a whole lifetime had been jammed into a few hours. She'd confronted Ryan only to be stunned by his plea for forgiveness. And then she'd run into Hudson.

While she might not have been as brutal to Hudson as Ryan had been to her, Coco needed to make her own amends. When she did see him next she wanted to tell him that she remembered him and was so sorry about how she'd behaved.

After saying good night to Coco, Katie returned to her own room.

Turning off the lamp on the bedside table, Coco nestled down in the sheets, pulled the covers over her shoulders, and closed her eyes.

It shouldn't have come as a surprise that she dreamed about Hudson and it was a warm, wonderful dream that left her smiling in its afterglow.

Chapter 20

Even though I was so tired, I had trouble sleeping. I heard Coco and Katie return to the inn around one in the morning, and it was well past that time before I was able to fall asleep. Then to my dismay I woke again long before the alarm went off. My eyes stung from lack of sleep and my heart felt heavy. It didn't take much to understand what the problem was.

Mark.

I was determined to put him out of my mind, but instead he dominated nearly every thought. On a positive note, his leaving and the chat with my mother had shaken me enough to be a wake-up call. It was time to reach out, stretch, grow, make new friends.

Date.

Date?

Then I remembered that I actually *had* a date this very evening. A sense of panic nearly swallowed me whole. I'd enjoyed my brief conversation with Rich Marlow, and after checking out his photo on Face-book I saw that he was reasonably good-looking. Thankfully, it was a double date, so I wouldn't be alone with Rich, and getting to know him would be a bit more natural and casual.

I brewed coffee and set the table for breakfast. Rover wasn't eager to leave his bed and lingered there until he heard me fill his food dish. I knew my guests had arrived back at the inn late. And it didn't seem likely the Daltons would be getting out of bed anytime soon. So I didn't start cooking breakfast until I heard movement upstairs.

Coco was the first one to show up. She bounced down the stairs with a bright smile, obviously a natural morning person if ever there was one. She was like a ray of sunshine to my cloudy mood.

"Morning, Jo Marie."

"Morning." I poured her coffee and orange juice, and set them in front of her at the table.

Katie joined her momentarily. Right away she reached for the coffee. She didn't look like she'd slept well, which made two of us.

"I hope you both were comfortable."

"I slept like a fairy princess," Coco answered.

"Not me," Katie confessed on the tail end of a yawn. She covered her mouth and yawned a second time. "I slept more like a troll under a bridge."

"You'd better catch a power nap, then," Coco advised, "because this is bound to be a long day, especially with the dinner tonight."

"I'm thinking I'll skip—"

"Don't go there, sister," Coco said, wagging her index finger at Katie. "I won't even let you consider missing the dinner and dance tonight. I know you're discouraged about James, but trust me, everything is going to work out the way it is meant to be."

I could see that Coco's words did little to encourage Katie. Frankly, I could understand all too well Katie's reluctance to face the day. I had my own doubts to contend with.

I finished cooking the eggs and carried the platter out to the table along with bacon and sausages and fresh blueberry muffins. These muffins were Mark's favorites and . . . no!

I absolutely refused to let Mark invade my thoughts. It was done, finished, over with, and so be it.

"We're meeting up with Steph this morning," Coco said, as she reached for a muffin. She glanced at her watch. "We have forty minutes."

"We are? That soon?" Katie's words were dipped in reluctance.

"Yes. Steph wants us to stop by her house. Then the three of us will have lunch before we head over to the school to decorate the gym for tonight."

"Oh yes, I forgot about decorating the gym." Katie didn't bother to hide her lack of enthusiasm.

"I heard Mercedes is having a sale, too," Coco said, and waved a half-slice of toast at her friend. "We should go. Who knows, I might find something irresistible for tonight."

"You want to shop?" Katie asked, as if the mere suggestion appalled her. "I thought you had your outfit already picked out."

"I do, but who in their right mind can resist a sale? Steph said all accessories are fifty percent off, plus some dress styles."

For the first time that morning, Katie smiled. "Resist a sale? Not you."

They ate their breakfast and then returned to their

rooms to get ready to go out. By ten-thirty they were out the door. I didn't expect to see them again until late afternoon.

I'd picked up on the sale at Mercedes's. I hadn't bought anything new in a good long while—most days I wore jeans—and I couldn't remember the last time I'd showed my legs. As an innkeeper, I was always running around, and skirts and dresses just didn't lend themselves to my days. Maybe I should check out Mercedes's sale myself. A new outfit would help get me in the right mood for my dinner date that evening.

My honeymooners had yet to make an appearance and I figured they probably weren't coming down for breakfast. I changed into my gardening clothes, planning to tackle a large package of tulip bulbs I'd ordered by mail from the Skagit Valley north of Seattle. I wanted to get those planted before we were hit by the October rains.

Rover followed me outside to the shed where I kept the shovel and other gardening equipment. The shed Mark had built for me. Just thinking about him irritated me so much that I was tempted to slam the door. It certainly didn't help that reminders of him were everywhere I turned.

I read the back of the package of bulbs. I'd heard years earlier that there were more tulips growing in the Skagit Valley than in all of Holland, though I don't know if that's true.

I'd ordered red tulips and wanted to plant them in the front of the yard around the sign that read THE INN AT ROSE HARBOR.

The very sign Mark had built and set into place.

I carried my equipment to the sign and slammed my shovel into the dirt, having a difficult time holding on to my irritation once again. It was a good thing Mark wasn't around, because the way I felt just then I'd probably punch him in the gut.

Rover's howl caught me up short. At times I swear that dog can read my mind.

"It's okay," I said, doing my best to calm him and swallow my pent-up frustration. All at once the urge to weep nearly overwhelmed me. I had one foot on the shovel and the other planted firmly on the ground as I stood, doing my best to suppress the tears. My precarious stance felt much like my life. Up and down, one minute feeling rooted and the next unpredictable.

"I'm better off without him," I told Rover, who'd positioned himself on the wet grass near the sign. He rested his chin on his paws and kept a close eye on me.

At my comment, Rover raised his head and twisted it to one side.

"I mean it," I said, as I continued to dig around the sign, creating a larger border where I intended to plant the bulbs. Mark had set the sign in concrete so there was no chance my digging would cause it to lean or topple. One thing I could say about Mark, when he took on a project he was determined to do a good job. I swore an atom bomb could go off and that sign would remain upright.

Once I had created the edging around the sign, I got down on my knees with the hand trowel and dug smaller holes for the bulbs. Rover ambled to my side and leaned his small body close to mine, offering me comfort.

"It's okay," I whispered. "I'll be fine. We both will." As soon as I spoke I needed to sniffle. Tears were a weakness that aggravated me more than just about anything, and here I was blubbering away.

Sitting back on my haunches, I removed my garden gloves and reached inside my jacket pocket for a tissue in order to blow my nose.

"God save me from irrational men," I told Rover.

"Good riddance, right?"

Rover did that head thing again.

"I mean it," I told him, a bit more forcefully than I intended.

I had about half of the bulbs planted when I heard the door to the inn open. Finn Dalton appeared with two overnight bags and walked toward the parking area.

My honeymooners were up and about. I stood and brushed the dirt from my knees and started toward the house.

"I've got coffee, juice, and muffins out," I told Finn.

"Yes, thanks, we've already helped ourselves."

He held the door open for me and I followed him inside.

Carrie stood at the end of the staircase and had her purse strap over her shoulder. "We slept later than either of us intended. I hate to rush off, but we need to hurry in order to catch our flight."

"No problem," I assured her. "It was a delight to have you."

"We'll be back," Carrie promised. "We had a wonderful time in Cedar Cove. Just wonderful."

Her gaze connected with that of her husband and I witnessed the strong flow of love between them. Seeing it produced an ache within me and I had to look down before I embarrassed myself by letting my emotions get away from me.

Just before Paul headed toward Joint Base Lewis-McChord for his deployment, my husband and I had shared that same look, that same connection. Twenty-four hours later he was on a transit to Afghanistan and I never saw him again.

After I finished planting the tulips, I took Rover on our daily walk. By sheer determination I didn't take our usual route past Mark's house. I needed to remind myself that he wasn't there and he wouldn't be ever again.

Once home, I tidied up the kitchen and cleaned the Daltons' room, hauling the sheets to the washer and making up the bed. When I finished I showered and dressed and drove over to Mercedes's Boutique.

Sure enough a large SALE sign was slanted across the big display window. I'd heard about the shop any number of times since moving to Cedar Cove. However, I had yet to have an opportunity to buy anything new.

I recognized Mercedes from the Chamber meetings, and when she saw me she broke into a huge grin.

"Jo Marie," she called out, greeting me, "how nice to see you."

"I've got a blind date tonight," I blurted out. *What is wrong with me?* I was fully incapable of making small talk or carrying on a conversation these days. I really did need to get back out into the world.

Mercedes's smile widened. "Ah, so you're looking for something new to wear?"

"I'm looking for a whole lot more, but let's start with the outfit."

"Dinner date?"

I nodded. "I checked him out on Facebook and he looks decent enough."

"Casual?"

Again I answered with a nod.

"Something just came in and I think you would look stunning in it."

She led me away from the sale rack, which at this point looked like it'd been pretty much picked over, to an area toward the front of the store.

Mercedes pulled a white tank top and a maxiskirt with a gray-and-navy-blue geometric design off the rack. "Don't you love these colors together?" she asked.

The price tag dangled from the waistband, and when I saw it my eyes bulged.

"I'd pair it with this white top and Caribbean-blue sweater, and I have the perfect necklace to complement the outfit."

I took the complete set into the dressing room, and once I tried it all together I had to admit Mercedes had a good eye. For a long time I remained inside the cubicle, studying my reflection. I looked good and my TOMS wedges would be a great addition. Admittedly, I could use a haircut and my brows needed some attention, too, but all in all I was satisfied. The outfit was casual enough for a walk along the waterfront but dressy enough for dinner at a nice restaurant.

"What do you think?" Mercedes asked, when I came out of the dressing room.

"I'll take it, plus the necklace."

"Excellent. You really do look lovely, Jo Marie."

"Thank you."

On my way back to the inn, I stopped at a local hair salon that welcomed walk-ins and had my hair trimmed and my eyebrows shaped. I was about as ready for this date as I was going to be.

It was well into the afternoon by the time I got home. It'd been so long since I'd gone shopping for myself that I felt renewed. The thought of meeting Rich and actually going out on a date had started to feel fun rather than daunting. This was progress. However, if I needed a new outfit to get me in the mood every time I met someone new, I'd soon be penniless.

Rover wanted out soon after I arrived back at the inn, so I stood on the porch and waited until he finished. I couldn't help but wonder what my intuitive pet would think of Rich Marlow. His reaction to this other man would say a great deal. If Rover took an instant shine to Rich, that would tell me everything I needed to know about Rhyder's brother.

I heard the approach of a vehicle coming down the driveway and right away recognized Bob Beldon's car. He'd been with Mark the day before, helping Mark clear out his garage.

Bob parked in the slot vacated by Carrie and Finn Dalton.

"Hi, Bob," I said, crossing my arms over my chest. As far as I could remember Bob had never made a trip to the inn without Peggy. I couldn't imagine the reason for this unexpected visit.

"Jo Marie." He removed his Seahawks cap and slapped it across his knee.

I wasn't sure what that was supposed to mean, so I waited for him to explain. He stood on the sidewalk and braced his foot against the bottom step.

"What can I do for you?" I asked, when he wasn't immediately forthcoming.

"Mark asked me to stop by."

"Mark?" I repeated, my voice strange to my own ears. I strived to look calm and collected and knew I'd failed.

"He wanted me to tell you why he left."

Right away the anger was back. What respect I had for Mark evaporated. "Mark couldn't tell me himself?" I demanded, not bothering to disguise my exasperation. "He asked you to do his talking for him?"

Bob slapped his cap against his knee a second time. "I wasn't keen on this myself, until he explained."

"What possible excuse did he have?" My voice vibrated with anger.

Bob's look held mine. "He loves you."

So he said. "He has a peculiar way of showing his feelings." If this was the way Mark chose to prove his love, then I was better off without him. I'd said it before and I'd say it again. *God save me from irrational, unreasonable men!*

Bob discounted my outburst with a hard shake of his head. "Mark knew if he explained what he was about to do, you'd attempt to talk him out of it, and because he loves you, he feared you'd convince him to stay. He said he couldn't take that chance."

"What?"

"Perhaps we should go inside and talk, Jo Marie. I think you're going to need to sit down for this."

Chapter 21

The morning had flown by, and Coco couldn't believe it when she looked at her watch and discovered it was time to head to the school to decorate for the evening's events. At Steph's house she reconnected with several of her classmates she hadn't talked to in years. It was a kick to catch up with those she hadn't seen since graduation. And, naturally, there was the gossip. Apparently, Tom Peters had arrived driving a Porsche that was said to cost six figures, and then one of the guys discovered it was a rental. Hailey Gentry was going through a divorce and this was her second marriage. There'd been lots to learn and lots to share, too.

Katie was quiet most of the time they were at lunch. Coco knew Katie was brooding over James. Her expectations for this first encounter had been far too high.

Katie had always been overly sensitive. That wasn't necessarily bad, it was the reason her friend was an excellent social worker. From the moment they'd first connected, Coco knew Katie had a big, generous heart.

She championed the underdog and did her best to right the wrongs of others. She cared, and that was what made her so endearing as a friend.

Coco sincerely hoped that after sleeping on it, James could accept that Katie would never intentionally hurt anyone, least of all someone she loved, without good reason. Perhaps tonight Katie would find him more receptive.

Once at the gym, Coco made her way to Angie Palmer. She'd hoped to talk to her at lunch, but Angie had been seated three chairs down and a discreet conversation would have been impossible.

"Hey, Angie, do you have a minute?" Coco asked, once the reunion organizer had parceled out tasks for everyone to prepare for that evening's dinner.

"Sure thing. What do you need? And by the way, thank you."

"I'm sorry?"

"For helping with the decorating."

"No problem," said Coco.

"I wanted to ask you about Hudson Hamilton."

Angie frowned. "Who?"

"Hudson Hamilton."

"I know he was in our class," Angie said, looking thoughtful. "Wasn't he?"

"Yes. If I remember right, he was the class valedictorian." *How could anyone forget that?*

"Oh right. Hudson—shaggy brown hair, sort of nerdy? I have so much on my mind, sorry. Now, what was it you were asking?"

"Is he coming to help decorate?"

Right away Angie shook her head. "Not Hudson. I would never ask Hudson."

"Why not?"

"Come on, Coco, you're not serious, are you? I can barely remember who he is."

She was serious, but it was best to let this pass. Coco had wanted to see him again as soon as possible. She hoped she'd get the chance at the dinner later that evening. "He's coming tonight, isn't he?"

"I think so."

"Can you check?"

Looking frustrated, Angie glanced around at the team of decorators. "Can I do it later? We've got a lot to do here, Coco. Why the sudden interest in Hudson, anyway?"

"I bumped into him last night. Literally."

"Has he changed? Did he evolve into a hunk or something?"

"No . . . yes. I didn't recognize him, but that was more me than it was him. He looks pretty much the same, though a lot better dressed, I'd say. We've all changed, right?"

"Not Donny Applegate," Lily Franklin called out.

A flurry of activity was going on around them. There were six-foot ladders positioned by the basket-ball nets and signs hung around the room. Posters were taped to the wall with highlight photos from their glory days at Cedar Cove High.

"Remind me who Donny Applegate is," Coco said to Angie.

"Donny was the lead in the play our senior year. He played Atticus Finch in *To Kill a Mockingbird.* Remember?"

Coco didn't.

At her blank look, Angie giggled. "I'm not the only one who doesn't remember everyone in the class."

"What about Donny?" Katie asked, joining Coco. "What makes him so special?"

"Nothing really," Angie admitted. "Well, other than the fact that he's still acting. Ashley Lambert claims she saw him in a television commercial."

"Was he?"

Angie shrugged. "Don't know. He didn't return the information sheet."

"So he isn't attending the reunion?"

"I guess not, but Ashley said she recognized him immediately, and she should know because she went to Homecoming with him when they were sophomores."

"But just think, Donny getting a role on national television."

"It wasn't national," Lily corrected. "It was local. For Flush King Plumbing."

Coco rolled her eyes. It apparently didn't take much to impress her classmates.

"Okay, Coco, are you ready to help now?"

"Ready, willing, and able. Just tell me what you need me to do."

Her assignment was to decorate the tables. Angie had rented tablecloths in their school colors of maroon and gold. With Katie's help, Coco covered each table with memorabilia from the year of their graduation: CD covers, old magazines, class photos and such.

When Lily noticed, she called out, "Hey, Coco, that's supercool."

Again with Katie's help, they arranged the centerpieces on each table. The decorations were cheap and tinselly, but when they finished, Coco had to admit the tables looked nice.

They'd completed everything by four o'clock, which allowed the group two hours to change clothes for that night's events.

Angie stopped Coco just as she was about to leave.

"You asked about Hudson."

"I did." She didn't bother to hide her enthusiasm.

"Did you see if he's paid for tonight?"

Angie set her laptop on the table and opened it. She balanced it on one arm while she did a quick search. "Let me see. Hudson Hamilton. Does anyone else find the name Hudson rather odd?" she mumbled, as she searched her records.

"It's probably a family name," Katie suggested.

"What a terrible name to give some kid," Lily said, coming to stand behind Angie.

"It distinguishes him," Coco argued, uncertain why she felt obliged to defend him. "Besides, I heard it's a name that's trendy."

"Hudson?"

"Actually," Katie said, entering the fray, "there's a famous Christian missionary who worked in China named Hudson Taylor."

"Really. How'd you know that?"

"I read about him."

"You always did like to read, didn't you?" Lily said, studying Katie.

Angie looked up. "He's here, but he didn't fill out the questionnaire, so there's nothing here that I can tell you."

"Oh," Coco said, doing her best to disguise her disappointment.

"Would you mind rechecking to be sure James Harper is signed up for the dinner?" Katie asked.

"Of course he is." Coco was convinced of it.

Again Angie looked down at the computer screen. "I just closed out of the program. Can't you two just wait until tonight and hook up with old friends?"

"I guess," Katie said wistfully.

"All right, all right," Angie muttered, reopening the program and focusing on the small screen. "Yes, James has paid up, too. Didn't I already tell you that?"

Katie didn't bother to answer.

They headed out of the gymnasium. Angie and Lily stayed behind to let in the catering group while Coco and Katie started toward the parking lot.

As they neared Coco's car, Katie slowed her steps. "I should have asked if he'd paid for one or for two," she said.

"Why didn't you?" Coco asked, and unlocked the car.

"I was afraid. If James is bringing a date or a girlfriend, I don't think I could bear it."

"Katie——"

"I know. I know. I've got to let go," she said, cutting Coco off. "After tonight I'll have my final answer and I'll accept whatever it is. I won't have any other choice."

Coco didn't feel she was in any position to lecture her friend about relationships. Because of her personality and being a people person she'd never had trouble meeting men. However, any time she began to get close to serious with someone she found an excuse to back out. It went without saying she had trust issues. She wanted to blame Ryan, but the truth was—and she'd recognized it long ago—the problem was hers. Several really wonderful men had drifted in and out of her life, and she'd let them go out of fear.

"I'm afraid," Coco said, choosing her words carefully, "that you've built up James in your mind. He was your hero, your first love, and over the years you've turned him into some knight or prince who can do no wrong. In your eyes he's perfect, and the reality is that like every one of us, James is flawed."

"Of course he is. We all are. All I'm asking for is another chance with him. Is that so hard?"

Coco opened her car door and shook her head. "You're putting way too much pressure on him and on yourself, Katie. You can't expect to make up for ten years in a single weekend."

What her friend said was true. Nonetheless, Coco realized Katie couldn't help but hope.

"Let matters evolve naturally," Coco continued. "Now that James has had a chance to see you and know that you want to talk, he needs time to absorb it, to open his mind and his heart to you. I believe he will, but if not, then it's his loss. And"—she hesitated—"something he will eventually regret."

Katie nodded and seemed to realize the wisdom of Coco's words.

They drove back to the inn in silence. Katie immediately headed to her room. "I'm going to shower and change for tonight."

"Yeah, me, too." Coco stepped across the hall but as soon as she was in her room, she changed her mind. She was more curious now than ever about Hudson.

Sitting on top of the bed with her legs crossed, she logged on to her laptop and Googled Hudson Hamilton's name. She found three Hudson Hamiltons.

Three. So much for all that talk about his *unusual* name.

One looked to be a mental case. Obviously that wasn't the Hudson Hamilton who'd graduated from Cedar Cove High. The second Hudson's bio caught her attention immediately. She scrolled down and found his photo, confirming it was him.

"Hudson," she repeated, her heart pounding. "Really?" Goodness, she wondered if any of her other classmates had a clue about him. He wasn't anything like what he'd been in high school. She remembered Hudson being utterly socially inept. Every time he'd talked to her it seemed his tongue had gotten tied up in knots and the words had stumbled out of his mouth making little sense.

Taking her laptop with her, she leaped off the bed and scooted across the hall and pounded on Katie's door.

"It's open," Katie called out from the other side.

Coco nearly fell into the room in her eagerness to share what she'd found. "You won't believe this," she said, bouncing onto Katie's bed.

Her friend stood wide-eyed with one towel wrapped around her head and the other around her torso. "Believe what?"

"Hudson."

Katie frowned and narrowed her gaze. "Will you please tell me why you're so stuck on Hudson?"

"I don't know; the fact is I've been trying to figure it out myself. Maybe it's because I discounted him when we were in school." And maybe because she'd felt this sudden connection with him. Whatever the reason, he'd captivated her. He was her alluring mystery man. Rather than invent an excuse, she whirled her computer screen around for Katie to see. "Hudson works at the University of Washington. He does cutting-edge medical research."

Katie remained emotionless and stuck out her hand as if to say, *And . . . ?* "That surprises you?"

"Yes . . . I mean, okay, so he's smart, really smart. We knew that in high school; I admire the fact that he's doing something with his life and making a difference."

"You're smart, too."

"Oh hardly, but I'm good at what I do, building apps." She didn't mean to discount her own abilities. She enjoyed her job, but Hudson's work was important, life-changing.

When he'd asked her to Homecoming all those years ago, she'd turned him down. Regretting that now, she hoped to rectify things tonight. She would turn the tables and ask him to dance.

Chapter 22

I stared at Bob for several uncomfortable moments before I started toward the house. "Come inside," I said, my heart rampaging inside of me. I yearned to hear what he'd come to tell me and at the same time dreaded finally hearing the truth about Mark.

Bob followed me and Rover trotted with him, then rushed ahead and led the way up the porch steps. My faithful companion waited for me to open the door as if he was just as eager to hear what Bob had to say as I was.

"Should I make tea?" I asked, knowing tea could be an excellent shock absorber. My mother had always brewed tea when she wanted to have a serious discussion or when she felt the need to comfort me. In the weeks following the news regarding Paul we drank enough tea together to warrant a stock investment in several name brands.

"Sure," Bob said. He made his way into the living room and sat close to the very edge of the sofa cushion while I went into the kitchen. Once again, his hat was in his hands and he slowly rotated it, his gaze focused on it as if looking to read an inscription on the inside of the brim.

My hands shook as I poured the boiling water into the ceramic pot over the tea leaves. I didn't trust myself to carry in a tray, fearing I might drop it in my nervousness.

"I'll leave it to steep," I said, as I joined Bob. I sat in the chair directly across from him and tucked my hands prayer-wise between my knees. Rover sat on the rug next to my feet, his chin resting on top of my right foot as if to secure me in place. I held my breath and waited.

Bob raised his head and held my look for the longest moment before he spoke. "Mark moved to Cedar Cove a few years before you—two, I think. He mainly kept to himself and took on odd jobs. Peggy and I didn't see much of him until you moved to town. We recently talked about the difference in him shortly after you arrived."

"What difference?" No one had mentioned any of this before now.

"Peggy deserves the credit; she's the one who noticed Mark coming out of his shell. For one, he showed up at the farmers' market on Saturday mornings and then Peggy and I started seeing him around town more often. He did his work, and collected his paycheck. You have to admit the man is a talented craftsman. But he didn't go out of his way to make friends—that is, until you arrived."

"What does my move to town have to do with any of these changes?" I wasn't sure I followed Bob's line of thinking.

"Peggy says Mark fell for you. I don't know that

much about these things; I leave that up to the wife to explain. Peggy thinks Mark was waiting for you to get over the loss of your husband before he declared himself. It makes sense, I suppose. Mark was smart not to rush you or make a move when you were vulnerable and grieving."

Thinking back over the last year, I could see what Peggy believed could be true. I had been blind to his feelings, but none of this mattered now. "I want to know why Mark left."

"I'm getting to that," Bob said. He set his hat aside and slowly rubbed his palms together, as if warming his hands. "Peggy told me a few weeks back that you were asking questions about Mark. How I met him and the like."

I nodded. "I know he has a deep, dark secret and I wanted to dig up what it was." I felt embarrassed to admit that now.

"When Peggy asked, I mentioned that I thought he might speak German."

"Yes," I said eagerly. "Peggy did say something about that."

"As it happens, Mark has an affinity for languages. I believe he speaks six or more. Fluently. German, Spanish, Italian, Chinese, and Arabic."

"Mark?" He'd never let on. Not even once. "Arabic?" I repeated. "Really?"

Bob glanced down at the rug and nodded. "Yes. Before he left, Mark told me his story. In order to understand him you need to know that his family has a strong military background. Both his father and grandfather were career military. His grandfather was a World War Two hero and his father got the

Silver Star in Vietnam. It was expected that Mark would enlist as well, and he did. He joined the army, the same as his father and grandfather, following his college graduation."

"His given name is Jeremy," I whispered. That much he'd voluntarily told me. "Mark was actually his father's name."

Bob straightened. "I thought he might have told you that. I still think of him as Mark."

"Me, too." It was what I'd always known him as, and Jeremy felt foreign to me.

"His father died just before Mark moved here."

It hurt that Mark had given Bob this information and had left me almost completely in the dark. All this had to be tied to the reasons he felt the need to leave, but it still pained me that he hadn't been the one to explain it himself.

"He had a sister who died when she was in her early twenties. Cancer, I believe. His mother took it hard and died shortly afterward and then a few years later his dad fell ill and died as well. His entire family was gone, and all within a short amount of time."

"So there's only Mark left?"

"Only Mark," Bob confirmed. "He was especially close to his father."

That much I knew. The one and only time Mark had mentioned his father to me, his words and his voice had revealed the depth of his love and pride for the man.

"Mark served three tours of duty in Iraq."

"As a translator?" Seeing that he was fluent in several languages, it made sense.

"I'm not completely sure of his role other than the

fact that he worked gathering intelligence. I don't know how much you know about how the military works."

"I only know what I learned when married to Paul." That had been such a short amount of time that I hadn't had the experience of many of the other spouses.

"I was in 'Nam myself and it was hell on earth. And you can bet it wasn't any Sunday School picnic in Iraq, either."

"I don't suspect it was," I said.

Bob started rotating his hat again and leaned forward. "Mark worked with a young Iraqi man who, at great personal risk to himself and his family, fed Mark information. The two became as close as brothers. When Ibrahim married, Mark attended the wedding, and when his wife gave birth, Ibrahim gave his son a name that loosely correlates to Jeremy."

I tensed, afraid of what Bob was about to tell me next.

"Ibrahim and his wife had a second child. A girl. Mark loved both children and celebrated their births with this man who'd become as close as family."

"And . . . ?" I could feel my throat tightening.

"Toward the end of his third tour Mark's unit was ordered to pull out of Iraq. He wasn't allowed to tell Ibrahim what was happening or why. The American military installation disappeared overnight."

I tensed. If Mark hadn't been able to tell his friends what was happening or why . . . "What about Ibrahim and his family?"

Bob looked away and didn't answer, as if carefully weighing his words. "Mark's orders were specific. He was to tell Ibrahim nothing. The less the other man knew about the orders, the better it was for him in case he was taken and interrogated later. He'd served his purpose and was no longer an asset. I know it sounds harsh, but the military felt the Iraqi army had been properly trained and it was time to go."

"You mean to say Mark was ordered to leave his friend and family behind?" Surely the army understood the possible consequences to Ibrahim and his wife and children if the country was overtaken . . . as currently seemed to be happening. Anyone known to have relationships with Americans would have been vulnerable.

"Yes, the military knew and so did Mark. The worst of it was that after all the help Ibrahim had given the Americans, and at great personal risk, he would now be left to the mercy of those threatening to take over the country."

A chill shot down my spine.

"You don't need me to go into the gory details of what's been done to the men and the families of those who collaborated with the American forces."

My hand flew to my mouth. Mark had told me he was a coward, crawling out of a black hole, and his abandonment of Ibrahim must be what he'd been referring to. But he'd had no option. No choice but to follow orders and leave behind this man he considered family.

"He left his friend, didn't he, and now his friend is dead."

"I'll get to all that in a minute."

"Okay." I was sitting close to the edge of my seat.

"Against every dictate of his conscience, Mark followed orders. He hated it; he argued and was nearly court-martialed for insubordination. Remember, his family has a long military history and Mark had to choose between putting a black mark on his family name or following orders."

"He followed orders." That went without saying, but I said it anyway. "And hated himself for it."

"As you can imagine, he became deeply depressed. When it came time to re-up, no one expected that he'd leave the military, especially since his father and grandfather had both made it their career. It was expected that Mark would do the same, and he probably would have, if not for what happened with Ibrahim."

"It was about the same time that he lost his family, too, wasn't it?" Everything Bob told me started to make sense. The depression, the self-recrimination, the sense that he'd failed everyone he'd ever loved.

"You were his salvation, Jo Marie. You, who came to town, grieving and lost yourself, and you were exactly what Mark needed. Falling in love with you gave him purpose. It took this long for him to accept what he had to do."

I wrapped my arms around my stomach, my grip tight, as if to hold myself together for what was about to come next. "You're about to tell me Mark decided to return to Iraq, aren't you?"

"That's what he did, Jo Marie. He got word from an old army buddy that Ibrahim and his family needed Mark's help. They were in dire straits. I tried to talk him out of it myself, without success."

"He went alone, too." It wasn't a question, because I already knew the answer.

Bob's face was bleak and colorless. "He went without government sanction, without any political clout or connections. He was basically on his own and alone."

"Ibrahim is alive?"

"Yes, according to the most recent word he'd gotten. Mark doesn't know for how much longer."

"Mark's going back for his friend and Ibrahim's family?"

Bob lowered his gaze again. He didn't need to say it for me to know how incredibly dangerous this would be.

There had to be a reason why he would decide to go right now. Some evidence that prompted him to act. "Did he somehow get further word of the situation there?"

"No. Mark has no new information regarding his friend."

"But he must have some idea of where Ibrahim or his family might be living and . . . and even if he's able to find them, how can Mark possibly help Ibrahim now? It's been years."

"Yes, nearly five years. You're bringing up the same questions, doubts, and objections I did. No one knows for sure if Ibrahim is alive or dead. Mark's not even sure where he is."

My heart was beating at an alarming pace. "But portions of Iraq are under control of radicals." I wasn't telling Bob anything he didn't already know. The news reports were filled with stories of the killings, and especially anyone connected to Americans. My head refused to think of what would happen to Mark if it were learned he had once been part of the

American military and he were captured. My breathing went shallow with fear.

"Jo Marie, Mark asked me to explain all this to you. He wanted you to understand the situation, so that if he didn't make it back . . ."

"He left knowing there was a good chance he'd die there." His reasoning was beyond understanding. Tears clouded my eyes, but I blinked furiously, refusing to let them fall. That explained what I'd heard when I'd inadvertently stumbled upon Mark giving Bob his woodworking equipment.

Bob continued to hold my gaze. "You should also know he's made you the beneficiary of his life insurance policy."

I gasped and shook my head several times. That Mark would think that I would want his money was beyond comprehension. I'd already been the beneficiary of Paul's policy. Surely Mark understood how painful it would be for me to collect his.

"He also asked that you be the executor of the funds from the sale of the house. He'd like for you to give that to the charities of your choice in his father's name."

The thickness in my throat made it nearly impossible for me to swallow or speak.

"I'm sorry, Jo Marie, I know hearing this is hard."

I was capable of speaking only one word. "But . . . ?"

Bob's own face clouded with grief. "I had the same questions. It's extremely risky, but nothing I said swayed his decision. He was returning to Iraq to help his friend if at all humanly possible."

"Why . . . ?" Again I choked out a lone word, which was all I was able to manage.

"Jo Marie, he did it for you."

"For me?" This made no sense. If he was doing anything for me, it would be to stay right here in Cedar Cove and love me. We were the best of friends. With time, we might have built something more. The potential was there and now Mark was throwing it all away, and for what? I didn't want a hero.

"Mark didn't consider himself worthy of you," Bob continued.

I cried out in disbelief.

"Mark felt that he was a coward who went against his conscience and followed orders he knew in his heart and head were wrong."

"He had no choice."

"He believes otherwise. He won't give up until he finds out what happened to Ibrahim and his family. And frankly, with the chaos going on in Iraq, I don't even know if that's possible. It would be best for you to put him out of your mind. He probably won't be coming back, Jo Marie. Accept that and go on with your life."

I stared at him in shocked disbelief.

"That was what Mark wanted me to tell you. What he was unable to tell you himself."

"That is his final message to me?"

"No," Bob insisted. "His final message is that he loves you and is grateful to you for giving him the courage to do what he knows to be right."

Chapter 23

❀

"I'm ready," Katie said a full half-hour before they were due to depart for the evening's reunion events. She was anxious, more than anxious. Tonight was it. It was her last chance with James.

"It's a bit early, isn't it?" Coco protested.

Katie knew her friend tended to be fashionably late, but she saw that Coco was dressed and ready as well. She looked great, but she always did. She wore a simple, sleeveless white shirt with a blue-and-white awning skirt and a kelly-green sweater.

"You look amazing," Katie said, a bit in awe of her friend's natural style.

"You do, too," Coco insisted.

"Do I?" Katie had taken great care with her own outfit. The only person she cared about impressing, however, was James. If he told her again this evening that there was no chance for the two of them, then she would accept his decision. With everything in her, she hoped that wouldn't be the case. Her one hope was that if he would just hear her out and understand why she'd done what she did, he'd be willing to give them another chance.

"I really do want to get there early," Katie said, pressing her small clutch against her stomach as she paced the hallway outside of Coco's room. "I want to be there when James comes in the door, that way he won't be able to ignore me."

"Gotcha. No problem," Coco said, and gave Katie's arm a reassuring squeeze. "Let's do this."

The fact that Coco agreed without an argument surprised Katie. "You don't mind? I mean, you don't normally like to get there early. If you want, you can just drop me off."

"I don't mind in the least," Coco said, and reached for her own clutch. "I have my own reasons." Her smile was wide.

Together the two women walked down the stairs. Jo Marie wasn't around, though they'd briefly talked about Jo Marie taking their photo on the way out and posting it on the inn's Facebook page. Actually, Katie was glad not to be waylaid. She was so anxious to speak to James right when he first showed up.

As she suspected, they were the first to arrive. The high school gymnasium looked as if they were stepping back ten years. Posters lined the walls with photos from their school years, along with movie and music memorabilia. Katie hoped these reminders would bring James's heart back to that special time and the love they'd once shared.

Coco left Katie to stand by the door. While she might have looked outwardly calm, her heart was in turmoil. It was a wonder her purse remained in one piece from the grip she held on it.

Several of their classmates arrived around six. Katie felt like she was one of the welcoming committee, steering her fellow graduates toward Angie and Lily, where they were to get their table assignments.

It was around six-ten when she first caught sight of James. Right away her pulse accelerated.

He must have spied her, too, because he hesitated briefly, his steps slowing as if he dreaded another confrontation. She offered him a tentative, shaky smile, which he didn't return.

Standing where she did, he couldn't very well avoid her. "I hoped we could talk for a few minutes," she said as he approached.

He glared at her. "Katie, we already had this conversation last night. As far as I'm concerned, there's nothing more to say."

"You're wrong," she challenged, grateful that her voice remained strong and even, especially when every other part of her body seemed to be shaking.

"I want nothing more to do with you, Katie. You're not important to me and haven't been in a very long while."

She chose to ignore his words, painful though they were. "I understand why you'd rather avoid me," she told him, doing her best not to let emotion bleed into her voice.

"Do you?"

"This is retaliation for the way I treated you."

He shook his head in a pitying way, as if he felt sorry for her. "What happened between us was a long time ago. It's over."

"It isn't, James, and won't be until you hear me out."

"I've heard all I care to hear," he said, his voice dropping below the freezing point. The chill was enough to make her blood run cold.

He stepped around her and she reached out and laid her hand on his arm. "All I ask is that you give me three minutes," she pleaded. "Three minutes," she pleaded.

Other couples passed as they entered. Katie realized that standing in the doorway to have this conversation probably wasn't the best idea.

James's look remained skeptical.

"Is three minutes too much to ask?" she said quietly. "If at the end of that time you don't like what I have to say, then we'll part ways with no hard feelings."

He exhaled and crossed his arms. "On one condition."

"Anything."

"I'll give you three minutes, and then you'll leave me alone the rest of the evening. I want to enjoy tonight without worrying about it being interrupted. I don't want to be mean or cruel. Katie, please, just accept that it's over between us."

Her eyes widened as she took in his words.

"Agreed?" he asked.

It took her a moment to agree and then she smiled. James might want her to think he was immune to her, but his request proved otherwise, bolstering her spirits.

"Agreed," she answered, when she realized he was waiting for her response.

He wasn't finished. "Then, after this evening, you promise never to get in touch with me again."

"Never?" She swallowed hard.

"Never," he said emphatically. "As I said earlier, I want nothing more to do with you. Stay completely and totally out of my life. Don't put me on your Christmas card list, and don't try to friend me on Facebook or any other social media."

"I already tried that. You wouldn't accept me as a friend."

"One would think you'd take the hint," he muttered under his breath.

Katie had learned a long time ago that the line between love and hate could be laser thin. That he would so adamantly want her out of his life told her that he was unwilling to admit how deeply he continued to care for her. This gave her hope, and she grabbed hold of it with both hands.

"Got it? Do you agree to my terms?" he asked impatiently.

"Okay. Got it." Despite how anxious she was about the conversation, his officiousness made her smile. Again, perhaps he was protesting a bit much? She could only hope. She moved away from the entrance and led him to the far end of the gym, where they stood beneath the basketball hoop.

When he joined her, he looked at his watch. It was as if he was literally starting his timer. She fully expected a buzzer to go off in three minutes. She took a breath and launched into her speech.

"It about killed me to break up with you, James, whether you believe me or not. You wanted me to come with you to California and I wanted that more than anything, but I had to know if you had your family's support. I talked to your mother, and she told me everyone was against it. Your grandparents were adamant this would be all wrong for you, and your parents as well. You never told me that. You let me assume none of that mattered, but it did. It was then that I knew if we got married or lived together the way you wanted it would have caused nothing but problems in your family. It would have been the two of us against your parents and your grandparents. They loved you and wanted the best for you and me, and at that time of your life a serious commitment to me wasn't it. I didn't have family and I refused to self-ishly destroy the relationship you had with yours."

"Two minutes and thirty-three seconds," he said, studying the face of his watch.

"You loved me then more than anyone had ever loved me. Even more than my parents or my family . . . well, other than my grandmother, but she was gone. I was alone."

"Are you looking for *my* sympathy?" he asked, giving off the impression he was bored with the conversation.

"Not your sympathy but your understanding."

"Katie, it's over. I don't know what more you want from me."

"But I've already told you," she pleaded, needing him to let go of the bitterness and see things from her side. The wall he'd built between them was thicker than concrete and just as difficult to crack. "It wasn't an easy time for me, either."

His face grew red. "I was away from home for the first time. I missed my family, but mostly I missed you. It drove me crazy that you could break things off as if what we'd shared meant nothing. You cut me completely off without a reasonable explanation. You wanted to date others?" His laugh was devoid of humor. "Overnight you went from hot to cold on me. I was frantic, wanting to know what was going on. You completely shut me out. I didn't know what I'd done wrong other than love you."

"I had to cut all ties between us," she said, lowering her gaze. "It was the only way I could do it."

"You could have talked to me, told me about this conversation with my mother, and suggested we hold off. Yes, I know my grandparents were against us, but eventually they would have come around. They were married when my grandmother was a teenager. She knew at a young age what it meant to find love. What you did was wrong on so many different levels, Katie, and now you expect me to let it go. You have no idea of the hell you put me through."

She closed her eyes. She'd been through hell, too, but she'd done it for him.

"You waited until I'd left for college and threw this emotional bomb at me and now I'm supposed to forget it ever happened," he continued, his voice tight with anger. "Sorry, but I can't do it."

She tried again, growing desperate. "It would have been too hard to maintain a long-distance relationship. Your mother warned about that . . . she said if we continued it would distract you . . . you'd be worried about me and your schooling would suffer."

"Do you think what you did was any easier on me? Do you have any idea of how cruel and heartless you were?" His voice gained intensity and garnered several glances from around the room. James must have noticed, because he lowered his voice. "Now you seem to think a few words of explanation and an apology are enough to turn everything around as if it didn't happen? This is a joke, right?"

"I'd hoped . . ."

"Then you're living in a fairy tale. I'm glad you did what you did."

"Glad?" She couldn't believe what she was hearing.

"You taught me a lot about myself. Thank God we never got married, because I'm fairly certain that we would have grown to hate each other."

Katie gasped, unable to hold back the shock.

"Your time is up."

From somewhere behind Katie a woman's voice reached out. "There you are, James."

The woman joined them and wrapped her arm around James's elbow and smiled up at him. "I thought you said you'd wait for me by the door," she said. "I should have known you'd get sidetracked. Class reunions are like that, aren't they?"

Katie stared at the petite auburn-haired woman who regarded James with her heart in her eyes.

"Is this one of your classmates?" she asked, when neither James nor Katie responded. She held out her hand to Katie. "I'm Emily Gaffney," she said.

Katie couldn't have said a word, even if her life hung in the balance.

"This is Katie Gilroy." James finally spoke up and made the introduction.

"Hello, Katie," Emily said, her smile warm and open.

"Emily is my fiancée," James explained.

Katie's gaze flew to James and then back to the other woman. Although shocked, she managed to recover enough to extend her hand. "I'm pleased to meet you."

"So you and James were friends in high school," Emily said, looking to James to confirm. She must have sensed the tension between the two of them, because her smile faded.

She was lovely, just the kind of woman James would want for his wife. No wonder he'd gone out of his way to tell Katie it was too late. He had indeed moved on with his life.

"Yes, yes," Katie managed, when she realized Emily was waiting for her answer. "James and I graduated together. He might have mentioned me," she said, wondering if he'd told Emily about their relationship.

"I believe it's time for us to mingle," James said pointedly. He wrapped his arm around Emily's waist.

Katie remained too stunned to answer.

"Nice chatting with you, Katie," he said, gracing her with a phony smile. "We'll catch up at our next reunion . . . say, in another ten years?"

The two left and Katie remained standing under the basketball hoop, frozen, hardly able to breathe normally.

How long she remained there she didn't know. What she remembered next was Coco joining her.

"Katie, what happened?" she asked, placing her arm around Katie's shoulders and steering her toward the closest vacant chair.

They both sat, facing each other so close their knees touched.

"Who's that woman with James?" Coco asked.

"His fiancée."

"James is engaged?" Coco sounded as shocked as Katie had been.

"I asked for just a few minutes to talk . . . I figured if he listened he might have a change of heart. In exchange he made me promise that I'd never make an effort to see or talk to him again."

"Oh Katie."

"For just a minute I thought, you know, that he still might care . . . that he'd never stopped loving me, but I was wrong."

"No one forgets their first love, Katie. In his own way James does love you, just not the same." Katie nodded. "He loves Emily. He can barely stand to look at me."

"I'm not convinced that's true."

Katie didn't want to argue. She had her answer. She'd hoped and prayed with all her heart for a second chance with James, but it wasn't meant to be.

"Did you get a good look at Emily?" Coco asked, breaking into her thoughts.

"Yes, of course. She stood right in front of me."

"And did you notice anything unusual about her?"

"She's very pretty." Katie didn't have a clue what Coco was getting at.

"Oh, Katie, please, take another look."

Katie searched them out and saw James and Emily about halfway across the room, talking to friends of James's. His back was to her and she was confident he stood that way on purpose.

"Do you see it?" Coco asked.

Katie gave her friend a blank look. "I don't know what it is I'm supposed to notice."

"Emily, the woman James is engaged to."

Just hearing the words was like a knife in her heart.

"Katie, she looks just like you! James is looking for someone just like you, because he's never been able to get over you."

Chapter 24

I sat on the edge of my bed and stared blindly into space. By all rights I should change clothes and get ready for my dinner date, but I found it nearly impossible to move. My mind continued to reel with the news Bob Beldon had delivered.

I heard Coco and Katie leave for their reunion. I'd mentioned wanting a photo for the inn's Facebook account but didn't have the wherewithal to take it. All I could think about was the fact that for the second time in my life I was about to lose the man I loved under very similar circumstances.

Mark had returned to Iraq and by his own estimation didn't feel confident he'd make it back to the States alive . . . and still he went, leaving me behind, even though he loved me. I thought about the intricate cradle he'd built and wondered if deep down he'd had a child of his own in mind. Our baby. I'd been shocked when he'd given it away. In retrospect, the timing was right—it was around then that he'd made his decision to return to Iraq.

My cell dinged with a text message from Gina.

Just off the ferry. 25 min eta.

For all the care—the hair, the nails, and the new outfit—that had gone into preparing for this dinner date, I now had to force myself to finish getting ready. I had no idea how I'd manage to get through this evening.

Gina's text got me moving. I changed clothes and filled my head with self-talk, promising that I'd shuffle through the emotions, doubts, fears, and hopes of Bob's news later.

Rich had sounded like a decent guy who was looking to make a good impression. He was the soon-to-be brother-in-law of one of my best friends. Besides, I knew Rhyder well. I should be able to do this.

The anger and sadness I'd experienced earlier regarding Mark had dissolved. All I felt now was . . . no, I didn't have the luxury of time to dwell on this now.

I slipped on my TOMS and was stunned by how strange it felt to be in a skirt. It reminded me of my days working in the bank. Although it'd been only a couple years since I'd left the corporate world, it felt as if it'd been a lifetime ago.

Rover barked, indicating my guests had arrived. Dragging in a deep breath, I knotted my fists, squared my shoulders, and started for the front door.

Gina was already halfway up the sidewalk with the two brothers behind her. She wore a huge smile and her eyes were bright with anticipation and joy. I'd never seen my good friend in love before, and I had to say it suited her.

"Welcome, welcome," I said, hoping my greeting sounded far more cheerful than I felt.

Gina hugged me and then turned to introduce Rich.

"My future brother-in-law, Rich," she said, swinging her arm out in a wide arc. "And of course you remember Rhyder."

"Hi, Rich," I said, hoping my smile looked genuine. Rover barked as if requesting an introduction. "This is Rover."

Rich stepped forward and extended his hand. "Jo Marie."

He has nice eyes, I mused. Kind and friendly, warm, and a dark shade of brown, like chocolate. Rich was about an inch shorter than his brother and beefier, with broad shoulders. I guessed he'd played football at one time just from the look of him.

Rich reached down and petted Rover, who eyed him a bit suspiciously.

"He's a friend," I whispered to my canine companion. Rover, however, continued to stay close by my side and didn't let his eyes wander away from Rich. My dinner date must have noticed Rover's scrutiny, because he kept a close watch on Rover as well.

Following the introductions, I led everyone into the house. I gave the three a quick tour and then led them into the living room. Earlier that afternoon I'd made up a plate of cheese and crackers.

Rhyder and Gina took the sofa, and Rich sat on one of the two wing-backed chairs while I set out the cheese plate. I brought it in on a tray along with the wine bottle and four glasses. When I entered the room, Rich stood and took the tray from me and then proceeded to open the bottle and pour the wine.

Rover continued to keep a close guard on Rich, following the man's every move and positioning himself between the two chairs as my protector. Heaven help Rich if he made one wrong move. I found it curious that Rover would be so on his guard with Rich.

Now that we each held a glass of merlot and a small cheese plate and napkin, I took my seat.

"The meeting with Rhyder's parents went well," Gina offered, starting the conversation.

"Frankly, Mom and Dad were so grateful to find a woman willing to marry Rhyder that they're doing cartwheels," Rich said, teasing his brother.

Rhyder frowned at his brother and then smiled. He raised his wineglass in a toast. "To love and marriage."

"Here, here," Gina added, and we all clinked the rims of our wineglasses together.

After a brief conversation and the wine and cheese, we left for the restaurant. Knowing that Gina enjoyed Thai, I suggested a local place I'd heard had great reviews online and from my guests. I'd been meaning to try it but hadn't.

Mark enjoyed Thai food. I'd discovered that quite by accident when I happened upon a recipe for Tom Yum soup in a magazine. Mark had stopped by right around dinnertime, something that had become a habit with him. When I told him what I planned to cook he'd gone on the Internet and found a recipe for a similar soup called Tom Kha, which was made with coconut milk. He claimed it was one of his favorites.

At the time, I'd been annoyed. I'd already decided on what I wanted to cook for dinner and he'd done his best to persuade me to try something else. Being generous in spirit, I'd agreed. Now I had to wonder if Mark had spent time in Thailand, either with his father as an army brat or later in his own military career.

We were seated right away and the waitress delivered menus. Rich sat in the chair next to me, glanced at the menu, and set it aside.

"Do you know what you're having?" I asked, looking for a recommendation. I knew Pad Thai was a popular dish, but I wanted to venture out a bit.

In the end I wasn't sure I'd remember the official name of the dish I ordered. Whatever it was, I found it incredibly delicious, probably because it was covered in peanut sauce. Unfortunately, I didn't have much of an appetite and struggled to swallow more than a few bites. The waitress looked concerned and I assured her it was an excellent recommendation and that I'd take the leftovers home and enjoy it later.

Thankfully, Gina and Rhyder carried the conversation, full of news about their wedding plans. Gina said she wanted me to serve as one of the bridesmaids. Rhyder wanted Rich as his best man. A good part of the evening was taken up discussing the pros and cons of a small, private wedding. Rhyder wanted to go on an exotic honeymoon. The question was whether to forgo the large wedding and honeymoon and purchase a house instead.

"The thing is," Gina said, raising her voice to be heard over the two men, "I only plan to marry once in my life, and I want a nice wedding."

"That's what I thought, too," Rich said sarcastically, bringing up his failed first marriage for the first time. "It was what I thought Melissa wanted, too, but I was wrong."

Gina looked toward me. "You had a small wedding when you married Paul, didn't you?" She didn't wait for an answer. "Do you regret not having the big wedding of your dreams?"

I didn't need to consider her question. "I regret nothing with Paul. Every minute we had together was precious, a gift I didn't fully appreciate until it was too late. With Mark it's different. I was blind to so much that I should have picked up on sooner. How could I have been so dense when it was all right there for me to see?" When I finished I realized all three of my dinner companions were staring at me like I'd recently stepped off a spaceship.

"Mark?" Gina repeated, looking at me strangely. "Who's Mark?"

Wow. What did I just do? I was clearly more rattled by Bob's news of Mark than I'd realized. "A . . . a friend."

Rich frowned in my direction. "He sounds like more than a friend to me." His gaze swiveled from me to Gina, as if looking for an explanation.

"Mark was a local handyman and carpenter," I said, hoping I wasn't digging myself into a deeper hole. "He built the gazebo and the sign for the inn and did a number of other projects for me."

"Was?" Rhyder asked. "Past tense?"

"He left," I said simply, thinking it was best not to go into the details.

"You mean he quit?" Gina asked.
"No, he left as in moved away . . ."
"Where did he go?"

I wasn't sure how to answer, or even if I should.

"To war," I whispered. "He went off to war."

"You mean he joined the military?" This came from Rhyder.

"No, he was in the military, or used to be. He went back . . . of his own accord, to help a friend." It didn't seem I was going to satisfy them with tidbits of information, so I blurted out the whole mess.

"You're in love with him, aren't you?" This came from Rich and was more a statement than a question.

I swallowed hard. "I'm afraid I might be. I know he loves me . . . but not enough to stay." Something Bob had said immediately flashed into my mind. I'd basically said the same words to Bob—that Mark didn't love me enough. Right away, Bob had argued and claimed Mark's love for me was stronger than I could ever imagine or could possibly accept, which was why he'd decided to return to Iraq.

"I just found out this afternoon," I whispered, and despite my best efforts, my voice cracked. "He wouldn't tell me why he was leaving or where he intended to go."

"That's rough," Rich said. "If I'd known, I would have suggested dinner another night. I wish you'd been more honest with me, especially given that you're falling for another guy."

"Give it a rest," Gina snapped.

I felt Rich deserved an answer, so I gave him one. "Like I said, I didn't know the reasons Mark had left until after you and I talked. The truth is I decided to go to dinner with you because I was angry but thought I had to move on. I hadn't talked to Bob yet . . ."

"Who's Bob?"

"Oh sorry, a friend. He came late this afternoon to fill in the details as to why Mark left. Until then I didn't know. All Mark would tell me was that he had to leave."

"Mark and now Bob?" Rich grumbled under his breath. He raised his arm in order to get the waitress's attention and then called out loud enough for the entire restaurant to hear, "Check please."

"Grow up, would you?" Gina said.

"Gina," Rhyder said, and gently placed his hand over hers. "I think it's time we left."

"I'm sorry," I said to Rich. "I really do owe you an apology. I shouldn't have come . . . please let me pay for the meal. It's the least I can do."

"No way," Gina protested. "We'll split it down the middle."

Rich crossed his arms and pouted while Rhyder and I split the check.

"You're kidding me, right?" Gina said pointedly at Rich. "You're seriously going to let Jo Marie pay for your meal?" she asked, looking outraged on my behalf.

"It's fine," I assured her, not wanting to make a fuss. "This was really awkward, and it's my fault."

It took several uncomfortable minutes before the waitress returned with our credit card slips. No one seemed eager to linger over tea or coffee and we left the Thai Palace almost right away. The ride back to the inn was uncomfortably silent.

"Thank you," I said, the instant Rhyder pulled to a stop in front of the inn.

"Listen, Jo Marie," said Rich. "I apologize for the way I behaved earlier. I was hoping . . . you know."

"No hard feelings," I assured Rich, as I opened the car door. I squeezed Gina's shoulder before I climbed out of the car. "I'll keep in touch," I promised.

"Please do," Gina said back.

"Good luck with Mark . . . or was it Bob?" Rich added.

I smiled ruefully and closed the car door, watching as Rhyder backed out of the driveway.

Rover stood inside the front door when I let myself into the inn. I knelt down on the hardwood floor and hugged his neck. I felt incredibly emotional.

My first attempt to get on with my life had failed miserably. Even if I hadn't had the other shoe drop with Mark leaving right before this date, I wasn't sure I was ready. I'd barely recovered from losing my husband, and now had been left reeling with Mark's determination to get himself killed.

I'd give just about anything to talk to Mark. I knew exactly what I'd say, too, exactly what I'd tell him. I'd tell him almost the same thing I had said to Paul just before he shipped out when we learned he'd been stationed in Afghanistan.

Live. Do whatever possible to stay alive. I'll be waiting. Praying, faithful. Just live.

My words, my prayers, hadn't made a difference when it came to Paul. I could only hope they would with Mark.

Chapter 25

Coco had waited all day for this night, eager to connect with Hudson again. Actually, she'd waited ten years for this night, plotting and planning her revenge against Ryan, only to have things turn around in a matter of minutes. In forgiving him it was like a huge retaining wall had been breached. In the matter of a single day she saw the world in a different light.

In the past twenty-four hours she'd done a lot of thinking about Ryan—and surprisingly, Hudson, too. For years she'd kept all her relationships with men at arm's distance, never dating one for long, never quite trusting men, fearful of giving her heart away. A sense of adventure now filled her, a desire to break out of this protective cocoon, spread her wings, and soar.

The first person she thought to test this new sense of self with was Hudson, who at one time had so obviously adored her. The truth was she hadn't been able to stop thinking about him and now she understood why. Every time he came to mind, a happy feeling stole over her. He was quiet, sincere, intelligent, and unlike any man she'd dated. Instinctively, she recognized this was a man she could trust, a man who, given the chance, would treasure her. And for the first time in her adult life she wasn't afraid to let down her guard and open her heart.

Hudson showed up at the dinner about thirty minutes after Coco, and she noticed that once again he attended solo. After greeting several others he walked around the perimeter of the room and took a seat in the back. Coco made her way to him, weaving around the obstacle course of tables and chairs. Although intent on reaching Hudson, she was stopped a number of times by classmates she hadn't chatted with earlier. It seemed to take forever to make her way to where she'd last seen Hudson, only to find that he was no longer at the table.

Anxiously, she searched the room. It didn't take her long to locate him. Hudson stood with a group of three guys who'd once been members of the science club. Coco remembered that this club was often referred to as the Geek Squad.

The two other men with Hudson formed a tight circle. He'd been the president of the group—that fact had slipped her mind completely. She hadn't known Hudson was even part of the club until she checked her yearbook last night. Actually, she learned a good deal about him from those pages.

Coco ordered a drink and then joined the group of three men. "Hi," she said, inserting herself into the circle. She looked at Hudson and sent him a warm smile. Right away the conversation among the men came to a screeching halt, as if she'd interrupted a confidential meeting.

"I'm Coco Crenshaw, remember?" she said in the uncomfortable silence that followed.

"I think we all remember who you are," Hudson said, when no one responded.

"Especially Hudson," one of the others commented.

They all looked at her rather coldly.

"You weren't a member of the science club, were you?" the guy with the badge that identified him as Willard asked.

Coco had no memory of him. "Not me," she said, making light of the question. "Did I interrupt something?" That would help explain the frosty reception she'd received.

"Yes, I'm afraid you did," Hudson said.

"Oh, okay, but when you can I'd like to talk to you, Hudson." She purposely said his name so he'd realize she did remember him. "Privately," she added. She wanted to make it clear that it would be between just the two of them.

The others stared at her blankly. She backed away and practiced a few of her power-schmoozing techniques while she made her way to the table where she'd first seen Hudson. Although she chatted with Katie and a few of the others, she kept an eye on Hudson. When he'd finished talking with his science club friends, he drifted away.

Coco followed. "Hey, Hudson?" she said, softly laying her hand on his arm.

He looked down at her fingers, which had curved around his forearm. When he glanced up his eyes were wary. "Is this a joke, Coco?"

"A joke?" she repeated, and then slowly shook her

head and smiled. "No, I really want to talk to you. It won't take long, I promise."

"Why?" The question was filled with hesitation. Coco didn't blame him. She was afraid that he might feel the same way about her that she'd once felt about Ryan.

"It took a bit of work to find out who you are," she said, starting out. "I wish you'd told me your name on Friday."

He held her gaze. "The truth is I didn't really expect you to remember me. No reason you should."

"We were in two classes together and you asked me to Homecoming."

"I wish you'd forgotten that," he muttered and frowned.

"I turned you down," she said regretfully, "and I wasn't very gracious about it. I'm sorry for that, Hudson, and want you to know I wish I had gone to the dance with you."

"Considering what happened that night—"

"This has nothing to do with Ryan. This is about you and me. I was rude, and I want you to know how sorry I am."

Surprise flickered in his eyes. "Don't worry about it," he said, brushing off her apology. "It was a long time ago. I got over it." He turned to leave, but she stopped him.

"Hudson," she implored, "I really am sorry."

He grinned as if to thank her. "We're both ten years older and hopefully wiser."

"Thank you," she whispered.

He nodded and started to leave again.

"There's a dance later this evening . . . following the dinner," she blurted out, detaining him again.

His frowning gaze held hers, but he said nothing, as though unsure what she meant.

"Would you consider dancing with me?"

He hesitated.

"Just one dance?" In her mind it would confirm that he had indeed forgiven her.

His eyes rounded. "The thing is, Coco, you did me a huge favor by turning me down. I was a terrible dancer then and I'm probably even worse now. I appreciate you asking, but it isn't a good idea."

"I don't care how coordinated you are on the dance floor, I'd still like to dance with you."

He blinked as though shocked she'd persisted. "I'd embarrass us both."

Mentally she thumped her fingers, looking for a way to reach him. "Your refusal tells me that you aren't willing to forget the past."

"It's nothing like that. I'm saving us both from humiliation."

"Au contraire."

His smile was genuine. "I'm glad to see you haven't forgotten what we learned in first-year French class."

We? "You weren't in French class with me, were you?" How could she have been so oblivious to him? She had absolutely no memory of Hudson from before their senior year.

The smile disappeared. "I was so hung up on you—you were the only reason I signed up for French."

She felt foolish. "You did? Oh Hudson, how could I have been so oblivious?"

"Like I said, it was a long time ago."

She wanted to talk with him more, but he excused himself and left. Coco remained, standing alone for several moments in an effort to absorb what had just happened. Hudson had accepted her apology and while he insisted he had no lingering resentment toward her, she suspected otherwise. His reaction said as much.

Coco had never been one to give up easily. Wondering how best to reach Hudson, she sought out his friend Willard. She caught sight of the other man in the buffet line.

Willard stood in the line that snaked across the polished gymnasium floor, chatting with those around him. By the time she joined him, he was close to collecting his plate and silverware.

"Hey, Willard—"

He bristled. "I go by Will now. I asked Angela to change my name tag, but she said they were already printed."

"Okay, Will," she said pointedly, beaming a bright smile at him. "You're one of Hudson's good friends, right?"

His eyes narrowed. "Yeah?"

"From what I understand, he had a crush on me in high school."

Will snickered a laugh. "He was crazy about you. It was nuts the way he felt about you."

"Really?" She couldn't hide the smile that came over her. "I didn't know—"

"You were into Ryan Temple and couldn't be bothered with Hudd." He frowned as he spoke. "It took him a solid week to get up the courage to ask you to Homecoming. He had it all memorized. Afterward he wouldn't talk about it, and heaven help anyone who had the guts to ask. And then after the dance when the rumors started about you and Ryan, Hudd was livid."

Coco felt her face heat up with shame and swallowed hard. "Yes, there was that."

"Hudd wanted to fight Ryan for you. He was that crazy about you, but Gilbert Reynolds and I told him fighting Ryan was like a death wish. Ryan had muscle, you know, and friends with even bigger biceps. It would have been no contest. Ryan would have taken Hudd down in seconds."

Will was close to the food now and far more interested in dishing up his plate than continuing this conversation with her. "You blew it," Will said, planting a large scoop of coleslaw onto his plate. "Hudd would have done anything for you." He hesitated for just a second and then added, "And I do mean anything, if you catch my drift."

Hub? The way Will said it made the hairs on the back of her neck stand straight up. She had to wonder what he meant by that slow, deliberate way in which he spoke.

Then it hit her.

It must have been Hudson who'd slashed Ryan's tires. That had been his method of defending her. Ryan had assumed Coco had been the guilty party.

Shocked, she whirled around and searched the room until she saw Hudson. He was standing next to a table, chatting with one of their older teachers— Mr. Bellerman, the chemistry teacher, who'd retired the year they'd graduated, if Coco remembered correctly. Without giving thought to what she intended to say, Coco hurried to the other side of the room.

When he saw her advancing toward him, Hudson stopped talking, his face full of curiosity. The determined way in which she moved in his direction caused him to square his shoulders as if bracing himself for an assault.

"Hello, Mr. Bellerman," Coco said, nodding toward the older man. "I hope you'll excuse Hudson and me for a few minutes."

"Of course, of course. You two young people need to get in line for dinner."

It was a good thing they were close to an exit out of the gymnasium, because it was clear Hudson didn't appreciate the way she'd interrupted his conversation.

"Now what?" he asked, leading her into the hallway outside the gymnasium.

For the longest moment all Coco seemed capable of doing was staring at him as tears filled her eyes.

"Coco?" he asked, frowning.

She covered her mouth, embarrassed that an incident from all those years ago had the power to reduce her to tears now. "Thank you," she whispered.

"Thank you? For what?"

"That's all I have to say." She would have returned to the party, but she'd be mortified if anyone saw the tears that swam in her eyes, ready to roll down her cheeks.

The cafeteria was across the hall and she walked over to one of the tables and sank down into one of the molded plastic chairs. Her party purse was in her lap and she frantically dug through it, searching for a tissue.

Hudson walked over and stood behind her.

She could feel his presence, his warmth so close, the almost imperceptible sound of his breathing.

After a long moment he asked, "You didn't answer my question. What's wrong? Why are you thanking me?"

Despite the emotion that clouded her head and her heart, Coco smiled. "You know why, Hudson. We both know why. It was you, wasn't it? You slashed Ryan's tires."

He didn't acknowledge her words either way, not that she expected he would. He placed his hand on her shoulder, his touch so light that for a moment she thought she might have imagined it.

"After you left the social on Friday, I offered to make it right with Ryan. I told him I'd reimburse him for what I did back then."

Twisting around, Coco looked up at Hudson. She was nearly blinded by her tears. "What did Ryan say?"

Hudson shrugged. "Not what I expected. He said he deserved what I'd done and that he wouldn't take anything."

Coco bit into her lower lip to control the trembling. "I hated him with a passion and hoped to use this reunion to pay him back for what he did to me. Before I could get out a single word, he apologized to me."

"And me," Hudson said.

"You?"

He shook his head as if he regretted saying that. "Never mind."

Coco was left to wonder what it was Ryan had

done to Hudson that required an apology. One day perhaps he'd tell her.

"Do you hate me?" she asked, her voice dropping to a whisper. He tried to show indifference, but she badly wanted to believe that was all a front.

"Hate you?" he repeated thoughtfully, and then shook his head. "No. I didn't think I felt anything toward you any longer, but now . . . now I'm not so sure."

His answer made her smile.

He shifted restlessly. "We better get back inside."

She agreed and sniffing once, stood, and followed Hudson back into the gymnasium. Almost everyone had filled their dinner plates and was seated at tables. The DJ had arrived and the dancing would be starting up soon. Coco had taken a glance at the song selections the reunion committee had chosen and knew it would be like stepping back into their high school days.

Right away, Coco looked for Katie and saw her friend sitting at the table with her head lowered. It didn't look like she'd been through the buffet line yet.

Hudson headed off toward his friends, but Coco whispered his name.

He glanced over his shoulder.

"I'm serious about that dance later," she reminded him.

His eyes narrowed. "Coco, please, it's not necessary. I don't dance."

"Just one dance. That's all I ask."

He looked as if he was about to decline yet again, but Coco said, "One dance, Hudd, please."

"I don't have the moves," he argued.

"No moves required."

He hesitated.

She held up one finger. "Just one?" She smiled.

Hudson's eyes grew softer. "You make it hard to say no . . ."

Her smile was wide and warm. "Thank you," she whispered.

Chapter 26

Katie and Coco were standing in line at the buffet table when Katie looked up and noticed that James and Emily were sitting at a nearby table with friends from high school. Their heads were together and they were laughing at some shared amusement. Looking at the two of them so wrapped up in each other produced a sharp physical pain, and Katie forced herself to look away.

Coco caught the direction of her gaze. "Remember what I said. James is looking for a replacement for you."

Katie didn't believe it. She was a realist, and while she wouldn't argue, she knew she was right. She'd finally seen more than enough evidence to prove otherwise.

"Don't tell me you don't see it?" Coco argued. "You're about the same height, same coloring. She even wears her hair the way you did in high school."

Coco might see it, but Katie didn't. Really, it would prove nothing, even if Coco was right. The woman James had chosen to marry was Emily.

In order to move on in her life she had to accept that James was lost to her. From this point there was no turning back.

They both helped themselves to salad, prime rib, and potato casserole, then made their way back to the table.

"I saw you talking to Hudson," Katie said, once they were seated. She was eager to turn the subject away from her and James. "How'd that go?"

"Surprisingly well," Coco said between bites of prime rib. "He's a lot different than what I remember."

"He is?" Katie thought he basically looked the same as he had in the photo Coco had showed her in the yearbook. No question he'd filled out some, and he was dressed less eccentrically. But then in his graduation photo he'd looked older than his years.

"I'm dancing with him later." Coco's eyes brightened with the prospect. "He hasn't exactly agreed, but I'll convince him."

"No doubt you will." Despite her own misery, Katie smiled. Coco had moved quickly from being a bit obsessed with Ryan to being a bit obsessed with Hudson. She was like that. She could be persuasive, that was for sure, and Katie felt confident she would get her dance. Her gaze drifted in James's direction, and to her surprise their eyes met and held for just a second before he determinedly looked away. Katie turned her attention to Emily Gaffney, his fiancée. She'd like to believe that James had chosen to marry the other woman because of their resemblance, but frankly Katie didn't see it. Okay, maybe the hair. Emily had curly red hair, too, but that was it.

Coco finished eating and was ready to hit the dance floor. Katie, who had only taken a few small bites, felt her stomach tighten.

The music had started up and already two or three couples had taken to the floor. James stood and reached for Emily's hand. Watching the two of them would be much too painful—Katie couldn't bear it. Not knowing where else to go, she told Coco she was headed toward the ladies' room.

Coco didn't stop her; Katie knew Coco could tell what she was feeling.

Outside the gymnasium, Katie wandered down the familiar hall. The school cafeteria was adjacent to the gym and she walked around the area until she found the very table where she'd once sat across from James as he tutored her in algebra.

She ran her hand along the top of one of the chairs and smiled. Memories floated by like they'd happened just yesterday: the first day that James had sat down on the chair next to her, instead of across the table. Their first kiss outside the swimming pool after that disastrous meet.

With her hand on the back of the chair, Katie closed her eyes and allowed the best days of their relationship to scroll through her mind.

He'd moved on and now it was time for her to do the same.

"It's you, isn't it?"

The disembodied voice came out of nowhere, and Katie opened her eyes and slowly turned around. James's fiancée stood only a few feet away. Katie's mouth went dry as she stared at the other woman. "I'm sorry?" she said, pretending she didn't understand.

"It's you, isn't it?" Emily repeated. "You're the woman James once loved."

Once loved.

Emily moved a couple of steps forward. "He told me about you, but he didn't mention your name."

"I'm Katie . . . we met earlier."

Emily crossed her arms as if experiencing a chill. "I know. I should have guessed when I saw the two of you in that intense conversation."

Katie wasn't sure what she should say, if anything. The best thing she could do, she decided, was to offer the other woman reassurances. "Don't worry. You have nothing to fear from me. What happened between James and me was a long time ago."

"You broke his heart," Emily said.

"Yes," she responded sadly.

Emily moved even closer. "I told James I was going to find the restroom."

"It's that way," Katie said, pointing in the right direction. "Just around the corner."

"It was a lie. I saw you leave and came to find you."

Katie frowned. "Why?"

Rubbing her palms together, Emily glanced down at the floor. "I saw the look the two of you exchanged a few minutes ago. The longing and pain in your eyes struck me here." She placed her balled fist over her heart. "You're still in love with him, aren't you?"

Emily was too smart; she had clearly seen through Katie. "Yes. I came to the reunion, hoping . . . but then I met you, and I could see that it was too late."

Emily didn't say anything for a long moment, as if

absorbing Katie's words. Slowly she walked over to the table where James and Katie had once studied together. "He didn't tell me a lot about the two of you, but I do remember that he said he'd tutored you in algebra. Was this where the two of you sat?"

Katie nodded. "It's the same table."

Emily held her look. "How can you tell?"

Katie ran her finger over the slight depression, a small divot on the edge. When James had first started to tutor her, she'd lowered her head and focused on that slight imperfection. At the time she'd felt overwhelmed. She'd been convinced she'd never understand those mathematical concepts. James could have given up on her, but he didn't. For weeks, he faithfully met with her until she started to get it.

"He was patient with me, and kind. After a while he got over being annoyed having to tutor me."

"And you were heartless." Emily's voice was hard and angry.

Katie's head snapped up at the emotion in the other woman. "Not heartless. I had my reasons."

Emily's short laugh was more scoffing.

Without fully understanding why or how she knew, Katie looked at Emily and said, "Someone you once loved hurt you badly, didn't he?"

It all made sense now.

The attraction between James and Emily had nothing to do with any physical similarities between the two women. What they shared was loss. They had each been forced to give up someone they had once loved.

Katie knew she'd hit the mark when Emily's eyes widened as she shook her head. And while she might want to deny it'd happened, she couldn't. "That was years ago and long forgotten."

"High school? College?"

"College." She didn't elaborate.

Katie could see that Emily struggled to hide the truth and was in no mood to divulge the story. The other woman's throat worked in an effort to swallow the pain.

"It's not so easy to forget, is it?" Katie asked, her voice dropping to a whisper.

"Like I said, it happened a long time ago."

"Time is relative."

Emily's shoulders stiffened, and when she spoke it was with conviction and determination. "I'm marrying James."

"Yes, of course. I . . . believe you'll make each other happy."

Surprise showed in Emily's face, and Katie understood that, too. "You have nothing to fear from me. James has made his decision."

The other woman held her look for a long moment, and then to Katie's surprise she pulled the chair away from the table and sat down and she motioned for Katie to join her. Once she had, Emily placed her hands in her lap and said, "I need to know why you hurt him."

"There's no need—"

"Please."

Katie swallowed hard and resisted. "It's in the past. It doesn't matter any longer." What a strange and unexpected conversation to be having with James's fiancée.

"It matters to me. I need to know."

And so Katie told her, doing her best to keep it short and explain what she could. Looking at Emily was difficult, so she focused once more on that small impression in the table, just as she had ten years earlier.

Emily listened and interrupted only once with a question. When Katie finished, the other woman remained silent.

"And you?" Katie asked.

"Me?"

"Who broke your heart?"

Emily shook her head. "It doesn't matter; like we keep reminding each other, it happened a long time ago."

"No fair," Katie protested. "I poured out my story to you; the least you can do is tell me yours."

Emily lowered her head and rubbed her hands back and forth. "Jayson's parents disapproved of me." She paused and then added, "I wasn't raised in the same faith as him and his mother in particular insisted that Jayson marry in the church. It was a difficult decision for him because I believe he genuinely loved me. In the end he did what was right."

"Right for whom?"

"For his family and for Jayson. He's married now to a woman who shares his religion. Last year he mailed me a birthday card and told me his wife was pregnant."

Talk about a knife to the heart. "That was a bit insensitive, don't you think?" Katie asked.

Emily shook her head. "The truth is I was glad for him. I knew that he felt terrible about what had happened between us, and the hard decision he made to break up with me. He hoped to hear that I was happy, too, in order to ease his conscience. I let him know that I'd fallen in love and was about to be married myself."

Katie smiled, though tears filled her eyes.

Emily frowned and leaning forward, she placed her hand on Katie's arm. "I'm sorry . . . what did I say?"

"No, no, it's fine . . . I'm the one who should be sorry." Embarrassed, Katie smeared the tears across her cheek. "You see, I understand. I so, so understand. You loved your Jayson enough to want him to find happiness. You realized that he never could be with you because there would be this constant pull between his faith, his family, and his love for you."

Emily bit into her lower lip. "Yes, I want him to be happy."

Katie gripped the other woman's hands in her own, squeezing her fingers. "Don't you see? That's why I can promise that you have nothing to worry about between James and me. I love him enough to want the same for him. Make him happy for me, Emily. Love him for me."

Tears shone in Emily's eyes and she wrapped her arms around Katie's shoulders and the two of them hugged.

Footsteps sounded behind them.

Neither Katie nor Emily broke off their embrace. Their hearts were linked with understanding and shared loss.

"What's going on here?"

Katie didn't need to turn around to know it was James who'd spoken.

Chapter 27

The minute the music began, Coco started to shake her hips. The Britney Spears song "Do Somethin'" brought her right back to when she was eighteen years old. Right away she looked for Hudson.

Before her courage failed her, Coco sought him out. She found him at a table with Willard (*Will*, she reminded herself) and two other former members of the science club, along with their dates.

As she approached, Hudson caught her look. Before he could hide it, appreciation and desire flashed in his eyes. His look did crazy things to her heart.

"I would really like to dance with you," she said.

He pushed his glasses up the bridge of his nose and sighed, as if refusing her demanded more of an effort than he could muster. "Just remember, I gave you fair warning."

"You did," she agreed, but it wasn't enough to dissuade her.

"Would you just dance with her?" Will said, elbowing his friend. "A few years back you'd have sold your soul for the opportunity."

Hudson sent him a harsh look.

Coco held out her hand. "Come on, Hudson, show me what you got."

His smile was almost boyish as he stood and gripped her fingers with his own. "Don't say I didn't warn you."

As soon as they reached the dance floor, the Britney Spears song ended and a slow one started.

"Now we're really in trouble," Hudson muttered as he turned her into his arms.

Coco fit nicely in his embrace and looked up at him and smiled. "This isn't so bad, now, is it?"

He grinned and rested his chin on the crown of her head. He did little more than hold her and shuffle his feet a little, and she was content with that. He rubbed her back, and she twisted her chin up just enough to kiss the underside of his jaw. Hudson faltered and although they were barely moving he nearly lost his balance.

"Sorry."

He cleared his throat. "My fault."

Coco tilted back her head and smiled up at him. "I'm enjoying myself, and while you might not want to admit it, you are, too."

He had his eyes closed and nodded. "I used to dream about dancing with you." No sooner were the words out of his mouth than he inadvertently stepped on her foot.

Involuntarily, Coco grimaced.

Hudson cursed under his breath. "It's probably best if we don't talk, okay?"

"Okay." They moved nice and slow, swaying gently to the music of the Black Eyed Peas. After a moment,

Coco closed her eyes, relishing the feel of his arms around her. Hudson held her close and she looped her arms around his neck, surprised by how comfortable she felt.

When she opened her eyes she noticed that Hudson's concentration was keen, his brow furrowed slightly as he watched his feet.

Coco pressed her head against his shoulder. Another song played, another slow one, and they barely moved. The music was soothing and romantic. Coco had her eyes closed when Hudson stepped on her foot.

She released an involuntary yelp. It was something of an accomplishment to trample on her foot when their feet were moving only inches at a time. She might have suspected he'd done it on purpose if not for the flash of irritation that showed on his face.

"That's it," Hudson said, dropping his arms. "I told you earlier that I'm no good at this."

"You don't like dancing with me?" she whispered, looking up at him. She hated the thought of breaking the contact.

"I like it just fine. Too much, if you must know, but I don't want you leaving town on crutches."

The *too much* part of his answer made her smile. "Is it warm in here or is it just me?" she asked, fanning her face with her hand.

Hudson stared down at her.

"Would you like to go outside and cool off for a bit?" she asked.

He didn't answer but continued to stare at her. "It is warm in here," he conceded, and reached for her hand, holding it firmly in his own as he led the way off the dance floor and out of the gymnasium.

On their way outside Coco grabbed her purse. Hudson led the way around the building to the football field and then into the stands. He sat down on the concrete bleachers about the third row up. Coco followed him into the row and sat next to him.

Leaning against his side, her head on his shoulder, she looked into the night sky. The evening was clear and the moon was full, casting a golden glow over the lush green football field. Coco couldn't have asked for a more romantic setting. The moon, the stars, and one of the biggest surprises of recent memory was sitting right next to her.

"This is perfect," she whispered.

Hudson remained stiff at her side as if he didn't trust what was happening. Perhaps she was getting ahead of herself—Coco didn't know. But for that moment, that evening, she wouldn't have changed a thing.

"You can put your arm around me if you want," she said, welcoming his touch.

"If you're cold you can put on your sweater."

"I'm not cold."

"Oh," he said, still sitting with his back rigid.

Hudson turned and studied her, his gaze narrowed with what could only be doubt. "You know, you and I are about as different as any two people can get."

"Haven't you ever heard that opposites attract? And might I remind you that you were attracted to me at one time? It just so happens that I find you strongly appealing and I was sort of hoping you felt the same."

Hudson seemed to give in and placed his arm around her. She nuzzled closer to him and laid her head on his shoulder again.

After what seemed like a long minute, he exhaled a deep sigh, the air rushing from his lungs. "Question."

"Okay," she said.

"Are you playing me?"

"Playing you?"

"This isn't a joke, right? You actually meant what you just said?"

She nodded, and then, as if to prove her point, she stood and scooted so that she stood directly in front of him.

Hudson looked up at her, his eyes wide and curious. "What are you doing?"

Smiling, she leaned down, planted her hands squarely on his shoulders, and then gently pressed her mouth over his. She heard the soft intake of his breath as he wrapped his arms around her waist. The kiss was long and deep. From the moment her mouth touched his, Hudson took control, bringing her down so that she sat on his lap. His mouth devoured hers, stealing her breath away.

By the time the kiss ended, Coco's head was swimming. It'd been a very long while since she'd been kissed like that. It took her a moment to compose herself.

"That was really nice," she whispered, hardly sounding like herself. He held her close, and she tucked her head against his neck. After a prolonged silence she said, "Hudson?"

"Yes?"

"Are you playing me?" Coco felt his smile.

In response he lifted his hand and turned her face toward his and kissed her again, as if he couldn't get enough of the taste of her. It was a good thing she was seated, otherwise she was convinced her knees would have given way. His kisses were potent and she felt them all the way from the top of her head to the soles of her feet and back again.

They were both breathing hard by the time he eased away.

"You might not be much of a dancer, Hudson Hamilton, but you have other talents." This man was full of surprises.

Again she felt his smile. He kissed her neck and shivers raced up and down her arms. Feeling as she did right that minute, Coco didn't ever want this night to end.

"I loved your spirit," Hudson whispered. "You were, then and now, always original. Do you work in fashion?"

"No."

"No?"

"I started out in fashion but after I graduated from college the only work I could get was part-time at the Seattle Fifth Avenue Theater in costume design. Part-time doesn't pay the bills."

"And now?"

"I'm a partner in a company that develops apps for cellular and tablet technology."

"Phone apps?" He didn't bother to hide his surprise.

"Quit asking me so many questions. Just kiss me again, okay?"

He readily complied until it felt as if her entire body was humming in tune with his.

"There's a question you aren't asking me."

"Why?" she asked.

Once more he went rigid. "I'm avoiding it."

"Guess I'm afraid of the answer."

Coco kissed the top of his head. "Ask me."

"Okay, fine. You're involved with someone, aren't you?"

She let him suffer, but only for a moment. "As a matter of fact, I'm not."

"But you were?"

The way he said it seemed to suggest that the thought she'd recently gone through a breakup and was on the rebound.

"I've dated some." She hesitated, looking to reassure him and find the best way to describe the last ten years. The truth was since high school she'd felt the need to protect herself and not be vulnerable. Instinctively, she felt she could trust Hudson. "After Ryan, dating became something of a trust issue with me."

She felt his body relax.

"So you're single?"

"Yep. What about you? Is there someone important in your life?"

"Several, actually."

"Several?"

"My brother and his wife have two daughters I'm especially crazy about."

Coco playfully slapped his shoulder. "That was mean," she said, and then promptly kissed him again. "Are there any other relationships I should know about?"

"No."

"That's good to hear."

Hudson Hamilton and her? Coco couldn't keep from smiling. Drawing in a deep breath to regain her equilibrium, she said, "Okay, you know about me and my apps job. Tell me about you." Her head was back where it was earlier, tucked against his neck as she snuggled into his embrace.

"What do you want to know? There really isn't that much to tell. The thing is, I live a pretty boring life."

"I want to know everything." His earlobe was right there and, unable to resist, she caught it between her teeth and gently sucked on it. His reaction was instantaneous and she felt the response move through his body.

"Coco!"

"Sorry." Only she wasn't. Teasing him was fun.

"Maybe it would be best if we went back inside."

"No." Her protest was immediate. "You were going to tell me what's been happening with you since graduation."

"Okay. I work for the University of Washington in their biotech laboratory. Right now my group is developing breakthrough technologies to complement protein design in nucleic acid and protein sequencing, with a secondary interest in high throughput activity screening." He continued to speak with animation for several minutes, clearly excited by the research in which he was involved. Most of what he said went completely over Coco's head, but clearly he was passionate about it.

After a few minutes, he hesitated. "I went on too long, didn't I?"

"No," she said, and meant it. "What you're doing is wonderful. It has the potential to save lives, right?"

"It's early stages yet, but yes, I hope so. I find my work exhilarating."

"I love how excited you are about your work." It might be a mistake to admit how much she liked being with him, but Coco couldn't help herself.

He went quiet.

"I mean it. I think you're wonderful." Coco leaned her head against his shoulder and glanced up at the stars twinkling in the clear night sky.

"It's just nostalgia—because of the reunion," he said, discounting her words.

"It's you," she countered. "And the fact that you were willing to risk life and limb defending me against Ryan . . . that you're a trustworthy friend and honest. You didn't have to admit to Ryan that you were the one who slashed his tires. Everything I've learned about you in the last twenty-four hours appeals to me."

They sat quietly for a long while, content just to be together.

"We should probably go back inside," Hudson suggested, after glancing at his watch.

If it was up to Coco they would have remained outside for the rest of the evening. But she knew Katie was miserable and wanted to get back to the inn, and her friend would need a shoulder to cry on. She felt for Katie and wanted to be there for her.

Hudson helped her up and then, holding her hand again, led her back toward the school.

"Will I see you tomorrow at the picnic?" Coco asked.

"Sorry, no. I'm heading back to Seattle in the morning."

"Oh." That was a disappointment. "I'll give you my contact information."

"No need," he said.

He must already have it. Of course, updated information on the entire class had been supplied by the reunion committee.

"I had a wonderful night, Hudson. Thank you."

"I did, too," he said, and looked at her with such intensity that it was hard not to kiss him again.

Once inside the gymnasium he reluctantly left her and returned to his friends. His gaze followed her as she sought out Katie and he smiled as if to say "Thank you for a lovely evening," but really she should be the one thanking him.

Chapter 28

It came as no surprise that I had a problem sleeping. I don't know when I'd had a more emotional day than Saturday had been. Naturally, my head was full of Mark and what I knew of his determination to save his friend. Every time I tried to sleep I felt his presence as strongly as if he were in the room with me.

I would always remember the look in his eyes as he said good-bye. He knew then what I didn't—how dangerous what he was about to do was going to be. Oh, how I'd misread him. I'd been so wrapped up in my own sense of loss that I'd missed the anguish Mark must have been experiencing. If only he'd been comfortable enough to share his past with me instead of leaving it to Bob Beldon.

In retrospect I understood why he hadn't explained his reasons, although I wished he'd had more faith in me. But knowing me as well as he did, he was probably right to hold back. I would have done anything within my power to persuade him not to leave Cedar Cove.

The evening had been complicated by the disastrous dinner date. It'd been a huge mistake to ever agree to go out with Gina's future brother-in-law. Rich was a piece of work. Then again, he probably felt the same way about me.

I knew neither Rich nor I would be seeing each other again. If I could have canceled our dinner at the last minute I would have. The devastating news I'd learned about Mark had badly shaken me.

I hadn't meant to bring up his name. Although in retrospect it was probably best that I had.

It was still dark when I gave up the effort to sleep. My two guests were scheduled to check out in the morning, and thankfully no one was set to arrive until Monday. I'd have a rare Sunday to myself. After Coco and Katie left I'd get their rooms cleaned and take an afternoon nap.

It was barely five-thirty when Katie came down the stairs, wearing her robe. She must have smelled the brewing coffee because she wandered into the kitchen.

"I didn't expect you to be up," she said, looking surprised to see me there.

"I'm not generally awake this early," I answered, on the tail end of a yawn.

Katie reached for a mug and stood in front of the coffeemaker while she waited for the brew to filter through.

"You couldn't sleep, either?" I asked, not wanting to pry but leaving the gate open in case she wanted to talk.

"Not a wink."

"I'm sorry."

She kept her back to me, standing in front of the coffeemaker. When she spoke, her voice was so low I had to strain to make out the words. "James is engaged. I met his fiancée."

The pain in her voice was evident in every syllable. "Oh Katie, how disappointed you must be."

"Her name is Emily . . ."

I stretched out my arm, wanting to reassure her, but hesitated, unsure she'd welcome the touch of a near stranger.

"The thing is, I really liked her. We talked, just the two of us, and she told me a little about herself. Then James found us."

She didn't elaborate and it looked as if she was swallowing hard in an effort not to show tears. After a brief pause, she continued: "He wouldn't look at me, but collected Emily and took her back into the gym. They were about to start the program . . . I didn't go back inside. Coco found me in the cafeteria and asked if I wanted to come back here and I did. I don't think I could have lasted another minute."

"So neither of you stayed late at the reunion?"

"No. I told Coco she should go back but she wouldn't hear of it. She . . . she didn't want to leave me." She paused and then added, "She's a good friend."

The coffee finished brewing and Katie filled the mug and carried it into the living room. I felt she wanted to talk and so I poured my own mug and followed her in. Rover, who'd already done his business outside, came along with me, as he almost always does.

We sat in the wing-backed chairs next to each other by the fireplace. Rover curled into a ball on the carpet between us.

"I didn't have a good evening myself," I told her. Since she was sharing confidences I felt comfortable doing the same.

"Oh?" She blew into the hot coffee before taking a tentative sip.

"I got some pretty intense news about my friend Mark—the guy I mentioned yesterday. I was intent on moving forward in my life, proving . . . I don't know what." In light of what I'd learned, I was furious with myself for my attitude.

"You're a widow, aren't you?" Katie asked.

I held my mug between my two hands, letting its warmth seep up my arms. "Yes."

"Do you find living alone hard?"

I wasn't alone. I had Rover and my guests, but I understood what she asked. "Some days, I do. I didn't get married until I was in my thirties, so I was accustomed to my own company. Love caught me by surprise, and when I fell, I fell hard."

Katie seemed to soak in every word. "I wonder if that will happen for me."

"Keep your heart open," I suggested.

"Was there a reason you hadn't married before . . . I mean, were you involved with someone else and it didn't work out? Sorry if I'm asking questions that are too personal."

"No, it's fine; I don't mind. The truth is I wasn't involved. I enjoyed my life in the business world, rising up the corporate ladder, independent and self-assured. And I guess I just hadn't met the right person." That seemed like another life now.

Katie stared down into her coffee. "I have to let go of him."

I had the feeling she said it more for her own benefit than mine. "Me, too," I whispered.

Katie looked up. "Your husband?" she asked.

I nodded rather than go into a long explanation about Mark. What I said was true, though. I'd learned that lesson when I lost Paul. Sooner or later I had to accept there was a strong likelihood that Mark was out of my life, too.

Footsteps echoed coming down the stairs. "Hey, are you two having a party without me?" Coco asked. Her smile was brighter than the rising sun. She radiated happiness. Apparently, unlike Katie and me, last night had gone well for her.

"Yeah, a party—a pity party!" Katie told her.

"Oh Katie. You didn't sleep, did you?"

"I didn't even try . . . I know, I know, I've got to get over James, and I will . . ."

"In time," I finished for her. "Time is the great healer." And I was in a position to know.

"I'm glad you had a good time at the reunion," Katie said to her friend. "I wish you'd just dropped me off and gone back. You should have."

"You needed a friend."

"I ruined your reunion."

"Nothing could have ruined last night," Coco said, and a happy, dreamy look came over her.

"Coffee?" I asked, ready to pour one for her, when Coco stopped me.

"Stay put, I'll get it." She momentarily disappeared and returned a couple moments later, a steaming mug in hand. Sitting on the ottoman in front of Katie, she wore a smile as wide as the Mississippi River.

"Coco reconnected with a guy from our class," Katie explained.

Coco glanced at Katie. "Who would have thought Hudson would turn into such a great guy?"

"He's not what I would consider your type," Katie said, seeming to enjoy seeing her friend this happy.

"That's so true, but I find him amazing,"

"She's like this, you know," Katie said, explaining her friend's behavior to me. "She doesn't do anything halfway."

The dreamy look was back as Coco released a slow, contented sigh. "He's simply wonderful, and if you must know, he's a really good kisser."

For the first time that morning, Katie smiled. "You went outside together, didn't you?"

"We sat on the bleachers and talked for the longest time."

"I think they did more than talk," Katie said out of the corner of her mouth.

I was impressed with Katie. Instead of being depressed and envious of her friend, she seemed to take pleasure in Coco's new relationship. In my view, that was a sign of true character.

"When will you see Hudson again?" Katie asked.

Some of the happiness drained from Coco's eyes. "Actually, we didn't set up a time. I hope he texts me sometime this morning, but it's still too early, I guess."

"How about some breakfast?" I said, thinking it was time to get the stuffed French toast casserole in the oven. I had fresh blueberries I wanted to cook into a compote to go along with it, plus cut the chives and grate the cheese for my special egg scramble.

"We're going to head back to Seattle after breakfast," Katie told me.

"What about the class picnic?" I'd seen the notice about Manchester State Park in a flyer Coco had regarding the reunion.

"Hudson told me last night that he has to get back to Seattle," Coco told me, and sounded regretful, "and really he's the only one I would want to see."

"And I . . . I'd rather head back into the city," Katie added.

I started toward the kitchen to get the breakfast cooking. Once I had the oven heated and set the casserole inside to bake, I headed to my room to change clothes. Rover trotted along behind me and paused in front of his food dish.

"Don't worry, you'll get your breakfast soon enough."

I grabbed a pair of jeans and a shirt and then made my bed. Everything I did was routine, but it wasn't an ordinary day and I knew it. I felt it.

Mark wouldn't be stopping by. He wouldn't be peeking inside my cookie jar to see if I had set aside his favorite cookies. Nor would he find an excuse to stop by for coffee that evening so we could sit out on the deck and watch the sun set.

He hadn't been "unexpectedly" stopping by for a few weeks now, but this was different. Way different. Mark was gone for real, and maybe for good. I had no idea if I'd ever hear what happened to him in Iraq, or if Bob's message was the last I'd ever know.

Breakfast was on the table at eight and both Katie and Coco came downstairs dressed. I noticed that Coco was busy looking at her cell phone. It dinged with the message sound and she grabbed it, read the text, looked confused, and then frowned.

"I thought we'd leave around ten," she said to Katie a few minutes later. "If that's good for you."

"Oh sure," she said. "Was that Hudson?" she asked, looking pointedly at Coco's phone.

Frowning, Coco shook her head.

"Text him," Katie suggested.

"No," Coco returned with a determined shake of her head. "I came on pretty strong at the dance last night. I made it clear that I'm interested, but the next move has to come from him."

"He was crazy about you."

"Was," Coco reiterated. "I need to know how he feels now. He has my contact information. If he wants to get ahold of me he knows how. It's up to him now."

Katie shrugged. "I don't think you have anything to worry about. He couldn't take his eyes off you all evening. You've got him wrapped around your little finger."

Coco didn't look nearly as convinced. "That remains to be seen."

The two sat down for breakfast and I noticed that Coco grabbed her phone after every *ding*. Katie's eyes flashed to those of her friend and Coco would shake her head indicating it wasn't the text or email she'd been hoping for. I didn't know anything about this guy they'd been discussing, but I had to believe he would be in touch soon enough.

"Let's head out," Coco said, once they'd finished with breakfast. "I'm more than ready to leave."

"I'm ready, too," Katie said.

It took only a few minutes for them to load their

suitcases into the car. They'd already settled the bill with me. Rover and I stood on the porch and watched the two of them back out of the driveway.

I stood there as they drove away, trying to absorb how, in the space of just a few days, my world had changed so completely.

Mark was gone, and I was devastated.

And the inn had failed me. Paul had told me in a dream after I'd purchased the inn that it would be a place of healing for me and all who came to stay.

But Katie had left with a broken heart, and Coco looked let down.

The inn had disappointed us all.

Chapter 29

❀

Friday night, two weeks after the reunion, Katie let herself into her small apartment and kicked off her shoes. She worked with adoptions and had been in court earlier that afternoon when two little girls, ages three and four, half-siblings, had been adopted into a loving family. It was cases like this that gave her a huge sense of accomplishment and joy.

By habit she turned on the evening news and checked the freezer for a frozen entrée. She was still making her choice when her phone rang. Caller ID told her it was Coco. Her friend never had heard from Hudson and it had bitterly disappointed her.

Holding the phone against her ear, Katie sorted through the selection of frozen meals, preferring something simple and easy after a hectic day in court.

"Hey, Coco, whatcha doing?" she asked.

"Not much, what about you?" They'd texted a number of times after leaving Cedar Cove and the reunion but hadn't spoken.

"Do you have any plans for tonight?" Coco asked.

"Not really. You?" The Lean Cuisine pasta looked

to be Katie's best dinner option. She removed it from the freezer and set it on the kitchen countertop.

"Want to go out for a while?" Coco asked. "A friend of mine is having a party. He wants to set me up with someone, and frankly, I'm not in the mood."

"What makes you think I am?" she asked, reading the directions on the back of the package.

"I figured you're probably in the same place as me. Getting out will do you good and this guy doesn't sound like my type."

Katie smiled. "So in other words, you want to use me as a buffer?"

"You might find Christian interesting, who knows. Come on, we could both use an emotional boost."

Katie tossed the frozen entrée back into the freezer. "All right, I guess I'll go with you."

Coco snorted. "We're pathetic, you know that, right?"

Katie laughed. She was half tempted to ask if there'd been any contact from Hudson, but she knew Coco would have said so if there had.

"I'll pick you up in thirty," Coco said.

"I'll be ready." Katie didn't have a better way to spend Friday night, and a party might be fun. She wasn't in a party mood but she needed to break out of this self-imposed shell and step out of the past.

By the time they arrived at the party it was in full swing. Everyone knew Coco and there were cheers when she arrived. It didn't take long before Katie was handed a beer. She took a tentative sip and stood back as Coco threw herself into the melee with full abandon. No more than ten minutes after they arrived, Coco was in the middle of the living room, arms above her head dancing and flirting. Coco was the life of the party. It was as if everyone had been waiting for her arrival.

Although she knew only a couple of people, Katie enjoyed herself. Sitting on the sofa arm, she watched the others dancing and laughing while sipping her beer.

"Hi there, I'm Christian."

"Katie." They clicked their beer bottles together.

"Coco said I should come over and introduce myself."

It was hard to hear him above the music and the noise. "So you're the one."

"The one?" he asked, frowning.

"Never mind," she said, studying him. He was actually quite attractive, with thick dark hair and a ready smile.

He glanced toward the others. "Would you like to dance?"

"Sure, why not?" The beer lent her courage.

The first dance led to another and then another, and by the end of the evening she'd exchanged phone numbers with Christian. With the loud music, conversation had been difficult, and she didn't know much about him other than the fact that he worked for Boeing and was a sheet-metal worker, the same as his father and uncle.

Coco, who had limited herself to two beers during the course of the evening, drove Katie home.

"Did you have a good time?" she asked.

"I did. Christian seems nice."

"I thought you'd like him."

It came to her then, what Katie should have suspected all along. "This was a setup, wasn't it? He was never anyone *you* were supposed to meet. You arranged for me to connect with Christian."

"Sort of," Coco admitted.

"Right," Katie said with more than a hint of sarcasm.

"One day you'll thank me. Christian's a great guy and I thought it was time for us both to have some fun."

Her friend was right. "I had a great time; thanks for inviting me."

"I had a good time, too," Coco said, and sounded surprised.

"You didn't think you would?" Katie asked.

"I didn't . . . well, sort of. I just wish I could stop thinking about Hudson."

Seeing that Coco had opened the door, Katie took advantage of it. "No word?"

"None." The word was stark and lonely.

"He's an idiot."

Coco shrugged. "His choice, I guess."

"You could always call or text him," Katie suggested. She could understand why Coco hadn't.

"No. I got the message. He's not interested."

Katie understood all too well.

To her surprise, Katie slept better that Friday night than she had any other night since her return from the reunion. She woke and checked her phone for messages and saw that she had one from Christian.

Meet for coffee? Starbucks on 45th. 10?

Sure. See you then.

By the time Katie arrived Christian had secured a table. He stood and hugged her when she approached.

"You're even prettier in the daylight," he said. "I ordered you a pumpkin spice latte. I should have asked what you wanted—is that okay?"

"That's perfect."

They chatted for nearly an hour and Katie felt herself beginning to relax. Christian was nice and they seemed to get on well enough. But the spark just wasn't there. Katie wasn't sure if he realized it or not, but she definitely did.

On the drive back to her apartment, she couldn't help wondering if she'd ever feel that connection to another man the way she had with James. As hard as she tried to let go of him, she was beginning to think that she might never be able to move on. In letting go she would have to relinquish the way he'd made her feel, the love he'd given her. She didn't know if it was possible to find someone who loved her as much as James had.

Had. Past tense. He was marrying Emily and she had to accept it.

One day, she promised herself, she would fall in love with someone equally wonderful.

Once back at her apartment, Katie started in on her cleaning that she did on Saturday mornings. She dragged out the vacuum and went at it with a vengeance. It'd been a while since she'd done the bedroom carpet. As she ran it around her bedroom set, she hit a solid object stored under her bed, causing another box to scoot out the other side.

Turning off the machine, she went to kick the box back to its hiding place when she realized what it was.

The letters.

The box contained James's letters to her, the ones he'd sent when he'd gone off to college. Katie stared at the box. It'd been months since she'd last read through them.

She'd kept every one and had read them countless times. Some of them she could almost recite from memory. There were several where he pleaded to hear from her that were stained with her tears. The angry ones had crumpled edges as his pain vibrated off the page. The last ones had read like journal entries, full of details of his life. He wrote about his classes, the teachers, and the friends he'd made, as if trying to stay connected even though she wasn't responding.

At the end of each letter he'd explained that he would never stop loving her, even if she didn't care about him any longer. She couldn't help but wonder how long he would have continued if she hadn't returned the last letter and asked him not to write again. It had about killed her, but she knew she had to be the one to end it. Just as he felt now that he had to be the one to move forward by marrying Emily.

It came to her that she would never be completely free of James as long as she held on to the letters. She had to destroy them before they destroyed her. The one place she felt she could do this was Manchester State Park, where they had so often met.

Her fear was that she wouldn't be able to make herself do it. She didn't know if she had the courage to burn them without someone there to hold her hand. The one person she knew who would understand was Coco.

She texted her high school friend.

Do you have plans for today?

What's up?

I need some hand-holding in Cedar Cove.

Cedar Cove?????

You coming with me or not?

If you need me, I'm there.

Thank you.

As soon as Katie picked up her friend, she explained the mission.

"You're sure about this?" Coco asked.

"No." Katie knew she could be honest with Coco. "It's going to kill me to burn these letters, but I know I'll never be able to let go of James unless I do."

"Why Manchester State Park?" Coco asked as they waited in line for the ferry. "Couldn't we do this someplace closer? I don't have a lot of good memories of our last visit to town."

"I know . . . I don't, either. I guess it's because it will be full circle for me."

Coco seemed to understand. They didn't talk much on the ferry ride over and the drive around the cove. The autumn drizzle had started. They paid the entrance fee into the park and found a campsite with a picnic table and a fire pit.

They soon discovered that neither one of them had thought to bring something with which to start a fire.

If it wasn't so tragic it might have been amusing. A camper took pity on them and they soon had a few sticks of kindling lit and the fire going.

"You ready?" Coco asked her, opening the box.

Katie swallowed hard and nodded. She reached inside the box and took out one of the last newsy letters James had written and after a brief hesitation threw it into the flames. For just an instant she regretted burning it and resisted the urge to grab it out of the fire. The paper was quickly consumed by the flames. The smoke rose and with it went one of the relics of her first love.

Katie's throat clogged. She'd understood burning the letters would be hard, but not this hard.

"You okay?" Coco asked, studying her and looking concerned. "You're pale and you're shaking."

"Am I?" she asked, her voice weak and trembling. She couldn't stop now.

Coco hesitated. "You sure you want me to do this?"

"Yes, please." It would help because there were three, perhaps four that she didn't know if she could burn on her own. She'd need Coco to do it for her.

Coco reached inside the box.

"Not that one," Katie cried, her voice in a panic. "Not yet . . ."

Coco dropped the letter back into the box. "You decide which one," she said.

Several minutes passed before Katie was able to choose the next letter. Coco unceremoniously tossed it into the flames and Katie swallowed down a cry. Her entire body started to shake and she felt the need to sit down. It was a good thing the picnic table was close at hand.

Coco kept a close watch on her. "I don't think you're ready for this, Katie."

She disagreed. "I have to get it done."

"I know, but do you need to do it all at once?"

Katie was too traumatized to answer.

Coco sat down on the picnic bench next to her and suggested, "Why don't you take out the ones you feel you can let go of and take the rest home until you're more comfortable with doing this?"

"I'll never be comfortable—"

"You know what I mean," Coco said, interrupting her. "This is killing you. You're shaking like a leaf."

"Okay, we'll only burn half today." She could manage half, she thought.

Only Katie was wrong. By the end of the afternoon they'd managed to destroy only a dozen. Each one had felt as if it cut away a section of her heart.

They loaded the box into the car and headed back to Seattle. Next week she'd destroy the rest. Katie was determined.

Chapter 30

It'd been nearly a month since Mark had left Cedar Cove. I'd more or less adjusted to life without him, although the days felt empty. Mark was constantly in my thoughts and prayers. I couldn't help wondering if he'd been able to get into Iraq, and if he had, whether he was safe. My prayers centered on him, praying for his safety and for God to send him back to me. Praying gave me little comfort. I'd prayed daily for Paul, too, and despite all my petitions to God I'd lost my husband. The one positive aspect of prayer was that it gave me an outlet for my worries.

I resisted the urge to contact Bob Beldon for news of Mark, certain that if he heard anything he would be in touch with me. On a positive note I'd started my spin class and loved being more physically active. The funny part was that by the time I finished my hour workout I felt incredibly weak and found it almost impossible to walk. Despite my daily exercise taking Rover out, I was sadly out of shape.

Another benefit of the class was that I made friends with Dana Parson, who was around my age, married, and had a couple of kids. Her husband worked at home, which enabled her to take the spin class while her son and daughter napped in the early afternoons.

I continued to get plenty of bookings for the inn. If I kept at this pace I might actually show a profit by the end of the year. Monday I had a rare free morning to myself. My guests from Sunday had left and my next guests weren't due to arrive until later that evening. It was a couple from Kansas City who'd come to visit their son who was stationed at the navy base in Bremerton.

Rover was eager for his walk and waited impatiently for me to finish my morning tasks. "All right, all right, I'm coming," I assured him, shaking my head. I'd spoiled this dog and had no one to blame but myself.

As soon as I got his leash, Rover did a happy dance and hurried to the door, looking over his shoulder as if to say it was about time. I attached the lead and started outside, surprised by how chilly the weather had turned. It was October now and the wind was whipping up the leaves. I'd no sooner raked up the multicolored foliage when a new batch would obliterate my yard again. It was a never-ending chore.

I started chugging up the hill, following the same two-mile path I took every day with Rover. The sky was overcast and the wind swirled up the leaves as I wrapped my raincoat more securely about me. Although it was relatively early in the month, there was evidence of Halloween all around. Several neighborhood yards were decorated with jack-o'-lanterns displayed on porch steps and a few angel-hair spiderwebs spread over low-lying bushes. One house had a scarecrow in the front yard with bundles of hay at the base and a few cornstalks.

Rover and I approached the street where Mark had lived. Ever since he'd left I'd avoided walking past his house. The FOR SALE sign out front upset me and I thought it best to keep away from the reminder that he was gone. Not that I needed anything to prompt my memory. I felt his absence each and every day.

For whatever reason Rover decided to turn down Mark's street that morning, determinedly tugging me in that direction. "That's not part of our walk," I reminded him.

Rover wouldn't hear of it. He glanced over his shoulder as if insisting this was the way we should go.

"Oh, all right, if you must, but Mark isn't there. You know that, right?" I might not need a reminder, but it seemed Rover did.

Rover's short legs gathered speed and he urged me along. By the time we approached the house I was struggling to hold him back. When we got to the driveway that led to Mark's shop, Rover let out a sharp bark as if he expected Mark to come out and greet us.

"He's not here any longer," I reminded him a second time, as Rover strained against the leash.

Then I noticed it.

The FOR SALE sign in front of the house had a large band slanted across the front that said SOLD.

I stopped and studied the sign as if it could fill in the details. For whatever nonsensical reason I'd held out hope that the house would remain on the market until Mark returned . . . if he ever did.

Seeing that SOLD sign had a curious effect on me. I

placed my hand over my heart as if to protect it from the sense of loss. This was one more indication that I needed to let go of Mark. I was surprised Bob hadn't told me. Right away I wondered if there were other things he hadn't told me about Mark and this mission he'd undertaken.

By the time I returned to the inn I was frazzled and upset. Rover was as well, because I hadn't taken him on the full two-mile trek the way I normally did, cutting short our time.

The first thing I did once we were back was put water on to boil for tea.

This was one of those times when I needed my mother. I hated to admit how fragile I felt, when the sale of the house was something I should have expected. Mark's house had been on the market for a little over a month; I just hadn't anticipated it would sell this quickly.

Once the tea was ready I sat down at my small kitchen table, reached for my cell, and punched the number that would connect me with my family.

Mom answered on the third ring. It took her that long to get to her landline in the kitchen, depending, of course, where she was in the house. Although my mother had a cell phone, she rarely kept it with her, and my dad never seemed to have his phone charged.

"Jo Marie!" she said. "It's good to hear from you."

"Hi, Mom."

My greeting was followed by a short hesitation. "You heard something, didn't you?" Right away she sensed something wasn't right. "I can hear it in your voice."

I'd said all of two words; I'd tried to hide my distress, but apparently not well enough.

"I need a little pick-me-up talk with my mother," I told her. I leaned forward, set my elbow against the tabletop, and pressed my hand against my forehead as I struggled within myself.

"What's up?" she pressed. "Did you hear from Mark?"

"No, nothing like that." There was no need to hide what had upset me so badly. "I took Rover out for his walk this morning and he insisted we turn down the street where Mark's house is."

Mom hesitated for just a brief second. "It sold, didn't it?"

Sometimes it was like she could read my mind. "Yes. I know, it's irrational. This is what real-estate people do: they sell houses. And he listed it with a company that has a reputation for selling quickly."

"And you're upset."

"I know. It's ridiculous. It was inevitable . . . it was bound to happen sooner or later."

Mom's voice softened. "We feel what we feel. Don't discount your heart. It isn't about what's right or wrong, Jo Marie. You're experiencing a loss; it makes sense that you'd be upset. The sale is one more connection to Mark that's been severed, so naturally it's going to affect you. It would anyone, so stop beating yourself up."

My mother was right. I shouldn't berate myself. I swallowed against the thickness that clogged my throat. "I'm so afraid I'll never see him again." There, I'd said it out loud. I was afraid and the fear was strikingly familiar to what I felt when Paul left for Afghanistan.

"Jo Marie, are you crying?"

"I'm trying not to." But it was hard, especially when my throat was tight and tears stung my eyes. "I'll be fine . . ."

"Of course you will," she said soothingly. "No word from him? Nothing?" she asked again, lowering her voice, as if afraid if she said the words too loud that it would upset me even more.

"Not a thing. But I'm doing well." Or I thought I was until this morning. "I've made a couple of new friends."

Again the briefest of pauses before she asked, "Male or female?"

"Mom!"

"Sorry. I've heard you mention Dana, but I didn't know if that was a man or a woman."

"Woman. We're in spin class together." Dana and I often stopped off at Starbucks after the class and ordered a skinny latte. We both felt the need to unwind before returning home. I could laugh with Dana and I needed a friend who would lift my spirits.

Mark could be a real pest at times but what stood out in my mind was all the times we'd argued and laughed together, often in the evenings when we sat on the deck and talked. I missed those times.

I missed Mark. Oh how I missed him.

Mom and I chatted for several more minutes about this or that. Nothing important, just girl talk. I was grateful to have a mother who understood me so well. She was able to pull me out of the mire of self-pity better than anyone, and I knew I could be honest with her about my feelings.

No sooner had I hung up the phone when my doorbell chimed. I checked my watch and realized it was too early for my guests to arrive. Rover was already at the front door when I got there, his tail wagging. Whoever had decided to make a call was clearly a friend, otherwise Rover would be on his guard. How the dog could tell before seeing who was at the door was beyond me.

I wasn't surprised to find Bob Beldon standing on my porch. His eyes met mine and his look was dark and serious. I opened the door farther in silent invitation for him to come inside.

"I know why you're here," I said, leading him into the living room.

Bob followed me and took a seat on the sofa. He wore a jacket and his hair was damp with small droplets of rain. I was grateful I'd taken Rover out earlier.

He held my gaze. "So you know. I wondered if you'd been by the house yet or not."

"When did it sell?" I didn't mention that it'd been nearly a month since I'd last walked past Mark's house.

"I believe the offer came in over the weekend."

"I expected it to take longer." The real-estate market had been slow the last few years, and in the back of my mind I'd hoped several more months would pass before an offer came in. Not that it mattered. One month or three or longer, eventually someone else would be living where Mark once had.

"It was a good offer," Bob explained.

"If the offer only came in over the weekend, then

why did the sold sign go up so quickly?" That usually took a while—it had when I purchased my Seattle condo and then later the inn.

"It was a cash sale. The closing will happen sometime this week and then I'll be bringing you the check."

Although Bob had told me Mark wanted me to donate the funds from the house, I had yet to decide what to do with it. In an effort not to think about it, I asked him another question. "Do you know anything about . . . the new owners?"

Bob shook his head. He sat close to the edge of the sofa cushion and braced his elbows on his knees. "I stopped by for more than just to update you about the house."

"Oh?" A chill came over me, although the inn was warm and cozy.

Bob looked down at the carpet. "Peggy wanted to come with me but got hung up in some volunteer meeting at the library. She said I should come without her, otherwise it might take us another week or two before both of us could connect with you."

Whatever it was he had to say must be serious. I stiffened, certain he was about to relay bad news. "You heard from Mark?" I didn't bother to hide my anxiety.

Bob shook his head, but he didn't meet my eyes.

"You heard from someone who knows about him?" I asked, eager for him to get on with whatever he had to tell me.

Bob nodded.

"And?" I didn't understand why he wanted to keep

me in suspense unless it was something he dreaded telling me. "It's bad news, isn't it?"

"It's news. Not good. Not bad. Mark made it into Iraq."

"Did he locate his friend?"

"Ibrahim, I . . ."

Too eager to wait, I plowed ahead. "Yes, yes. Did he find him? Is he alive? Ibrahim, I mean, not Mark? If so, how soon can he get him and his family out of the country? Is it possible to bring Ibrahim and his family to the United States?"

"Jo Marie," Bob said, and held up his hand. "I don't have answers to any of those questions."

"Tell me everything you know, and please don't hold anything back. Whatever you found out I can take."

"Okay." He leaned forward a bit more. "All I know is that Mark is in Iraq."

"How do you know?" I demanded. "Did you speak to someone?"

"No." Bob shook his head. "I got this in the mail." He reached inside his jacket pocket and pulled out a postcard and extended it to me.

The picture on the front was of skyscrapers in Dubai. I turned it over and in tiny print the message read: SAFE ACROSS BORDER. And that was it.

"Who mailed this?" I asked, studying the back of the card for any indication of who might have sent the postcard.

"I don't know."

I focused on Bob, wondering if he was telling me the truth.

"That isn't Mark's handwriting, is it?" he asked me.

I knew it wasn't. "No."

"The way I figure it, whoever put this in the mail was with Mark long enough to know he made it into Iraq safely."

"You think Mark gave someone your address?" I demanded, fighting back my irritation.

"I can't tell you that, either. I'm sorry, Jo Marie, I wish there was more, but this is all I have."

Chapter 31

Coco wrapped her multicolored nylon raincoat around her as she slid out of her car and made a dash from the parking lot into her favorite Starbucks. Normally she would have gone through the drive-through, but the line was really long and she didn't have time to spare.

Nearly all the baristas knew her by name if not by face, as she was a regular. With the holidays approaching she decided to order a peppermint latte and then head directly into the office.

"Hey, Coco, love the coat," Jill, the barista, greeted her.

"Thanks."

"Is it new?"

"Yeah." She'd created it herself, although she didn't mention that to Jill. The last couple months she'd spent a lot of time at her sewing machine. She enjoyed creating Christmas gifts for family and friends. Keeping her mind active while away from the office helped her push aside thoughts of Hudson. He hadn't contacted her, and after all this time she had given up expecting that he would. A hundred times, possibly more, she'd reviewed the night of the dance, wondering what she might have done differently. No matter what she came up with, the one fact remained: Hudson simply wasn't interested. If he had been, she would have heard from him before now. Yes, she was disappointed, but she'd been disappointed before and she'd get over it. If he was looking to pay her back from rejecting him all those years ago, he'd succeeded, although she found it difficult to believe Hudson was that petty or that unkind.

In an effort to get past his rejection, Coco threw herself into the social whirl, going out nearly every night, dating two and three guys at a time. To those around her, it looked as if she was having the time of her life. Coco wished that was the case. The bare, naked truth was that she was bored silly. It'd taken her a good six weeks to find her equilibrium.

One positive had come from the reunion, however. Coco and Katie had become even better friends. They'd stayed in touch before, connecting through the years. They'd met for lunch or dinner or sometimes a movie, once every couple of months. That had changed since their visit to Cedar Cove. They either talked or texted nearly every day. If Coco had been asked why, she'd guess it was the shared disappointment—it just felt like it had brought them closer.

To her credit, Katie was moving forward. Her friend hadn't asked her to accompany her on any more letter-burning expeditions, and she also seemed to be coming out of her shell. Although she claimed she didn't feel any romantic spark with Christian,

Katie had gone out with him several times. They were seeing more of each other. In fact they'd gone out two weekends straight. Katie told Coco in detail about their drive to Leavenworth for the last remaining weekend of the Oktoberfest celebration. Just recently Katie and Christian had attended a rock concert at the Columbia Crest winery. Christian liked Katie, and it did Coco's heart good to see her friend with someone who genuinely appreciated her.

Lately Coco had cut back on her social life, playing it more low-key. She realized the frantic dating was how she'd chosen to deal with the disappointment of not hearing from Hudson. What took her by surprise was how much his rejection had affected her. She'd genuinely been attracted to him. She liked him better than any man she'd dated in a long while.

"Your latte is ready, Coco," Jill said, interrupting her thoughts.

"Oh sorry, I was a million miles away." Coco reached for the peppermint latte and turned to go. She noticed two men approaching as she went to the exit. One of the men opened the door for her and she stepped through. She glanced up to thank him and went completely numb.

It was Hudson Hamilton.

Seeing him no more than a foot away came as such a shock that the latte slipped out of her hand and fell onto the ground. Immediately, the contents spilled all over the concrete sidewalk. Coco gasped and leaped back to avoid getting splashed.

All these weeks she'd half wondered if she'd run into him, seeing that they both lived in the University district. But considering the fact that she hadn't happened upon him in ten years, the likelihood of their being in the same place at the same time seemed fairly slim.

"Coco." Hudson sounded as shocked as she was.

For one crazy moment all they did was stare at each other.

"I'm so sorry," she said, recovering when she found she could breathe again. She bent over and scooped up the empty cup and tossed it into the waste receptacle. An employee came with a pitcher of water and washed the remainder of the liquid off the walkway.

"Did any of my latte get on you?" Coco asked, fearing some might have splashed on his white lab coat or his pants.

"No. What about you?"

"I'm fine," she assured him, eager now to escape.

"Let me buy you another drink," he offered, apparently blaming himself for the accident.

"No . . . no, it's fine, really."

"Coco," he said firmly. "I insist."

She looked at her wrist without actually registering what her watch said. "Another time, perhaps. Sorry, I can't be late for work." And with that she dashed across the parking lot, heedless of any traffic, finding it imperative to leave.

By the time she was inside her car, her hands were trembling so hard she had trouble inserting the ignition key. She felt like such an idiot. As soon as she was out of the parking lot, she called Katie.

Katie answered right away. "Morning," her friend greeted cheerfully, full of positive energy. "You're out and about bright and early."

"I bumped into Hudson," Coco blurted out, her

voice in a panic. Even now her heart continued to race at the speed of a freight train.

"What?" Katie repeated and then started again.

"Okay, okay, tell me everything. Where are you?"

"I'm in my car now. It just happened."

"Where were you?"

"Starbucks. I ran in for my morning latte and was on my way out. I saw a couple of guys in white lab coats, and didn't think anything of it. I wasn't really paying attention, you know?"

"Sure," Katie said.

"Hudson held the door open for me and then I looked up and saw that it was him, and Katie, oh Katie, you won't believe what I did. I was so shocked I dropped my latte and it spilled all over the sidewalk."

"Oh Coco, how embarrassing."

"Hudson must have assumed it was his fault, because right away he volunteered to buy me another. I said no and flew out of there like Freddy Krueger was after me. I'm still shaking."

"Is this the same Starbucks you stop by every morning?"

"Yes."

"You've never seen him there before?"

"Never."

Katie paused. "Do you think he was seeking you out?"

"I doubt it. He looked as shocked as I was. This makes me so angry. I can't tell you how mad I am."

"Angry?" Katie repeated, sounding surprised. "With Hudson?"

"No," Coco insisted. "I'm furious with myself.

How is it that after all these weeks he still has the power to rattle me? What is it about him that unsettles me so?"

"I can't answer that." Katie's response was gentle and full of understanding.

"The problem is that I can't, either."

They chatted a few minutes more and then disconnected. Coco made it through the day and later that night sat at her sewing machine, working on her Christmas gifts until the wee hours of the morning, seeking a distraction. When her alarm went off the next morning, her eyes burned and she was out of sorts. The last thing she needed was another run-in with Hudson, and she almost decided to skip her stop at Starbucks.

"You are way overreacting," she told herself as she climbed into her car. "It isn't likely that you'll see him again anytime soon. He'll probably avoid that particular Starbucks for the rest of his natural life." She went through the drive-through and of course there was no way to run into him there.

In fact, she went through the drive-through every day for the next week with no sighting of Hudson, which suited her just fine.

On Wednesday before the Thanksgiving holiday, she rolled up to the drive-through to find Jill, her favorite barista, at the window.

"Morning, Coco."

"Happy Thanksgiving," she returned, smiling and thankful for the upcoming holiday. Not that she had any real plans—well, other than stuffing herself with turkey at her brother's house and Christmas shopping later with Katie. Stores in downtown Seattle were so beautifully decorated this time of year.

"Can't say. Why?"

Jill half leaned out the window. "You know that guy you bumped into last week?"

Right away Coco's heart went into high alert, pounding hard against her ribs. "Yeah, what about him?"

"He's been here every morning since. He's asked about you a couple of times. Said he knew you from high school and wondered how often you stop by."

"What did you tell him?"

"Just that you're a regular. Maybe I shouldn't have, because he's been here like clockwork every day about the same time you usually are."

Coco thumped her fingers against the steering wheel, not knowing what to make of this.

"Maybe I shouldn't have said anything," Jill said.

"No, no. It's fine."

Jill glanced over her shoulder. "He's here now."

"Now?"

Jill nodded.

The driver behind Coco pressed impatiently against his horn. Coco beeped back and then pulled forward onto the street. So Hudson had made a point of returning to Starbucks. Fascinated at his reasoning, she circled the block and returned, parking in the lot.

His behavior didn't make sense. If Hudson wanted to contact her all he had to do was text or call. He had her contact information and he'd made no effort

"When are you coming back inside again?" Jill asked, lowering her voice.

to reach out to her. Coco sat in her car for a couple minutes until she felt capable of making a decision.

Curiosity won out.

Grabbing her purse, she climbed out of her car and headed inside the Starbucks, leaving the latte she'd recently purchased behind. When Jill saw her she nodded toward Hudson, who sat at a table with his laptop open, intently studying the screen. Coco might as well have been invisible, for all the attention he paid her.

Not knowing what else to do, she got into the long line, ready to place her order. Feeling more foolish by the minute, she purposely turned her back to him and pretended not to notice that he was anywhere in the vicinity. Despite her best effort to be calm, her heart continued to pound. It was a wonder no one else could hear it.

She was close to the counter when she sensed someone approach.

"Coco?" Hudson said her name.

Although she knew it was him, she glanced at him and smiled as if surprised. "Hello, Hudson."

"I'd like to buy your latte."

"Why?" she asked, again sounding perfectly calm.

"Please, let me," he answered. "I wanted to replace the one you dropped last week then, but you said you had to get to work and didn't give me a chance."

"Really, that's not necessary. It wasn't your fault. I was the clumsy one." This all rushed out in one giant breath, as if she couldn't get the words out fast enough. She inhaled in an effort to calm her pounding heart and started again. "There's no need," she said, clenching her wallet.

"I wouldn't feel right if I didn't replace the one you spilled."

In other words, he'd been hanging around Starbucks every morning for the past week out of obligation. This had nothing to do with any desire to see her or talk to her. The disappointment was keen. Her first inclination was to argue, but that would have been ridiculous.

"All right," she finally said.

He stood beside her until it was her turn to order. When they reached the front of the line, he gestured for her to place her order and then asked for black coffee for himself. Hudson paid for both and then waited for his coffee while she stepped down to the end of the counter to collect her latte.

"Didn't you have an order come up earlier?" Dan, another of the baristas, commented.

Coco glared at him and pretended she didn't hear the question. Dan set her latte down on the counter.

Hudson joined her but remained silent.

"Thank you," she said, and reminded him once again, "but it wasn't necessary." She waited, giving him ample time to start up a conversation.

He didn't.

Coco tucked her purse strap over her shoulder. "I hope you have a nice Thanksgiving," she said, and started for the door.

To her surprise, Hudson scrambled and hurriedly gathered his things and followed her outside, securing his laptop under his arm. "See you," he called after her.

"Right. See you," she echoed.

This was perhaps the strangest encounter Coco had

ever had, and she didn't have a clue what to make of it. The one person she felt she could ask was Katie.

"He felt guilty," Coco said, talking on her Bluetooth as she drove into work.

"Didn't you tell me that the barista said Hudson had shown up every day for the last week?"

"Yes, but that's only because he felt guilty."

"That's more than guilt, Coco. He wanted to see you."

"When he did see me he didn't seem to have anything to say," she argued, although she wasn't sure why she felt the need to debate the issue, especially when she wanted to believe every word Katie said.

"If all he wanted to do was pay for your drink, he could have left you a gift card," Katie insisted. "Every day, Coco. He's been at Starbucks every day since he first saw you. Think about it."

"I'm thinking, but it doesn't make sense."

"Has anything with Hudson ever made sense?" Katie asked.

Her friend had her there. Coco had no choice but to admit that was the case. "Not a thing. He's unlike any man I've ever known." He was completely unpredictable.

Coco wanted to believe there was a possibility that Hudson had had a change of heart, but she was afraid of being disappointed again. She found it impossible to read him.

"Test it out."

Katie lost her. "How am I supposed to test this out?"

"You normally do the drive-through, don't you?"

"Yeah." She didn't get out of her car unless it was necessary.

"On Monday go inside and see if Hudson shows."

"He won't be there," she argued again, without knowing why, when that was the very thing she wanted most.

"You don't know that," Katie argued back. "And didn't he say he'd see you?"

"Yes, but that's just an expression."

"If ever there was a person who takes something literally, it's Hudson Hamilton. When he said 'see you' he meant that he intended to see you."

Coco's back stiffened with pride. "If that's the case, then he can find me. He knows where I live. It's in the reunion booklet; if he wants my number he knows where to find it. I won't go chasing after him."

"All right, if that's the way you want it," Katie said.

"Listen, I've got to go. I've got a meeting I need to get to."

"Sure, no problem, see you," Coco said automatically, without thinking.

"Yes, you will," Katie confirmed, "and my guess is that you'll be seeing Hudson again soon, too."

Chapter 32

Katie's radio station had started playing Christmas music long before Thanksgiving. Hearing her favorite holiday songs seemed apropos as she stood in her kitchen, assembling everything she needed to bake apple and pecan pies for Coco's family Thanksgiving. The meal was being held at Coco's brother's house in the north end of Seattle. Coco had invited Katie and she was happy to accept. For the last several years Katie had spent Thanksgiving with one of her coworkers and their families.

With an apron tied around her waist, she had the flour canister on her kitchen counter along with a tub of lard. She baked pies once or twice a year and took the task seriously. None of those store-bought piecrusts for her. She insisted on doing everything from scratch.

With the radio playing, Katie hummed along to the music as she peeled the apples. At first she didn't hear the doorbell, thinking it was part of the song. It rang a second and third time before she realized someone was outside her door.

Setting aside the knife, she dried her hands on her apron and called out, "Coming." She checked the peephole before she turned the lock.

Emily, James's Emily, stood in the hallway outside her apartment.

Her immediate thought was that something terrible had happened to James and Emily had come to tell her personally.

"Emily," she said, throwing open the door.

The other woman looked apologetic. "I'm so sorry to show up unexpectedly like this. I took a chance you'd be home . . . I realize I probably should have called first."

"Don't apologize. Please come inside."

The other woman continued to look uncertain as she entered Katie's apartment. Her heart was racing and she had to know. "Is everything all right with James? Has there been an accident?"

"As of last week James is perfectly healthy, as far as I know."

The implication was that Emily hadn't seen him in that time. Clearly something had happened and Katie was fairly certain that Emily was about to tell her what it was.

"Please sit down. Can I get you anything? Tea? Coffee? Water?" Katie realized she sounded like a waitress in a diner, but she was nervous and unable to hide it.

"Nothing, thank you." Emily took a seat on the sofa. She looked pale and weary, as if she hadn't slept well in quite some time.

Katie removed the apron and set it in the kitchen and then joined the other woman.

"I interrupted you," Emily said, looking into the kitchen with the bowl of half-peeled apples and pie plates lined up on the counter.

"I was baking pies for Thanksgiving," she said. "Coco and her family invited me. You met Coco, didn't you?"

Emily shook her head. "I don't think so . . . I might have. I met a lot of people the night of the reunion."

"It was a bit overwhelming, wasn't it?" Katie said gently.

Emily stared down at her hands.

The room went silent and Katie waited for Emily to speak. It went without saying that Emily hadn't come to pay a social visit. Clearly, she had something she wanted to say, and Katie didn't feel the need to rush her now that she knew James wasn't in physical danger.

"Everything changed for James and me following the reunion," Emily said, glancing up but only briefly.

"I take it whatever changed wasn't for the good?"

"No, it was just the opposite."

"I'm sorry."

"I'd like to say it was all James, but it wasn't." Emily straightened and offered Katie a feeble smile. "I changed after that night, too."

"Oh?" Katie wasn't sure what to say, but her training as a social worker had taught her to let people talk and explain matters at their own speed, especially in difficult circumstances, which this seemed to be. She had questions, lots of them, but she was patient enough to know the answers would come.

"That time with you in the cafeteria opened my eyes to a lot of things," Emily said, and paused as if she needed a few moments to compose herself before continuing. "I know what it is to love someone to the point that you feel your life isn't worth living if you can't be with that one person."

"I'm better now," Katie whispered, wanting to assure Emily that she'd moved forward since that night.

"I've actually been dating a great guy."

"Do you love him?" Emily asked, pinning her with her gaze.

Katie knew she had to be honest. Emily would see through any lie far too easily. "No."

She smiled as if she was proud of Katie for telling the truth.

"He's a good person," Katie rushed to add. "He's kind and thoughtful and he makes me laugh."

"And in time you're convinced you'll eventually come to genuinely care for him, right?"

Katie hesitated before answering. "Yes," she admitted. "That's what I'm hoping for."

"I assumed the same thing when I agreed to marry James. We met just a few weeks before I got that card from Jayson telling me that his wife was pregnant. It took me a long time to understand why he sent it. Like you, I assumed he wanted to hurt me, but I know Jayson, and he would never do anything intentional to cause me more pain. It took me longer than it should have to realize it was his way of telling me I needed to find someone else to love."

"And then there was James."

"Yes. We dated for a while and like this man you've met—"

"His name is Christian," Katie supplied.

"Like it's been with you and Christian, we started

slow and easy. We both came into this relationship with wounded hearts. It didn't take me long to realize that James is a good, solid man. Like Christian he's kind and thoughtful."

"Sensitive and caring," Katie added.

"That, too," Emily concurred. "We dated for two years before we decided to get married."

"That long?" Katie asked.

"We're good friends."

Katie knew what a good friend James could be, too. "He told you about me, you said, but he never mentioned me by name?"

"All I ever knew was that he'd once loved with his whole heart and the relationship had ended. He didn't fill in the details and there was a reason for that."

"Oh?"

"There was no need to bring up the past for either of us. The relationships were over. I never gave James any of the details about Jayson and me, either. We were both determined to put the past behind us and look to the future . . . to start again, so to speak."

Katie had done her best to do the same. "I know what you mean. I burned some of James's letters. He wrote me, you see, almost every day for months on end . . . his letters were heart-wrenching. Even though they tore me apart, they were filled with love, too . . . but they're gone now."

"You saved the letters until just recently," Emily said this as if she understood.

"Every one of them in a box."

"And since the reunion you've destroyed them," she whispered, and sounded saddened by this news.

"It took several weeks . . . there were a few I held

on to . . . fifteen in total. I couldn't bring myself to burn those. I was convinced that if I got rid of the letters it would be a physical sign that the relationship was completely over. The two of you were engaged, and more than anything I wished you happiness."

Emily smiled, but it was one that revealed more pain. "I . . . know. I loved . . . love Jayson enough to want him to be happy, too. He was close to his parents, especially his mother, and marrying me would have done irreparable harm to their relationship. I couldn't do that to him or to her. His mother never understood how much I admired and loved her." Tears filled her eyes and she quickly blinked them away.

Katie hardly knew what to say.

"Like I said, things changed between James and me following the reunion."

Swallowing, Katie waited for the other woman to continue.

"I realized you loved James the same way I love Jayson."

"Yes, but——"

"And more important," Emily said, cutting her off, "I discovered James was still in love with you."

Katie was unable to hold back a soft gasp. She shook her head several times, discounting the other woman's words. "I'm sure you're wrong. He could hardly look at me; he made it abundantly clear that whatever we once shared is over, dead."

Emily responded with another of those sad smiles. "That was what he wanted you to believe. It isn't true, Katie. He's never been able to stop loving you."

The tightness in her chest moved upward and into her throat. Covering her face with both hands, Katie's shoulders shook. Bending over, she pressed her forehead against her knees and waited for the swell of emotion to pass. She couldn't quite let herself believe what she was hearing.

"I came to tell you I broke off our engagement," Emily whispered. "James and I won't be getting married."

"Oh no," Katie cried.

"It was the right thing to do," Emily insisted, reaching out and briefly squeezing Katie's hand. "James and I could have gone through with our wedding plans, but we each would have been accepting less than what we deserve."

Slowly, gathering her composure, Katie straightened. "And James? How did he react when you told him . . . what did he . . ." she started, unable to get out the full question.

"He wasn't surprised. At least he didn't act like he was. It was almost as if he'd been expecting it. To be fair, he did try to talk me into keeping the engagement ring and postponing the wedding while we sorted through all this."

"That seems sensible."

"No," Emily countered. "Nothing is going to change. Deep down James recognized it, too, only he didn't want to admit it."

"That was a week ago?"

"Yes. This last weekend we told our families we were calling off the wedding."

Katie could only imagine the disappointment James's parents must have felt.

"I wanted to do it together as a couple, but James said it would go better with his family if he went alone. My parents didn't take the news well. They want me to be happy, but unfortunately, they seem to believe that will only happen when I'm married and have a child. What they don't understand is that getting married when it's not the right person doesn't accomplish anything."

"What happens now?" Katie asked, knowing how painful and difficult the last few months must have been for this woman.

"I . . . I don't know what the future holds for me. It isn't necessary that I do. As for James's future, I believe that's up to you," she said.

"Up to me?" she repeated.

"If you still love James, and I know you do, then you will need to let him know."

"James already knows how I feel about him. I couldn't have made it any more clear."

"You won't go talk to him?" Emily's gaze probed hers.

Katie shook her head. "I can't. At the reunion I asked him to hear me out, and he agreed with the stipulation that I not contact him ever again. I think it's his choice to make now."

Emily continued to stare at her. "Are you telling me after all this you're going to actually let pride stand in your way?"

Katie gave one short laugh. "This isn't pride, Emily. I came to the reunion with my heart on my sleeve. I wanted nothing more than to explain why I had been forced to break up with him when he left for college."

"James believes if you'd sincerely loved him, it wouldn't have mattered what his parents thought, or anyone else," Emily told her.

Katie's head came up. "So he talked about me following the reunion?"

She nodded. "We had what was quite possibly our first honest conversation, baring our souls to each other. He told me everything. He was so badly hurt by what happened between you, but you already know that. I think he was so hurt, he couldn't see your point of view. You were both teenagers and you didn't have the support of family! You knew what it would be like for James if he lost that himself and didn't want him to suffer what you had."

Emily understood her situation far better than James ever had.

"I promised not to contact him, but it's more than that, Emily. James has held on to his anger. The only way I can be convinced that he is truly over the past is if he came to me."

"Katie . . ."

She held up her hand, stopping her. "I don't know that a relationship from this point forward would survive with that resentment and anger hanging between us."

Emily took a few minutes to absorb this before she slowly nodded. "I understand."

"What about you?" Katie asked.

Emily shrugged as if to say she would let the future take care of itself. "I can't say. I teach first grade and love my job. I'd found contentment before I met James, and I think I can again." She stood then, as if the reason for her visit had been accomplished.

"The last time we met, you asked me to love James for you. That deeply touched my heart. I want to give those words back to you. If you two can find your way to each other, I hope you'll love James for me in a way I've never been able to do. Fill his life with laughter and joy. Give him children. We'd talked about starting a family—he'll make a wonderful father one day."

Katie's throat tightened and she nodded, and when she spoke it was through tears. "I don't know if that's possible, but I would love nothing more."

Chapter 33

Thanksgiving morning I was up even earlier than usual. Within a matter of hours I'd be joining my parents for the traditional meal, taking the Southworth ferry into Seattle. The trip across Puget Sound from Southworth took less time than the ferry that left the Bremerton dock, and there would be less traffic from West Seattle.

My mother always went out in a big way for Thanksgiving. I wasn't concerned about leaving my guests unattended for the holiday—I'd only be away from the house for a few hours, and each guest had an individual key and their own holiday plans.

Although I'd offered to bring a side dish or dessert to contribute to the dinner, my mother refused. She had been cooking for days and had more than enough.

My mother was an excellent cook. Thanksgiving was her opportunity to show off her culinary and decorating skills. She loved this day and planned for it weeks in advance.

As soon as breakfast was served I took Rover for his walk, and on the way back I stopped at the mailbox. I'd been busy and hadn't collected yesterday's mail. The first thing I noticed as I sorted through the bills and junk mail was a card with the return address from Yakima, Washington. It was from Maggie Porter. Maggie and Roy had stayed at the inn a few months back, and I remembered them well.

The inn had provided its healing magic for the Porters. Maggie discovered she was pregnant, and apparently this pregnancy was unplanned, unexpected, and unwanted. Reading between the lines, I'd guessed that Roy believed there was a possibility that the child wasn't his. Unlike what had happened with my two guests who'd been in town to attend their class reunion, Roy and Maggie had found their way back to each other during their time at the inn, and had left at peace.

I slid open the card, happy to hear from Maggie.

Thanksgiving 2015

Dear Jo Marie,

This year I'm taking time to count my blessings and wanted you to know that I will always treasure my time with you in Cedar Cove while staying at the Inn. Roy and I are doing well and our boys are growing like weeds and are eager to greet their baby sister.

Yes, the ultrasound showed that Roy and I are having a girl. I can't tell you how pleased and excited we are.

Roy has been busy painting and decorating everything in the baby's room the most lovely shade of light pink. Grace already has a complete layette from family and friends. I can already see how spoiled she'll be.

We decided to name her Grace Margaret Porter. Roy insisted she have my name as well, and we settled on the name Grace because she is a special gift God has given us to help strengthen our marriage and our commitment to each other. She's an active baby, and I can tell she's going to give her two older brothers a run for their money.

When you see Mark, please let him know how much we love the cradle and how blessed we are to be the recipient of this treasure. I wrote him recently but his letter was returned. Apparently he's moved?? It meant the world to Roy and me that Mark would give us such a beautiful piece of woodwork.

I'm using the word blessed a lot, aren't I? That's because this is how I feel—so very blessed. Like I said, I'm in good health and have been well. For the most part, this has been an easy pregnancy. The truth is I've never felt happier, despite what we've been through.

Roy and I would like to return to The Inn at Rose Harbor, but probably not this year! I'll send you a picture of Grace once she makes her debut.

Thank you again, Jo Marie, for everything.

Roy and Maggie Porter

I returned the card to the envelope and started walking back to the house with Rover straining against his leash. Maggie's words tugged at my heart.

I remembered the talk Mark and Roy had had

shortly after Mark had started work on the gazebo. I'd been at the side of the house, working in my garden. Neither man knew I was there. I hadn't meant to eavesdrop on their conversation, but I couldn't ignore it, either.

Mark had been calm and reasonable with Roy, who was hotheaded and angry, convinced the only course of action was for him to divorce Maggie. His ire had been so strong that he could barely stand still.

My respect for Mark grew by leaps and bounds that day, listening to him talk to Roy. Mark hadn't argued with the other man nor had he tried to reason with him. Instead Mark had asked Roy a series of questions in what might have looked like a casual conversation. Those questions had helped Roy recognize for himself what his life and that of his children would be like without Maggie. In the end Roy had decided to do whatever it took to save his marriage. I really believed Maggie and Roy were together and happy in large part thanks to Mark.

My thoughts were on Mark as Rover led the way back into the inn. My guests were all going out for the day, spending the holiday with extended family and friends. I was about to head out myself when a sudden thought hit me.

The cradle.

Mark had worked on that cradle for months, carving an intricate design into the headboard. I'd been shocked when he offered to give it to the Porters, who were little more than strangers. He could have sold the piece for hundreds of dollars. Perhaps more. It was a beautiful work of art.

I never had understood why he'd build something

for which he had no personal use. Really, it wasn't any of my business. If Mark wanted to spend ridiculous amounts of time on something that hadn't been commissioned, that was up to him.

I thought back to my conversation with Bob Beldon, and what had prompted Mark to create such a beautiful cradle—he'd built it with the hope that one day he would be a father. That, at some time in the distant future, he would get married and have children of his own.

He'd built it for us.

The truth of this realization hit me with renewed force. Stumbling into the kitchen I sat down while I sorted through my thoughts. When I felt my legs would hold me, I put on water for tea.

Over the last month, I'd tried to push thoughts of Mark from my mind, although it seemed like an impossible task. It was time I fully owned up to the truth. I'd fallen in love with him, though I'd been oblivious to my own feelings mainly because I'd been wrapped up in my grief after Paul's death.

Looking back, I realized that Mark had done his best to hide his feelings for me. He recognized that I wasn't in a place where my heart was free to love again, grieving for Paul as I did. It'd only been in the last nine months that I'd been receptive as our relationship blossomed into more than friendship. Even then I'd been blinded to what was right in front of my eyes.

Mark had been the one to point out to me that I'd started to have feelings for him. As dumbfounded as I'd been when he said it, I realized now that he'd been right.

Mark hadn't wanted to love me. He fought it, feeling unworthy because of what had happened to him in Iraq. It had clearly shaken his sense of self. In the end he didn't feel he could live with himself by abandoning Ibrahim. He made what must have been a heart-wrenching decision to return. He was prepared to die in order to right a wrong.

Sipping the tea helped calm me. Maggie Porter had sent me this beautiful card telling me how grateful she was for her time at the inn. Despite the fact that I was a widow who'd already buried one man I loved, and that another was in danger, I tried to feel grateful for what I had, and this was the day to give thanks.

I was about to head out to my parents' when my office phone rang. "Rose Harbor Inn," I said.

"Jo Marie, it's Peggy." She didn't stop, but continued, speaking so fast her words ran together. "Do you have your television on?"

The urgency in her voice immediately put me on edge. "No. Why?" The only television on the main floor was in my personal area. "What's happened?"

Peggy hesitated, and when she spoke again she sounded undecided. "Listen, it might be best if I come over. I don't want you watching the news alone."

I rushed into the other room and turned on the television, holding on to the phone with one hand and the remote with the other. The Macy's Thanksgiving Day Parade flashed onto the screen and I started pushing buttons in an effort to locate a twenty-four-hour news channel.

"Just tell me," I blurted out, every part of my body starting to shake. "What's happened?" Did she seriously think I would sit around and wait, not knowing, while she hurried to the inn?

"There was a news flash . . . we don't know—information is sketchy at best. It's just so hard to tell. An American's been captured in Iraq—"

"Is it Mark?" I demanded, desperate to hear what she was trying to tell me. Whatever it was had badly shaken her. Before I went into a panic I forced myself to calm down. "There are lots of Americans in Iraq," I argued, unwilling to believe this one, whoever he might be, was Mark. My Mark.

"We don't know for sure, ISIS didn't announce the name," Peggy went on to give the details of the largest and most fanatical of the terrorist groups whose name had been all over the news.

" . . . the news agencies say it isn't one of their journalists," Peggy said.

"Couldn't it be an aid worker?" I said. My mouth had gone so dry that I found it difficult to talk. She didn't need to remind me what had happened to other Americans held by this terrorist group. I struggled to swallow down the panic that started to build inside of me.

"You think it's Mark, don't you?" I couldn't think of any other reason she'd call me. For reasons, possibly ones Peggy and Bob had never told me, they believed the man in the hands of ISIS was Mark.

Peggy didn't answer me.

"Peggy," I cried out.

"I . . . don't know. I just don't know."

Although I asked, I felt I already had my answer. My worst fears had been realized.

Chapter 34

Monday morning, Coco pulled up to the drive-through at Starbucks and was grateful to see that her friend Jill manned the window. Silly as it seemed, her stomach was in knots and she was jittery.

Out of habit, she placed her usual order, but she wasn't interested in drinking her latte. She wanted to know if Hudson was inside. Katie kept insisting he would be. Coco so badly wanted to believe her friend was right about Hudson, but she had doubts.

As soon as she rolled up to the window to collect her latte, Coco asked Jill, "Is he here again? You know, the guy you mentioned last Wednesday?"

Jill wriggled her eyebrows up and down several times. "Front and center. He parked himself by the front door and carefully watches everyone who steps inside. You gonna put him out of his misery?"

Coco joyfully pumped her fists in the air. "I think I will."

Without hesitating, she drove around the building and parked in the lot, and then walked inside, holding on to her latte. Sure enough, Hudson sat at the table closest to the door. Without waiting for an invitation, Coco took the chair across from him and set her drink down on the table next to his closed laptop.

He stared at her as if she were an apparition.

"You know, it's kind of silly for us to keep meeting like this," Coco said, and crossed her legs as if she were completely relaxed, though she was anything but.

Hudson blinked.

"Are you here to see me?" Maybe she'd misread the entire situation, which would be highly embarrassing; that, however, seemed unlikely.

He pushed his eyeglasses up the bridge of his nose and slowly nodded.

"You do realize there are other ways of contacting me, don't you? I have a phone. I live in a condo nearby." With a bit of flair, she uncrossed her legs, stood, and prepared to leave. Then she decided she might give him a bit more encouragement, and leaned across the table and kissed his cheek.

Hudson blinked again. Twice this time.

"See you," she said, on her way out the door.

For the entire rest of the day she found it impossible to concentrate on her work. Her mind went in a dozen different directions, wondering how long it would take for him to make his move. If he finally did make a move. She glanced at her watch every ten minutes, wanting the day to pass, hoping with everything in her that Hudson would either call or stop by her condo that night. She'd been blatant enough that even he should be able to understand it was his move. As soon as she arrived home, Coco called Katie, telling her about what'd taken place that morning with Hudson.

"Don't worry," Katie insisted. "He'll be in touch."

"I hope God is listening," Coco moaned. If she didn't hear from him this time, she was finished.

Katie's smile was evident in her voice when she spoke next. "I've never seen you like this over a guy."

"I know, and I'm not even sure I know why. I mean, I do and I don't. He's so smart and so dense at the same time. He loved me from afar and I was such a jerk to him and oh, I don't know—I can't stop thinking about him. We seem like we're totally mismatched, I know, and any relationship we have will probably go down in flames, but I don't care, I want a chance with him."

"I don't agree that you're wrong for each other," Katie countered. "You'll make a great couple because you balance each other perfectly."

"Do we really?"

"Coco, you hardly sound like yourself. Where's that confident, gutsy girl I know so well?"

"She's still back in high school, praying a certain boy likes her enough to ask her to prom," Coco admitted, pacing her living room floor like a prowling lion ready to spring into action.

"Don't worry. Hudson's a smart guy, he'll figure it out."

"I swear to you, Katie, if he doesn't connect with me soon I will never go to that Starbucks again. I mean it. I can't play these games; I don't do well with this."

"Coco," Katie said, sounding serious now. "Hudson isn't the kind of person to play games."

Coco sincerely hoped her friend was right.

"My guess is that he regrets not contacting you after the reunion and he's trying to let you know how he feels, but a guy like Hudson isn't good at expressing his emotions. But he feels so strongly about you that he's willing to do whatever he can to let you know he's interested in dating you. Hence the waiting game at Starbucks. This is probably about as good as it gets with someone like Hudson."

Coco mulled over her friend's words. "When did you get so smart?" They chatted a few minutes longer and ended the call.

At loose ends after talking to Katie, Coco continued to pace her living room, convinced she'd go crazy if Hudson kept her waiting for days on end. A hundred different things were calling for her attention. She had Christmas gifts to sew, cards to mail, books to read, dinner to cook, and laundry to do, and yet she found herself incapable of doing any one of those things.

Her phone rang and she nearly fell on it in her rush to answer. It was her brother, looking for suggestions of what to buy his wife for Christmas. Disappointment hung on her like a dead weight. By nine-thirty she was convinced it was a lost cause for that night.

Then her doorbell rang.

The peephole told her it was Hudson. At last! It was Hudson. She was so relieved she wanted to cry.

He wore a shirt and tie under his open jacket. His hair was combed and he held a potted poinsettia.

Coco opened the door, smiled serenely, and then grabbed hold of his tie, causing him to stumble into the condo. She slammed the door closed with her foot.

"I didn't think you'd ever get here," she said, so happy it was impossible to hold it inside.

"I brought you . . ."

"I know." She took the plant out of his hand, set it aside, and then backed him against the door and kissed him. She realized she'd probably come on way too strong, but she wanted to make sure Hudson got the message of how happy she was to see him.

His glasses were slightly askew when she lifted her head. "Okay, glad we've gotten that out of the way. Should we sit down and talk?" she asked.

Instead, Hudson reached for her and pulled her back into his arms. He kissed her again, ravishing her mouth with his until she was so weak, it felt as if her knees were about to give out. When he released her, if anyone needed to sit, it was Coco. She sank onto the sofa, and after a moment Hudson joined her. He looked like he had something he wanted to say, but all he could do was look at her as if she were the most beautiful woman in the world.

"Okay," she said, smiling so big her mouth hurt. She doubted Hudson realized what a powerful punch his kisses carried. "I need to know where we stand . . . or sit, as the case may be. And it'd help if I knew why I didn't hear from you after the reunion."

"I . . . I just couldn't believe you were serious." He tilted his head ever so slightly to one side and his mouth was set in a hard line. "Coco, you're beautiful and I'm this nerdy guy who is in way over his head when it comes to understanding women. By the next morning, following the reunion, I was convinced there was no way you were genuinely interested in me."

Coco hung her head and looked down at her hands, which were clenched in her lap. "But I was . . . I am."

Hudson went still and quiet for several moments.

"I'm not exactly a GQ kind of guy."

"And exactly whose opinion is that?" she demanded. While he might not be a cover model, there was more to Hudson than a dozen men she'd known through the years.

"Come on, Coco. I know my strengths and I know my weaknesses, and relationships, especially with women, aren't easy for me. You felt bad about what happened in high school. I get that, and when you found out it was me who'd slashed Ryan's tires I became something of a hero in your eyes. In reality, that was the act of a coward. I figured that night with you on the bleachers was like the perfect storm. Everything came together at once, but it wasn't meant to last. I figured you were probably happy I didn't text you."

Raising her chin, Coco stared at him, finding it hard to believe he would even think such a thing. "That's crazy. It doesn't make sense that you'd even think that."

"Maybe it doesn't make sense to you, but it does to me."

Coco blinked. "Okay, but what changed your mind?"

"Bumping into you that day," he said, his look anxious. "You saw me and dropped your latte."

True, that hadn't been her finest moment. She

should have played it much cooler but had been taken by surprise. "I was shocked to see you, is all."

"I was surprised to run into you, too. I had no idea you went to that Starbucks. I'd only been there a couple of times."

Coco didn't want to get hung up on the coincidence of their meeting. "But I don't get what changed." Coco needed to know if she was ever going to understand this man.

Hudson lowered his eyes. "Truth is, I haven't been able to stop thinking about you. Every night I go to sleep and you're in my dreams. I keep thinking about kissing you and how good you'd felt in my arms. Then I wake up feeling empty and alone."

"You could've called me," she reminded him gently.

He shook his head. "I lost count of the number of times I wanted to text you, but I didn't know what to say. I felt like I'd missed my chance. Weeks passed and I felt even if you were interested, which I was convinced you weren't, that I'd probably blown it and you wouldn't want to talk to me."

"But I did," she whispered.

His eyes were full of regret. "I'm sorry, Coco," he said with such sincerity she couldn't doubt his words. "That day when we bumped into each other everything changed. When you looked at me I saw something that almost made me run after you."

Coco frowned, not understanding what he was saying. Sure, she'd been shocked to see him, but she'd recovered quickly, or so she'd thought. "What did you see?"

He hesitated and then admitted, "Pain flashed in your eyes. In my stupidity, I realized I'd hurt you."

"Stop saying you're stupid, Hudson, because we both know you have the highest IQ of anyone I know."

"When it comes to you—"

"Stop," she insisted, interrupting him again.

"I couldn't get your look out of my mind. It ate at me. I had to do something to make it right, only I didn't know what and so I started hanging out at Starbucks every morning in the hope that I'd see you again."

"But when I did show, all you did was buy my latte." She didn't mention that she already had a full one in her car.

He snorted as if disgusted with himself. "I couldn't get my tongue to work. I am so in awe of you. I was still convinced I'd read you wrong and that it was best to leave matters as they were. There you were, so perfect and so beautiful, and I couldn't imagine why you'd want anything to do with me."

Coco cupped his cheek, holding her palm against his face. "I waited for you to talk to me, and when you didn't, I wasn't sure what to think."

"I don't blame you. I didn't know what to think, either. After you left, I wanted to kick myself. I'd let you go and there was so much I wanted to say and then this morning." He paused and chuckled. "It's a good thing you left when you did."

"Why's that?"

"After you kissed my cheek, I jumped up and did a jig around the table. It's an Irish one. My mother is Irish from County Cork and she taught it to me. I'll show you, if you like, one day."

"Really?" She laughed.

"Oh yes, and then you said, 'see you,' and it was like a personal invitation."

"I meant every word."

"That was what I hoped. I was here about seven, parked outside your condo building. I think one of your neighbors must have called the police because a patrol car came by and asked me what I was doing sitting in my car for hours on end."

"What were you doing?"

He shrugged. "Working up the courage to come inside."

"Oh Hudson, if only you knew how antsy I've been, hoping you'd contact me. I've been on pins and needles all day, wishing so hard that I'd hear from you."

He smiled then and relaxed. "Can I kiss you again?"

"Yes!"

Hudson gathered her close and kissed her as if he was dying for want of her, as though he couldn't get enough of what he needed in a single kiss.

By the time he pulled away they were both breathing hard and heavy, sagging against each other. Coco balanced her forehead against his. "You aren't going to change your mind again, are you?"

"No, but . . ."

"But?" There always seemed to be a *but* in conversations with Hudson.

"There's something you should know about me. I don't have much experience."

"With what . . . relationships?"

He tensed and his hands tightened around her upper arms. "That, too, but I'm talking about sex. I know you've probably had partners with far more expertise and—"

Coco placed her hand over his mouth, stopping him. "It's a bit early to be talking about sexual compatibility, Hudson."

His eyes widened. "See what I mean? I'll screw this up sure as anything."

"Stop. You're doing fine, just promise you're not going to leave me again."

"Okay."

"As for my vast sexual experience, you might be surprised to know there hasn't been anyone since . . . since that awful night with Ryan."

He shook his head as if he found it impossible to believe.

"I didn't feel I could trust another man or give my heart away," Coco explained.

"You can trust me," Hudson said.

"I believe I can," Coco whispered. "In fact, there's no one I'd trust more than you, Hudson Hamilton."

Chapter 35

❦

Christmas was fast approaching and Katie knew it would be a happy one for Coco and Hudson. The two were so much in love it was almost painful to be in the same room with them. They were so darn cute together, and happiness radiated off them like sunlight, warming those around them. Katie had never seen her friend this happy, and it did her own heart good to know that finding love was possible.

Perhaps not for her, though. Katie had yet to hear from James, and frankly she doubted that she would. Enough time had passed since her talk with Emily that Katie was convinced he was incapable of letting go of the past. She hadn't heard from Emily, either, not that she'd expected she would.

Dusk approached around four in the afternoon this time of year in the Pacific Northwest, and Katie took pains to leave her car beneath a streetlight in the office parking complex. She often stayed late and the lot could get deserted.

That wasn't the case, though, when she left work on the Friday a week before Christmas. Several cars were scattered about the lot. The sky had been overcast, and with temperatures dropping below freezing there had been talk of snow flurries that night. Katie suspected every kid in Seattle hoped that was the case.

Bundled up with her coat buttoned all the way to the top, a knitted scarf wrapped around her neck and a hat covering her head, she left the building. With her shoulders hunched and her head down, she strained against the wind and walked toward the parking lot.

The first time she noticed she wasn't alone was when she spied a man standing close to her vehicle. Immediately alarm filled her and she looked up, her car keys in her hand in a position to do damage, should someone choose to attack her. Katie wouldn't be an easy victim.

As she drew closer she realized the man standing next to her car was no stranger.

It was James.

Dumbstruck, Katie froze and straightened. No more than a few feet separated them as she waited. For a long time all they did was stare at each other.

"You're working late," he said, breaking the silence.

"I often do."

He stood with his hands buried deep in his coat and wore a watchman's cap. He didn't look overly pleased to see her. "Can I buy you a cup of coffee?"

"Sure."

They decided on a place to meet, a diner about a mile away, but when they got there it was crowded with the dinner rush, and the wait would be as long as forty minutes.

"It's the time of year," Katie said.

James looked across the street to a bowling alley.

"Want to try there?" he asked.

"Might as well," she said, laughing. *A bowling alley?*

They raced across the street with the light. James's hand cupped her elbow in case she lost her footing. He'd always been a gentleman, polite and considerate. It was one of the many reasons she'd fallen in love with him.

The restaurant in the bowling alley was busy, but they were able to get a seat right away. They left their coats and hats on the rack by the front door. Katie rubbed the cold from her hands as they found an open booth.

As she slid inside, Katie noticed the café charged a minimum for anyone sitting in a booth. James seemed to notice the sign the same time she did.

"Guess we'll need to order more than coffee," she mentioned, as she reached for the plastic-coated menu.

"We can leave if you'd rather."

"It's fine."

He, too, reached for the menu.

"I don't mind paying for my own meal," she told him.

The look James shot her cut straight through her.

"It was just a suggestion." Katie read over the specials of the day and discovered, for a bowling alley, the menu was impressive. Although she had to wonder how good the cordon bleu would be.

The harried waitress came for their order, set aside

the coffeepot, and then grabbed the pencil tucked behind her ear and the pad from her apron pocket.

"I'll have the black bean soup," Katie said, although she wondered if she'd be able to swallow a single spoonful.

"Make that two," James said, and tucked the menu back behind the napkin dispenser.

Once the waitress left, silence lay between Katie and James. She waited, looking down at her hands. She took a sip from her water.

James spoke first. "Emily broke off the engagement."

"I know. She told me."

He frowned. "I suppose she insisted that I was in love with you and if we got married that she would be my second best."

Katie shrugged. "Something like that."

"It's not true, you know."

She didn't agree or disagree. "You wanted to talk to me?"

"Yes."

If that was the case, he seemed to struggle with what he intended to say. After several awkward moments, she gestured to him. "Well?"

"I don't love you," he said once more, and it seemed he needed to convince himself more than her.

"Any longer," she added.

His frown darkened as if he didn't understand.

Katie clarified it for him. "At one time you did love me, James; you can't deny that any more than I can deny loving you," she explained.

"Okay, you're right." His jaw clenched. "I did care

about you at one time, but not anymore, and the sooner you understand that, the better."

"It sounds like you're looking to convince yourself more than me, James." If what he said was true then it didn't make sense he would seek her out, ask her to coffee to reiterate a fact he'd already made crystal clear on more than one occasion.

Their soup arrived and Katie reached for her spoon, holding on to it in a tight grip. If he hadn't come to clear the air between them then there had to be another explanation. "Do you blame me for the broken engagement?"

He glared across the table at her. "I blame you for everything."

Katie probably shouldn't have smiled, but she couldn't help herself.

"Do you find that funny?" he demanded, glaring at her all the more intently.

"No. The truth is, it's rather sad." She meant it, even though she could see how upset it made him.

James leaned against the edge of the table, clenching hold of his own spoon, which was pointed toward the ceiling. "I loved you, heart and soul. I would have died for you."

"I know, and I loved you that way, too."

"But it's over," he insisted.

"So you keep telling me." Katie forced herself to take a bite of the soup. Under ordinary circumstances she would have enjoyed it, but these were far from ordinary circumstances.

James watched her and then followed suit. He kept his gaze lowered. "Emily said you're dating someone."

"His name is Christian." So James had already known that Emily had talked to her. Christian and she hadn't gone out much lately. It must have been a couple weeks since she'd seen him or talked to him.

"Do you love him, too?" His question was gruff.

"No. The one I love is you."

"Sure you do." Then, to her surprise, he slid out of the booth, slapped a twenty-dollar bill on the table, and walked out of the bowling alley.

Katie watched him go, defeat weighing down her heart. She wasn't sure why James had sought her out or what he'd expected would happen. He'd been angry and he blamed her, as he said, "for everything." It was a sad commentary on his life, and heartbreaking for her as well. Perhaps all he'd wanted was to prove to himself that he no longer loved her.

The waitress stopped by the table. "Everything all right with the soup?" she asked.

"It's fine. I don't think either one of us was hungry."

"I'll get you the bill."

"Here." Katie retrieved the twenty and handed her that. "Keep the change."

"But the tab comes to less than twelve bucks."

"Merry Christmas," Katie said, as she scooted out of the booth.

She collected her coat at the front door and stepped outside to find snow flurries raining down from the night sky.

Her car was parked on the other side of the street and she waited to cross at the light. As she approached her vehicle she saw that James's car, which had been parked next to hers, was still there. When she approached, he opened the door and climbed out, closing it behind him.

They stared at each other and once more Katie waited for him to take the lead. When she couldn't stand the silence any longer, she said, "I would have thought you'd be gone by now."

"I should be," he muttered.

"You are."

"I'm not stopping you."

Traffic sped past and someone in the distance leaned on a horn. The loud, discordant sound cut through the night.

"How am I stopping you?" she asked, and realized he wasn't talking about tonight.

James walked back and forth, creating a path in the fresh coating of snow. "I thought if I saw you . . . if we talked, I'd be able to purge you from my mind." He slammed his fist against his chest. "And my heart."

"Did it work?"

"No," he said, and closed his eyes as though fighting himself. He tilted his head back and stared up at the sky.

"James," she whispered, unsure what was happening.

"No one has hurt me more than you . . . I should hate you, but God help me, I can't . . . I can't make myself do it."

"I know. I'm so sorry," she said. Deep down, Katie knew he could never really hate her.

"I'm so in love with you I can't think anymore." He shook his head. "I can't trust you."

"You can trust me," she assured him softly. "I may

have made a mistake when we were eighteen, but I was doing the best I could, and everything I did, I did for love. I have never loved anyone else but you, James."

Katie watched as the indecision played across his face. He wanted to believe her, wanted to give her his heart, but still he hesitated. For what seemed like an eternity, James stood frozen.

"You'll never understand what it was like for me to have you just break it off with me back then, without a single word of explanation. How could you have done that? I still don't understand why you didn't just come to me and tell me what was going on."

"I don't know, James," she said. "I thought I was doing a brave thing. A selfless thing."

Staring into the falling snow, she said, "I was a kid, James. Trust me, to say I learned a lot from what happened would be the understatement of the year. I would never hide something from someone I loved again."

"You made a decision that affected both of us," James said.

"Yes. But I'm twenty-eight now, not eighteen. And people are capable of learning and growing."

After several moments she felt a hand on her shoulder. Katie turned to find James, his face looked blurred through the tears that clouded her eyes.

"I can't do it," he said, his voice raw. "I can't let you go."

With that he hauled her into his embrace, half lifting her off the ground, hugging her until she feared he was about to steal the very breath from her lungs.

Katie looked down on him, her hands cupping his

face. Tears streamed down her cheeks, before she slowly lowered her mouth to his. They kissed urgently as if to make up for the last ten years in a single exchange.

"I've always loved you," she choked out.

James wouldn't let her talk. Instead he kissed her again and again, holding her against him and whirling around in the snow like they were kids on a playground. When he lifted his head, Katie threw hers back and gazed up at the sky, laughing and weeping both at the same time.

Chapter 36

I'll admit I went overboard when it came to decorating the inn for Christmas this season. Not until January, when I had to take everything down and place it in storage, did I acknowledge that this excess of Christmas cheer was a blatant attempt to lift my own spirits. Now, with the decorations down, the inn looked stark and bleak to me.

My guests came and went with rapid regularity. A few special ones returned. Mary Smith, who had stayed at the inn a few months after I purchased the bed-and-breakfast, had come with her husband. She'd originally visited while she was battling breast cancer, and had reconnected during her visit with a Seattle attorney she'd once loved. Mary's cancer was in remission and she and her husband seemed blissfully happy. Perhaps the healing power found at my inn was stronger than I realized.

If only that had been the case for Coco and Katie when they were here back in September for their ten-year class reunion. Coco and Katie. It saddened me to remember that the inn had failed them both.

In an effort to brighten the bleak days that followed Christmas, I decorated the inn for Valentine's Day, although it was early yet, still January. I felt like a hypocrite, hanging hearts from the ceiling over the dining room table.

There had been no further word since the news reports of the ISIS kidnapping. I had no way of knowing if it was in fact Mark, as Peggy had worried. But if Mark was alive I felt certain I would have gotten some form of communication by now . . . and I hadn't. The hard part was that there might never be closure for me with Mark.

When I had first learned Paul's helicopter had been shot down, I clung to the hope that my husband had somehow survived. It took a year for his remains to be located and identified. I steadfastly refused to believe my husband was dead and when I was forced to accept the truth, it was like losing him all over again. The grief and pain had been debilitating. I wouldn't do that with Mark. It was too painful to live my life in limbo. As far as I was concerned, I had to move forward as if he were gone from me forever. For the sake of my sanity, I accepted that Mark was out of my life.

As I stood on a chair with a shiny red heart dangling from a thread, I glanced out the window and heard a car pull into the driveway. I recognized the two women who got out and walked toward the inn.

Coco and Katie, my high-school-reunion girls. The very ones I'd just been thinking about.

I jumped down off the chair, and Rover and I were at the front door and had it open before they reached the top step.

"Remember us?" Coco asked, smiling broadly.

"Of course I do," I said, inviting them inside. I hugged them both.

"We were in town and decided to stop by and tell you our news."

"Come in. Tell me." I led the way to the living room. "The coffee's on if you'd like a cup."

Katie glanced at her wrist. "Sorry, but we're due at a friend's house in fifteen minutes."

"What's going on?" I asked eagerly. They both looked wonderful. Happy.

We sat together, the three of us, in my living room.

"You first," Katie said, gesturing to her friend.

Coco thrust out her arm and wiggled her ring finger, displaying a diamond engagement ring. My eyes went from the ring to Coco. She must have read the question in me, because she rushed to add, "It's from Hudson. You gotta love this guy. He knows what he wants and so do I." Her face shone with joy. "He couldn't decide if he should give it to me January eighteenth on Stephen Hawking's birthday or January twenty-second on Sir Francis Bacon's birthday, and Carl Sagan's somewhere in there, too. So he chose January twentieth."

"Tell her what he did," Katie urged. "This is so romantic."

Coco's smile covered her entire face. "He insisted on showing me this scientific experiment he'd first tried as a kid using household items. He had baking soda and vinegar and a bunch of other stuff out on my shelf. We were in my kitchen and then his experiment bubbled over and there was a huge mess. I laughed and told him he wasn't allowed to use the kitchen any longer to teach me about science. When he finished, I dutifully applauded and then he frowned and said something had gone wrong because there appeared to be an object in the bottom of the glass. I looked and sure enough there was, and it was a diamond ring."

"Hudson isn't the most romantic guy in the world, but he outdid himself with this proposal." Katie smiled at her friend as she spoke.

"Then Hudson proposed. He got down on one knee and asked me to marry him," Coco said, her eyes dreamy with the memory, "and then I got down on both knees next to him and said yes."

"Through her tears," Katie added.

"Okay, I'll admit I was crying, but Hudson was so sweet and so sincere and so wonderful."

"That's marvelous," I said, genuinely pleased for her. "Congratulations."

"He wanted to put the ring in my latte because we meet up every morning at Starbucks, but he changed his mind, which is probably a good thing. Knowing me, I would have probably swallowed it and Hudson would end up doing the Heimlich maneuver." Coco turned to her friend. "Okay, Ms. Know-It-All, your turn."

Katie turned toward me. "My story with James isn't as dramatic or romantic as Coco's."

"It is, too," Coco insisted. "It's every bit as romantic and wonderful."

"Wonderful for sure," Katie concurred.

I held up my hand. "I thought you told me he was engaged to someone else."

"Was, past tense," Coco supplied. "Oh sorry, Katie, this is your story."

"I won't go into the broken-engagement part although it does play a key role in the story. Really all I have to tell you is that James and I have gotten back together and our relationship is better than ever."

"You should see the two of them," Coco said, and then grew thoughtful. "They both realize, I think, how close they came to living completely separate lives. If any two people need each other, it's Katie and James. They're perfect together, two halves that make up a whole."

"What about you and Hudson?"

"Talk about yin and yang," Coco said, and laughed. "We're two people who are exact opposites but we agree on everything that matters. Well, other than the names of our children. I am not going to saddle a son with the name Francis or Albert. Besides I think Hudson Junior is a perfectly fine name."

I hesitated and then asked, "Are you pregnant?"

"Not yet, but I plan to be shortly," Coco cooed.

I couldn't help smiling. Both my reunion girls had found happiness, and their faces were a reflection of their joy.

"We came back to Cedar Cove to let you know how happy we are and how much it meant to us to meet you," Katie explained. "Even when you were emotionally down yourself you encouraged us. Besides, we were curious. Did you ever hear from your handyman?"

I shook my head. "Not directly. He's . . . he's out of the country."

"That's disappointing."

"It is. Thank you for asking," I whispered, doing my best to hide the effect Katie's words had on me.

"And we're late to see Lily Franklin," Coco said, scooting off the sofa. "She wants to get a group of our friends together and plan a wedding shower for me and Hudson. She was one of the reunion organizers and is giddy, claiming credit for our romance."

"She does have a point," said Katie.

"Okay, maybe. If it hadn't been for the reunion, I can't imagine I would be with Hudson now."

I hugged them both in turn and then they were off. Rover and I followed them out to the porch and watched as they backed out of the driveway.

It excited me that the inn had kept its promise to me after all. When I returned to the house, I heard the office phone ringing and rushed to catch the call before it went to voicemail.

"The Inn at Rose Harbor," I said. "How can I help you?"

"Hello," the disembodied voice spoke from the other end of the connection. "My name is Emily Gaffney and I'm calling to ask if you'd consider taking in a boarder for a couple of weeks until I can find a place to live."

The question gave me pause. "I . . . I don't know. I've never had a long-term guest."

"I recently accepted a teaching position in Cedar Cove. Funny thing is I was there late last summer. It shouldn't take long. But I don't want to make a hurried decision."

It was something to think about. To this point no one had asked to book the inn for more than a few days.

"I'm quiet and I won't cause any trouble," Emily assured me. "I looked online at what was available in town and was immediately drawn to your inn. It's a special place, isn't it?"

I could tell by her voice that Emily was someone who needed the healing powers of the inn. "I'll put your name down and we'll work something out. My rates are reasonable and I'll hold the room for you on a week-to-week basis. How does that sound?"

"Perfect." I heard Emily sigh with relief. "Thank you. Thank you so much. I'll be in touch."

"Okay, then I'll wait to hear from you."

Emily gave me her contact information and we ended the call. I decided that, on reflection, it might be nice to have some live-in company for a while.

Although I was loath to admit it, I was lonely. I'd been managing to fill my time but the nights were bleak. While not wanting to dwell on Mark, I missed him.

The rest of my day went well and by the time I crawled into bed, I was exhausted. I'd added hot-water bottles to all the beds in the inn and tucked one between the sheets of my own, surprised by the warmth and comfort it offered. It was an old-fashioned pleasure, but one I'd become addicted to this winter.

I don't know how long I'd been asleep when my phone woke me. I kept it in the charger at night on my bedside table. I didn't often get calls this late and when I did they were mostly the wrong number.

"Hello," I said, resting on my elbow.

Nothing.

I was about to disconnect when I heard a weak voice that sounded like it was coming from the moon.

"Jo Marie?"

A voice from the grave. I nearly dropped the phone. "Mark," I cried, tears instantly in my eyes and in my voice. "Is that you? Please, please tell me I'm not dreaming this."

"It's me," he said. "It's me."

"Oh Mark," I sobbed, resisting the urge to cover my mouth with my hand. "Where are you? Are you safe? Are you coming back?"

"I'm still in Iraq, but I found Ibrahim."

Relief washed over me that not only was Mark alive but he'd been able to locate the man he felt as close to as a brother.

"I'm traveling with him and his family," Mark continued. "We're trying to get across the border. We're constantly on the move."

My heart stilled.

"I just couldn't go any longer without hearing the sound of your voice," he whispered, "and go without telling you I'm in love with you. You are my heart, Jo Marie."

The sob that sprung from my throat jarred me and I struggled to hold back tears. The static faded and I was sure the connection had been broken. "Mark. Mark." Frantically I cried out his name.

"... I'm sorry I had to leave you the way I did," he was saying, when the connection caught again.

I was afraid that I'd missed part of what he'd called to tell me.

"I understand now," I said, talking around the

thick knot in my throat. I was afraid he wouldn't be able to hear me.

"It was the only way I could leave you."

"I know. Bob told me. He got a postcard," I told him. "He brought it to me so we knew you'd gotten into Iraq safely." My hand tightened around the phone. "Then there were photos on TV of an American being held captive. We thought it was you."

"It wasn't, but it was someone I knew. A friend who helped me. He's dead now."

I gasped and bit down on my lower lip. I wanted to reach through the connection and bring Mark back safely to me, but I knew that was impossible. I whispered the words I hadn't been able to tell him before he left. "I love you."

"I know. I didn't want you to love me . . . not when I considered myself a coward. But I couldn't stop myself from loving you."

"Come back," I pleaded. "Just come back . . . you can explain everything then."

My plea was met with silence. "Mark, Mark," I cried, fearing the connection had been cut off.

"I'm here," he whispered. "Jo Marie," he whispered. "Jo Marie, I'll do everything within my power to make it back to you. If I don't . . ."

"Don't even say it. You're coming back, Mark. I can't think of anything else."

"If I don't . . ."

"Mark," I pleaded, doing my best not to sob, "don't even say it. Please, I can't bear the thought of losing you."

"Jo Marie," he shouted, "please listen to me. If I

don't make it, then I need you to do something for me."

I bit down on my lower lip, swallowing down my fear as best I could. "Of course. Anything."

"I need you to help Ibrahim and his family. It's possible they'd make it across the border without me. If they do, will you help them?"

"Mark—"

"Promise me," he said, cutting me off.

"I promise."

"Thank you."

I was sobbing openly now, and nearly incapable of speech. "Just come home."

"Home," he repeated slowly. "I've learned something important through all this."

"Yes?"

"My heart is wherever you are. I could no more stop thinking about you than I could stop breathing, although there were plenty who would enjoy giving me the opportunity."

"Just make sure they don't get the chance."

"I'll do my best, my love."

And then suddenly the connection was broken.

I held on to the phone for a long time, unwilling to let go of Mark. All I could do now was wait and pray God brought him back to me.

The much-anticipated conclusion to
Debbie Macomber's beloved Rose Harbor series

SWEET TOMORROWS

Set in the picturesque town of Cedar Cove,
a vibrant and poignant novel of
letting go of fear, following your heart,
and embracing the future—come what may.

Available from Ballantine Books

Continue reading for a special sneak peek

Jo Marie

Life is filled with the unexpected. I know that sounds
rather dramatic—sort of like: *It was the best of times,
it was the worst of times.* Trust me, I've been through
both, but then I suspect everyone who breathes in
oxygen has experienced this.

I started my career as a bank teller and eventually
worked my way into the corporate office, taking on
more and more responsibility. I liked my job and ad-
vanced quickly, but that driving ambition to succeed
came with a price. I got so wrapped up and focused
on my career I didn't have time for relationships. Oh,
I had a few close friends, but when it came to dating
and true love, I blew it off, thinking there would be
time for all of that later.

Then one day I woke up and discovered the majority of my friends were married and raising families. When I did become interested in finding my soul-mate, the men I dated, well, suffice it to say, and I'm being as kind as I can be, were a sorry disappointment.

Then I met Paul Rose and I fell head over heels in love. Within the first week I knew he was the one. He was career military and hadn't married, either. It felt like a miracle that I would meet this wonderful man when I'd given up hope of ever finding anyone.

Just like the lyrics of a country western song, we got married in a fever. Paul was an Airborne Ranger and a few months after he placed a diamond ring on my finger he shipped off to Afghanistan, then died in a helicopter crash.

It was as if life had hit me with an atom bomb.

My husband, who I'd loved so briefly, was forever gone from me. I've read books that talk about the different stages of grief. They were filled with good advice, most of which I ignored. I was in so much emotional pain that I could barely function. It took every ounce of energy I could muster to force myself out of bed. Overnight everything, and I do mean everything, that I'd once considered important—my career, my home, my lifestyle, my hopes and dreams of one day having a family with Paul—were gone in the blink of an eye.

Poof, destroyed.

Still reeling from the loss, I did the opposite of what everyone told me: *Don't make an important decision the first year after the death of someone close.* On a complete whim, I quit my corporate job and purchased a bed-and-breakfast and named it after my deceased husband. It became known as the *Rose Harbor Inn. Rose,* naturally, for Paul. And *harbor* because I'd gambled that this next unexpected curve in the roadway of my life would become a harbor of healing for me. And, thankfully, it has. As a bonus, it seems the inn has the power to help others heal as well.

I seldom mention this insight to people for fear they'll suggest I consider counseling. Even now, almost four years later, I sometimes wonder if I'd imagined that first night I spent after moving in. I'd been half asleep . . . it might have been a dream. You know the kind where you aren't really asleep but not fully awake, either? Paul came to me in that dreamlike state, so real I was afraid to breathe for fear he would disappear. It felt as if all I had to do was reach out and touch him, but I knew I dared not.

While it was enough that he stood next to me, and I could see him and feel his love for me, as a bonus he spoke. Not that I heard the words out loud; they were spoken inside of me, in my heart.

I know it's hard to believe, but I swear that's what happened. He told me as plain as anything that I would heal here and all those who came to stay would find solace and healing of their own. Authentic or not, I've held on to that promise, clung to it with both hands, desperately wanting it to be true. Desperately needed hope, a reason to continue.

When Paul told me I'd heal, the last thing in my mind and certainly in my heart was the possibility of falling in love again. Finding Paul was miracle enough; I certainly didn't expect I could be so lucky again. But discovering love a second time was even more of a surprise than it was the first time. Certainly my relationship with Mark Taylor didn't start out as a lovefest, but I'm getting ahead of myself.

After my husband was killed, I retreated from life, which in retrospect is perfectly understandable. For three years I lived in a shell. I took up knitting and gardening, adopted a dog named Rover. All of these were things I'd never have considered in my previous life.

The one constant the first three years I owned the inn was Mark Taylor, my handyman. He was grumpy, noncommunicative, and sometimes downright unpleasant. But as time progressed, Mark became a friend. I still found him irritating, but in a comforting sort of way. I suppose that doesn't make much sense, but it's the best way I can think to describe my feelings. In truth, it's hard to explain.

Mark was around the inn a lot, mainly because I hired him to do a variety of projects and odd jobs. After a while, despite our clashes and differences of opinion, we grudgingly became friends. We argued, but our disagreements weren't serious. I enjoyed teasing him. He loved my home-baked cookies, and I found I could get him to do most anything with the promise of hot-from-the-oven sweets.

The first time I laughed after learning about Paul was with Mark. He'd been painting, and when climbing down the ladder he stuck his foot into a five-gallon paint bucket. I thought it was hilarious and laughed until tears rained down my cheeks. Mark, however, wasn't amused.

Over the years he took on a number of projects I

wanted done around the inn, which included building a rose garden and gazebo. I saw him nearly every day, and often more than once. Spending time with Mark became part of my daily routine. Even when he worked elsewhere he would invariably stop by the inn for coffee. We routinely sat on the porch and chatted about our day. There were times when we said nothing at all. We didn't seem to need words to communicate. Certainly there was no hint of romance; he was a friend and that was what I preferred. I was completely oblivious to the fact he might have come to care for me as more than that.

Just as I was coming out of my self-enclosed shell, Mark let me know that he'd fallen in love with me. His words shook me as powerfully as the 2001 Seattle earthquake. And then it hit me . . . and when I say that, I mean the shock of it turned me upside down. I discovered Mark had become more than a friend to me, too. Bottom line: I'd fallen in love with him. It'd been gradual—so gradual, in fact, that I wasn't even aware of the subtle shift of my feelings for him. This was so utterly different from falling in love with Paul that I remained oblivious to what had happened until Mark revealed his love for me.

No sooner did I come to accept that my heart was open and ready for Mark's love when he hit me with another shock. This one even bigger than the first. He announced he was leaving Cedar Cove, with no intention of returning.

What?

I didn't have a clue what that was about. He made no sense.

"I love you, Jo Marie. Sorry, but I'm leaving and I won't be back."

Who does that? And for the love of heaven, why? And then he was gone. Really gone. Sold-his-house gone. Gave-his-belongings-away gone. Simply gone.

Not until later did I learn the reason for his abrupt departure. At one time in the distant past Mark had been in the military, the very service that had claimed my husband's life. Mark had gotten out of the Middle East unscathed, but at a terrible price. He'd been forced to leave behind an Iraqi friend he'd worked with, an informant who'd become as close to him as a brother.

Even though the circumstances were beyond his control, Mark viewed himself as a coward for not doing everything humanly possible to save Ibrahim and his family. Mark had struggled with his conscience every day since returning to the States. The only way he felt he could properly love me was to go back and rescue the man who'd fed him vital information to help with their mission. But going back held life-threatening risks. He didn't bother to sugarcoat the danger. He let it be known that there was every likelihood he wouldn't return.

Now he was gone. I suspected he never really intended to let me know how deep his feelings were for me. Telling me was an accident. In retrospect, I realize he'd wanted to spare me the pain of dealing with another loss, the death of someone else who loved me.

If Mark thought that by leaving me he was doing me a kindness, he was wrong. I learned later that he couldn't tell me for fear I would talk him out of taking on this risky mission and he was right. I would have done everything within my power to keep him in Cedar Cove. He had basically gone on a suicide mission.

When he left I told him, mainly because I was bitter and angry, that I wouldn't wait for him. I'd already cracked that protective shell in which I'd hidden for three long years, and I wasn't retreating. I was going on with my life. I would date again, and I had, although I hadn't met anyone who made me feel alive, at least not in the way Paul and Mark had. Still, I went out and had started to forge a new life for myself.

Mark has been gone almost nine months now, and I've heard from him only once. One time. It happened late in the night when I was woken out of a sound sleep by a phone call. It was Mark letting me know he was in Iraq and had found Ibrahim. The connection was bad and I was able to catch only part of the conversation, which upset me terribly. I hungered for every bit of information he could tell me, longing to hear the sound of his voice, which came in sporadic spurts. As best I could understand, he was making his way out of the country along with Ibrahim, his wife, and their two small children. Where exactly he intended to go and how he'd get there remained a mystery.

In our broken, frustrating conversation, Mark asked for my help. If he was able to get Ibrahim and his family out of Iraq, he needed to be sure I would help them settle in the United States. What he didn't say, or what I was unable to hear due to our faulty connection, was that he needed me to do this in case he didn't make it out of the country alive.

With no other option, I promised Mark I would do everything in my power to see to the needs of this family. How could I not when Mark had risked his life for their sake?

Like I said, that was nine months ago, and since that time I'd heard nothing more.

Nada.

Zilch.

Not a single word.

No letter. No phone call. No communication of any kind.

I could only believe that after this amount of time he'd failed, and Mark, like Paul, was forever lost to me.

It was June now, and I'd grown downright comfortable with avoidance. I chose not to think about Mark. Or at least I tried, but, frankly, I hadn't been successful. What I had managed to do was keep everyone else from talking about Mark. Mostly my mother, who took pains to remind me that she continued to pray for him and the success of this undertaking.

I didn't want to hope Mark was alive. It was easier to accept that he was dead. Harsh, I know, but you have to understand, Paul's remains weren't recovered and identified for a full year after the helicopter crash. Every single day of that year, every single minute I held on to the hope, clung to it like someone hanging off the ledge of a twenty-story apartment building that against all reason Paul had managed to survive.

I refused to do that a second time. For my own mental well-being I had to let go. I'd rather go down in a flaming free fall than continue to live on empty hope.

Peggy Beldon was someone else who refused to ignore my determined effort to move on. Peggy and Bob Beldon own Thyme and Tide, another B&B in town. After I bought the inn, they more or less took me under their wing and helped me figure out what I was doing. They're good friends, along with Grace Harding. Her husband died before I moved into town, and she fell in love and remarried. She understood what it meant to be a widow and shared some insights into this new stage of life I'd entered. I appreciated their friendship.

The one person who seemed to understand and appreciate my attitude was Dana Parson. She was a relatively new friend I met in my spin class. We were about the same age. She was married, with two small children, and worked part-time as a real estate agent. Her husband's job allowed him to telecommute, and that gave her an opportunity to take an exercise class when her two kids were down for a nap.

Before he left, Mark confided in Bob his reason for selling his home and leaving Cedar Cove. It was Bob who came to me after Mark departed for the Middle East and explained where Mark had gone and why. At the time I was understandably angry, but I'd mellowed out since and understood his reasoning. Mark did what he had to do.

Thankfully, the inn was booked solid for weekends from June through August. Unfortunately, the weekdays were so-so, depending on what was happening in the area. I'd taken a chance and decided to accept a resident over the summer, renting on a week-to-week basis.

Emily Gaffney was due to arrive later this month, as soon as the Seattle schools let out for the summer. We'd talked briefly on the phone months ago and a few times since then. Emily had accepted a teaching position in Cedar Cove. Up to this point she'd lived in Seattle, renting an apartment. She'd been able to sublease her apartment to someone she knew and trusted. However, her friend needed to have the apartment starting in the middle of June.

To sum it up, Emily needed someplace to move and fast—like now would be convenient. She wanted to possibly buy a home in Cedar Cove, but she didn't want to be rushed into making a hasty decision. That was why she contacted me. She found my name online and called to inquire about renting week to week, possibly as long as a month or two, depending on the housing market.

I'd never considered taking in a boarder, and basically that was what Emily would be. It wasn't what I'd had in mind when I purchased the inn. But the truth was I was lonely and looked forward to having someone on hand. Rover was good company, but I needed human companionship. Even after nine months I hadn't gotten used to life without Mark. Some days it felt as if a huge void threatened to open up and swallow me whole.

Emily was due to arrive soon, and I looked forward to meeting her.

Checking my watch, I saw that it was time to leave for my midafternoon spin class. I'd always enjoyed exercise. Not necessarily while I was involved in it, mind you. I didn't like pumping my legs on a stationary bicycle to the point that my buttocks went completely numb and my legs felt like they were about to fall off. What I liked was the aftereffects. The emotional high and all those endorphins coursing through my body, giving me both a mental and physical lift.

"I'm leaving now," I told Rover as I moved toward the door. I wore my tight exercise pants and a sleeveless shell, plus a white-and-black polka-dot headband.

Rover refused to look at me. He considered it his right to follow me wherever I went, but I couldn't take him to spin class. He lay on his stomach, his chin on his paws, and purposely turned his head away from me. This was my punishment.

"Stand guard," I muttered and closed the door, locking it behind me.

Dana was already at our assigned bikes. After all this time one would assume my butt would have molded itself to this narrow seat. Not so. Most of the time I climbed off that bike with my legs bowed out like an eighty-year-old rancher who'd spent the majority of his life on a horse. What I needed, I decided, was a more comfortable seat. Something the size of one on a tractor.

"You having a good day?" Dana asked. She had her hair up in a ponytail and was already atop the bike, arms raised, flexing her shoulders, raring to start. I, on the other hand, looked at the bike and tried with everything in me to come up with an excuse to leave.

"Jo Marie?" Dana pressed.

"I've had better."

I didn't state the obvious—that my thoughts were wrapped around Mark. The night before I'd gone to the movies with a guy named Ralph. He was nice, divorced, but there wasn't any spark. There wasn't even a book of matches. I thought going out would be good for me, but the truth was I came home feeling depressed and out of sorts. I don't know what I was looking for. What I did know was that I wasn't going to find it in Ralph. The evening ended on a sour note when Ralph asked me out again. When I refused, I was then obliged to tell him why. Were all men this dense? Really?

I felt Dana's eyes on me, and from her look I could see that she was debating if she should say anything or not. Frankly, I didn't want to talk about Ralph or Mark or anyone else. I helped her decide by getting on the bike, leaning forward to brace my forearms against the handlebars, and said, "You ready to get this show on the road?"

"Ready," Dana returned.

And so was the rest of the class.

We were off, wheels spinning, heads and shoulders forward, intent on working our hearts to the point of imploding in order to stay healthy and live longer. It didn't make sense to me, but what do I know? I did it. I had a love/hate relationship with it, and afterward I was glad I'd made the effort.

I wiped the sweat off my face with a towel and let out a deep sigh.

"Are we to Paris yet?" I asked. As incentive, Dana and I had been adding our miles up for the last six months, mentally biking our way to Europe. Dana, who was naturally athletic, was miles ahead of me. I was no quitter, and while she might make it to Paris before me, I preferred to laze away in the imaginary

French countryside, sampling freshly baked bread with cheese and a lovely bottle of red wine.

"We're almost there," Dana assured me.

I didn't believe her for a minute. "See you Wednesday," I said on my way out the door.

"Wednesday," she called after me. "If not before."

When she got a free minute, which wasn't often, Dana stopped by the inn for tea and talk. I enjoyed her visits and was glad to have a friend who understood me.

I looked forward to my shower and sitting on the porch. We'd been having a beautiful spring to this point. The weather was unusually warm and sunny for Seattle. My mind was occupied with what I would make for dinner. I tended to eat a lot of salads, mainly because they were fast and easy.

On the way into the house I stopped at the mailbox. Inside were a couple flyers, a food magazine—I'd taken to reading those like novels—and naturally a couple bills. I laid the mail down on the kitchen countertop and went in for my shower.

Rover had forgiven me now that I was back. He cocked his head and stared at me.

"You've already had your walk for the day," I reminded him. I spoiled him terribly, and he appeared to have our roles reversed. I had to remind him every now and again that I was the one in charge, not him. Okay, I'll admit it, I hadn't been all that successful.

After my shower I felt worlds better, and seeing that it was a bit early for dinner, I decided to take my food magazine out on the porch, bask in the sunshine, and relax. After the workout I'd just had, I needed it.

I poured myself a glass of iced tea and took it outside with me. Plopping myself down on a white wicker chair, I set my feet on the ottoman. Because I sat in exactly this same spot so often, I nearly overlooked appreciating the view. The cove stretched out below, the marina thick with boats of every size bobbing on the surface. The peaks of the Olympic mountain range poked against a radiant blue sky. After I let myself be mesmerized by the view, I flipped open my magazine.

That's when it happened.

A postcard with a foreign stamp fell out from between the pages.

Not just any postcard.

Although he didn't sign his name, I knew it was from Mark.

Enjoying Jeddah Beach Swim Reef.
Bad connection. No ANDC
Lost suitcase okay, but mine is badly damaged, making its way home.
Love you.

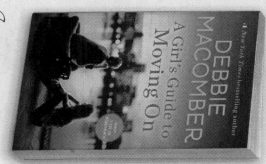